THE LOVE OF A BAD WOMAN

'You're an obdurate woman,' said Elli, 'and an intolerant one.'

'You think I should give them my blessing?'

'I think you should be more laid back. And play a shrewder game. It isn't as if she's run off with your husband.'

Kate made a prayerbook of her hands, sent up an entreaty for patience and restraint. 'She could have *had* my husband,' she responded tonelessly. 'Why not? Everybody else has. But what she's doing is far, far worse. This I can never forgive.'

'Tush. You're being silly.' With David on her mind, now, Elli turned to the mirror above the fireplace and made a routine assessment of her neck, her chest, her clavicles. Her eyes, in the glass, appraised her. Not quite *everyone*, Kate Garvey, she thought. *I* haven't had your husband. Not yet.

Rose Shepherd is a freelance journalist and has written for numerous publications, including the *Sunday Times, Independent, Good Housekeeping, Woman's Journal* and *Marie Claire*. She lives in London and is not so bad herself.

Rose Shepherd

The Love of
a Bad Woman

Mandarin

A Mandarin Paperback
THE LOVE OF A BAD WOMAN

First published in Great Britain 1995
by William Heinemann Ltd
and Mandarin Paperbacks
imprints of Reed Consumer Books Ltd
Michelin House, 81 Fulham Road, London SW3 6RB
and Auckland, Melbourne, Singapore and Toronto

Copyright © by Rose Shepherd 1995
The author has asserted her moral rights

A CIP catalogue record for this title
is available from the British Library
ISBN 0 7493 1798 1

Typeset by Deltatype Ltd, Ellesmere Port, Wirral
Printed and bound in Great Britain
by Cox & Wyman Ltd, Reading, Berkshire

For my mother

CHAPTER

1

When the bell rang, the sound seemed to pierce Kate's heart; her whole body pealed with the shock of it, but this was just her usual nervous over-reaction. She had no real presentiment of trouble, no inkling of the calamity that had come to her door, just an obscure horror of being 'found out', surprised in her natural state (and she had in mind something more abstract than a grubby, shapeless T-shirt, filthy white plimsolls, or uncombed, unconformable hair; she was thinking of her public persona stripped down like a bicycle, in bits about the house).

Still, she decided as her reason returned, the caller would be no one who figured in her life. And, expecting at worst some modest demand on her purse – from the milkman, perhaps, or that earnest young man from the Wildlife Trust, or another of those well-intentioned, well-fed, fatuous schoolchildren contemplating, of all the nonsenses, a sponsored 'famine' – she swept assorted coins from the dresser into her palm.

'Who the hell . . .?' she enquired of the deserted kitchen, which a moment ago had been invited to share in her enjoyment of *The News Quiz*, to applaud as she yelled out the answers. Then, 'Nobody we know,' she concluded as she reached across to mute the radio.

Through the bubbled glass of the front door, however, she could just make out a wilting female figure, and, opening up, she received into her arms Naomi Markham, drenched in Arpège and weeping with abandon. 'What is it? What's happened? Are you hurt?' Kate, shoeless and stocky, with her fist still closed around the coins, supported the taller woman as best she could, and, as Naomi sobbed immoderately on her shoulder, the two of them staggered in a grim boxers' clinch down the narrow passageway.

'I've left the bastard.'

'Not again?' Kate steered an uncertain course past the ugly hall stand, with its stubby brass antlers, its shapeless accretion of anoraks and overcoats. Fleetingly she visualised the bastard in question; she recalled a gaunt, silent man with a domed head, hair worn thin by constant raking, and a permanent air of preoccupation, the intense inward gaze of one who would get his mind round differential calculus – or around those countless little Versace numbers in which Naomi must be kept. She could not believe Alan Neish guilty of any real atrocity. He might, at his nastiest, with all his worries, be a bit liverish, tense, uptight.

'Yes. This time it's for ever.' Naomi, momentarily galvanised, rigid with dudgeon, made a grand, dismissive gesture, a lofty flourishing of the hand, flashing her pearly fingernails in the direction of the gaping front door and the cab that stood fretting at the kerb beyond the shorn privet hedge. On the pavement beside it, items of Gucci lugage stood assured of a porter, for all the world as if this were the Savoy Hotel, Strand, London

WC2, not number 28 Larkspur Road, Tooting. 'Lend me a tenner, will you?' she implored. 'Pay the wretched man for me, there's a darling.'

Perhaps unfortunately, Kate had been to the cashpoint that morning and had drawn out fifty pounds. She manoeuvred Naomi into the front room, which smelt of warm, gloss-painted windowsills and tired pot-pourri, ditched her on the sofa in the bay, then went thudding upstairs to fetch her bag, breathless and shaky with exasperation, rehearsing as she went how she would remind her friend of the debt – or else how she would write it off, forget it.

Naomi was shamelessly negligent about such trans-actions, apt to deny all recollection of them, to pay up only on demand, and then sulkily, disbelievingly, raking the contents of her purse with long, manicured fingers, counting out the sum in small change, slapping it down on the table, offering no apology for any deficit. (On the contrary, 'You've cleaned me out,' she would say, not in so many words, but with a look. 'Go on, take the lot, take my last penny, why not?')

Every time this happened – and it happened too often – Kate would vow to make her no more loans. But in this, as in so many matters, her resolution failed. Now she decided that nothing under twenty pounds was worth reclaiming, so fraught with ill feeling was the whole business. And she rendered the debt inconsequential by averaging it out over her possible lifetime, mentally reducing it to twelve pence a year.

'The young lady all right, is she?' The taxi driver, a man in his sixties with corrugated grey hair, regarded her from behind gangster sunglasses, which returned to her twin images of her harassed self, as Kate stooped to peer in at him, to enquire about the fare.

'I expect so,' she told him curtly, squinting in the fierce sunlight which ricocheted in all directions off the baking black bodywork. The dusty pavement seared the soles of her bare feet. Never mind Naomi, she wanted to snap at him. What about *me*? What about my space, my time, my freedom, my privacy, my precious Saturday?

Familiar sensations of pique stole upon her and overran her. Her skin crawled with irritation. The two miniature faces in his mirror lenses flushed a petulant scarlet and ballooned at her as she leant into the cab to address him.

Why were her needs and desires always discounted? Why did Naomi Markham and her like command attention, when she, Kate Garvey, so patently did not? How did she fail, despite her size, to appeal to some strong, protective instinct in the human male? Men seemed to see her – in so far as they saw her at all – as a good sort, capable, dependable and inconsiderable. They barged her out of the way in their eagerness to open doors for their glamorous wives and girlfriends; they stampeded her in their rush to light cigarettes for luscious blondes; they showed her their backs, shunted her and her shopping into tight corners, as they ceded their seats on the tube to sultry redheads. And it was useless to tell herself she didn't care, because she did, disproportionately. She bitterly resented the way they subordinated her to more beautiful women, for in so doing they confirmed her most abject feelings of inferiority.

4

'You should send for the doctor.' The driver oppressed her with his counsel. 'Get him to prescribe a sedative. She's very overwrought.'

But it would be an uncondoling Dr Body who would call to minister to so wispy a patient on this fine weekend. He would afterwards be punishing in his satirical way; he would treat Kate and her female ailments, more than ever, with wry disdain. So she set her face against the idea, set her lips in what she hoped was a forbidding line, expressed her words in a thin stream through them. 'I doubt if that will be necessary.'

'She was in a fine old state when I picked her up,' he persisted, undiscouraged, jabbing at his sunglasses with his thumb, hitching them up his nose so her twin reflections jinked. 'Crying her eyes out.'

'I can imagine.' She stared fixedly at the dashboard, which was a shrine to the man's family, adorned with framed photographs of his wife and children or grand-children, with a plastic flower in a holder and a deodor-ising 'tree', a kind of talisman to ward off evil-smelling passengers.

'I thought someone had been having a go at her.'

'Yes, well, I don't suppose –'

'I asked her straight, "Has someone been having a go at you?" You'd best take good care of her.' His tone carried a strong hint of reproof, as though Kate herself were charged with the whole sorry state of affairs.

'Why?' she asked acidly. 'Am I my sister's keeper?'

'You're *sisters*?' His incredulity was as comic as it was uncomplimentary. His eyebrows shot up. You don't *look* like sisters, was eloquently implied.

'Identical twins. I should have thought that was obvious.'

'Eh?'

'Oh, no, look. We're just pals. What are you owed? Here.' She thrust a folded ten-pound note at him. And, rancorously, figuring that this amount was derisory, 'Keep the change,' she bade him, turning from him, lumbering herself with suitcases, then staggering with them up the black and terracotta chequered path, to dump them at the foot of the stairs.

'Thanks.' Naomi greeted her wanly from the scuffed and cracked leather sofa where she reclined on a scratchy Navajo blanket, bathed in syrupy afternoon light. She raised her hand a mere fraction, as an invalid might who was not expected to make it through the night. 'I'll settle up on Monday. Don't let me forget, you hear?'

'Not a chance.' Kate stood in front of the fireplace, hooked to the mantelpiece by her fingers, and studied herself in the gilt-framed mirror, where she featured between a bowl of desiccated brown roses and a raffia elephant, trying to discover who or what she was. Whoever said that by the age of forty we get the face we deserve, didn't know what he was talking about. He didn't know shit.

For, look at her, so good-natured and kind and, yes, sure, quite pretty, but essentially ordinary, unexceptional ('passable', she would have called herself; she would have put it no higher than that). Then look at Naomi lounging there, so thoroughly selfish, so spoilt, so utterly undeserving yet so altogether exceptional.

'You'd better tell me the whole story,' she prompted,

pushing her springy, brown-blonde hair back at the temples, searching for strands of white, wondering at a face which seemed to her to lack some crucial element (one nose, it had, one mouth, two eyes, and yet . . .), leaning into the glass till she bumped against it and momentarily blacked out her senses. She blinked back sudden tears and the room behind her came into focus, homey, cluttered, eclectically furnished, with a distinct but not displeasing air of tat.

Against the far wall stood an old upright piano, from which no one would ever milk a tune. The chairs were sole survivors of three very different suites. Nothing matched, the pieces had no common history, no shared geography or culture, yet somehow, mysteriously, all corresponded, as if their coming together had been entirely meant, a matter merely of time. Only Naomi apeared out of place – appeared, indeed, in her elegance, slightly preposterous, the way we all may be in anxious dreams when, inappropriately dressed or undressed, we see no choice but to brazen it out. 'What's been going on, eh?'

'Oh, it's been a living hell. You have no idea.' Naomi gave a pained sigh as if it fatigued her to talk about it. She pressed her brow into her palm and her hair closed about her thin forearm. She had pale, swishy, expensive-looking hair, which hung in silken skeins about her shouders, softly coiled. Her eyes were wide-set, beguiling, blue, lustrous now with unspilt tears. Her complexion was like buttermilk. She had high and prominent cheekbones, a wide and useful-looking mouth which – when it was not engaged in passionate advocacy, pouting, protesting, pleading her case – settled itself into a

7

smile of quiet self-satisfaction. Her chin had lost nothing of its youthful purpose, her body none of its promise. But there was about her beauty a hint of instability, of volatility. At any moment it might vaporise. She'd just *go*. Or was this Kate's acrimonious fancy, some meanness of spirit, the wishfulness of envy?

'I'll make a cup of tea,' she offered, supposing she must play the gracious hostess to her uninvited guest. And, ashamed of herself, hoping to atone for her uncharitable impulses, 'Poor you,' she added gently.

'Have you nothing stronger?' Naomi plucked at her clothing, picking neurotically at imagined cat fluff. And, as if she were considering what better use might be found for his brindled fur, she turned a hard and calculating stare on Pushkin, who dozed pneumatically, blissfully unknowing, in a pond of sunlight on the threadbare patterned carpet. 'I could kill for a vodka and tonic.'

She was wearing flares, Kate noted to her chagrin. The watery satin spilled over her slender knees and shimmered as Naomi nipped and tweaked at it. Bloody flares! Bloody fashion! Kate herself wanted no part of it. Wide trousers would not suit her any better this time around than they had the last. She had not been built to wear them, as old photographs all too vividly testified (there was one in particular, at the sight of which she shuddered and went hot and cold, of herself in hippie days, in bell-bottoms, with fringes at the knee like the feathers on a shire horse). For Naomi, however, with her narrow gauge, her long, long legs, the style might have been specially created.

What goes around comes around, Kate reflected idly to

8

herself in the matter of dress. To Naomi she said with something like triumph, 'Booze, you mean? No, nothing. Sorry.' Even so, she cast about her rather wildly, as though a bottle of something alcoholic might be hiding thereabouts. 'I don't keep spirits. Well, neither of us has a taste for them. And we drank the last of the holiday wine yesterday with supper.'

'Well, then, tea will have to do.'

'Too right it will.' But Kate only muttered this, tucked it away under her breath; she could not bring herself to speak it out loud. Already she was sick with self-reproach, feeling she had been stingy to the cabbie. She worried that he might have thought her a hateful person. She worried about those children of his, or those grandchildren, out of whose mouths, as it now seemed to her, she had taken the very bread.

Whistling like a boy, though more from pent-up stress than from high humour, she went to the kitchen, stood at the sink filling the kettle, listening to the drizzling of water, watching Alex through the window, wondering at the miracle of him as he toiled up and down behind the rusty mower.

He was sweating from his exertions. The hems of his jeans and his white Reeboks were wet and stained and furred with clippings. At the sight of him, her heart felt enlarged with love and pain and gratitude and huge, possessive pride. Sighing, she filled her lungs with gusts of juicy, grassy air, held it there for several seconds as if to green her insides, before noisily expelling it. She should buy a new machine, she told herself, a nice nippy electric model. But then she had a vision of blades biting into flex, she pictured Alex going up in a puff of black smoke, her stomach lurched and she changed her mind. It was, after all, a minute lawn, it demanded minimal attention.

She had first seen the garden, all that time ago, in the early morning, when the small enclosure had been filled with sunshine like a cup. Enchanted by it, wildly ambitious for it, she had bought the place, only to find that it faced the wrong way, north or north-east, so the sunlight drained to the dregs before noon and left it chilly until nightfall.

That was, of course, before horticulture became her livelihood and her obsession. In a spirit of reckless optimism she had put in pinks and delphiniums, honey-suckle, aquilegia, azaleas, geraniums, candytuft and Canterbury bells, which grew in such brilliant abundance on the front of seed packets, but in sorry straggles, if at all, in this dank and cloddy soil.

Alone among her early plantings, the magnolia had survived. It stood now, unblushing, *en déshabillé*, amid its shrugged-off petals. The bench seat beneath was warped with damp, felted with moss.

These days, knowing so much more, she grew waxy-looking cyclamen, sappy, stripy hostas, shaggy ferns, and various climbers, hardy Outward Bound types which, for all they were meant to be shade-loving, bunked off over the back wall when she wasn't looking, into the summery plot beyond.

Nevertheless, she quite loved this little house, which the two of them had shared for twenty years. She delighted in its sturdy structure so firmly footed in

London clay; its square two-storey bay topped off with a jaunty tiled hat; its brave wrought-iron embellishments, the flaunting front balcony – a cosmetic feature, an architect's conceit – on to which no one would ever venture. Even its sameness to its neighbours, its replication up and down the street, was to her an obscure comfort. To be overlooked at the rear by the bedrooms of Broomwood Road was reassuring. And the way all those identical strips of ground butted up, side to side, end to end, was positively cosy.

The mortgage on the place had come to seem trifling, and anyway was soon to be redeemed. The bills were paid by instalments, by direct debit, they did not impinge upon her consciousness. She was earning quite decently, and Alex rather better. She was as well off as she'd ever been, she was managing nicely. This had given her, finally, a sense of control and of deep, deep security. She was, by and large, fulfilled.

As she waited for the kettle to boil, she let her gaze dart aimlessly about, to gather in impressions of disarray, to report back to her conscience the unholy chaos that it everywhere encountered. There was so much stuff in her life, so many possessions strewn about. The thought of ever having to move, of packing up and transporting this muddle, made her dizzy and distressed.

On the dresser she noted balled-up, umatched socks; a broken bicycle bell; a bent fork; radio batteries, dead or alive; a Vogue pattern, crumpled sheets of tissue crammed anyhow into their envelope; a pink and smiling clockwork pop-up toaster from a Christmas cracker . . . A place for everything, she joked to herself as she rapped on the window pane, and everything in its place.

When Alex glanced up, she beckoned him. The mower swerved and dug in. With a rueful grin, he abandoned it and came to the back door, stood there leaning on the jamb in his relaxed manner, folding himself up, arm over arm, leg over leg, poising his right foot, resting it balletically on pointed toe.

'Naomi's here,' she informed him in a low, confiding voice and with a martyred smile.

'Yes?' He assumed the expression of amused tolerance that he reserved for discussion of her close circle of friends.

'She's walked out on Alan.'

'Again?'

'This time for good – or so she claims.'

'We-ell, that remains to be seen.' He uncrossed his arms, dashed the hair out of his grey eyes, which were full of all they saw and all they knew.

'She came here in floods of tears and a taxi.'

'No Clapham omnibus for our Naomi, eh? No Northern Line for her. She does these things in style.'

'Oh, always.' Kate, unseeing, checked her watch. 'Goodness knows what she'd have done if we'd been out,' she grumbled. 'She hadn't a brass farthing on her for the fare.'

'So who paid the guy?'

'Need you ask?' She put her hands apart as if to enquire, What could I do? What choice had I? 'I'm wondering if I should ring Elli. See if she can come over.'

'You could, I suppose,' he reflected, scratching his

nose which the pollen teased, twitching his nostrils. 'I mean, if you need her help.'

'Well, you know how she is. She can be very solid.'

'As a rock. But she is also a rancid old bag,' he observed, not without affection, and now when he smiled his whole face went on the tilt with humour, his features sliding to the right. 'What you have to ask yourself is: will her being here make matters twice as bad?'

Alex was not exactly handsome (although she could not have said why not), but he was so attractive, and so thoroughly personable that she was moved to squeeze his elbow hard, to grip the strong, suntanned arm that protruded from the loose sleeve of his T-shirt, then to touch her lips to his shoulder, to breathe through moist, detergent-impregnated cotton the sweet, warm smell of him. 'It'd be a gamble.'

'Depending on her mood.'

'Precisely.'

They had such a good rap, she and Alex, such an open, honest relationship. In all her life, of all her achievements, she held this to be by far her greatest.

'Could you bear the spare room?' she wheedled. 'Just for tonight? Or for a couple of nights? I'm not clear what her plans are – how long we are to be honoured with her presence.'

'I don't mind,' he agreed, with the merest hesitation. He had the same grudging instincts as everyone else, but an ability, also, immediately to set them aside, and he would give no thought afterwards to his own generosity, or to those who presumed upon it. Unlike Kate, he did not keep a tally. 'Look, the kettle's boiling its head off. Shall I do the tea while you do the sympathy?'

'No, *you*, Alex. Bags I be the tea lady. You be on sympathy duty – for five minutes at least. Look in on her, there's a darling. Sit with her and murmur "There, there". Keep her company. Soothe her. Imprison her soft hand and let her rage. Make sure she doesn't open a vein. You know what a drama queen she can be.'

'Don't I just!' He sauntered through the hall to the front room. Kate, clattering Bourbon biscuits on to an antique willow-pattern plate, its glaze cobwebbed with cracks, heard his cheery greeting, the low, reassuring rumble of his voice, heard Naomi's querulous responses.

At once she moved to the phone, snatched up the receiver, replaced it, snatched it up a second time, and for a second time replaced it. She wanted very much to call for reinforcements, to summon Elli who, at her best, in such situations could be a brick.

On the other hand, she could be a bit *too* tough, too powerful, too abrasive. At her worst, Elaine Sharpe could be very . . . well, very Elaine. And very sharp.

Geraldine Gorst, née Garvey, sat, a stubborn Canute, enthroned on complaining canvas in the dwindling black shadow of the rhododendrons, as the sun stole inexorably upon her.

She was not a great one for the heat. She had said as much to Mrs Thingie yesterday, conversationally, in the kitchen over coffee, at pains as always to treat the woman as her social equal. She had said it to a denim-clad backside, as Kate grubbed around among the floribundas. She had said it to the window cleaner, tipping back her head so her voice might pursue him up his springy ladder, which knock-knocked against the brick back elevation of Copperfields, her handsome Surrey home. ('I'm not a great one for the heat,' he had heard as he set to work on her gable end.) And she had said it again this morning to the girl at the cash-desk in Marks and Spencer, who, pausing in the act of flurrying and folding a white nylon nightie, a billowing ghost of a garment, had turned her head, turned her vaguely curious regard upon the distant street door, perhaps to see for herself across the bright rails of blouses and beachwear the putative splendours of a summer of which she, in her fluorescently lit, electrically cooled, whispery work environment, heard only rumour.

One woman's perfect English afternoon is another woman's purgatory. The day seemed to Geraldine to be wearing the weather like an extra layer of clothing; it seemed wrapped and muffled in it. Fanning herself, she tutted aggrievedly.

Flaming June. It got into her crevices, which were many and deep and did not bear thinking about. It stole her energy, reduced her to the consistency of ripe Brie so she ran out of her sandals, and out of the sleeve holes of her cotton sundress.

Now, to further try her, there hovered in front of her face a yellow and black stripy insect, like a baby wasp (did wasps have babies, or did they emerge, fully formed, from some ghastly pupa arrangement?), its diaphanous wings a blur. She swatted at it fretfully, ineffectually, and a sort of emotional blow-back inflated

15

her cheeks. Such a fortune the Gorsts lavished on their grounds, their green acre. Yet, much as the idea of it tantalised her, she had substantially less than her money's worth from the reality. (That life was like this – that nothing would ever quite measure up – was a notion she chose not to entertain.)

Only on the occasional Sunday, when she opened their lovely landscaped garden to public view – when people came to wander around, to ooh and aah at her agapanthus, to beg cuttings of her Comtesse de Bouchaud, or to praise to the heavens her *Pelargonium x hortorum*, when the gleaming line of Vauxhalls, Volvos, BMWs and Saabs, parked nose to tail, stretched out of the gravelled drive into the lane – did it seem truly, truly worth the expense. And often, as at this moment, she fell to wondering if Kate's charges were not a mite on the steep side – if they were not, indeed, extortionate.

Geraldine had always been very generous, very giving to Kate, to whom she felt – soft-hearted bitch that she was – some measure of responsibility. If she hadn't introduced the girl to David . . ., ran one vague line of reasoning. Kate was family, after all, ran another. But there was a limit, surely, to one's obligation. One could do *too* much for a fellow human being. And, as both Elli and Naomi would agree, Kate was rather apt to take advantage; she did have a tendency towards over-dependency, which should, for her own sake, be discouraged.

She closed her eyes and heard sounds of splashing from the swimming pool, the cavilling voices of her children beyond the shrubbery, Lucy and Dominic

16

engaged in perennial, perpetual squabble. Presently, the self-righteous slap of rubber soles, and a disagreeable, chemical, chlorine smell signalled Lucy's approach.

'Mummy.'

'Yes,' said Geraldine, shading her eyes, framing a picture of a fourteen-year-old girl, plump as a peach in her one-piece swimsuit, filling it out with her pubescent form (exotic flowers blossomed madly at her bosom), dripping all over the path. 'What's the matter?'

'Dominic tipped me off the Lilo.' Lucy folded her arms across her chest, thrust her chin out and tossed her plaited hair about. Pique enlived her complexion; her eyes were ominously bright.

'Well, I dare say you'll survive.'

'But I'd just put my cream on. My factor eight.' Lucy, with head tilted, made a caressing motion, mimed the application of Soltan to her shoulder and upper arm, exaggerating to herself her own tenderness and vulnerability. Her round face, normally quite pretty in an unresolved manner, was transformed by a scowl. Her brows meshed, her nostrils curled, her lower lip took on a life of its own.

Even as a baby, Lucy had had this way of turning, quite literally, ugly. It was hereditary. Mother had remarked it in daughter – and daughter had remarked it in mother. What neither of them recognised, although it was hilariously apparent to Dominic at least, was how precisely they mirrored one another. 'Now it's all washed off, thanks to *him*.'

'Then put some more on. Goodness me. Don't make such a song and dance about nothing.'

'The water will be oily. We're supposed to shower the stuff off before we go in the pool, Daddy said.'

'You children. I don't know.'

'It was Dom. I was just lying on the side reading *Eventing*. He rolled me in. The magazine's ruined as well.'

'Then that was very wrong of him.'

'I told him you'd be livid.'

'Well, so I am.' But she felt only weary. And effete. Exhausted by parenting. And unequal to the situation. Dominic, in spite of her efforts, in spite of the best education money could buy, was increasingly beyond her control. He was David, that was the thing. David all over again. The spit and image of his reprobate uncle. At seventeen he was the boy her brother had been nearly thirty years before. He was more like David's son than David's son was. And just as there had always been problems with David Garvey, there were bound to be problems with Dominic. It was innate. Genes had a lot to answer for.

Despairing, she watched the youth's ambling approach, marked his confident mien, his height, his breadth, the set of his features, his bronzed and glistening torso, his brown hair tinged copper by the sunlight. He was wearing wet swimming shorts which left very little to the imagination, and there was something louche about his whole presentation. What was the use, after all, in scolding him? What would it achieve? The word 'incorrigible' came to mind.

Still, 'Dominic,' she reproved him as maternal duty demanded, 'say you're sorry to Lucy, please. That was a nasty trick to play, and so childish. You should be very ashamed.'

'Sorry, Lucy,' he said indifferently, sitting on the lawn, spreading his knees, hunching over, tearing up hanks of grass with restless energy and strewing them about. Hormones didn't help, of course. Geraldine shrank from contemplation of his hormones.

'So you should be,' Lucy sniffed. 'My heart could have stopped. I could have died.'

'Oh, *please*.' Dominic, derisive, chucked in her direction a confetti of clover and daisies.

'Well, I *could* have. There is such a thing as thermal shock, in case you don't know.' She was quivering with affront.

'You're out of your head.'

Geraldine pressed her hands to her ears. 'Can't you ever stop? Either of you? Keeping on and on.'

'She's such a little cry baby.'

'It's *him*. *He* started it.'

'But now it's finished. Over.'

'Till the next time,' said Lucy sententiously.

Till the next time, thought Geraldine, as she checked her watch. Ten to four. 'I'm going indoors now to make the tea. Lucy, run and tell Daddy. He's cleaning the Rover. Ten minutes, say to him. Dominic, you must buy Lucy a new magazine. And I don't want to hear another word about this.'

'You won't,' Dominic promised, flopping out on his back, flinging his arms wide, addressing the cloudless blue heavens, closing his eyes, which glinted with both silver and gold. 'Not from me, at least. I can't speak for goosey Lucy. Ouch!' For Lucy had delivered a well-aimed kick to his ribs.

Geraldine, defeated, went inside.

'Want a drop of this? Too late, tough, you missed your chance.' Elli Sharpe tipped the last of the Pinot Grigio gloatingly into her glass, waved the green-tinged bottle around, tilted it before her eyes to be certain that it was indeed empty, and lobbed it into a patch of nettles under the wall. 'Bloody brilliant weather,' she remarked. Then, creaking back in her wicker chair, setting the drink aside, she uttered a snore of contentment and turned her hands palms upwards so that the sun might do its stuff on the deathly white undersides of her arms. 'I could stand any amount of this, couldn't you?'

If she had expected an answer – and she could apparently take one or leave one – none was forthcoming. Juin sat on a sofa cushion, on the margin of the lawn, with a magazine draped across her knee, dipping into a bag of smoky bacon crisps, popping them alternately into her mouth and into Muffy's snapping jaws, and made no sign of having heard, or any sound beyond a concentrated munching.

A funny, awkward, intractable kid Elli thought her. A challenge, all right. With her close-cropped dark hair, her huge black eyes, her poignantly thin limbs, her washed-out pallor, and in her grungey, faded frock, Juin looked like a street urchin – she looked for all the world like the orphan she so often avowedly wished she might be.

Sixteen last Thursday, the girl had been named for the month of her birth, but in French, which was so much

20

more stylish, so much less *ordinaire*. Yet she stubbornly eschewed the correct form, representing herself always as Ju-in. 'Jwan,' she would complain, travestying the pronunciation, 'sounds so affected. I feel a complete tit when people call me Jwan. Like I'm right up my own bum.'

Elli, puckering her face against the punishing afternoon light, smiled to envisage this contortion. 'Going out tonight?' she asked after a few minutes' silence – a loaded question, requiring a response.

'Maybe,' said Juin, discarding the crisp bag and offering her hand to the tousled mongrel at her feet, so he might slaver at her salty fingers. 'Maybe not.' He was notionally her dog, bought for her by Elli three years ago, in a fine demonstration of conspicuous thrift. If you could afford to buy and keep a pedigree pooch, went the reasoning, what need had you to do so? 'Oh, Muffy's a bitsa,' Elli loved to declare. 'Bitsa this, bitsa that.' And, somehow, no one was left in any doubt that she could run to a Weimaraner if she wanted, she could afford an Afghan. Poor old Muff was, in other words, as Juin dimly perceived, the noisome, larky, barky equivalent of a fun fur.

'I don't understand you lot.' There heaved around in Elli's chest a sigh for youth, so wasted on the young. Dullards, she thought the modern generation. Disappointing. There might be no possibility of living vicariously through them. Thank goodness, then, that she had her own life, a pacey, varied and endlessly social one, rich in incident. 'When I was your age I was out every night. No one stayed in on a Saturday unless they were dead. There was always a party to go to, or a club.'

'So I'm told.' It was Juin's turn to sigh, to issue a grudging little breath through her teeth.

Elli knew she had said it before, many times, knew it bored her daughter witless to hear the same old riff. Christ, she even bored herself with it! But she could not help herself, could not stop herself from puzzling aloud. She remembered her own strict upbringing, based in ignorance, set about by sanctions and constraints. 'You don't know you're born. All the freedom you have. All the licence.'

If only *her* mother had been half so laid back! If only she had talked to her as Elli talked at every opportunity to Juin! If only there had been that honesty and openness between them! Scare stories, Elli had had in place of sound advice. And, in place of a listening ear, moral lectures.

She dwelt now, for an instant, on this dereliction, with such concentrated malice that, if poor old Sybil Sharpe, innocently tending the busy lizzies on her south-facing balcony as the sea slid up and down at the periphery of her vision, felt a sudden stabbing pain between her shoulderblades, it might not have been the arthritis or the 'old bones' to which she would naturally attribute it.

'We're very grateful, I'm sure.'

'You should be.'

As soon as the young Juin had shown interest in where babies came from, Elli had apprised her of the facts of life, fully and fairly, with a wealth of anecdotal material, setting out her own past for inspection like a rummage sale, so that her daughter should know she had been there, done this, done that, and would realise that she was unshockable.

An enlightened parent, she had recently offered, if Juin only said the word, to go with her to the doctor's, to demand the pill. But, 'Leave it out, will you?' Juin had said crossly, bringing her bony shoulders up to her ears, which she had stopped with her Walkman, filling her head with what these days passed for music – 'house' or 'garage' or some such manufacturered noise – not the least appreciative of the gesture.

'You know . . .' Elli hooked a second chair with her toe, dragged it bucking and squealing across the patio tiles towards her, sat with her poor, mangled, bare feet up, her knees bent, and raked with her nails at an angry gnat bite on her calf. She wore white cotton shorts with a pink bandeau top. Her shoulders and chest were patterned by the wicker, lumpy, like wattle and daub.

Still, she was not, she was pleased to think, in bad shape. Her waist was maybe thickening, but not so as you would notice once she'd cinched it with a wide belt, offset it with big, padded shoulders, beguiled the eye with a miniskirt, drawn attention to her shapely legs.

Her flesh reproached her rather for her excesses, with its poor quality, with a certain lack of resilience, but this was a small price to pay for the undoubted benefits of booze and fags. She smoked to keep her weight down, drank to keep her spleen topped up, to keep herself good and uppity, and she *needed* her toxins.

She was essentially plain, with heavy-lidded eyes and slightly lardy features, but she had confected a look of vivid, brassy, breezy attractiveness, a kind of ersatz glamour; she had worked up her image, along with an assumption of her own appeal, which did her quite as

23

well, probably, as patrician beauty ever could. It was a confident woman who came at her out of mirrors, who shot her looks of affirmation across crowded restaurants and bars, or twirled in the glass in the changing-rooms of South Molton Street boutiques.

If she was soft at heart, she seldom showed it, carapaced as she was in self-assurance. She was very smart, strident, bold, unshrinking, and thus eminently qualified for her work as a newspaper columnist. A former Maoist, she had once pulled a policeman off his horse, but her politics had, with the decades, lurched unevenly to the right, her values informed by expediency, resolving themselves around her ego, so that no one could now guess where she might stand on any question, and her weekly polemic in 'The Sharpe End' of the *Globe* never failed to surprise or to antagonise her readers.

She could not pretend to the title First Lady of Fleet Street, but she arguably ranked fourth or fifth. People stopped her in the street and said 'You're Elli Sharpe.' They said, 'I'd like to shake your hand.' They said, 'I'd like to slap your face.' She relished all this – particularly the face-slappers. She was delighted to be controversial.

'What?' said Juin.

'What?'

'You said "You know . . ." I said "What?" ' As Muffy lolled on his back with his eyes rolling up in their sockets, with his ears flopped inside-out to reveal their pink silk linings, Juin rubbed his tummy and wobbled him about. '*What* do I know?'

'I was only thinking. You should have a party. Ask all

24

your mates. I'd hire a band. Why not? We'd have a great time.' Momentarily, Elli envisaged their tall, white house in Hackney – which area of north London, on Juin's recalcitrant lips, was made to sound like a skin complaint – throbbing with loud rock music, thrumming with life. A few of her own friends could be invited, also. They would show what was meant by a good time.

'Nah,' came the unsatisfactory response.

'Why not?'

'Don't fancy it.'

'But *why* not?'

'I just don't, that's all.'

'You *are* a funny girl.' With her two hands, Elli swept up her frosty blonde hair, flicked it back to reveal large silver hoop earrings. 'Give Lucy a call, then,' she persisted, worrying about Juin, worrying *at* her, hell bent on flushing her out.

'Lucy *Gorst*?'

'Sure. Invite her over. Next weekend, say. She'd be company for you.'

'But she's such a baby.'

'She must be fourteen.'

'Going on four and a half.' Juin sniffed with contempt.

'The child's repressed, that's the thing. It's Geraldine's fault, she's too protective. And a shocking prude. I've tried to make her see sense, I've said "You're retarding the poor little cow", but she won't be told.'

'I don't know why you bother. What's it to you?'

'And that silly school. Straw boaters and lacrosse rackets. In this day and age. Well, I *ask* you . . .'

'Sticks.'

'Huh?'

'You play lacrosse with sticks.'

'Very well, if you insist,' Elli, yawning, allowed. 'Sticks and stones . . . what's the difference?'

'It's up to them, isn't it? To John and Geraldine. It's their choice.'

'John? You think John has a say in it? I doubt that. He's so irredeemably wet. I don't imagine he has a good fuck in him.'

'Just the same,' argued Juin, squirming visibly, 'if they want to send her private –'

'If they want to blue their money . . .'

'Yes, that's their affair.'

'They have enough of it, of course, as is constantly being borne in on us. But the fees are astronomical. An arm and a leg. And for what? It's not as if she's even very bright, poor kid. It's not as if she's destined for great things. With Dominic, yes, arguably it might be worth it. There's something of David in Dominic. He has a future.' Elli's eyes took on, for an instant, an avid gleam. 'But Lucy will get married to the first fuckwit to ask her, you mark my words. She'll be like her mother and get hitched to a solicitor or a stockbroker or some such, and get hugely fat.'

'I think John's nice,' protested Juin, a person of fierce and – in Elli's view – aberrant loyalties. 'And Geraldine's not *hugely* fat.'

'I didn't say she was.'

'Yes you did. You said Lucy'd get hugely fat like her mother.'

'What I actually said was, she'd get married like her mother. And hugely fat.'

'Which amounts to the same thing.'

'No it doesn't. Besides, what I'm really getting at is, what is it all *for*?'

'What *is* it for?'

'It's the motive I distrust. The thinking behind it. Do they want to send their kids private so they become brain surgeons or research scientists or – as it might be – award-winning journalists? Or do they send them private so they can boast to their snooty pals at the golf club that they send them private?'

'Does any of it matter?'

'Yes,' said Elli hotly, because it did, very much, to her. If state education was good enough for her own daughter, she often and loudly declaimed, it was good enough for any child (although not so good – as Kate had wryly remarked to Geraldine only recently – that she did not have to make regular visits to Juin's school, to harry the teachers, to tell them where they were in error). She offered this up as a principle, one of those that had survived intact since her days at the barricades. But, like all her values, then and now, it was at the disposal of her vanity. Never mind Juin: if state education had been good enough for Elli Sharpe, it was good enough for all.

'Then why stay friends with the Gorsts?' Juin queried. 'Why bother to see them, ever? Why get on at me to invite Lucy? I should have thought you wouldn't want her under your roof.'

'It's you I'm thinking of. You need company. I honestly do feel, Juin, that –'

Just then the cordless telephone began to ring. 'Saved by the bell,' declared Juin tritely. She grabbed it, marked

27

time with it, let it ring once, twice, three times, before clicking the switch. And wasn't it weird the way, the instant she did so, it seemed a hole opened up in the ether, an echoing tunnel miles long, and wide enough for two voices to meet and pass each other? 'Yeah?' she said gruffly into the mouthpiece. And, 'Yes, she's here.'

She did not, however, immediately pass the phone to her mother, but sat there weighing it in her hand, frowning, still wondering at the miracle of technology that provided a breach into someone else's life – a conduit to Larkspur Road, Tooting, where lived . . .

Abruptly and with flushed cheeks, she got to her feet and thrust the handset at her mother. 'Kate,' she said shortly. And, unnecessarily, 'For you.'

'Me?' As Elli stretched out to take the instrument, she remarked her daughter's arousal and – horribly shrewd – guessed the reason for it. 'Kate, hi,' she said into the mouthpiece, as her eyes rested surmisingly upon the wretched Juin. And, 'Yes . . . Yes . . .' she continued, drawing herself up, rising physically to the occasion, becoming visibly braced. 'Oh, gawd . . . Of course I can imagine.' Conducting, as was her wont, a kind of conference call, she drew Juin into the discussion, speaking to her in loud asides. *'Kate has Naomi with her,'* she relayed. 'No, no, Kate, I was just telling Juin. *Naomi's having one of her breakdowns, apparently* . . . Yes, sure, I can come over. *She wants me to go round there and reason with that light-minded friend of ours.* No, that's all right. I'll come straight away. *Can't you picture the scene? Poor old Kate!* Yes, I was just saying to Juin, "Poor Kate". Give me an hour. I'll be there. Ta-ta.'

'What's it all about?' asked Juin with studied insouciance, as her mother handed back the telephone.

'Just Naomi doing her nut as usual.'

'What about, though? What's up, actually?'

'She's flounced out on Alan. Fetched up at Kate's and is inconsolable.'

'So what are you supposed to do?'

'Well, console her.'

'But if she's –'

'*I* shall talk her out of it. You have to be firm with her, which of course Kate can't be. She doesn't know the meaning of the word. She really is a bit of a drip, to be brutal about it. I mean, very nice and sweet and well-meaning and all that, but . . .' A derisive twitch of the lips said it all for Elli, it said just what she thought about niceness, an overrated virtue, only for the craven. Let no one ever call *her* nice. 'She's been pleading with La Markham for the past hour, she claims, and the more she pleads, the more the tears flow. She's at her wits' end, wherever that might be.'

'So you're riding to the rescue?' Juin was putting up a fine show of indifference.

'Yes. Do you want to come?'

Juin inspected a gnawed fingernail, gnawed it some more, inspected it again minutely. 'I don't think so.'

'Suit yourself.'

Elli drained her wine glass and, brushing past the hydrangea, setting the pink mopheads bobbing, she bore it up the steps, in through the french windows.

Juin stayed on the lawn for a further five minutes, trying in vain to teach Muffy to give a paw, then the pair of them, also, in a mood of mutual disenchantment, traipsed indoors.

They found Elli in the hall in red halterneck jumpsuit and staggeringly high heels. 'Do you have to wear those shoes?' Juin protested, wincing, though the shoes were the least of it. (Elli's love affair with clothes had been the longest and the least requited of her life.)

'What's wrong with them?'

'They look really Shazzy. Dead common.'

'These, my sweet child, are Valentino. Two hundred and fifty quid touch.'

'They still look common.'

'My darling daughter. So conservative.' Elli took from her handbag lipstick and compact, drew herself a savage snarl to frighten the horses. 'You'll grow out of it, I have no doubt. Now, I may be gone for some while, as the man said.'

'What man?'

'*That* man. Captain Oates.'

'Ah.'

'A very gallant gentleman. Now, don't forget to eat, you hear me? There's salami and all sorts in the fridge.'

'You know I hate salami. All the white bits.'

'Well, have cheese then. Or one of my Healthy Options.'

For answer, Juin poked a finger down her throat and squinted down her nose.

'Give us a kiss.' Elli offered a cheek and Juin feinted at it. 'You'll be all right?'

'Of *course* I'll be all right. I'm not completely incapable, you know.'

'I know, honey.' Elli paused to look at her an instant, considering. She thought how like her dad was Juin, how like nice Tim, who had so sportingly impregnated her and then, as agreed, had made himself scarce. Funny to think that, despite all her efforts, despite his absence, Juin was still more her father's than her mother's creature. There must be some conclusions to be drawn from this about nature or nurture, if she could be bothered to ponder it.

'Give my love to . . . Kate.' Juin, balanced stork-like on one leg, and, clawing her toes, inspected the black and puckered sole of her foot.

'Naturally.'

'And to . . . you know.'

'Oh, sure.'

Juin trailed her mother on to the step. 'Don't drink and drive,' she pleaded finally, futilely. 'Sleep over if you have a skinful.'

'Oh, thanks very much. Is that how you see me? As some kind of lush?'

'Well, it's not unheard of, is it, for you to have a few too many?'

'Very, very occasionally, I'll admit. On high days and holidays.'

'You get stinking drunk. All the time. Ratted. *Please*, Mum, be careful.'

'You can rely upon it. Toodle-oo.' Then, precariously balanced, pitching forward in her four-inch heels, Elli headed for her sporty Toyota.

Juin, waiting on the step with Muffy, heard the engine roar, heard the car go tearing down the road, leaving in its wake a smell of scorching rubber. As it swung into the high street, she heard, too, a squeal of tyres and a long blast of someone's horn.

What now? She went upstairs to wash what little had been spared of her hair.

'If you *must* know,' said Elli, 'it's Martin Curran.'

'Oh, dear,' responded a distracted Kate, who must know about Elli's latest love affair, only inasmuch as Elli must tell her. She would have far preferred, indeed, given the choice, to be left in ignorance. She felt burdened mightily by confidences. Ruth Curran, Martin's wife, came at once to mind and reproached her. Kate had always liked the woman, whose recipe for *penne* with tomato and ricotta, scribbled down for her on the back of a Sainsbury's till receipt, she had followed often and to great acclaim. How could she face her if by chance they met? How could she look her in the eye? She did not care to think of her being cheated in this fashion.

'Ruth is no angel, I'll have you know.' Elli, reading Kate's expression, reading her thoughts, was quick to extenuate.

Maybe not, conceded Kate. Yet there was something of the angel in the way Ruth looked, with her wide-set, forget-me-not eyes, and with her strangely serene – as it now seemed, deluded – expression: it was hard to believe her guilty of mortal sin.

'Besides . . .' Elli sloshed into a smeared glass, on Kate's cluttered kitchen table, an apparently generous measure for herself of the Piper Heidsieck which she had bought on the way here to 'toast Naomi's new-found freedom', as she had so bullishly expressed it. The champagne, thus heedlessly poured, frothed like shaving foam, subsiding slowly to a disappointing insufficiency. 'Now look. I've gone and given myself short commons.' With greater care she topped up the drink. 'Besides, what the eye don't see . . .'

'Hmph.'

'And what is that supposed to mean?'

'It means, I think that's balls. It won't do, Elli. It won't wash. In a way, it only makes it worse, the eye not seeing. It compounds the wrong.'

Kate thought of David, who had packed more infidelity into their few months of marriage than most men manage in a lifetime. She thought of the pitying looks she had inspired. And of all the phone calls – strange women's voices, David's guarded responses ('It's a bit inconvenient . . . Yes, I know I said . . . Well, of *course* I do').

Then, because these things were stored in the same cluttered compartment – in a box in her brain marked 'Humiliations, misc' – she thought of the time when she'd gone round all morning with her school skirt tucked into her pants at the back.

'And if Ruth *were* ever to find out?' she challenged Elli. '*Then* she'd certainly have something to grieve over.'

'She won't, though. Find out. Why should she?'

'Because these things have a way of coming to light, don't they? People are caught all the time. Someone tells tales. Or they get tripped up by their own lies. Or they leave a trail of evidence – hotel receipts, plane tickets, Access bills, knickers in the glove compartment, stuff like that.'

'Only if they choose to.' Elli waved aside this objection. 'Only if they secretly, subconsciously, deep down *want* to be caught. If they want to be punished and then forgiven. Or to force a showdown. They'd destroy the evidence, wouldn't they, if they didn't mean it to be discovered?'

Not, reflected Kate, if the whole thing was on expenses, if incriminating tickets, bills, credit card slips might, through creative misaccounting, be worth money. (Such petty satisfaction she had had from going through David's pockets, and from destroying those precious scraps of paper, for which the cost of his philandering might have been redeemed.)

'It won't happen with Martin and me, we're both far too clever and balanced and adult and discreet. Besides . . .' *Another* besides? 'It's just a mad fling. A bit of fun. It won't last. It will be over by Christmas, as they said about the First World War.'

'Yes, exactly. And look what happened then.'

'Pfoof.'

'In any case, it was the American Civil War.'

'What was?'

'That they said would be over by Christmas.' Kate had listened very hard at school for fear of missing anything, and was precise almost to a fault, preoccupied with inconsequential details, unable somehow to let a fact pass unfinessed.

'It was not.'

'Yes it was. Originally it was. I mean, yes, they said it about the first war as well, but . . .'

'Have it your way, then,' Elli told her indulgently, as

you might an impossible child. 'I'm not going to argue with you. Enough with the wittering, OK? Cut out the sanctimonious claptrap and get some of this Hide-n-Seek down your neck.' Then, taking a swig, 'Archbishop,' she shouted to cover a belch. 'We are here, after all, to rally round our comrade, to cheer her up and stifle her regret.'

'Ah, yes. Naomi.' Kate got to her feet and went to the dresser, snatched up a bicycle bell which she found there and rang it idly. 'Thanks,' she said over her shoulder as Elli slopped out champagne for her. 'She seemed better, I thought, after you spoke to her.'

'You have to tough it out with her, you realise? It's no good just pandering to her the way you do, it's no good pussyfooting around her.'

'I guess not,' agreed Kate with humility. It was true that no amount of soothing seemed to do the trick with the distraught woman. Elli had achieved, in a few minutes, with her brisk, no-nonsense attitude, what Kate had failed to achieve with two hours of murmured platitudes. And, when the tears were dried, it had been a subdued and tractable Naomi Markham who had been packed off upstairs to 'repair her face', to 'make herself respectable'.

'Believe me, it ain't.'

'I say . . .' Kate cast an eye at the clock. 'She's been for ever. D'you suppose she's all right? Should one of us nip up and check?'

'Are you kidding?' Elli grimaced, and they shared a moment of shouty mirth. Once, long ago, in their teenage years, at the flat in Holland Park, it used to drive them mad. *Then*, it had been an issue, the way Naomi

35

hogged the bathroom, locked the door against them for an hour, two hours, drained off the hot-water tank, refused to respond to their knocking and pleading, or emerged, indignant, for no more than an instant, swathed in towels, to offer some compelling reason – that she must treat herself to a Toni, must apply her Tanfastic, must Val-Pak her face or Veet 'O' her legs – why she should not be disturbed.

'I never could imagine what took her such ages,' Kate remembered. 'God created woman, if we can believe what we're told, in a fraction of the time it takes her to get ready to go out to lunch – and with a great deal less fuss and bother.'

'Using fewer raw materials,' agreed Elli.

'Oh, *yes*, she always spent a fortune on cosmetics.' This with a sniff, a hint of disparagement. Kate was privately contemptuous – and not a little envious – of cultivated beauty, having neglected even to try to cultivate beauty of her own. These days she devoted all her energies to the cultivation of beautiful gardens. Was there something to be inferred from this?

'It's time she grew out of these histrionics,' said Elli tersely, tapping a Stuyvesant from its pack. 'She's a big girl now. We all are.'

'I guess she's a bit unbalanced.'

'Mad as a snake,' Elli cheerfully confirmed. 'Mind you, it must be rough for her. When you've been a top model, with all that that involves, the rest of life must seem something of a let-down. And when you've been as drop-dead gorgeous as she was –'

'She still *is*,' reacted Kate, springing to the defence of

36

that which, only seconds ago, she had deplored. 'She takes such care of her appearance. I think she looks as good as she ever did. She's hardly changed a bit.' Then, 'Nor, for that matter, have you,' she added dutifully, complaisantly.

'No.' Elli narrowed her eyes, clicked the lighter, chased the wagging cigarette end with the flame, puffed it alight, coughed with abandon and slapped the smoke about. 'Whereas Geraldine *has* aged, hasn't she? (In her case of course, it's wilful.) And so, my love, I am bound to say, have *you*.'

'Ooooh!' Kate, caught unawares, could not disguise her hurt and outrage. Her pulse thundered. Elli should have known better, she should have played by the rules. Out of kindness and politeness only, Kate had paid her a compliment: and kindness and politeness had been her due in return. How dared the woman sit there, all raddled and bloated and gone to pot, in her preposterous playsuit, and make wounding personal remarks?

'Don't get on your high horse,' Elli told her smoothly. 'And don't glare at me like that. If the wind changes you'll get stuck like it, then you *will* be in trouble.'

'For God's sake!'

'I was only thinking you do look a bit tired. Worn, you understand? You need a holiday.'

'I just *had* a holiday, in case you don't remember. Alex and I went to Brittany at Whitsun. I sent you a card. The seabird reserve at Cap Sizun. Or a girl in traditional Breton dress for the Pardon of St Anne.'

'Ah, yes.' It was a bit rum, Elli remembered thinking at the time, for a guy of nearly twenty-two to go away with

37

his mum. If Alex had not been so much his own person, she might have quite despised him for it. 'Also,' she added, 'your hair is going grey.'

Kate sat down hard and gripped the table edge, to restrain herself physically from leaping up and rushing to the mirror to verify this. '*You* could be too,' she snapped. 'You could be completely grey, for all anyone knows, under that . . . that peroxide wig. You could be quite white.'

'I could be,' Elli tranquilly allowed, '*for all that anyone knows*. And the great thing is, no one does know. *I* certainly don't, so why should it bother me? It's the jolly old unseeing eye again, and the ungrieving heart.'

'In which concept, as I told you, I don't believe.'

'In which you don't believe. You suit being older, you see, Kate, that's the thing. Some women do. You have a very English face. And what it lacks in beauty, it makes up for in character, which is, after all, the more enduring quality.'

'I am bound to say . . .' began Kate. But it seemed she was not bound at all, for at that instant Alex appeared in the doorway, and twisting in her chair, smiling up at him sweetly, she discarded the thought, discarded the remains of the sentence, the entire conversation.

'I've been mucking out the spare room,' he reported, adding to the debris on the dresser an overflowing ashtray and two mugs with hard black-coffee glaze. 'Ah, my socks! I've been looking everywhere for them.'

'They're not a pair, you will notice,' Kate told him.

'No, but they exactly match another non-pair I found in the drawer.'

'A coincidence.'

'Yes. A stroke of luck, eh?'

'Hey, handsome,' Elli called, cutting across this interchange. 'Come over here, big boy, and give your Aunt Elli a kiss.'

Amenably, with a roguish quirk of the mouth, Alex went to her, stooped over her to peck her on the cheek and, as she seized him by the neck, was forced to submit to a deep, wet, sexual snog.

'I do wish you'd be a pal,' Elli cajoled him when finally she released him, 'and give my Juin one. She's dying for a fuck – can't wait to find out what it's like – and I so want it to be a goodie for her. I mean, first time and all. Get her off to a flying start. Besides, she has the hots for you, I can tell, I recognise the signs.'

The effrontery of the woman! The infernal cheek! Kate was winded with shock. Such a way to speak to her Alex! Such a way to speak of poor little Juin, who would be mortified if she knew!

Alex, however, with no hint of discomposure, offered a courteous reply – only, really, half heard by the shaken Kate – to the effect that, while he could think of nothing more delightful, he did feel Juin should be left to make her own arrangements. 'In any case, she's barely sixteen. What's the rush?'

'What's the rush?' Elli rolled her eyes. 'What's the rush, he asks. We were at it like knives at your age.'

'Ah, well, Elli,' he affected regret, 'times change, I guess.'

Such charm, he had, and innate grace. From where did that come? Not from David, surely, thought Kate in a rare fit of pure detestation (on the whole she bore scant ill will towards the man who had given her the greatest gift of her life). Not from her, either, for she was truly gauche, tongue-tied one minute, blurting the next, never able to say what she meant, or to mean precisely what she said.

She ached with devotion as she watched him walk from the kitchen into the garden. With her eyes on his retreating back, she tilted her glass, missed her mouth altogether, and slopped cold champagne down her front.

Sitting on the back step, minutes later, propped against the wall with the brick nibbling the fabric of his T-shirt, Alex Garvey grinned to himself as he thought how he and Kate would hoot with laughter over all this, when at last they were rid of their preposterous guests. Drawing up his knees, he squinted down between them at the paved square, at scurrying black ants as unreadable as small print, a dyslectic's nightmare.

A splutter in the downpipe a few feet from him, a sudden, scented debouchment, signalled that Naomi was at last out of the bath, so things were moving.

He breathed the smell of the warm water in which she had been steeping, her perfume, the very quintessence of femininity, intimate as body fluids, at once familiar and infinitely strange. And deep within him something stirred.

A memory came to him, dazzling and distorted as a scene reflected in a Christmas bauble. Faces bulged and warped in the foreground. Sounds resonated down the years.

Naomi had been there, and Kate, towing him through

the cosmetics department of . . . Selfridge's, he supposed it was. Baskets, handbags, the hems of jackets dashed his face. ' . . . the last bus,' said a voice somewhere above him, with terrible portent (the end of the world, no less, it had seemed to him, must be nigh).

He saw – but mistily, through a cataract on his mind's eye – Naomi pause at a counter, saw her pick up a spray and anoint herself with . . .

Faster and faster the lights spun. The voices boomed. Then there he was, sitting on the steps to the food hall, with his head between his knees. 'Better now?' Kate was asking him, her hand on his shoulder staying him. And – to Naomi, presumably – 'Low blood sugar, d'you think? He could be hungry. Should we get something to eat?'

The recollection, though it brought with it disorientation and faint nausea, was not altogether disagreeable. Rattled, aroused, feeling almost furtive, he got up and got busy, stowing the mower in the shed, padlocking the door against intruders. And he tried to put from him a powerful intimation of sexual otherness.

He was used to the company of women, to their moods and cycles, their highs and lows, to the peculiar, confiding nature of their conversation, the heart-searching, the soul-bearing, the occasional lewdness, intensely personal revelations, raucous laughter, copious tears. He had grown up among thrusting bosoms, bumping hips, fleshy thighs, swishing nylons and snapping elastic. He had grown accustomed to the ripe anatomy of the older female, held together as it seemed to be, or dependent upon, straps, suspenders, hooks and eyes. He had heard

41

of the pencil test, and of pelvic floor exercises, press-on towels, tampons, D and Cs, PMT . . . He was at ease with all that. And on the whole he felt favoured to be privy to it.

But there were moments, as now, when he felt suffocated, moments when it overwhelmed him, when he longed for the swagger and the superficiality of the public bar fraternity, for a game of darts and a pint of lager, for an hour or so of light relief.

I shall go down to the pub tonight, he decided, slipping the shed key into his jeans pocket with satisfaction. I shall leave them to get sloshed and maudlin together. They can have a real girls' night. They can talk about old times.

At which his mind positively boggled.

CHAPTER

2

The news was not all bad. In the matter of grey hairs, for instance, Kate was reassured to find that Elli had, if not exactly lied, at least been uneconomical with the truth. Her own rigorous investigations in remorseless morning light, using, literally, a fine-tooth comb, had revealed no more than the few strands for which she had already accounted. So there was little cause, really, for despondency.

On the other hand, there was Naomi. Or, rather, there Naomi was. 'Let me stay,' she had implored – and stay, it seemed, she meant to do, in an odd, exalted position, somewhere above either guest or resident, required to make no appreciable contribution, while enjoying the complete run of the house.

Ten days, and she had apparently no idea of when she might go, still less *where*. The subject so pained her, she could not address it without closing her eyes, furrowing her brow, pinching the bridge of her nose between thumb and forefinger, and hauling her breath in across her tongue.

'You'll have to give her an ultimatum,' Elli had advised Kate when she'd rung on Sunday morning for what she was pleased to call 'a natter' (too benign a word, in Kate's

43

view, for the kind of vituperation in which this woman routinely indulged). Elli had claimed to have a hangover, but, in spite – or because – of this, had been more than usually bumptious. 'Set a limit on it,' she had urged. 'Tell her she's got until the end of the month. Be quite ruthless. I would. Otherwise you'll have her there till Christmas.'

'How *can* I?' Kate had pleaded in a stifled undertone, wrapping her mouth with her hand lest her words carry all the way upstairs to where Naomi lay sleeping. And, indeed, how could she? She *would* be grey, she told herself ruefully, she would be stooped and lined if this went on for very much longer. But how to end it, given her soft, appeasing nature? She had no wrath in her but that which she catalysed from the slights, hurts and affronts which came her way from other people. Naomi must provide her with the necessary strength of feeling before she could find in herself some more spirited response. Mere self-absorption, laziness, want of con-sideration were minor annoyances, not the stuff from which she might manufacture ire. And she could not, in all reason, be mad at Naomi for something she did to the air.

'There's no harm in her, after all,' she had weaselled, then, pushing her fringe back off her forehead, clamping it down with the flat of her hand, wondering if she could begin to explain about the Naominess that pervaded the place.

'I'm not saying there is. However . . .'

'Hm?'

'Have you thought about the council?'

'What?'

'You can call them in, can't you, for infestations? There's a special department. They send round men with masks and sprays.'

'Don't be vile, El. She's your friend, too, remember. And she needs us. Couldn't she come to you for a bit? Wouldn't that be an idea?'

'An idea, yes. One of your worst. An absolute stinker. I'd rather eat sick.'

'I think you might cheer her up.'

'I am not in the business of cheering people up. If Jesus had wanted me for a sunbeam I should have had notice of it long ago.'

'For one thing, you have more space.'

'Which is how I prefer it. I can't stand to be crowded. Besides, I have no time. My life is all taken up, as you must realise.'

'And mine *isn't*, I suppose?'

'Not to anywhere near the same extent.'

'Ha!' Kate had scratched around under her T-shirt, worried with her fingers at her brassière, which seemed to have welded itself to her flesh. To have Elli in one's life was, she had reflected, insufferable. Yet *not* to have her would be unthinkable, as if one's least favourite colour – a peculiarly lurid shade of mauve – had been discontinued, removed for ever from the spectrum.

'Well, let's face it, it isn't.'

'For another thing, Elli, you're so persuasive. You might be able to din some sense into her.'

'I don't see why. I can't din any sense into *you*, can I? What did I just say to you? Lay it on the line for her.

Tell her you can't be doing with her. It really is that simple.'

'I can't honestly say that she's a nuisance,' Kate had further demurred. Which was so, or it was not, depending on one's definition of nuisance.

Kate did not mind, for instance, coming home to find unwashed cups in the sink, spent matches in the box, cold, flecky tea in the pot, the lid off the marmalade, in which wasps had met a sticky end. She did not mind clearing up after her guest, rinsing soap scurf from the basin, clawing nests of long hair out of the plug-hole, restoring the place to a more familiar state of disorder.

What she did mind was the trace, the faint but lingering spoor, of ennui. Everywhere she detected evidence of a day spent in idleness. Small items, ornaments, would have been moved – snatched up no doubt by listless hands, subjected to perfunctory scrutiny, then set aside. The crossword would have been trifled with, wrong answers sketched in, scored out, or overlaid with more wrong answers. Doodles on the jotter by the telephone, numbers, cryptic notes, hinted at desultory conversations held with God alone knew who.

'You won't face her down, of course,' Elli had persisted, with horrible acuity, 'because you secretly love being put upon.'

'I don't. I emphatically do not.'

'Then you are just a coward, aren't you? Afraid of confrontation? Can't stand to be disliked?'

'So? No one wants to be disliked, do they? Not even you.'

'It's a risk I'm prepared to take.'

'You just like to be provocative, that's your way, Elli,

46

though you're as needy of affection as the next person. Anyway, I am going to talk to Naomi, but I'm going to talk to her *my* way.'

Which was what Kate had done. And, as was her way, she had failed. 'Why not go and stay with Geraldine for a bit?' she had ventured yesterday, in a voice bright with dissembling. 'I'll be going over there myself tomorrow. I can drive you. You could do with a change of scene. It always helps to put a bit of distance between yourself and your troubles, I find. It gives you a whole new perspective. Besides, the country air would do you good.' She still, somewhere inside herself, believed the one about fresh air, its salutary effects. She quite saw how Naomi might perk up if she were exposed to it, how the roses would bloom again in her pale cheeks. 'You are looking awfully peaky.'

But, no, Naomi had been adamant, she must not leave town, she must stay in London for her work.

'What work?' Kate had, with reckless insensitivity, enquired.

More tears. Floods of them. 'I gave up my career for that bastard,' Naomi, who dealt heavily in half-truths, had protested, sniffing, rubbing her cheek with the heel of her hand. 'I gave up everything for him.'

She had been so dependent upon Alan, reflected Kate on this Tuesday morning, as she stood stripping the remaining flesh from the carcass of yesterday's chicken for Pushkin and Petal, who, breathing the slightly sulphurous smell, bumped around her ankles in thrilled anticipation and keeled over, purring, at her feet.

The kitchen was filled with fluttery early sunshine,

47

which would be gone by midday, mercifully taking with it the smears and finger splotches on the window pane, the teeming dust motes, the telltale signs of less than thorough cleaning.

On the dresser, the post lay unopened. There were two letters for Alex – from the bank and the building society, Kate had noticed, but unwittingly, for the times were gone when intriguing marbled envelopes arrived, addressed in girlish hand, in violet felt-tip, scented like a brothel and sealed with a loving kiss. Nothing about his correspondence these days required it to be sniffed at or held up to a strong light.

Long gone, too, were those desperate times when the clack of the flap, a flurry of paper, the postman's whistling made her ill with anticipation lest there be a cheque from David, or lest there not be.

Alex was coming down the stairs now, his tread cumbrous still with sleep. 'It's terrible, actually, isn't it?' murmured Kate almost complacently, directing her words to the doorway which would at any moment darken with his presence, as she stooped to deposit some unappetising ribbons of meat.

'What's terrible?' Alex indifferently enquired.

Straightening with a groan, hanging her hands in front of her, she went to rinse away the grease under the tap. 'It strikes me that there's something very wrong when half the world starves while our two mogs stuff them-selves on maize-fed chicken.'

'I doubt,' said Alex, 'that they would see it that way. I'm quite sure they would say it was only fair. That is one point of view.'

Pushkin and Petal, meanwhile, oblivious, cast covetous eyes upon one another's dishes, each fearful that the other had been better done by, until, finally, convinced of it, they changed places.

'You're probably right. Besides, what can you do? It's no use to send the scraps to Oxfam. Now, breakfast?' she offered, the pangs of conscience thus easily assuaged, and she slid under the lighted grill two slices of wholemeal bread.

'Not for me. But if that's fresh coffee I can smell . . .'

'Oh, you must have *something*.' She became slightly agitated. 'You'll be fainting by eleven o'clock.'

'Huh? Oh, all right, then.' He yawned into his palm. He would munch his way through a slice of sawdusty toast, but only to please her. He had a very male appetite, sometimes urgent, sometimes not, and he ate, as men do, if and when he was hungry – a strange concept to a woman such as Kate, in whom appetite and emotion were all confused.

'If you're quick,' she offered, 'I can give you a lift to the tube. But I must be on the road by eight.'

'That's all right. I'm not going to the office today. I have paperwork I can do here, then a lunchtime meeting.'

'Something interesting?'

'I've been asked to do a magazine redesign. Yeah, it's great, I should enjoy it.'

'Mmm.' Smiling she poured him coffee from the jug. 'My son the graphic designer', she liked to say to herself, and would have said to others at every opportunity – 'Help, help, my son the graphic designer is drowning!' –were her sense of self-parody less highly developed.

Her son the graphic designer sat now with his elbows on the table, listening courteously to *Thought for the Day*. If some chap had taken the trouble to ponder the nature and significance of human relationships, his demeanour implied, the very least one could do was to attend when the conclusions were made explicit.

'Butter or marge?'

'Yes thanks.'

'Which?'

'What? Oh, sorry. Either.'

She chose for him, for the sake of his arteries, polyunsaturated spread.

'How about you?' he wanted to know. 'What does your day hold?'

'Really nice things.' She inhaled deeply and veiled her eyes, as if drinking in the exquisite scent of a rose. 'A trip to the garden centre. Some planting at the Gorsts. Then, this afternoon, I'm in Barnes.'

'To Geraldine's first, eh?' He snuffled scorn into his coffee, for, almost alone among the human race, his aunt enraged him, patronising as she was to Kate. 'She gets her money's worth from you all right.'

'Hey, now,' Kate chided. 'Geraldine's all right. She was good to me when you were small. When David was all behind with his cheques, and I couldn't meet the bills.'

'And she has been exacting payment in kind ever since.'

'That isn't fair.'

'It is. You know it is. She runs you ragged.'

'Nonsense,' Kate soothed, suddenly abstracted, her

mind racing on. A trip to Neals, she thought, to fill the boot with polystyrene trays of smiling, nodding pansies. Then on to Surrey. 'Right, right, I'm off. Be good.' The crown of his head, the pale skin beneath a sweet whorl of dark hair, was eminently kissable: she tapped it with her fingertip and touched her lips to it. 'Hope the meeting goes well. Bye-bye.'

She went quickly, then, down the hall, slipped out into the morning's warm embrace. And, 'Hi,' she said, tangling with the surly paper-boy at the gate, trying to get by him, to let him pass, so that he might drop off the *Globe* for Naomi to hash up when she came wafting down three, four, five hours later.

There was a shimmer about the day, a false promise of eternal, glorious summer. The pavement was splattered with sunshine. The privet hedge appeared to have been polished overnight. There was sparkle even in the grass which grew in ragged clumps around the roots of the plane tree at the kerb.

It made her happy, it made her hopeful. She actually sang a few self-conscious, tuneless lines as she unlocked her little Fiat Panda – chosen not for its size, or for fuel economy, but because she had liked the name, because pandas were so cuddly. Easing in behind the wheel, she did a quick grey-hair check then adjusted the rake of the rear-view mirror so that the ceiling light, the trug and spade on the back seat, the Wiltons' silver Subaru, inconsiderately parked, all made themselves known to her. She had a pleasing sensation of standing off from herself, watching her own performance, she saw herself as able, emancipated and free.

Poor Naomi, to have relinquished all responsibility to her man, and to other men before that. She had yielded her whole self to her lovers. Alan had kept her, fed and clothed her. Leaving him, she had left everything.

Kate's single state seemed to her now to be one of immense privilege. Such good fortune to be self-sufficient! How much more blessed was the provider than the provided-for! In a way she had much for which to thank David. Had he not been so remiss, she would not have been forced to take hold of her life, to learn the trade which she so loved, to become an expert. That bastard from hell – as she now, good-humouredly characterised him – must often have spent more on one boozy lunch than his wife and son had lived on for a week. But, in the end, she was richer for it, so all might now be forgiven.

As she started the engine, her smile gave way to her driving face, an expression of mild apprehension. With her usual circumspection, she engaged first gear, let out the clutch and moved away in a series of short hops.

'If you would only listen to what you're told . . .' Elli in a boiling fury was a truly terrifying prospect. There was a thin film of moisture on her upper lip and she appeared almost to be fluorescing.

Trevor, however, was unmoved. His withers were unwrung. He could not, to put it bluntly, have given a bee's fart. 'You didn't tell me anything,' he reminded her woodenly.

'A note,' she ranted at him. 'I left a note.'

'One can't listen, exactly, to a note.'

'Unless it's a musical note,' put in Juin unhelpfully, though she then, to show willing, went down on her knees, patted about on the blond carpet, examined the flat of her hand, patted some more.

'Do be careful,' Elli rebuked her. 'You might kneel on the thing.' Grabbing up a cushion, she shook it about and pummelled it senseless. 'I left it for you to read, Trevor. There, where I always leave notes.' She indicated the chrome and glass table under the tall sash window, to which, sure enough, a yellow Post-it sticker adhered, with the day's ordinance scrawled upon it. Crossing the room, she peeled off the scrap of paper, advanced it trembling on one finger, invited him to read and to repent. 'You will see it says you are on no account to do in here.'

Mischievous, the morning light sought her out beneath her silky ivory robe: like a wick through pale candle wax her body might be seen. Splotches of shadow from a suppurating lime tree, playing upon her face, somehow intensified her scowl.

'It does?' The sun might not look through her, but Trevor could; by an act of will he caused her to dissolve. A familiar London street scene, a row of austere houses opposite, white rendered, with condescending front steps, impressed themselves upon his consciousness. And it occurred to him, in an idle way, how various were the aspirations of their owners, for this was one of those districts which seemed always in transition, going no-where fast, in which one's neighbour might be concert pianist or drug pusher, prostitute or film producer. Elli had been drawn here by the faintly bohemian atmos-

53

phere, the mix of dilapidation and gentrification, the 'street life' as she thought of it, for which there was a price to pay in punitive insurance premiums.

'I should be going in any case,' Juin fretted, getting to her feet, brushing her skirt fastidiously. 'I shall be late for assembly.'

'Bugger assembly,' Elli dismissed her concerns. 'And don't tramp about like that. Watch where you're putting your feet.'

'It's not as if you always leave a note,' Trevor argued. 'How am I supposed to know when you do?'

Elli folded her arms across her chest. The ornate ceiling mouldings, the dado rail, the marble fire surround, an urn of strangely inorganic-looking lilies, an Arteluce lamp seemed by turns to obsess her. Her lips moved in silent imprecation. The effect was of someone striving to control her temper, but she was probably just working up a head of steam. Finally, she spoke. '*If* I leave a note, *when* I leave one, that is where you will find it. It would not be asking too much, I should have thought, for you to check.'

'It's all right for you.' Juin snatched up her bag and, rummaging, produced a small square of mirror in which she registered her desperation. 'No one gets on to you about your time-keeping, you can come and go as you please. Oh, rats, look at my hair! And where are my keys? I have to dash. I'll get detention.'

'Take the day off, then. Take a sickie.'

'How can I? That's stupid. I'm about to sit my GCSEs any minute, in case you had forgotten. I can't go skipping lessons every time you have a crisis.'

'You've had a full five years to study for your damned exams. If you're under-rehearsed, that's your own fault, not mine. Oh, my God, get that stupid animal *out* of here.' For Muffy, drawn to the excitement, had come bursting through the panelled door and was embarked upon a tour of the knocked-through lounge, his tail waving like a pennant, and his snuffling nose to the ground. 'Shoo!' yelled Elli, beside herself, enraged by the lack of co-operation which she found on every hand. Blurred faces stared at her, uncomprehending. The dog, a dark splodge, ran all over the shop. Could nobody, *nobody*, in this unruly household be relied upon for anything? With a crackle of static, she went in pursuit.

The ominous whine of the vacuum-cleaner had roused her from a deliciously diverting dream. She had come flying down from her bed, in yesterday's make-up and foul humour, and she was not, at this moment, at her best. A night person, she did not even start to come together before ten. Squinting to bring the clock into sharper focus, to establish that it was not yet a quarter to nine, she took on a predatory aspect.

'Besides,' she went on, breathless, warming to her theme, once the unfortunate dog had been ejected, 'who needs exam passes? *I* didn't get to be *me* by being a swot. Look, I'll write a note for Miss Pushface, tell her you had a pain. How's that?'

'It isn't my problem, is it, really?' Trevor justified himself, as Muffy scrabbled and whimpered at the door, distressed at having been excluded. 'It's your own lookout, I'd say, if you can't take care of your possessions.'

'And it will be *your* lookout if I decide to fire you.' Elli fixed him with a stare so cold it would have chilled the blood of a more susceptible human being. (A basilisk, indeed, confronted by that stare, might have slunk off home to consider a career move.) Trevor, however, merely shrugged and matched his employer, glare for glare. So you fire me, his attitude conveyed. What do I care?

He was a lanky, emaciated youth with the greyish pallor of the undead. He lived, so far as anyone could tell, on taco chips and Thunderbird. An art student, he 'did' for Elli only to eke out his grant. He was not, he implied by his demeanour, a real housekeeper, and he carried around in his breast pocket, by way of credentials, snapshots of his work – of great, gloomy canvases, with their apocalyptic titles, impressive dimensions and audacious prices jotted on the back.

If he had a sense of humour, he kept it under his hat with his finer feelings and his political convictions. On this last, Elli had often tried to draw him out, regaling him with tales of Grosvenor Square in the glory glory days. He would, however, reveal nothing beyond the fact he had been a nihilist before disillusionment set in.

The threat to sack him, so often repeated, was, like a perennially dripping tap, no longer audible to either of them. Now and then it occurred to Elli to wonder if she wouldn't do better to employ some nice homebody like Geraldine's Mrs Slipper-Slopper, a motherly lady with blue permed hair and tired feet. By no stretch of the imagination, after all, could Trevor have been called a 'treasure'.

On the other hand he was a talking point, he was different. And it amused her no end to have a young man going down on her skirting-boards. In her lighter moods she treated him to the sort of constant, humiliating, low-level sexual harassment which so many young women workers must endure. In a bad mood, as now, she berated him horribly.

Trevor would ask himself, on occasion, which was the more tedious, the baiting or the bollockings. And always the answer came back: six of one, half a dozen of the other. The teasing he could, on the whole, take. The contumely he could cope with. What he really resented was the way she trashed the place, as if deliberately to increase his workload. He had heard tell of proud homeowners for whom domestic help acted as a discipline. These were people who, their minds intensely concentrated, actually cleaned for their cleaners. Loath to let their dailies glimpse a speck of dirt, they would be up at dawn dusting and polishing. It made him laugh a hollow, barking laugh, to hear of this phenomenon.

It was a bit much, frankly, Elli was fulminating, when you could not roll in from a night on the razzle, mislay a contact lens and leave the finding of it till the morning, without some busybody barging in and sucking the little mother up the vacuum pipe. She helped herself to a Stuyvesant from a silver box, lit up with an onyx table lighter, removed the fag from her mouth and studied the glowing tip consideringly. 'There's no help for it,' she decided. 'You'll have to empty out the Hoover.'

'You have got to be kidding.'

'Go on, take it into the garden. Tip it onto a sheet of newspaper. Sift through it. What was that you said?'

'Nothing.'

'What did you call me? You called me a name.'

'I said the old bag – the Hoover bag – needs changing anyway.'

'Then do so while you're at it. There are spares in the cupboard.'

'Yes, sahib.'

'And less of your lip.'

'Whatever you say, sahib.'

He lugged the vacuum through the french windows on to the terrace. There he spread out a copy of last Wednesday's *Globe*, open at Elli's column, weighted it with stones, tipped grey fluff all over her face and set about the winnowing process. A playful breeze bloated the curtains upstairs and down; it blew in by turns, from neighbouring houses left and right, the sounds of ragga and grand opera. The house filled insidiously with choking clouds of dust.

'Guess what I've found.' Juin, emerging triumphant from the bathroom to background music of singing plumbing, ambushed Elli on her way back to bed and held out her closed fist.

'What is that?' Elli touched a hand to her temple. She could not deny that she'd had one drink too many last night. But which one had it been? She was inclined to blame her poisoning on the glass of inferior dry white in the pub, rather than on the bottle of excellent red in Alastair Little's, or the champagne she and Martin had consumed by way of a nightcap at the Groucho. Yes, there had been something distinctly suspect about that first glass of plonk.

'Guess,' urged Juin tauntingly.

'I don't have time for guessing games. Nor do you. You'll be late for school. You'll miss assembly. You have GCSEs to consider.'

'Bugger GCSEs. Bugger assembly.' Juin uncurled her fingers. Couched in the soft flesh of her palm lay a tiny tinted disc. 'It was in the soap-dish. Stuck to the soap like a bubble.'

'My lens. How did that get there?'

'At a wild guess, I would say you put it there.'

'But I was sure I dropped it . . .'

'You can't have done, can you? Here, take the horrid thing, it gives me the creeps.'

'Thanks, honey. Are you off, then?'

'Yes, of course.'

Elli followed her to the head of the stairs, stood poised there like some large, ungentle bird. 'Tell Trevor for me, will you?' she commanded. 'Tell him to stop pissing about. He's wasted half the morning as it is. He'd better bloody well get on now and do the front room.'

Since she was up, she decided grumpily, she had better stay up. She would run herself a hot bath and soak away her tiredness. She could spend the morning in idleness. Then, at one, maybe two o'clock, she would retire to her study and clap out her copy.

On days when she had no looming deadline and little else to do there, she was usually to be found at the office soon after eleven. She would read her mail, bin most of it, dictate excoriating replies to an unfortunate few, catch up with the top news stories, scan other people's columns, check out the opposition, make a few personal phone calls, and chat at the wage slaves she saw all around her, who hunched over their terminals as if, she said, the race was on to see which of them would be first to suffer repetitive strain injury.

Elli liked to hark back to the era of hot metal, of real journalism, of subbing 'on the stone', of blood, sweat and tears, when men were men, and Fleet Street was Fleet Street, and everyone tipped out for interminable liquid lunches in the Cock Tavern, the Cartoonist or the Olde Cheshire Cheese. Her reminiscences went down a bomb, of course, with the new intake of junior reporters and graduate trainees in their high-tech, no-drinking, no-smoking environment, down river in London's docklands. Oh, they loved to hear all about it!

On Tuesday mornings, however, they were deprived of her insights, for she chose always to stay at home to write her page. In theory she was supposed to deliver before one o'clock, but it suited her to wait around, while her answerphone recorded ever more desperate appeals from frantic sub-editors, then to Tandy at four or five o'clock, when they would be too busy to mess with her text and would have no time to raise queries or to make problems.

Her behaviour was tolerated because, according to her editor (himself a hot metal man, an old Fleet Street hand), she was 'good value', and because – who could deny it? – she was one of the best. She was wicked and wily.

No one knew this better than Elli herself, and, as she slid down in her bath with a judder of flesh on ceramic, as the water slapped around her shoulders and tugged at her laquered hair, she felt lapped in self-gratification.

Her contretemps with the wretched Trevor had gingered her up no end. Today's column was going to be a scorcher. She had raised perversity to an art form. To this extent, at least, she was predictable. Her worst invective was reserved for noble deeds, acts of heroism, fashionable causes, popular figures, the cutesy, and the ideologically sound. She would see hypocrisy, pusillanimity, woeful naïvety, intellectual dishonesty, bad taste and cant where others saw only virtue. Meanwhile she would cheerfully espouse the mad, the bad and the dangerous. But just where she would come from on any question, and where her meditations might lead her, not even she could foresee.

She would sit down for but an instant at her desk, consult her conscious and subconscious, then off she'd go, rattling away at the keys, tapping the wellspring of private prejudice. They called this process work and paid her handsomely for it. But to La Sharpe her job was a doddle.

She showed no fear, favour or compunction. If her victims protested, if they were wounded or incensed, she gave not a fig; people should, she reasoned, be more like her, they should be robust. If they wrote to complain, threatened libel action, she would laugh out loud and claim fair comment. That her opinions were a matter of caprice in no way undermined her sense of her own unassailable rightness.

So-o . . . Who would it be today?

As this politician, that TV personality, the other minor royal went about their business, they could not have guessed what even now was cooking up for them, or

61

have known how comprehensively their Wednesday would be spoiled.

And there, if you like, was power.

'Fifty per cent of tetanus cases are fatal,' proclaimed Geraldine, for whom a piece of information was much like a new hat – something to be paraded and admired. Bacteria, she continued, lay dormant in the soil, just waiting to invade the body through a deep and dirty wound. Rusty nails were commonly implicated, but rose thorns were culprits too. She sounded inordinately pleased about this.

'I know,' said Kate, privately doubting Geraldine's statistics, as she held her hand under the gushing tap. Pink ran the water into the bluish steel sink. With appalled fascination she watched it curl around the plug-hole, watched her life blood wash away down the waste pipe. 'I do *know* about tetanus. We were warned on the course. I've had all my jabs.'

'Just as well, as it turns out.' Her sister-in-law, sniffing, soaked a wad of cotton wool in Dettol and offered it. 'The muscles go into spasm. The jaw locks tight. Here, take this, will you?'

'Thanks.' Kate, accepting the dressing, staunching the wound, detected beneath the public lavatory smell of disinfectant a strong whiff of disfavour. 'If that foolish girl would only wear gloves . . .' Geraldine would say of her to John tonight, when the pair of them sat down to pool their disapprobation. (There was a hoity-toity temper to the Gorsts' conversations, they were as one in reprehension: they could not credit the obduracy, idiocy and degeneracy of Other People, which caused them to sigh, to shake their heads, to stare meditatively into their seven o'clock gin and tonics.) Well, she would have a point, conceded Kate, inspecting with chagrin her begrimed hands, her split and broken nails, no two of them alike in length or shape. But she needed to touch, to feel, to make contact, to grub around among the tender roots and shoots, and could not bear the blinding of her seeing fingertips.

'I can't abide injections, me,' volunteered Mrs Slack, and, comfy in the knowledge that she need not endure one, perhaps ever again, she poured fragrant, amber Assam tea for the three of them, straining it into fluted fine bone china cups.

'Nor I, Mrs Slack, nor I,' Geraldine feelingly agreed as she peeled off the protective strip and slapped a plaster on to Kate's gashed finger.

The daily help had come with the house, and, five years on, was still very full of her former employers, the Robbies, who had been gracious, apparently, and generous to a fault. She had a forthright and confiding nature – indeed, no ache or pain went unconfided. Her name was actually du Slack, but Geraldine refused to indulge such aspiration in her domestic help. ('Oh dear, what a mouthful,' she had protested, when Mrs Robbie had so graciously, generously, introduced them, 'I shall never get my tongue around that.')

'I faint clean away at the sight of a needle.'

'Yes.' Geraldine, disappearing into the pantry, raised her voice. 'The dentist, now, I can tolerate. But, confronted with a hypodermic, I turn immediately to jelly.'

'Myself, I turn to drink,' called out Kate, a bit above herself today, a bit boisterous, as she visualised with amusement this unlikely transubstantiation: a Geraldine-shaped jelly wibble-wobbled, iridescent, before her inner gaze.

'All the same . . . ' Geraldine stood amid the shelves of tins and packets and preserves. And, as the mingled scents of vanilla, cocoa, flour seemed to fuddle her brain, she closed her eyes and clubbed her head but nothing came to mind.

It was a bothersome business, this, and it was happening more and more. A keen sense of purpose would carry her to fridge, to sideboard, to wardrobe, she would tug open cupboard or drawer, to find that none of the contents declared themselves to her, nothing connected. Then, at worst, she would be forced to retrace her steps, to trail back indoors or out, upstairs or down, to return to the job in hand, for only then would she recall the need that had impelled her.

She blamed all those who put upon her – not just her mutinous and combative children, or her mild, biddable husband (mildness is, after all, an imposition of a kind, biddability makes its own demands), but everyone who, by their comings and goings, caused such a run on her energies. Small wonder if she was distracted.

Lemon curd, pickled cabbage, rhubarb chutney . . . She had no use right now for any of them.

If others would only give a little more, if they would take a little less.

Suet, rice, cream crackers . . . She continued her futile inventory. The red and blue of Atora, the orange and black of Jacob's, the brilliant product livery, so insidiously recognisable, barely registered upon her consciousness. A fat bluebottle, now bumping angrily up against the zinc window mesh, now dipping, despairing, around the bleary light-bulb, seemed exactly to mimic her mental processes.

Then, 'Got any biscuits?' Kate cheerily enquired, and as if by magic the paralysing spell was broken.

'A little treat.' Geraldine emerged triumphant, in control once more, brandishing a chocolate swiss roll like a baton in its cellophane wrapper, proof, if proof were needed, that the sainted Robbies had no monopoly of grace or generosity. Behind her, in buzzing agitation, rather as if it had some uneasy attachment to her, came the big black fly.

'Great,' said Kate appreciatively.

'I think I'll take the weight off . . .' murmured Mrs Slack. Old friends, her bottom and the rush seat of the chair were reunited. Doubling at the waist to unhook the tight straps, to ease them over her chafed heels, she liberated her feet from their new, navy, summer slingbacks. 'They fit a bit snug,' she understated, 'though they were sold for a five and a half.'

'Perhaps,' suggested Kate absently, watching as Geraldine stripped the wrapper from the chocolate roll, 'you should have tried a six.'

'But I never took a six.' Mrs Slack was visibly affronted. There were billows in the tea which she lifted to her lips. 'Not in my whole life,' she insisted, steadying herself before taking a sip. And then, lest there be any lingering doubt, 'I never was a six,' she reiterated, for she had a

65

version of herself, unrevised since the age of fifteen, in which she could close her hands about her waist, kick one leg above her head, turn a perfect cartwheel, trip the light fantastic in a dainty slipper.

'Ah, well.' Kate was as mortified as she was amazed to have given offence. She liked Molly du Slack, whose true worth was far higher than Geraldine acknowledged. It went way beyond her diligence in dusting behind the radiators or going at cup rings on the coffee table with a meth-soaked cloth; it had to do with decency, integrity, a strong sense of self, and extraordinary courage in the face of unremitting ordinariness; it had to do with a stout heart. All the same . . . Her eyes, sliding furtively sideways, downwards, came to rest on one bunioned foot, a hammer toe. All the same, she decided, a six at the very least she was looking at here.

'You can't trust manufacturers' sizes.' Geraldine sliced the swiss roll decisively, handed the pieces on the knife. 'Not in shoes,' she said firmly. 'Not in dresses. Neither one.' For herself, she was finding lately that makers were skimping on their size 18s, she was finding increasingly that 'large' was an exaggeration, but she chose for some reason not to share this.

'It's true,' confirmed Kate in an effort to be agreeable, though it cost her in energy to shape such common-places, to think them up, let alone to give them voice. It was like dredging a pond in the dismal certainty that, at best, you'd come up with a rotten old pram or corroded bedstead. The effort was out of all proportion. 'Some cut so much more generously than others,' she concluded feebly.

'And now, Katharine . . .' Geraldine came on, without warning, all la-di-da, she assumed a distancing and a defining tone. 'How are you getting on with my parterre?'

'The weeding?' Kate, perceiving this change in manner, paused in an attempt to unwind in one continuous strip the furled segment of chocolate sponge. It had long been Geraldine's wish to disambiguate their relationship, to place her permanently somewhere between in-law and hired hand. For the moment at least, she found this amusing, and ducked into her cup to hide a smirk. 'It's done,' she said, with well-judged deference. 'Or almost.'

'It takes an age, doesn't it?' said Geraldine, with a meaning tut (a more efficient operator, Kate was made to feel, would crack through the job in half the time).

'It does. You'd be surprised.' The strip of sponge came apart. 'Forest bark,' said Kate puzzlingly, before popping a piece of sponge into her mouth.

'What say?'

'I was just thinking, if we were to put some shredded bark down, it would check the weeds. It is expensive, but –'

'But then, so is maintenance.'

'That's true. You would probably save in the long run.' On *me*, she meant, on *my hours*, you would save. Nor did she much care, since she could take the Gorsts' garden or she could leave it. She had spent years repressing it, discouraging rampant or irregular growth, cutting back, containing it, and it had come to dishearten her deeply. Geraldine favoured knife-sharp edges, bleached stone slabs, swept paths, striped lawns, neat drills or blocks of uncompromising colour. Nothing grew that had not been put to grow there. It was all by invitation only here at Copperfields, and the grounds had the primped and pristine aspect of a municipal park, a constant air of newness, dulling to the soul, all the more so when one remembered how it had been.

Some time in the 1940s the big house had been set down, four square, in long-established gardens, on the site, it was said, of a former priory. The Robbies, for all their grace and generosity, had obviously been very lax about the upkeep. Kate called to mind banks of rumpled shrubs, borders clotted with brambles and lacy cow parsley, a rotting door let into a wall of crumbling brick to which attached, with bindweed trammels, a rusty garden roller. She saw tortured pear trees, swishy orchard grass pregnant with fallen fruit, the whole glimpsed through a softening, saffron haze of pollen and seed-heads. Almost nothing had survived the bulldozers: an ancient greenhouse, only, and the theatrical backdrop of beech along the farthest margin had been spared. Given a free hand, she could have done very different things with the land. But a free hand she had absolutely not been given.

'It's worth considering then?'

'Oh, yes, I'm sure. Or stone chippings would be fine around the alpines.'

They sat a while in an unexpectant silence, Kate and Geraldine musing on the possibilities, Mrs Slack, for once, not disposed to speak, since she had – to her own small surprise – nothing much to offer on the subject of mulches and top dressings.

'Naomi is still with me, did I say?' Smiling, Kate advanced her cup, wordlessly solicited more tea. With a certain hauteur, Mrs Slack did the honours (and whatever happened to manners, she was bound to ask herself, to the proverbial ps and qs?).

'What, *still*?' queried Geraldine, squelching a yawn with the flat of her hand. 'How awkward for you. I really do think . . .' And it went without saying, what she thought.

'Yes, well.'

'No word from her friend, I suppose?'

'From Alan? Not a peep.'

'Has she plans? Does she say?'

'It seems not. I have no hint.'

'Then it's up to you, I suppose,' Geraldine concluded with a sudden and complete loss of interest, 'to put your foot down.'

'Mmm, that's what Elli reckons, more or less.' Kate picked up a teaspoon, twirled it between thumb and forefinger. 'It did occur to me she might come here.'

'*Here*?' A bizarre notion, Geraldine made it sound. The North Pole, to judge by her reaction, could scarcely be more impractical.

Silly of me, Kate thought, even to moot it. 'Anyway, she says she can't leave London, she's on call for work, so you can relax, you're in the clear.'

'But, naturally, if she wanted . . .' Geraldine expanded to fill the safe space thus afforded. 'I should be only too happy . . . if it would help . . .'

'Oh, we'll muddle through, I dare say. We always have.'

No thanks to you and yours, Kate told herself.

Thanks, in no small way, to me, thought Geraldine.

'If you ask me,' put in Mrs Slack, who liked to speak as she found, 'that young lady brings her troubles down on her own head.' Naomi had, in her view, the looks of a film star, and film stars were, notoriously, fools to themselves; they were the unhappiest beings in all creation.

'Well, I don't know about that,' replied Geraldine with a pursing of the lips and a hint of asperity. It was not Mrs S's place to pass judgment on her friends. But then, if a large part of her liked to observe the proprieties, there was another large part that warmed to a good old gossip. So, 'I never felt that Alan Neish was right for her,' she disclosed, wise in hindsight. 'Or she for him.'

A size six ego, Kate privately decided of Naomi, in a size five relationship. Her torn finger had begun to throb. The not altogether unpleasant sensation absorbed her. How soon began the body's healing processes. If only the spirit might heal half as swiftly! 'She seems utterly lost,' she murmured, more to herself than to anyone else. And, hearing her own words, she was moved along at last from resentment to compassion; she felt at once better and worse about her friend. 'That's why I can't, you know, simply tell her to push off. She is quite without resources of her own.'

Sucking in her lower lip consideringly, she studied Geraldine's face, still comely after its own fashion, but not somehow of its time. Deliberately, wilfully, according to Elli, Geraldine Garvey had aged. Unlike Kate, she had done it on purpose. Supposedly. Yet, to Kate's eye, the other woman appeared not so much old as out-moded. She might have strayed off the pages of a women's weekly magazine from the 1950s, when fashion had dictated a slightly daffy, feminine look: bright, appliqué mouth; stiff, cockled hair; fine, arched brows conveying perpetual surprise.

She had always been an anachronism though, possessor, in the Swinging Sixites, of such oddities as evening gloves, of sequinned bags and big, boned undergarments. Simply, in middle years, her earlier quaintness had been fully realised.

Now Geraldine drove her fingers into her perm, raised those ruthlessly tweezed brows a millimetre more, worked up a pout and wondered whether the bank, perhaps . . . Or, if not the bank, then Naomi's parents. Her mother. At a pinch, her father . . .

'God, no, I doubt it. Not from what we hear. Those two wouldn't give her the time of day. In any case, I'm not talking about financial resources,' Kate explained, 'although it's true she doesn't have a bean. No, I was thinking more of initiative, motivation, that sort of things. Coping skills.'

'Savvy,' interpreted Molly Slack.

'Yes, exactly.'

'I see.'

'Because she really can't manage, you know, on her own. She can't *do* anything. She's purely decorative.' Kate tapped her cup experimentally with the edge of the spoon. 'I've been wondering, actually, if I dare call Alan. If I could only persuade him to come and scoop her up and take her home . . .'

'But he would have been there by now, surely? If he meant ever to come. He knows where she is, I presume.'

'Well, he'd need just three guesses, wouldn't he? Where else would she be but with one of us? With thee or me or Elli?'

'If I were you, I'd hesitate to get involved.'

'So should I,' Kate told her vexedly. 'Given the choice, I should certainly hesitate. But I don't have that choice, do I? I am, as usual, the muggins who's been lumbered.'

'Look, I did offer, didn't I?' With breathtaking dishonesty, Geraldine voiced what was the truth, the whole truth, and yet, somehow, anything but the truth. 'Not a moment ago. Yes, by all means, I told you, she should come here to stay. If it would help, I said.'

'That's right.' Mrs Slack endorsed, once again speaking as she found. 'She did offer.'

'You did,' Kate moodily acknowledged. She dropped her head and glared at her thighs, plumping out the denim of her jeans. 'But . . .' But, she thought crossly, you did not mean a word of it.

In the ensuing hostile silence, each heard the click of a key in the latch, the clack of the bolt, the crash of the front door, an impertinent tread, shoe leather wrenching at the newly polished parquet. 'What's this?' queried Dominic, derisive, barging in on them. 'Mothers' meeting? It's all right, Mama, I'm not sagging off. Old Watmough is laid low with influenza. Double French has been scratched. I'm allowed out on licence. Hi, Katie, how're you doing? How's every little thing?'

'Every little thing is fine,' Kate informed him drily,

stifling her dislike. 'It's the big things that are giving me headaches just now.'

What was it about the accursed boy? Well, she knew what it was, of course. He was a fine, well-made youth, excessively confident, indecently handsome, all swagger and smirk. With a satirical air, he sported his school uniform: he did not so much look foolish in it as it looked foolish on him. With his shirt unbuttoned at the neck, and his tie tugged awry, he had a ruffianly aspect. His expression was roguish, his manner explicit. When he blithely declared himself 'shagged out', Kate no more than half believed him (the 'shagged' rang true; the 'out', somehow, did not). He was altogether too mobile about the mouth, too loose around the pelvis. She could not glance at him without thinking of her husband. She thought: David, you bloody bastard!

Nobody knew what it was to be Naomi Markham. Least of all did Naomi Markham know. She had very little insight, and that little which she did have she tended to discount, for she had never learned to trust in intuition.

Of one thing, though, she might be sure: whatever ailed her, it was not bound up with beauty. Oh no! Beauty is seldom the torment the unbeautiful are pleased to think it might be. One the whole, indeed, it is a tremendous asset. In any case, Naomi had been a late arrival at the ball. As a child, at that age when the real damage is done, she had been plain. She had been worse than plain. She had been tall for her age, and scrawny, stick-limbed, with lank hair through which her ears had poked pathetically beneath the brim of a straw school

73

boater anchored by elastic which cut like cheese wire. She had had, too, almost preternaturally pale skin, a blue, bruised look around the eyes, and the most solemn of countenances. (The smile had come later, with practice, with the profession, in the business of baring perfect pearly teeth, of mouthing 'hi' and 'cheese' and 'lesbian' at the camera lens.)

She had also been, then as now, less her own person than a mass of other people's attributions. Acquiescent, if not actively obliging, she had become as she was represented to herself, embodying without question the faults ascribed to her. Lazy, her mother, Irena, had said of her continually; sulky, her father, Geoffrey; spoilt, her mother's lover, her so-called Uncle Huw.

It was perhaps fortunate, then, that she had not stood accused of far more serious failings. No one had, for instance, ever suggested that she might have her mother's vile temper, her father's sly, sadistic wit. Conscious unkindness, sustained malice were beyond her. She was happy to bitch when it seemed to be required of her, but she had never really got the hang of it. She had neither the curiosity to divine others' baser motives, nor the invention to impute them. She sinned usually by omission, by her failure to comprehend those close to her, and she turned her tantrums mainly on herself.

Her infancy had been spent in Pimlico, in a tall, red, Gothic house with latticed windows. The panelled dining-room, with its imposing, carved stone fireplace and crest above it, had done duty as a waiting-room, where jittery strangers sat distractedly leafing through back numbers of *Queen* magazine, straining after the shrill whistle of the drill, poised to spring up when they were summoned, to go jaunting implausibly into her father's surgery.

Geoffrey Markham had made a fat living in private dental practice. He had loved Wagner and fine burgundy before wife and family – or so Irena had accused, and no doubt she had spoken true. He had taken a keen interest in Naomi's oral hygiene, had proscribed sweets of any kind, but had seemed otherwise, on the whole, in the matter of his daughter, to be largely indifferent. 'He doesn't give a damn,' Irena would rage, pacing the Persian carpet in the first-floor salon. 'Not for you, not for me, or for anyone but himself.' Then, 'I'm *bored*,' she would fling at him. And, B-O-R-E-D, she would spell it for him, her voice flying out behind her like a thin, bright scarf, as she stormed off down the passageway to revile the cook. At which Geoffrey Markham would subside into his button-back leather armchair, prop his feet on the brass fender, shake out the morning's *Times* and, with a sigh of supreme satisfaction, immerse himself in the latest floods and famines.

Home, to the small and sombre Naomi Markham, had meant wealth, opulence, high ceilings, crystal chandeliers. It had meant Minton vases, marquetry writing tables, ormolu clocks. And the sick, anticipating smiles of patients in the vestibule. And the antiseptic smell of the surgery. And the unremitting animosity between her parents.

These were the memories she would carry with her from the age of nine, when Irena had declared, to her husband's huge enjoyment, that enough was enough. The Valkyries, at full volume, had pursued mother and daughter down the long, curved staircase, out through the front door, between vicious black spiked railings, on to the street, where Daimler and liveried chauffeur had awaited.

They had fled with Uncle Huw, first to Capri, and then – more prosaically, but always in style – to Oxfordshire. Naomi had had to rough it emotionally, but materially she had always been indulged. The Holland Park year, the flat-share with Elli and Geraldine and Kate, had been, as she misremembered it now, a mere youthful adventure, a jolly, girly interlude, before her career took off and relays of men in velvet suits and platform shoes and Aston Martins came bearing gifts.

So it was a profound shock to find herself, at this time of her life, in a poky little room in godforsaken south London, with traffic passing just feet away, and a workman shouting for someone called Vick or Nick, and a skip lorry rattling the windows in their frames. It was a setback, once more to live out of a suitcase, to be forced to share a bathroom – to creep along the landing and to try the door, only to find it bolted. It was a comedown to eat one's evening meal off ill-assorted china at the kitchen table, with a flustered Kate springing up apologetically every few seconds to fetch butter from the fridge or to snatch a smoking pan from the stove.

She was just not in her element here in Tooting. And what kind of name was that, anyway, for a place? It sounded like a . . . Naomi lay among the piled pillows, sunk deep in heartsickness and hollowfibre filling, and sifted through the sorry remnants of her education, searching for the word 'gerund', which was not, after all, to be found. Tooting? It sounded like a noun formed from a verb. As in hunting and shooting. Rooting and Tooting. It sounded like a doing word, better left undone.

Some sin she must be guilty of, to deserve this fate. Some failure in herself, there must have been – but what? 'For God's sake, darling,' Alan used to plead with her, 'be reasonable.' And this was what had made it so impossible, since, always, by her own lights, by her own reasoning, she *was*. 'I'm a terrible person,' she told herself experimentally. But she felt only sorely mis-understood, and tears of self-pity welled up behind her eyelids, inducing another thumping headache.

How had Kate endured for so long such oppressive surroundings? How could she bear to be trapped in this bog-standard, three-up, three-down configuration? And Alex, now displaced to the box room? How could that big, strong, gorgeous boy abide it?

Unconsciously, Naomi checked her breathing, drew in little sips of air, as if it were on ration. Deep sleep and riven dreams had left her unrefreshed and anxious. Her limbs felt racked, her muscles sore. One of the cats (for such was its custom and – it had given her to understand – its inalienable right) snoozed in a solid ball at her feet, wheezing with contentment, anchoring the duvet, imprinting it with grime.

When she opened her eyes she felt rebuffed by the ugly wardrobe, and by the dingy, speckled mirror on the wardrobe door, which, refusing to latch, stood always agape, offering her its own depressing slant upon her situation.

This was a very basic, male bedroom, unrelieved by civilising feminine touches. Here had slept, in their time, all the different Alex Garveys – the engaging toddler, the scruffy schoolboy, the raw adolescent, the strapping young man. And here those Alexes had left their possessions – football, cricket bat, Scalextric, snorkel, squash racket – junked on top of that hideous piece of furniture.

Behind the slewed mirror-door hung his shirts and jackets, in disorderly line, like a bus queue; they had jibbed and chattered in indignation when she'd hustled them up to make space for one or two of her own blouses.

Her gaze travelled hopelessly, to arrive by turns at the small, tiled fireplace with stove-enamelled iron grate, the sagging armchair, the narrow glass doors, the inky-dinky balcony with all the brashness of the day beyond. It settled for an instant on the chest of drawers, in which resided among the socks and shorts – and wouldn't Kate just *die* if she knew it – an ambitious quantity of condoms, more Mates than you could shake a stick at.

The memory of this inadvertent find discomfited Naomi, who might be meddlesome, and a fidget, who might be into everything, but who truly hadn't meant to pry. She yearned to be far away from here, back in sylvan St John's Wood, where graceful houses in shades of pale pastel, swagged with wistaria, reposed on wide, sun-patterned avenues, behind high stone walls, and the brass door furniture gleamed, and the architectural ironmongery had meaning and function. She yearned for

78

her own room, for her own life, for the luxury she'd left behind.

Glaring at Pushkin, or at Petal (for she made no distinction), she tugged at the duvet in an attempt to dislodge the stupid animal, but it merely put out a contemptuous paw and unsheathed its hooky, horny claws as its face opened up in a pink, ribbed yawn.

If there was nothing now to hope for (and it seemed there might not be), such wretched circumstances could but compound her desolation.

'I feel so stuck,' she had confided yesterday on the telephone to Elli. 'And I'm so dreadfully in the way here. I'm completely *de trop*.' She was not so insensitive, after all, that she could fail to detect atmosphere when it pressed in upon her; she was not so stupid that she could not tell when she was supernumerary.

She had been accustomed, in the past, of course, to being one too many; she had grown up knowing in her bones, as children do, that she was misconceived. She had been underfoot in Capri, and in the Cotswolds. But at least Irena and Huw had not then had two decades of each other's company in which to establish arcane rituals, or to devise a secret language, a system of signing, of little coughs and collusive glances, subtly to exclude her.

'You could come here, of course,' Elli had told her sympathetically, 'if it weren't for Kate. One has to bear in mind her feelings. She would take it very badly, wouldn't she, if you were simply to decamp? She'd be mortally offended. She has such a chip on her shoulder, as we are all too painfully aware.'

'But I get on her nerves, I can tell.'

'Well, of course, she is, you know, the original contrary Mary. But, in any case, my lovely, it won't be for very much longer, will it? Things will sort themselves out, they're bound to.'

'I expect so,' Naomi had responded dully. But what? How? She could see no way forward, no possibility now of happy resolution.

At first she had assumed that Alan would come for her. Not straight away, perhaps, but in a day or so he would arrive. And she would be persuaded by his pleadings to return with him – subject to certain terms and conditions – in time to make ready for a promised holiday in Barbados.

Her intention to leave him absolutely and for ever had been real enough, but rash and unconsidered. And at Larkspur Road she had had ample leisure for repentance. She was sorry for her haste, for things said which might better have been left unsaid. In particular, when she had tried to draw on her account at Coutts and had learned that her allowance had not been paid, she had been very, very sorry indeed.

'My dear girl,' Irena had reacted with impatience when she heard her only daughter's voice on the telephone, 'don't ask *me* to bail you out. Huw keeps me so short, I can barely get by.' And, *sotto voce*, 'I'm so *bored*,' she had complained. 'We never go anywhere, we never see anyone. I was better off, frankly, with your father, monster though he might have been, God rot him.'

Then, 'My darling one,' Geoffrey had derided, 'fruit of

my loins, apple of my eye, don't look to me for a subsidy. I'm a pensioner now, you realise? I exist on a mite. Try that friend of your mother's. What's his name? Huw. Use your feminine wiles. See if you can't sting *him* for a bob or two.'

And, 'Nothing as yet,' Ariadne, her agent, had reported with a trace of irritation, when she had phoned in to check on progress. (Naomi had seen in her mind's eye this woman of sixty-several, for whom weight control was like a religion and required at least as much devotion. She had pictured her sitting po-faced at her inlaid mahogany desk, in her black Jean Muir, with her sleek bobbed hair, uncompromisingly chic and almost impossibly perpendicular). 'No, we've not forgotten you. Be assured, we'll get in touch with you the instant we have something for you.'

Be assured!

'Don't call us,' Naomi had muttered angrily as she slammed down the receiver, 'we'll call you.' The ingratitude of the old bitch! A small fortune, the agency had made in its time out of Naomi Markham. Yet today Ariadne could not even bother to pull out her perfectly manicured finger.

Whatever happened to loyalty? And to obligation? She supposed her agent's energies must be taken up with her younger clients, the so-called 'supermodels' who, she had read, would not get out of bed for much under a hundred thousand pounds. Huh! Herself, the way she felt now, she might not get out of bed at all. Ever.

Oh, what to do, what to *do*? She must make a new plan. But when she closed her eyes the hideous wardrobe bulked out her imagination. And she hadn't a thought in her head.

Globe Tower stood, very tall, very full of itself, a monument to proprietorial vanity, on the north bank of the toffee-coloured Thames. It was one of those glassy, galleried 1980s structures that seemed to have been built inside-out, with fresh air and daylight and rampant greenery up the middle, and with vital organs all exposed.

Here worked some of the finest minds in British journalism – among them Elaine Sharpe, who was even now arriving, under protest, in answer to a summons from the editor. Through the vast, marbled foyer she clattered, disdaining the uniformed commissionaires, disregarding the paper's nineteenth-century founder, who was raised up on a plinth behind a potted palm, cast in bronze. At the foot of the lift shaft she hovered, toggling the 'up' button, craning her neck as she watched for one of the metal capsules to drop down the transparent tube to collect her.

She was, to put it mildly, not best pleased. Her day, which had started so badly, seemed rapidly to be getting worse. How could she be expected to write her *bloody* column if she was also to attend a look-ahead meeting, convened on a whim by the big white chief? Christ, the way things were shaping up, she would not even have time for a proper lunch! A sandwich off the trolley was as much as she could hope for – some misbegotten combination of tuna and sweetcorn or cream cheese and raisins. Nor (this being a strictly dry outfit) any drop to drink.

'Come on, come *o-on*,' she agitated as, with infuriating slowness, one of the lift cars began its wheezing descent, stopping three, four times on its journey, to take aboard more passengers (minions, probably, from the post room – and, frankly, it would not have hurt those lazy little oiks to walk).

It was thus a very crabby Elaine Sharpe who greeted the lift's occupants when finally, and with small expressions of relief, they issued forth. But she set aside her glare in favour of a strained smile for Patti Henderson, the executive editor, a vision in Armani, in their midst.

'Elli, *hi*,' Patti greeted her, twinkling her fingers in a coquettish manner which Elli judged neither appropriate nor appealing. The woman was pushing fifty and had worked in the organisation, 'man and boy' (as her subordinates loved to joke), for thirty-two years. There were those who called her 'hatchet-faced' – and those who spoke up passionately in defence of hatchets. She was eminently fitted for her high-powered job, blessed as she was with those three sterling qualities – ratlike cunning, a plausible manner and modest literary ability – identified by Nicholas Tomalin in the 1960s as essential to success in journalism. Arguably, she was a mite short on quality number three, but numbers one and two she had in spades. She inspired fear and loathing on every hand, yet here she was, waving, simpering, going cooey.

Elli nodded her response as she stepped into the lift. And, in the instant before it sealed itself, 'I've messaged you,' Patti called to her. 'I'm inviting you to Il Podge in September. Do try and join –'

Oh, *wow*, Elli told herself, exultant. Wow-*wee*. She

leaned against the wall, wrapped her arms about herself and closed her eyes. This would be some message! She could not wait to get to her work station, to call it up on her computer screen, to see it written down in black and white, to be sure she had not misheard. An invitation to one of Patti's house parties at Poggio nel Vento, her holiday home in the Tuscan hills, was quite simply to *die* for. The favoured few who went each year were always insufferably smug, flashing their snapshots around, sharing noisy reminiscences, shrilling with laughter, exhibiting a nauseating camaraderie. Elli, who disliked La Henderson mightily, and who distrusted her deeply (the word 'ruthless' came to mind, and the word 'scheming'), now found herself warming to her strangely.

Indeed, so elated was she, so excited, that she could not manage more than half-hearted obloquy for the casual sub-editor who was squatting in her place.

The scale and opulence, the outward display which so impressed the casual visitor to Globe Tower, was not so much in evidence behind the scenes. The newspaper staff was crowded into just four of the twenty-three floors, many of its members were freelances with no security of tenure, a sweatshop atmosphere prevailed, and a 'hot desk' policy required lowly day labour to grab a seat and a computer terminal where it might.

'Out, out,' Elli commanded, baring her teeth at the poor guy as he snatched up his few belongings and made a bolt for Home News. 'Christ, Jan,' she hissed at her secretary, 'I hate to seem territorial, but . . .'

'Sorry,' Jan replied, though she wasn't remotely. She

absolutely never rose to Elli's provocation. She was a drowsy twenty-three-year-old, with a seen-it, done-it attitude, unbecoming – as Elli often told her – in one of her tender years. She was priceless, though, for her telephone manner, for the ease with which she saw off readers when they rang in to complain. Holding the receiver to her ear while they yattered on, she would assume a hazy, unfocused look, as one might when mentally compiling one's wedding list (a current obsession) or performing pelvic floor exercises (another of her preoccupations: her list must, according to Elli, by now be as long as a full stock inventory at John Lewis, while her pelvic floor must be as taut and as snappy as an Olympic trampoline). Then, 'I'll pass your comments on,' Jan would promise with supreme indifference, and 'Thank you for calling,' she would say, before hanging up.

'Make me a coffee, there's a love,' Elli urged her.

'In a minute.'

'No, no, no.' With one pecking finger, Elli typed in her log-on, and the password that would give her access to the computer system, then she sat back in satisfaction as the legend, MESSAGE PENDING flashed at her. 'Not in a minute. Not in half a minute. *Now.*'

Bringing the message on to the screen, she read.

LUCCA.
TWO WEEKS FROM 26 AUGUST. I'M INVITING A WHOLE GANG OF LIKE-MINDED FUNSTERS. MUST BE CARD-CARRYING GOOD-TIMERS, FULLY PAID-UP MEMBERS OF THE INTEMPERANCE MOVEMENT. HOW ABOUT IT? *VIENE?*

Viene? Are you coming?

Now, no one could accuse Elaine Sharpe of creeping. Let it never be said that she kowtowed to her bosses. No grovelling sneak, she!

But she fancied that trip to Italy. She wanted it so much it hurt. Pausing for no more than a moment to wonder about Juin – about where she might be billeted, or who brought in to keep an eye on her – she flipped through the directory, checked Patti's log-on, and tapped in her reply.

'*Vengo*!' she spelt out. I am coming.

Alex Garvey was not a habitual liar. He knew the objective truth from a bar of soap when he came across it, but he saw no virtue in being profligate with it. His mother need not, after all, be privy to everything he thought, or to everything he did. That would be just *too* oppressive.

His sex life, for instance, was none of her concern, as hers – if she had one – was none of his. And his inner life must be strictly in; and soul-baring was strictly out. He was devoted to Kate. She was without equal, the best person on the planet. But that did not mean he wanted to live in her pocket.

Where he wanted to live, rather, if it met his eager expectations, was at number 11 Chafford Road, Fulham, in a ground-floor flat with a through lounge, a decent-sized kitchen and brick patio beyond. He wanted out of here and into there. He wanted his own space.

His 'meeting' at noon was with a selling agent. The magazine redesign of which he'd spoken, though real enough, was not on the day's agenda. Two facts, laid end to end, had amounted to a falsehood. For reasons of his own, he had dissembled. A voice in his head had urged circumspection. Time enough to tell all, it had counselled.

Kate would have the story from him as and when . . . As soon, that is, as his purpose was firm; when he was on the point of making an offer. To involve her just now in what was still, for him, a moral dilemma would be premature and pointless.

Eleven o'clock. Already the day was cooking up and thickening. When he opened the door to the front sitting-room, something came quickly past him, murmuring of yesterday. Catching a soft whiff of unexpired perfume, he was reminded: he didn't have the house to himself.

Nor was Naomi's the only lurking presence. In here the grandmothers, Garvey and Perkins, were condemned to eye one another wordlessly across the small expanse of stringy carpet, Eleanor Garvey peering sharply up from the mantelpiece, where she kept uneasy company with dead roses and raffia elephants, Pam Perkins gazing down from the top of the piano – an advantage she had not enjoyed in life.

Both women had vigorously opposed the marriage of Kate to David, and each for the same, sound reason that David was so obviously a high-flier, while Kate was so obviously not. The couple were quite unsuited, the mothers had asserted. They had given it six months. And six months, in the event, had been optimistic.

Poor Kate had been pregnant. He, Alex, had been on

the way. And David had deemed it his duty, or what-ever, to 'stand by her'. Attracted by some notion of his own nobility, or merely to annoy his parents, in a spirit of defiance David Garvey had plighted his troth.

Well, they were gone away now, the lot of them, Eleanor and Jack Garvey to Gloucestershire, where she seemed scarcely less remote than was Pam Perkins on the Other Side. Eleanor was a person of charmless whimsy. She had the fervid, seeking gaze, the empty, tinkling laugh, of one who, while talking endlessly, engages not at all in conversation. She had, in the early days, meddled intolerably in the upbringing of Alex, criticising Kate, whom she regarded as irredeemably lax. But the novelty having worn off, she had turned her attention from the first of her grandchildren to the second and third, to Dominic and Lucy, to whom she'd had far better access, and whose conception had been a more seemly, more acceptable affair.

Pam Perkins, who had died as she had lived, with humility, was scarcely the type to impinge upon him from beyond the grave. Her husband Cyril, Kate's father, meanwhile, was a virtual recluse. He lived in Woldingham, in a white cottage daubed green with nature's own graffiti. He tended his allotment on a strip of land beside the railway tracks, sowing long drills of East Ham cabbages and stalky Early Batterseas and blue curled kale, stopping only to eat a fingerprinted sandwich or to smoke a roll-up in the cold brick bothy, keeping himself to himself.

As for David – at the best of times erratic in his contact, unreliable in the matter of maintenance payments – he had been out of the picture for a decade. So there really had been no one but Kate for Alex. And, for Kate, there had been no one but Alex.

She'd done so well by him, he told himself, as he stood before the fireplace to establish himself in the mirror. She was a trouper. She emerged each day from the bathroom, innocent of make-up, scrubbed and soaped and heroic. She went out into the world, with her stumping walk, her feet inelegantly splayed, and she worked and worked, as she had always done.

'I owe her,' he said aloud, crossly, suddenly impatient with her, with himself, with their reciprocity. 'How can I desert her?' The envisaged flat – the through lounge, the white-tiled bathroom and the jolly galley kitchen – receded somewhat; they lost something of their gloss in his imagination.

He had striven, always, to help her. He was the sort of young man of whom older men despair, willing as he was to do the dishes unasked. He could sew on a button with quite the same competence as Kate – which is to say, barely competently. He was reasonably house-trained. He had made his contribution. But had he done half enough? Or was it too soon to leave her? Too soon to stop paying into the household kitty?

'You go,' she would be sure to encourage him, with a bright, brave gleam in her eyes. 'What a good idea, to get a foot on the property ladder. To have something of your own. Of course, you must.' And without him, she would return to her back-of-envelope budgeting, and she would not mind the penury half so much as she would mind the loss of his company.

Or might she feel herself to be liberated? Find herself a man? Remarry? Perhaps it was only he, Alex, who held her back.

He clawed at the neck of his T-shirt, dragged it over his head, to emerge with his dark hair rumpled and a faint flush in his cheeks.

He had a rather fine, well-muscled physique, of the sort that is achieved by playing recreational sport, rather than by serious training with weights. When he folded his arms across his chest, clamping his hands beneath them, his biceps made small but pleasing bulges.

Unlike his mother, who rarely combed her hair, and who simply never ironed a blouse or polished her shoes, he took some trouble with his appearance, methodically, and without great vanity, turning himself out.

He had grown into himself so perfectly these past few years, he fitted his skin exactly. He held himself erect, moved with effortless grace, assured of his body. He was no longer awkward and angular, no longer subject to sudden energy surges, as if from some inconstant power supply. Nor was he yet prone to minor malfunction, to the snapping knees and creaking back, the early intimations of degeneration which cause people laughingly to declare – and, in so declaring, somehow to deny – that they must be getting old.

He subjected his torso, now, to perfunctory inspection. He felt with the flat of his fingers a day's growth of beard, made a lathering motion with his hand, grinned in self-mockery and decided, arbitrarily and absolutely, that he would wear his light blue shirt.

Here, though, was a problem. The shirt was in his

wardrobe, in the bedroom above, from where there came not a sound.

Barefoot, stripped to the waist, and with exaggerated stealth, as though he, rather than Naomi, were the interloper, he crept upstairs and hovered on the landing. He laid a hand on the doorknob, pressed his cheek to the sour-smelling wood and heard the scritch-scratch and the plaintive mew of Petal on the other side.

Naomi Markham would surely sleep through World War Three, he wryly decided. She would wake with a start when the balloon went up and, blinking, enquire, 'What was *that*?'

He rapped softly with his knuckles. Then, receiving no reply, he turned the handle and pushed the door. Petal shot out between his feet as he edged furtively, even guiltily, inside. The wardrobe mirror marked his halting progress. He became conscious that he had suspended his breathing, and, inhaling, he took down into his lungs the slept-in air. When he drew the mirror-door towards him it gave him back his bedroom, or a tricksy version of it, an intriguing chiaroscuro, dream-distorted, some-where richer, more complex, less mundane than he'd remembered.

And it gave him, also, Naomi.

She was half-sitting in bed, borne up by pillows, watching him. One of her hands rested limply on the duvet, while with the other she clasped the front of a blue shirt – *his* blue shirt – fastening it at her breast. In the shadow she had about her a lambent quality, pale and flickering as candle flame. Her eyes were huge with sorrow so he saw right through them. And if she were shallow, as everyone said, why this sensation of going so deep, of going right in over his head?

Her misery was so genuine and so profound, it awed him (it would take a special kind of courage to abandon oneself in this way). Speechless, she revealed to him her utter desolation.

He went at once, sat on the bed beside her and, frowning, in a manner of a doctor, picked up her limp wrist, masssaged it with his thumb.

'Can I help?'

She shook her head. Tears started. Releasing the shirt she covered her face, regarding him through her fingers.

'Move up,' he said abruptly, with the intention only, probably, of holding her, of giving solace. But enclosed beneath the duvet was a sweet and dangerous warmth. Her skin was so soft to his touch. And there is, after all, one supreme way in which two people may give each other comfort.

'Don't cry,' he implored her. 'I can't bear it when you cry.'

Then, with infinite tenderness, without inhibition, with disbelief for the moment set aside, watched by the mischievous mirror, Alex Garvey made love to Naomi Markham as he had never made love before.

CHAPTER

3

Kate dreamt that she was in her childhood home, in her bed with the quilted plastic headboard melted at the corner by the heat of her fringed reading-lamp, which had illuminated for her the tempestuous worlds of Lowood, Wildfell Hall and Wuthering Heights.

To her right she saw how early sunlight busied in the half-dark. To her left it was stiller, softer, more opaquely grey. She sensed around her reassuring presences: her Beatles pin-ups plastered on the dressing-table mirror, the precarious, pink tufty stool with spindle legs which, if you sat on it too heavily, too perfunctorily, would put you off on to the rug.

Presently, the first train from Tattenham Corner to London Victoria would thread its way through her subconscious. The front door would vomit the *Daily Herald*, the *Croydon Advertiser*, the usual mess of bills on to the mat. A smell of frying bacon, fat and salt and piggy, would waft up the stairs from the back kitchen. Then in would come her mother with the day's misgivings, with a jittering cup of instant coffee and urgent admonishments to hurry, hurry, lest she be late for school. She was twelve years old, or thereabouts, and everything was as she'd always known it.

She could slip out of bed now, to sit on the padded linen chest beneath the window, and, pressing her chin into her forearm, gaze speculatively out at the backs of people, ranged in unsociable line along the garden wall, as they waited there for the bus to town, leaving festoons of litter in the flowerbeds and on the spotted laurel.

But it was easier just to lie here, bound with sticky webs of sleep . . .

When she did sit up, it was with a startled cry. And when she opened her eyes, she was dismayed to find the topography mysteriously altered, for there was no door where a door should be, just a big, rebuffing blank wall.

She knew, of course, almost instantly, where she was (in Tooting, in the 1990s, in middle age, in error). She knew it was ordinary old Thursday. Yet she was filled with obscure grief, with apprehension, with a sense of loss both past and impending.

Glancing at her travel alarm clock, she saw it was just five. When she was working, she set it for six-thirty, and in the daily race to be first awake, not to have it harry her, she would anticipate it, ordinarily, by a matter of a minute.

What, then, had roused her at this hour? Something inward? A loose memory racketing around? Or something outward? Something untoward?

Sliding from under the duvet, she tried to distinguish, in the fabric tangle on the floor, among the knotted legs and arms, a garment to cover her nakedness. The striped rugby shirt which she finally isolated was barely long enough to cover her. Hauling it on, tugging it down over her bottom, bunching the hem, holding it with one hand, she went to the door, opened it a crack, peeped out, then stepped on to the landing, which, though quite deserted, seemed faintly ruffled, as if by someone's swift and stealthy passing. The door to the spare room had about it a braced and purposeful aspect, a hint that it had just this second closed (almost, she seemed to hear the latch click into place). It was all very unrelaxed, some-how, and stirred about.

Alex must have been to the bathroom, of course. And she, at some unconscious level, must have heard him. But when she wandered down there, it felt chill and empty and unused. The long pile of the carpet sat up bushily. The porcelain maintained a stony silence.

So what . . .? She sat down abruptly on the loo, clasped her hands between her knees, rocked forward to stare at the sprightly carpet. What was going on here?

Kate had shared a house with illness, with birth, with death. She knew about these othernesses that could take up residence. But this was another other altogether. She could not identify it, but what had moved into her home this time was . . . well, *the* other. It was the incubus that has its evil way with all of us. It was sex.

'Not under my roof!' she would have protested, beside herself, had she known. But she didn't know. Not yet. Or even guess. Of course she didn't.

'Do we *have* to have her?' Lucy sat glaring down at her bran flakes, with the jug poised over the bowl, looking as if she might burst with bad temper. '*Why* do we? I can't endure her.'

Endure? That had come to her as if from nowhere. But

95

then, she had a way with language, Miss Goodman said. Her compositions were felicitous. Her poetry showed a certain flair. She breathed over the word adenoidally for a second, excited by its resonance, watching how her small breasts rose and fell beneath her cotton school dress. Then, 'I simply can't endure her,' she reiterated.

'Lucy, please.' Geraldine seemed to test with her fingers the flesh of her cheek, pressing it as one might a Victoria sponge to see if it were done. Spongily, the crumpled cheek puffed up again.

'Oh, *she's* all right,' put in Dominic, disagreeing, probably, for disagreement's sake. And, 'Whoops,' he shouted, jogging Lucy's arm with his elbow, so her flakes were drowned in a sudden shock of milk.

'Dominic, for pity's sake, grow up,' snapped Geraldine.

'Get a life,' said Lucy sneeringly.

'Now, you, Lucy, be quiet. Juin will be coming with us to Scotland. I promised Elaine. So we'll have no more discussion.'

'She'll spoil our holiday. I know she will. She's really weird. She and that stinking fleabag dog of hers.'

'What did I just say to you? It's been arranged. You should be thankful that you even *have* a holiday. There must be many poor, deprived children who don't.' Geraldine saw them clearly, suddenly, these large-eyed waifs from some recent invention called the 'inner city', who had probably never so much as glimpsed the sea. 'So let's hear no more from either of you, hmm?'

Her voice faltered. It was out of sheer frustration, however, for her own impotence, and not for the large-

eyed waifs, that she could have wept. The truth was –
though she could not confess it – that she was sick with
herself for having been persuaded. But Elli had asked her
on the phone last night, and Elli would always have her
way. She had this trick of begging a favour – often
something wholly unacceptable – for all the world as if
she were conferring one. To be burdened with her
awkward, truculent child while she swanned off for two
weeks in the Italian sun, Elaine Sharpe had somehow
given Geraldine to understand, would be the Gorsts'
privilege. 'She'll be company for Lucy . . . Nice for the
girls to be pals . . . Not as if Juin is any bother . . .
civilising influence on Dominic . . . tremendous help
around the place . . .'

There'd been nothing said – Geraldine now privately,
pettishly reflected – about that noisome mongrel, Muffy,
who jumped up slavering on the furniture, snatched
food off the table, rocked back on his haunches to guzzle
at his private parts, and had once, on a weekend visit,
done unspeakable things with a Dralon cushion behind
her living-room sofa.

Well, he must go into kennels; she would be firm about
it. You had to draw the line. The girl was one thing; the
animal quite another.

'I'll tell you what . . .' Dominic scraped busily around
the jam pot with his knife, spread his toast thickly with
apricot conserve. It was his pleasure to annoy people, he
was a consummate technician, but he never wasted on
his mother or his sister the infinite subtlety of which he
was capable, preferring to get straight to it. 'I don't mind
Juin. I mean, I wouldn't kick her out of bed.'

John had then urgently to be summoned. Or called

out, rather, from behind the morning's *Times*. Scandalised faces looked to him as, reluctantly, he lowered the paper. There had been, it was impressed upon him, an incident of sorts. He was to speak sharply to his son about some piece of downright insolence – 'Tell him,' Geraldine was exhorting, 'go on, *tell* him,' as Dominic waited, in a state of high amusement, to be told.

Uhm . . .'

'Daddy, do you *realise* what Dominic just said?'

'Ah, well . . .'

'Or, if *you* won't tell him, *I* shall. It is simply intolerable. We have to discourage this kind of lamentable attitude.'

'Sexist pig. He's utterly gross.'

'Well, of course.'

John Gorst had spent the past nineteen years effacing himself, getting himself down to a mere nothing. He fancied that by now he was almost invisible. If he stood against a hectic patterned wallpaper, he had every hope he'd disappear completely. In his office he was quietly effective, nodding gravely over clients' grievances, drawing up contracts and conveyances, drafting letters which he would sign neatly, legibly, with a minimum of flourish and a squeak of his fountain-pen. He brought home a handsome salary, wrote cheques for this and that, did little jobs around the house, cleared out the gutters, mended fuses, and was pleased to think he was perceptible more by his actions, the effects of his pottering, than by his actuality.

When he gazed in the mirror every morning, he saw someone quite, quite unexceptional. He ran his razor round the contours of a very average face. He was distinguished only by his baldness (though even that was incomplete, it was a half-hearted affair), and by his faintly lugubrious air.

Probably he exaggerated to himself his lack of presence. No one, really, can move through the world unseen. For all he knew, as he stood on some garage forecourt filling the tank of the thirsty Rover, he would attract the notice of a woman at the opposite pump, who, watching him through wafts of four-star and taking an unreasoning dislike, would remark that he had the look of a sexual pervert or serial killer (for isn't it always the quiet ones?). For all he knew, as he perched on a stool at a narrow counter in the baker's to grab a polystyrene cup of coffee and a bite, the kindly lady who served him would apprehend his weary air, a soup stain on his shirt, or the absence of a button, and, supposing him to be lonely and untended, would put into his roll, with the cheese and tomato, a little extra loving care.

But at home, on the whole, he had it just about right: to his family he was more or less a cipher. They had such robust views, such cacophonous voices, such strong, competing personalities, he need hardly add his own to the mix.

Now and then, though, they would call upon him to side with one or other of them, to get behind an argument. Like it or not, he would be drawn into their squabbles.

'We were talking about Juin, Daddy. About her coming to Scotland. *I* don't want her to. *Must* she come? And then Dominic said he wouldn't kick her out of bed.'

'Yes, yes. I do see.'

Boys would, John supposed, be boys. He only wished he'd had the wit to be one in his time. But, what with one thing and another, boyhood had sort of passed him by. I'm a dry old stick, he thought with a certain grim satisfaction.

Geraldine, however, for whom the spectre of teenage pregnancy loomed large and had long horns (one had only to think of David, and of Kate), was loath to let the matter drop. If Dominic was not all talk, if he was indeed sexually active, if he was indulging in adult behaviour, he must at the very least be reminded of his adult responsibilities.

Young people grew up so fast these days, as she was saying to Mrs Hoojit only yesterday. 'They grow up so fast,' she had remarked to her, raising her voice to be heard above the vacuum-cleaner. She had said it again, *sotto voce*, to the head librarian in the hush of the public library. 'Old heads on young shoulders,' she had commented. 'They're all wise beyond their years.' The lady had nodded in distracted agreement as she gathered up a pile of sex-and-shopping novels, much thumbed by eager schoolgirls, and arranged them alphabetically on the rack.

'Dominic, I want –' Geraldine began.

But the boy was already scraping his chair back. He yawned voraciously, as if air were meat and drink to him, as if he could never have enough of it. 'Can't stop,' he said on his way out of the breakfast-room. 'I have to be at the gate in two minutes flat if I want a lift from Hillier's old man.'

On the kitchen table, Lucy had laid out her lunch – ham sandwiches, a low-fat yoghurt and an apple – for later careful packing in her blue plastic lunchbox. The sight of it irked him madly. Christ, she was a little madam!

With half his mind on Azucena, the Hilliers' au pair – she of the dark eyes, the full breasts, the delicious tangle of dark hair, who coloured up prettily when he brushed against her or spoke her name – contemplating the things he might do with her if she only said 'Si, si', he grabbed up the apple, took a greedy bite, left it grinning on the table, and let himself out through the back door.

Juin made a ring of her right arm and put her face down into it, propping her forehead on the table edge. Elli was obliged to address her words to the top of her daughter's downy head, and to the poignantly thin stem of her neck, which grew, tulip-like, out of the collar of her school summer blouse. 'You're being selfish,' she said, with something less than her usual conviction.

Juin muttered thickly into her armpit, something to the effect that Elli, if anybody, was the selfish one. She brought up her face for the second it took her to hurl at her mother, 'You only ever think of Number One.'

'You're old enough and ugly enough, I should have thought,' Elli told her drily, shaking a cigarette from the pack, 'to do without me for a couple of weeks.'

Oh, she would not mind one bit, Juin mumbled, doing without her beloved mama for a week or two. She would not mind, if it came to it, doing without her for good and bloody all. In fact, it would be a blessed release. But why did she have to be dumped on the Gorsts, to be forced to keep company with boring bleeding Lucy?

'We've been through this, Juin. I've told you why.'

'I could stay here on my own. I'd be OK.'

'Oh, ho, yes. You'd be OK. And I shouldn't sleep a wink for worrying about you.'

'I can take care of myself.'

'Picture me if you will, hm, flying into Heathrow, straight into the arms of the Old Bill. I'd be up before the beak on a charge of neglect.' Elli drew on her fag so it glowed fiery red, hooked an arm over the back of her chair, and described with a measuring movement of the hands – largely for her own satisfaction, since Juin still refused to look at her – a screaming banner headline. 'Imagine it. "Home Alone Child of Fleet Street Star Columnist". My enemies would have a birthday.'

'But I'm not a child.'

'You're not an adult, either.'

'I'm old enough to leave school. To have sex. To get married with parental permission.'

'Which I should, of course, withhold.'

'But you're not my only parent, after all.' Under the table, as Juin watched him, Muffy circled the wood-block floor, on a hunt for breakfast crumbs. Wretchedly, she began to weigh up her options. These were, after all, pitifully few, and they took very little weighing.

She could spend the time with her granny, Sybil, in her retirement flat, which always somehow smelt of soup, and where Muffy could not be accommodated. She could listen to endless talk of who had died, or had nearly died, or was about to die. If she was lucky, she might slip out to the beach for an hour in the afternoon, to take up a towel's space among squalling families, while Sybil's friends came up to play canasta. She could be in bed by nine, and up at seven, and go clean off her head with the tedium.

There was Kate, of course. She would adore to stay with Kate, in whose gentle, undemanding company she felt so free to be herself. But she would not suggest it, for Elli would be sure to state the obvious: that the Garveys had a full house, that there would be standing room only at Larkspur Road for as long as rotten Naomi chose to hang out there.

Worse, Elli would give one of those self-congratulatory smirks, an amused curl of her mouth – like, 'I know what's in *your* mind.' And the bugger of it was that she *did* know. Because she, she, Juin, had got this crush on Alex. She had only to think his name for her heart to quicken painfully. And though she had never confided this to Elli, the woman had somehow fiendishly divined it.

It appalled her to think that her mother, indiscreet as she was when sober, and horribly garrulous in drink, might one day spill the beans; she might come right out and tell the guy. If that were ever to happen Juin would expire, she would drop down on the spot from shame.

She found it hard enough, as it was, to face Alex Garvey, to sit and make conversation with him, without betraying by so much as a flicker the strength of her passion. So here was another reason why Tooting was out: because how could she bear to confront him first thing in the morning, before her face had properly reconstituted itself? How could she sit and eat a meal with him, when, with each morsel of food, she was sure to lose a little of her female mystery? She would foozle with embarrassment, fumble with her fork, miss her mouth, spill gravy in her lap. As for making trips to the bathroom, and in so doing, betraying the hideous truth that she, like everyone else, must perform . . . well, bodily functions . . . It was all too terrible to contemplate.

So that left only . . .

She brought up her head abruptly, with a little exclamation, and too late blinked away the light of wishfulness. 'I could stay with my dad.'

'You know you couldn't.' Elli got up and paced angrily, folding her arms at her waist. This line of conversation made her defensive, which in turn made her tetchy. It was liable to end in tears.

'Why not? He's a nice man, you always said. I'm his creature, as you're fond of telling me. It would be good to get to know him.'

'Tim? He's a diamond. But, honey, that was never part of the deal.'

'You had no business, anyway, making deals,' said Juin, sniffing, self-pitying, infantile, regressing, 'without consulting me.'

'It was in the very nature of the deal,' Elli reminded her, 'that you were not around to be consulted.' She went to the sink, ground out her cigarette, turned on the tap, jabbed the stub down the plug-hole. 'Where's that blasted Trevor? He's late. I shan't stand for it, he'll have to go. No, Juin, be thankful that I planned my pregnancy. You were a wanted child – unlike poor Alex Garvey.'

'Hah!' Poor Alex Garvey? *Poor* Alex Garvey? Juin could

think of no human being on planet Earth less deserving of that epithet. 'There's nothing poor about Alex.'

'Ah, yes, of course.'

'What d'you mean, "of couse"?'

'I mean, I was forgetting about you and him.'

'What were you forgetting? What's to forget? Nothing, as it happens – except in your twisted imagination.'

'If you say so, angel.'

'I do.' Juin tugged the hem of her skirt down at her knee, then yanked it up almost to her crotch. She considered her skinny thigh, the spare flesh on the femur. There was this much, at any rate, for which to thank God: she didn't have fat legs. 'I only meant,' she protested (and perhaps she did protest too much), 'that Alex really lucked out, having Kate for a mother.'

'You figure?'

'Yes, I do. I think she's great.'

'Well, of course, she's very pleasant,' Elli was happy to allow, since the term was, for her, a pejorative one. Personally, she regarded pleasant people as cheats for their failure to engage with issues, to play the game. They were thoroughly intellectually dishonest. No one, after all, could *really* be so amenable.

'You realise I shall miss the first week of term,' Juin reminded her bitterly.

'Lucky for you. When I was your age, I'd have done anything to get time off. An extra week of holiday. Fab.'

'The first week of the new school year. Of the sixth form. I shall want to be there. I *need* to be. Otherwise I'll be left out. I won't hear the gossip. I'll get lumbered with the worst desk, have to sit at the front in English, next to soppy Sonia Stevens, within spitting distance of old Renton – literally. It'll be ghastly.'

'Lucy will be missing a week at her school, too. So will Dominic. I don't hear that there have been complaints from them.'

'They'll only miss a day or two. They go back after we do. Private schools have longer hols. You're never going to the office dressed like that, are you?'

'Like what? You are speaking of my Vivienne Westwood.'

'All this upset, you know, the insecurity, it's doing my brain in. I shall probably fail every one of my exams.'

'Oh, Juin, please, don't be difficult. You're a bright kid, you'll sail through. Or if you don't, so what? You can always resit. Look, I'd take you to Italy if I could. But the invitation was for me alone. And besides . . .'

'Besides?'

'You know, you'd hate it,' Elli told her. Then, under her breath, 'And you wouldn't half cramp my style.'

The company on the holiday would be interesting. The Chianti would flow. And in that romantic setting, under the Tuscan stars . . . well, who knew what might happen?

Something, Elli had learned the other day. Something, Patti Henderson had confided to her, sitting beside her at Friday conference, holding on to her sleeve in a show of cosy mateyness. (Coldly, across the room, Tina Hagan, the health correspondent, had watched this perform-ance. For some nameless act of perfidy, she had been banished from the charmed circle of Patti's friendship, never again to darken the doors of Il Podge.) 'Someone else will be flying in to join our little party. Now, guess who.'

'I can't. How should I guess? A he or a she?'

'Oh, a *he*. Hee-hee.' Keeling towards her, cupping her hand to her mouth, Patti had dropped into Elli's ear a name to bring red-blooded women out in rashes.

There had been a look, then, in Ms Henderson's eye, of smugness, satisfaction, and of sexual aspiration. So she fancied she was in with a shout?

Not if I can help it, Elli had grittily determined.

If any guy rated the title God's Gift, this was surely he. Martin Curran, beside him, was as naught. Ruth was welcome to him, actually. Suddenly, he bored her to distraction.

Only by mischance, it had always seemed to her, by oversight or error, had she failed in the past to have this other man. Some lapse of taste there had been on his part. Or else others had conspired to prevent her.

Well, not this time. No sir. She was long overdue for this close encounter. She had eight years on Patti Henderson; she was faster, she was looser, and the race would be to the swift.

In September, in Italy, come hell or high water, Elli Sharpe meant to get it on with David Garvey.

Naomi Markham was in love. She thought she'd never felt this way before. But then, perhaps love was like pain, which, it was said, you could never precisely recall. Was that true?

She shed herself like moonlight upon Kate's sofa, wan and ethereal, sighing for her situation, not minding too much any more about the cat hairs. And she tried to locate, in all her past, something comparable to her present condition; she went way, way back in her heart, and found no trace of such exquisite emotion.

By an effort of concentration, she pictured Alan Neish alongside Alex Garvey, but they seemed oddly disparate, out of scale, as if they had been snipped from different photographs: Alex in sharp focus, in the foreground, with his arms wrapped across his chest, beaming confidently; Alan more distant, indistinct, a stranger who had blundered into shot.

She yawned deeply, repeatedly, like someone in shock, until she was woozy. Her thoughts swam. Then some ambiguous need, which she interpreted as thirst, drove her to the kitchen in search of mineral water.

Alex was sitting there, straddling a chair, eating Jaffa Cakes from the box as he listened with enjoyment to a radio phone-in.

She wavered in the doorway, surprised to see him, vaguely abashed. 'I couldn't sleep,' she offered as an explanation, pillowing her cheek in one hand, as if this was the hour of the wolf, the darkest watch of the long night, not a quarter-past nine on a midsummer morning. (If ever she woke before ten o'clock, it was with a sense of disgruntlement, with the firm conviction that something or someone was to blame.)

He got up at once, and went to seize her elbows, to give her a sweet, chocolatey kiss. Then he dragged her – 'Come,' he urged her, 'come and listen to the unadulterated crap these dickheads talk' – across the room, and down on to his lap, where she sat tall and teetering, her legs swinging, and with an awkward, unaccustomed consciousness of self.

'Where is Kate?' She crossed her ankles to steady herself.

'Oh, long gone. Want some tea or something?'

'No.'

'Because I'll make you some.'

'No, honestly. You don't think she . . .?' Her gaze wandered to the sink, to the perilous stack of dishes on the draining-board, and it came to her as an alien concept that she might actually do something (put stuff away, swab down the surfaces) to help around the place.

'Not at all.' He pressed his splayed hand to her back, ran a finger down the knobs of her spine. She was wearing something thin and satiny, of the same texture as herself; he felt the warmth of her through it, and her insubstantiality. 'Not at all,' he said again, more positively.

In fact, Kate had been a bit off with him, almost grouchy, this morning, pleading a headache, which was how she represented every ill – 'headache' might mean anything, in her case, from minor malaise to double pneumonia – for she was a stoic about her health, and never very good on symptoms. 'I shall be fine,' she had assured him distantly, slipping the key-ring on to her finger, inspecting it minutely, frowning, palming the latchkeys so hard her knuckles bulged.

'Sure?'

'Sure, sure. I just don't feel very rested. As if I hadn't been to bed. You know how it is. I had a bad dream. It's stayed with me.' She had hung about for an instant, like a bad dream herself, unresolved. Did she look all right, she had wanted to know. Would she do?

'Do for what?' he had asked her, affectionate, bantering, but he'd failed to elicit a smile. Muttering something about lunch, she had turned on her heel. 'Right, that's me,' she had announced. 'I'm away.' And, true to her word, she had gone.

'She'll have to be told some time,' he said to Naomi, for her sake doing his best to dress up his disquiet. Because he was in love too, for the first and – for all he could know – the only time, with this helpless creature whom life had so rudely misplaced. Reason advised him that his mother would not favour the relationship. Thrilled, she would not be. Let's face it, she'd go ape shit. She would hit the roof.

'Yes,' she agreed. But neither of them knew when – or even, really, why. It was not as if they had pledged themselves, or made coherent plans. It was just nine days, for heaven's sake, since this thing had got into the pair of them.

'Shouldn't you be at work or something?' Naomi laid a hand upon his shoulder, her forearm against his strong upper arm. She was all in pieces. She was like a puppet, held together and unnaturally dependent upon string. It was an effect of loving, properly loving, and of being properly loved. It had quite unmade her.

Always, until now, she had had clear status. Always, too, there had been rules, not explicit, but completely understood. She had had a role – to lend lustre to a man's grey life – in return for which she had commanded all manner of goods and services.

Alex, however, wanted less of her. Or more (which *was* it?'). He wanted her for herself. And, in return, he pledged *himself*. Now, what kind of basis was *that* for a relationship?

Crazy. It was crazy. He could give her nothing ('I shall buy this flat,' he'd vowed – a *flat* – 'where we can have time together', and Naomi had seen so plainly the style of thing that he envisaged, a compromise upon a compromise), yet she wanted the nothing he could give as she wanted nothing else.

Perhaps he read her mind. 'You realise,' he said cheerily, 'that I cannot hope to keep you in the manner to which you are a custard.'

As if she had not thought of that – at least in so far as thought was demanded, for it was not, somehow, a matter of cool calculation (of pounds, shillings and pence, as she put it to herself, forgetting that shillings had had no currency in Alex's life), but of a profound sense of confusion and dismay. 'Well, I honestly don't mind,' she assured him with a little summoning of courage, compacting herself around the promise. And maybe, after all, she honestly did not. She was not so materialistic as she was insecure. She had shored herself up with luxury – but suppose she no longer needed shoring?

'You swear it?'

'I swear.'

'Not even a soupçon?'

'No.'

'Then soup's off!'

'So it would appear.'

111

'But you know what they say about love in a hut? I mean, with water and a crust?' He tipped his head back and she drew him a twirly moustache with her finger, then drew round his smile – his big, boisterous grin. He was always kidding around. She wondered about jokes – what their point was – and thought maybe she was beginning to understand.

'No, Alex, tell me, what do they say?'

'They say it's – Love, forgive us! – cinders, ashes, dust.'

'They do, do they?'

'To a man.' His chameleon eyes looked into hers, taking up his emotions, at first humorous, then with a dangerous penetration which caused her to fidget, to fiddle with her hair. 'In a moment,' he said, 'I shall be going.' Clasping his arms under her, he scooped her into him, stared hard at her bosom, down the V of the silk garment, then put his ear to her chest and listened gravely to her heartbeat. The sight of his fine, dark hair, the crown of his head, which so moved Kate, moved Naomi now in a different manner.

Alex was about to make a flippant comment, to say he thought that she would live. But then there was this paralysing horror that he might lose her, that this fragile heart might fail, and he was so appalled, he almost choked, he could not for a moment speak.

In the ensuing silence, Mrs Beesley from Bungay, loyal Radio 4 listener, staunch monarchist, devoted fan of Princess Diana, spoke up with spirit for the royal family, whose right to privacy had been so infringed.

'Love me?' he asked when he found his voice again.

'Uh-huh.'

'What's uh-huh?'

'What it says.'

He lifted the draped hem of her wrap, pulled it apart to the sash-tied waist. Together they solemnly considered the flat plane of her belly, the triangle of pubic hair, the perfection of her pale skin. He decided there was no one lovelier in all the world. 'We should get away somewhere,' he said, 'the two of us.'

'For . . . ?'

'For a holiday.'

'Ah.'

'Ah?'

'Ah, yes, a holiday.'

But where would they go, and in what style? Naomi was used to posh hotels which parodied with a desperate conviction their own illustrious past. She was used to liveried doormen, to piano bars with potted palms, vast suites smelling of damask and lace and the recent ministrations of the vacuum-cleaner, where room service might be summoned at all hours, dry martinis delivered up by brass-buttoned attendants.

In her limited imagination, with no experience to draw upon, remote as she had always been from most people's reality, she visualised for Alex a very different world, one of boarding-houses with swirly orange carpets, snappy seaside landladies, bossy notices forbidding guests to walk sand into the carpets or to take food into the lounge.

'We could get a gîte. In France. A cottage. Self-catering, you know. Kate and I took one at Whitsun.'

'You did?'

'She sent you a card, as I recall. Of birds with webbed

113

feet. Or some local girl with a doily on her head. So what d'you reckon? Should we go for it?'

'That would be nice,' she said, as visions of Sea View, of Blue Horizons, of brisk and bossy Mrs Burridges, receded like effluent in a tide of relief. Then, after a pause, 'Say that again. What you said about love in a hut.'

'You mean, with water and a crust?'

'Yes.'

'I said it was – not to put too fine a point on it – cinders, ashes, dust.'

'And would this apply to a gîte?'

'I hope not.'

'*I* hope not too.'

'On the other side of the coin . . .'

'Yes?'

'Love in a palace is perhaps at last, more grievous torment than a hermit's fast.'

She gnawed on her lip for a moment, reflecting on the sentiment, thinking of the palaces in which she'd languished. 'Who said all this, actually?'

'The poet Keats.'

'Well, I think he had a point.'

'Yeah, so do I. Hey, listen, though, you, it's high time I wasn't here.'

'Must you go?' she implored, but dreamily, unpersuasively, for she rather wished he *would*. She felt fatigued and not a little frightened. She needed to be alone, to check herself over, to investigate with hypochondriac attention her spiritual health.

When he left, she sat there for uncounted minutes, before evaporating from the kitchen and condensing

once more on the sofa, where she sat watching, unblink-
ing, as Petal or Pushkin fought to the death with a
balled-up tissue, wondering at the cat's ability to animate
a mere object, to bring the thing convincingly to life.

There *were* calculations to be made, of course, there
was some more basic arithmetic to be done than that
concerning Alex's income or their putative lifestyle. But it
might be left to others to reckon up the implications of
her age, his youth. Elaine Sharpe, for instance, might be
relied upon to state, although always in a caring manner,
the ineluctable truth that she was old enough to be his
mother. Because, oddly, besotted as they were, and in
their own minds well matched, the mathematics did not
seem to bear on either of them.

Introspecting fruitlessly, she picked up the *Globe*,
stared unseeing at the lead news items, before bracing
herself, flipping the paper over, and taking a stab at the
day's quick crossword, penning answers heedlessly.

Three across: 'Yorkshire town.' Eight letters. Begins
with B. Reckless, she wrote in Barnsley. But that must be
wrong, since five down ('Medieval mercenary') was
surely 'free lance'. 'I need an F,' she said aloud, but
softly. Then, falling back in an attidude of abandon,
closing her eyes against the day, thinking of Alex, so
vibrant, so alive, so eminently desirable, she said, again
aloud, and softly, 'I need a fuck.'

It was the wrong day. Or the wrong time. Or the wrong
place. *Something*, for sure, she had got wrong. Kate sat
wretchedly at a restaurant table, torturing a soft bread
roll, tearing into it with floury fingers, and struggled

against the impulse to twist in her chair, to gaze once more in the direction of the door, or yet again to check her watch.

Elli had invited her to lunch ('My treat'), and an invitation from Elli carried all the force of an official summons. No use to protest that she must work, that time was money, that she had appointments which she must honour. The thing was simply not negotiable. So, 'That will be nice,' she had said in resignation as she groped for a ballpoint to jot down her instructions, patting vainly around among the drift of papers by the telephone. And, 'La Cantina,' she had parroted, to imprint it on her consciousness, silently cursing Naomi for the disappearance of the pen. 'Butler's Wharf. One o'clock tomorrow. Right, I've got that. No, I'm sure I can find my way there. I'll look forward to it.'

How much more sanguine she would now feel if she had committed the details to her diary, if she could dip into her bag for a written confirmation. For, with no such hard evidence to reassure her, she was beginning to wonder if she'd invented last night's call from Elli. It had been that kind of flustery morning, with dreams assuming a bogus reality, and reality taking on a hazy, dreamlike patina.

She clamped her left wrist very tightly with her right hand, covered her watch, pressed it hard against the bone. Sit tight, she told herself. Stay calm. Don't lose your nerve. Elli has probably just been delayed. Count to a hundred, not too quickly, and before you are through she'll be here.

Loath to be the first to arrive, she had herself contrived

to be a little late. She had left her Fiat at the far end of the rutted car park, where dandelions cracked through the concrete in small, defiant bursts of yellow, and had loitered at the riverside, peering over the parapet at the water, her eyes narrowed against the skittering reflections.

She had watched as a rusted barge slipped soundlessly by, with an excited brown dog pointing into the breeze, hairy, oddly shapeless, like something blown inside-out, at its prow. She had counted off an excusable five, six, seven minutes. Then, rehearsing her breathless apologies (road works, traffic cones, diversions), she had gone swiftly over to the restaurant, had pushed through the glass door to find herself in a cool, bright room, peopled by media types – Elli Sharpe types – all talking nineteen to the dozen while doing themselves very decently on pasta and white wine.

But no Elli.

She had been ushered to a table, had ordered fizzy water, accepted the *ciabatta* roll which she was now unconsciously demolishing.

She had smiled a sickly go-away smile at the solicitous waiter: her face creaked with the effort of appearing screne. She had explained that her friend was due at any moment. She had sat tight for all of half an hour, reading and rereading the menu, failing to envisage a single item.

And still no Elli.

None of this matters, she told herself sternly. On your dying day you will look back over your lifetime, at all the silly little things that mortified or terrified you, and you will know, finally, just how trifling they were.

117

But even of this she was not persuaded, for had not Pam Perkins passed away still fretting over things she'd said or not said, reproaching herself for the smallest omissions and indiscretions, this slip of the tongue, that want of grace or generosity or tact, wondering what people must have thought of her?

It's monstrous arrogance, Kate further lectured herself, to suppose that anybody here gives a damn about you, let alone that everyone is looking at you.

Then her eyes swivelled to the next table, whose two female occupants were indeed staring at her with overt and malign attention (Kate fancied she intercepted some derisive remark: plainly, they thought her a sad-sack).

Blazing with embarrassment, she dropped her head, studied her hands which lay in her lap, examined her jagged, blackened fingernails, then rolled them up in her fingers.

She glanced miserably out through the window and across the Thames, to the clock on Fenchurch Street Station, which would not spare her the truth that it was five to two.

Right, that was it! She was out of here. She woud signal to the waiter, request the bill, pay for the bread and the water and walk away with her head held high.

The truly mature thing to do, of couse, would be to stay put, to brass it out, with an appearance of enjoyment to eat lunch. If she was any sort of person, she would call for a plate of risotto. If she was really together, really sorted, she would go through the card. But the idea of eating alone was desolating. She had never found pleasure or comfort in it, but would sit enisled, beleagured, like a friendless child, turned inward on herself, as she ground the food mechanically between her jaws.

She would have to get used to it, she supposed, when Alex left. When he found himself a nice girl and moved out. She would have to learn to cook herself a proper meal, to eat it at the table, with a knife and fork, with decorum. But at least in her own home she would not be the object of pity or malicious jest.

Would the staff let her leave the restaurant, though, without a proper meal? Had she, by her very presence, by her monopoly of the table this past hour, entered into some kind of contract with the management, whereby she must take lunch? Or, at any rate, pay for lunch? Pay for *two* lunches?

Then, what would they think of her, slinking away in this fashion? If only she could faint or something, and be stretchered out, no questions asked. She was hot enough and hungry enough to do so. But once before in her life she had almost collapsed – at the hospital, as a child, when she'd needed six stitches. Then they had given her orange squash and, as her mother stood awkwardly by, had told her brusquely that her own nervous tension was to blame, so she had felt she was a dreadful nuisance. She couldn't go through *that* again.

As she cast wildly around her, hoping to catch the eye of 'her' waiter, to beg a sympathetic hearing, she saw with disbelief, with a slight delay of recognition, the approaching spectre of Elaine Sharpe.

Elli came on as always with the air of the Queen; she made the same assumptions, had the same expectations, dressed though she was in something quite unqueenly, a very modern garment with distinctly saucy overtones.

'Sorry, sorry,' said Elli breezily, with no hint of contrition. 'The traffic was murder. Have you eaten already?'

'I didn't . . .' said Kate half hauling herself up, hunching over the table, the better to offer her face for a kiss. 'I wasn't . . .'

She was overwhelmed by relief. She could have thrown herself on Elli's neck and wept. She had never been more pleased to see her friend, or more thankful. Vindicated, now, she beamed around her. You see, I haven't been stood up, she announced by her smile. Here is my luncheon companion. Oh, ye of little faith, here is Elli. But the two women on the nearby table were deeply preoccupied, talking, talking. Nobody marked her triumph. 'It doesn't matter a bit,' she lied through her teeth. 'I was late myself, as it happened. Road works, you know. Diversions.'

'Isn't it sheer hell? And you came straight from your work?' Elli took in Kate's clothing – her cotton slacks, her faded blouse – with an eloquent hitching of an eyebrow.

'Well, yes, but I . . . Am I too scruffy? Is that it, or what? Because I wouldn't want to show you up, I'm sure.'

'No, no, you're all right. You're fine as you are. I simply wondered.' By a dismissive gesture, Elli relegated the matter. If Kate wanted to go about looking like the dog's breakfast, she signalled, that was a matter for her alone. It was a free country. 'Myself, I've had a pig of a morning. Boy, do I need a drink! But, look here, what *have* you been doing? You haven't even ordered the wine.'

'I'm sorry. I wasn't sure if . . .'

'No problem. I'll get some.' Elli put out a hand to arrest a passing servitor. 'A bottle of house white, please, darling, for two thirsty souls. No, Kate, as I was saying, I've been having the most frightful day. I'm invited to stay with chums in Italy in September, and Juin is cutting up rough. She's to go with the Gorsts to Scotland – they're only too delighted to have her along – but that's not good enough for her, apparently. These kids do make such a production out of everything. They go in for so much hand-wringing, don't you find? Well, of course you wouldn't. Not with Alex. He's a peach.'

'He is,' agreed Kate reflexively, yet with somewhat less than her usual animation. She felt strangely offish with her son, strangely at odds with him.

'But the rest of that generation do dramatise their lives so. They behave as though they were starring in some ghastly B movie. I find it tedious beyond belief.'

'I can quite see,' said Kate sensibly, 'that Juin might not want to be dumped on the Gorsts. It's not as if she and Lucy are of an age. And, though I hate to say it, she is an insufferable little madam. Oh!' She slapped her hand over her mouth. 'Lucy, I mean, not Juin.'

'But Juin can be a madam too, you know. Stroppy little cow. I love her dearly, but she drives me to distraction. As for "dumping her", as you so sweetly express it, that is hardly the case. Hey, what's on today? What do you fancy? I shall have a pizza. No, a big plate of spag. This lunch is on me, by the way. Did I say? Eat whatever you want. Fill your face.'

'I'll have whatever you have,' Kate responded meekly, for she had gone, at some point, beyond hunger.

'Excellent. I like a woman who knows her own mind. Then spaghetti it shall be, with melted onions and chilli. Now this talk of Geraldine reminds me, have you had word of David lately?'

'David? Not for ages, no,' said Kate, blinking. 'Not for a year, in fact. Why? Should I have done?'

'I just thought he might have been in touch. I mean, since he'll soon be back in town.'

'He will? I had no idea. Nor do I much care, to be frank.' Forgetting her manners, Kate flicked a bread-crumb across the table. The very mention of that name made her tetchy. 'So far as I was aware, he was to be at least another nine months in Washington, where he can stay till kingdom come for all the difference it makes to me.'

'No, he's due back. A fab job has come up for him at the *Inquirer*. A promotion.' There was a slight, uncharacteristic flush in Elli's cheeks, and her mouth showed the merest inclination to smirk. 'Or so my informants tell me,' she added grandly.

'Well . . .' Kate, scowling, continued to play a kind of Subbuteo, a version of her own devising. Ping. Another crumb of *ciabatta* shot across the tabletop. 'So what? What is it to you?'

'Oh, nothing.' Elli lolled in her chair, hooked her arm over its back, the better to smile up at the waiter, who – now she came to check him out – was himself quite a dish. 'We're both having the spaghetti, thanks. And some mixed salad. Make it quick, will you, hmm? We're a bit pushed for time.' Then, to Kate, 'Hey, don't get all uppity, you. I can *ask*, can't I? I can take an interest? I'm in the same business as David, after all.'

'The Fourth Estate,' said Kate foolishly, not knowing quite what the expression implied, but fancying it was freighted with contempt. And she laughed a mirthless little laugh. 'Well, certainly you can ask.' Although where this line of questioning was leading, she could not imagine.

'Have you ever wondered . . .' Elli raised the glass which the waiter had filled, considered it an instant, then took a sip and rolled the wine ruminatively around her tongue before swallowing noisily. 'That is, has it ever struck you as odd that, out of the three of us, it was you that he chose?'

Chose, Kate said to herself. *Chose*? But Elli knows full well – and we have talked about this often – that it was never a matter of choice.

She felt depressed and used up when she thought about it. It was all so long ago, more distant somehow, and less vivid than her childhood, as though life were indeed a circle and she were now headed back to where she had begun.

She squeezed her eyes, squeezed her mind, wrung out a thin grey stream of recollections. She remembered with what pride Geraldine had led her brother in to meet them, as one might a thoroughbred stallion, showing off to her friends this very fine specimen of Garvey stock. And there had indeed been much of the thoroughbred in

David, who was so physically refined, so powerful, and yet so uncertain of temperament.

Of course he'd had eyes above all for Naomi. Of course he'd had at least a passing fancy for Elaine. But he had been a young man consumed by personal ambition, burning up with a sense of higher purpose, assured of his own prodigious talents, and anguished lest they go unrecognised.

He'd been three years out of university, and was embarking on his writing career, determined to rise like a meteor through the journalistic ranks. Then, *then*, would come The Novel, a work so hot he almost feared to handle it.

And, yes, yes, Kate had soothed him, patiently, kindly, kneeling beside the sputtering gas fire, sitting back on her heels, reluctant to fidget, to move a muscle, to interrupt his streaming consciousness, though the skin of her thigh was scorching through her jeans.

Naomi might yawn and look distracted, Elli might be stuffed with aspirations of her own, but Kate had been always there for him, listening with her head slightly cocked, with a look of genuine concern and utter credulousness, nodding whenever a nod was appropriate, sighing over his dilemmas.

At last she had gone to bed, not with the man but with his monumental, needy, greedy ego. He had used her, as it now seemed, like a sick-bag, a repository for all his undigested angst. For his angst and for his teeming sperm.

'What I'm saying is –' said Elli.

'What you're saying is, you think I'd have been the last one he'd go for. I mean, seeing as I was by far the least attractive.'

'Darling, don't be paranoid.' Fastidious, with a pointed grimace, Elli picked a *ciabatta* crumb from her lap and twiddled it off her fingertips. 'But you must admit you weren't really his type.'

'That's true. I wasn't. You know as well as I do, it was just something that happened.'

As Elli rattled on about it, expounding some half-baked theory as to why David Garvey had never remarried, never settled down, Kate fell to contemplation of the woman's face. She would look awful without hair, she told herself irreverently. As would I, of course. As would most of us. There would be a very few – Naomi, for one – who could carry it off, I guess. But if women went bald the way men do, it would be a tremendous leveller.

Then, to further pass the time while Elli talked – because discussion of David was such anathema to her – she began to work around the room, to picture first this woman, then that one, the scheming, sarcastic bitches at the neighbouring table, with smooth, shining scalps. Oh, ho, ho, what sport!

'. . . need a very special woman,' Elli was saying. 'Someone with the character and intellect to stand up to him.'

It helps to be blonde, reflected Kate. Even though it isn't natural, it does give Elli a kind of aura.

'He would never do for Naomi, for instance. I used to think they were made for each other, pair of narcissists that they are. But I've come to the conclusion –'

'Oh, do leave it out,' begged Kate, exasperated, tuning in once more, with some reluctance, to the conversation. 'David is history to me.'

'It wouldn't bother you then? If he did find someone?'

'Not remotely.'

'Oh.' Elli looked, if anything, disappointed. Some of the energy went out of her. 'Here comes our pasta,' she announced, 'and not before time. I have to be back at the office by three to record a radio interview.'

'What a glamorous life you do lead!'

'Your crabbiness ill becomes you.' The Fifth Lady of Fleet Street reached over to the ice bucket and brought out the dripping wine bottle. 'How is Naomi, by the way? Still got her dainty feet under your table?'

'You know perfectly well she has.'

'No chance that you could move her on, I suppose? Then Juin could come and stay with *you* instead of Geraldine. She'd like that, I'll bet.'

'I should like it too, well enough. She would be a far easier house guest. Although I shouldn't mind if we had the place to ourselves for a change. It would be a real break.'

'And under your roof, who knows . . .' Now Elli began knitting up spaghetti with spoon and fork, with such fixity of purpose, such sheer determination, she might have been knitting up the ravell'd sleave of care itself.

'Who knows *what*?' Kate took her fork and redistributed the pasta on the plate.

'We-ell . . . you know, Juin and Alex might just . . . Because propinquity, you realise –'

'Pro-what-ity?'

'Nearness of place. The state of being not unadjacent. Propinquity and opportunity make for love affairs.'

'Yes, I suppose they do.'

'Absolutely. It's a fact. That's why there's so much bonking in offices.'

'In *offices*?'

'Or out of them, rather. I'm talking of extramural pleasures and pastimes. But it's all cooked up in the workplace, you see, with people thrust together day on day, week on week. It gets the old chemistry going like nobody's business.'

'I suppose it must,' allowed Kate, whose own work was so solitary.

'For that reason,' said Elli in her goading fashion, 'the sooner you get shot of Naomi the better. Or I dread to think what sexual chemistry she and Alex may cook up. Hey, hey, don't look like that. I'm only kidding. She's old enough to be his mother, after all.'

'Yes, I know. It's just that I feel . . .'

She'd had them since her early teens, these 'funny turns', as she described them to herself. It would be as if she were suddenly distanced from the here and now. Scraps of long-forgotten conversation, actual or fanciful, would return to her fleetingly, not as faint memories, but in ringing tones. And there would be a smell of hyacinths – or it might have been wet fish, or damp cellars – overpoweringly strong, yet elusive.

Thoroughly gripped, in a kind of thrall to the mystery of it, she would sit there, waiting to be returned to herself, when with depressing regularity dizziness and nausea would follow, and a most unpleasant searing sensation in her nostrils.

It was happening at this minute, the by now familiar syndrome. 'Excuse me,' she muttered, recovering the power of speech, 'I must nip to the . . .'

Black clouds were scudding across her brain as she lurched off to the loo, where she bolted herself in a cubicle, sat down heavily and put her head in her hands. She would be fine. She was always fine. But for a moment there, she had imagined she might have to be stretchered out after all.

Geraldine Gorst had lunch in town, a little treat, a small recompense to herself for her day's exertions. She loved to eat alone, in restful silence, without the family's rude impositions. She loved to address herself to food, free from distractions, assiduously to put a meal away, and she carried around in her subconscious some scrapbook images from early infancy – Jack Horner with his plum pie, Miss Muffet with her curds and whey, the queen with bread and honey – which celebrated solitary gluttony.

She relished, also, the atmosphere of olde worlde charm, the authentic feel of the 1960s Tudor, so faithfully preserved here in the Bay Tree Café. She had stationed herself in her favourite corner, in a banquette seat, and now, snatching up the menu, ran her eye down the typed list, which read like a roll-call of old friends.

The lamb cutlets, she decided happily, with buttered cabbage and minted new potatoes. Then gooseberry crumble to follow.

'They say it will rain,' reported the motherly waitress, thingamajig, with whom Geraldine was on cosy first-name terms, and with whom she always passed the time of day. 'Thunderstorms, they reckoned on the forecast.'

Well, confided Geraldine, *she* at any rate would not be sorry. A good storm would clear the air. Besides, she had never been a great one for the heat. Then, as she was at the point of declaring her preference for lamb, the impulse moved her to plump for fish and chips.

'Will that be cod or plaice?' queried the waitress, her stub of pencil poised above her pad.

'Plaice, thank you, Agnes,' responded Geraldine firmly, for she held plaice to be a lady's fish, and cod a man's, with haddock somewhere in between (neither fish nor fowl, as she put it to herself). 'I'm very fond of plaice.'

The kitchen, like some vital organ, a ruptured gut, gave out a hot and odoriferous hiss, a foody waft, as the busy little body in starched cap and pinny went banging through the swing doors with her order. Content to find herself in safe and caring hands, Geraldine subsided in her seat and smiled vaguely, benevolently, around her.

Unnoticed at her feet, a Boots carrier-bag capsized, to spill on to the patterned carpet tubes of this and tubs of that across-the-counter remedy – preparations to free the bowels, or to bind them up, to ease the pain of tense, nervous headache, to soothe the itch of insect bites, to relieve the misery of acid indigestion. A holiday, after all, lay not very many weeks ahead.

She had no need, at this moment, however, for palliation. She was in her element. This was her sort of restaurant, with its black oak beams, its branched candlestick wall-lamps and copper kettles; her sort of place where old ladies sat long over poached eggs on toast, the brims of their felt hats almost touching as the magnetism of gossip drew them ever closer.

Elaine and her crowd were welcome to their trendy brasseries and bistros, to their smoked duck breasts, sun-dried tomatoes, balsamic vinegar. Geraldine knew of these things, which featured increasingly in her weekly magazines, but she wanted no part of them, for they seemed to her merely faddy, as much subject to fashion as the latest length of skirt or style of shoe.

Her own preferences (some might say 'prejudices') had been inculcated by her mother, received as a complete set. From Eleanor Garvey, Geraldine had learned what she must wear or not wear, what she must approve and what not. No issue, it had seemed then, was in the slightest doubt. The rights and wrongs of every-thing had been manifest to Eleanor, who had never stinted in her duty to dash off letters to the district council, to Her Majesty's government, to Spar Grocers, South Down Buses, Express Dairies, to bring to their notice these absolutes.

There was, perhaps, something almost too devotional, so many years later, in daughter's adherence to mother's rubric. But then, if mother love is conditional on highly polished shoes, on neatly brushed hair and pretty ribbons, a girl can go one of two ways: she can buff up her shoes and brush her hair, or she can neglect to do so. And Geraldine Garvey was still, metaphorically, buffing her shoes, she was brushing her hair. She was still wearing those pretty ribbons.

Or maybe she simply saw no need to rearrange or renew her mental furniture – when the old lot, though handed down, was still perfectly serviceable.

Geraldine's problem, if indeed she *had* a problem, was a lack of selfhood. She seemed to have been born without imagination or conviction of her own. She could be said to be like her mother only in so far as an image on a blotter can be said to be like the original; and she was like herself not at all.

But then, when she thought of David, so richly imaginative, so utterly convinced, so chock-full of self, she was bound to wonder what it profited him. As the waitress brought a pot of tea ('Thank you, Angie,' said Geraldine absently), as she poured for herself a refreshing cup, she fell to fretting for her brother, to wondering wherein might lie his salvation.

Once upon a time she had fancied that he and Naomi might . . . It would have gratified her, somehow, if the two of them had tied the knot. She had seen in her mind's eye this exceptionally attractive couple, seen herself in matching pastel coat and dress, in pillbox hat with a frippy bit of veil, showering the bride and groom with paper hearts and silver foil bells and horseshoes.

Almost speechless with pride, she had introduced him to their girlie Holland Park ménage. Then what had happened? He'd gone straight for Kate, of all people. And Alex had been the consequence.

Since then, David had settled to nothing, committed himself to no one. He lived the life of a roué, he brought no credit to the family. Nor had he been entirely generous, she was aware, over payments for his child.

He had shirked his responsibilities rather. Yet, while she, Geraldine, had tried to atone, to help Kate to stay in funds – not with patronising handouts, but through the dignity of work – she could not help but sympathise with her brother, who had missed his chance with Naomi, and seemed quite comprehensively to have lost out.

Now it appeared he would be home in a matter of weeks. An important and prestigious job had come up at the *Inquirer*. He would touch base by the end of August, then he'd be off once again for a short break in continental Europe, before taking up his new situation.

This Geraldine had learned, not from David himself, by means of a loving letter, but from Elli Sharpe if you please, who had rung her yesterday, ostensibly to beg a favour, to foist her daughter on to them, and then, insouciantly, as if by way of afterthought, had deigned to deliver the bulletin.

It was coming to something, Geraldine reflected, when complete strangers . . . not that Elli was a stranger, exactly, but nor was she family, nor was she *that* close . . . It was coming to something when you got to hear of your brother's movements, as it were, on the grapevine.

He had moved so far away fom her, she realised with compunction, and she had somewhere other than Washington in mind: she was thinking of planes of existence. As the waitress set her meal before her, as she picked up a wedge of lemon and squeezed it, she was all at once beset by ineffable despair. She felt quite, quite lost. She saw herself starkly as a silly fat woman in a tight blouse and ridiculous dirndl, hunched greedily over a plate of calories.

But it was, after all, one of those momentary depressions to which certain sensitive females are prone. And, when she sniffed and dashed her hand under her eye, it was only because a squirt of lemon juice had found its mark.

'Thank you, Alice,' she murmured with a distant smile. 'I'm partial to a nice bit of plaice, aren't you?'

The girl lay on her side, in an elegant curve, with her knees drawn up – he could have counted her vertebrae, right down to sacrum and coccyx – with her chin pillowed on one arm. She looked almost too perfect, too posed or *com*posed, like someone merely feigning sleep, but her breathing was so shallow, and she so inert, that he sensed she was dead to the world.

Objectively, in the hard morning light which came in tranches through the slatted blinds, he could see that she was beautiful. But her beauty no longer aroused him. His appreciation of her long, strong limbs, her tiny waist, her well-made face, was of the sort he might feel for some merely competent piece of sculpture. And unreasoningly he blamed her for her failure to find in him intense erotic response.

Her teeth were very white, her gums a healthy pale pink in a wide, uncluttered mouth. She had a neat, glossy cap of fine, dark hair. Her skin was smooth and golden. The eyes that might at any moment flutter open to gaze appetently upon him were of an intense blue, belying her guile. She worked in public relations, drove a beast of an old Buick, dressed always in black. He had met her at a gallery, at an opening, five months ago. Her name was Kirstin, she was twenty-six years old, and she had set her heart on marrying him.

This last she had, by her very insouciance, communicated to him. She affected a casual disregard for conventional relationships, declared herself a free spirit, two or three nights a week declined to see him, insisting that she must have her own space, or must have time with her women friends. She was, in other words, a creature of low cunning.

He felt sudden and profound disgust, not with the girl, not with himself, but with mischievous lust. Time and again it cheated him, taking him over, making him almost demented with wanting, moving into him, then without notice moving out and on.

Round and round and round it turned him, in an endless cycle of desire, devotion, disaffection. The woman he wanted with a passion today, he would weary of utterly tomorrow – which would have been fine, it would even have been fun, if it weren't for the grasping nature of womankind.

They were so possessive of him. And they had no notion of consummation: he would fuck them rigid, but they never stayed fucked. Always, always, they came back for more. They clung to him so he must tear himself away from them, and thus, each time, lose another little piece of his vital being.

He was so heavily burdened with sexuality, he was limping with it. His appeal was all-powerful, his technique unsurpassable. He knew that when he slept with women they would be spoiled for other men, perhaps for ever. He just could not leave them as he found them. Onerous was the responsibility he had to bear.

And the wiles they would employ! The stunts they would pull to entrap him! Once only, many years ago, he had fallen for it. He had allowed a woman to misappropriate his sperm to make a baby. Well, never again! No way! He was on to them, now, he knew their games.

Extricating himself from the tangled sheet, watching as he did so her perfectly unaffecting face with its faint flush of slumber, he eased off the mattress. Treading softly on bare sanded boards, he crossed to the window. He parted the snappy metal blinds and stood for minutes in the pale wash of day, with his shoulder surrendering warmth to the cold plastered wall, peering down at the traffic, at the frenzied eight o'clock rush. He was six foot two without shoes, and loosely jointed. He wore his nakedness with the same languid grace as he wore his clothes. Years and experience had robbed him of nothing; rather, they had endowed him. His brown-blond hair still grew with vigour. Deep vertical grooves lent his face an intriguing, wolfish quality. Above all he had acquired with maturity a manner that compelled not just women, but men also.

Forty-five last February. There could be no better age for a man. 'You must have been through college,' Kirstin had said to him last night in the restaurant, 'before I even started kindergarten.' No doubt she had intended to endear, to enchant him with an image of herself as tiny child. Her smile had been one of fond indulgence for cute little Kirstin. Or it had been one of misplaced self-congratulation: she had been scoring off him in that

135

cheap way that young people will (as though youth were not given to all at some time). But he, who had never really seen the point of children, could only think that the infant Kirstin had been singularly favoured, fated as she had been to meet him (to this end, it had seemed to him, all her years of growing up and filling out might have been bent). And, with a sudden, unaccountable impatience, up to here with anchovies and mozzarella, he had shoved aside his half-eaten pizza.

Behind him, he heard her stir, heard her breathing quicken, deepen. The hairs on the back of his neck prickled with this apprehension. Let her not wake, for a while at least, to intrude upon his precious solitude.

David Garvey was a tortured soul who, like so many tortured souls, had very partial insight into his torment. He blamed his mother, somehow. Well, everybody does, of course, but perhaps he had more reason than some.

He, who had always so wanted to be his own idea, must forever be reminded that she had thought of him first. She seemed less to have conceived him than contrived him. 'David will be tall like my brothers,' she had declared, when he was five, six, seven years old. And, lacking the power to disoblige her, he had grown to her specification. Not that he didn't glory in his stature; but he should have far preferred to feel that she had not commanded it.

Then there was 'David will make his mark, you'll see, David is going to *be* someone', so that his every small success might have been ordained by her. When he won this award for political commentary, that one for his war reporting, she had assumed an insufferable 'I told you so' attitude.

Meeting her eye, he would find himself transfixed by the intent and purpose he saw there. Worse even than this, though, was to see, with appalled fascination, his own self looking out of her at him.

'David has his artistic talents from me,' she would repeatedly claim, and in this, for once, she had perhaps got it wrong. David was not, after all, artistic. But then, on the available evidence, nor was she, unless there was art in the hanging of a brocade curtain, the scattering of tapestry cushions, the arrangement of frigid pink carnations in a cut-glass vase. (He could picture her now, with her set expression, hammering the stems on the scrubbed pine draining-board, then jabbing them in, with precision, one by one, as though according to some higher symmetry apparent to no one but herself.) And, in subjective matters such as this, it was impossible to gainsay her.

How much more fortunate had been Geraldine, the irrelevant daughter, for whom, in girlie girlhood, a long series of mere distractions had been found. He remembered her as a plump kid with a preposterous froth of curls, working away ham-fistedly with embroidery silks, sewing mutant chain stitch, or banging out 'The Blue-bells of Scotland' on the piano. Geraldine in short white socks and black buckle shoes, always obedient and good, with no aptitude for anything beyond obedience and goodness.

And here was an irony: for while he, who was born in her image, who was truly his mother's son, struggled endlessly to be unlike her, Geraldine, who was not her like, struggled endlessly to be so.

The many perverse, pig-headed things he had done in his life, he had done principally to confound his mother. Would he have married Kate, for instance, had Eleanor not vehemently opposed him? Then, with heart-sinking inevitability, in leaving Kate, he had handed her vindication on a plate.

Eighteen months away from his tiresome family had done nothing to distance him emotionally. In a curious way, indeed, they horned in on him more here than ever they had done at home. He could have forgotten them more thoroughly, could have blanked them completely, if they were just in the next room watching television.

Well, he would be seeing them again soon enough. Seeing England, too, which in spite of himself he missed, for America had not absorbed him as he had hoped it might, into its very warp and weft. And he had not absorbed America into his.

The prospect of the new job stirred in him both excitement and anxiety. What if it were not up to him? In his nightmares he was underestimated, either grossly or – perhaps worse – subtly. He dreaded that the world might fail to get his measure. It was this that prevented him, even now, from sitting down to write his novel. For suppose it should go unremarked, its sheer importance overlooked?

Before the job, of course, he had the expectation of a holiday, a trip to Italy with those raucous old hags from the *Globe*. It would be refreshing, actually, to be among them, to be, for a week or so, less than earnest. He had known them throughout his working life, for he too went back to the old Fleet Street, to hot metal, blood, sweat and alcohol. In hindsight those days seemed almost healthy, free as they had been from today's obsessions with passive smoking, with safe drinking limits and cholesterol counts.

Kirstin's breathing further quickened. She could be heard struggling up to consciousness. Now would be the moment to tell her, while he had this hard edge on her, that he was including her out of his plans.

She was a free spirit, he would remind her. She wasn't into commitment. She needed her space, and might soon have all the space she needed.

'Ur,' she said softly. Then, 'Hi.'

He turned from the window, rubbed his frozen shoulder, felt sorry for her, rather, and deferred the conversation. He, too, just said 'Hi', and from some-where found for her a smile.

CHAPTER

4

The summer was not, after all, to be endless or uninter-
rupted. That evening, as threatened, the weather broke.
And 'broke' was the word for it, thought Kate, gazing out
as a rogue streak of lightning ripped through the cloud. It
was all somehow coming apart.

She ground her knuckles into her eyes, which felt sore
and gritty. She had a bad taste in her mouth, and was
distinctly out of sorts. Drinking at lunchtime did for her,
she realised. It did her in. And, with a sense of grim
inevitability, supposing that she had better finish what
she had started, she uncorked a bottle of Fitou,
poured herself a brimming glass.

Weird, bat-winged fancies still flapped about inside
her head as she set salted water on the hob to boil. She
would have liked to lie down in a darkened room, to
write off what remained of the day. But there was the
evening meal to be prepared. Besides, if she slept now,
she would be sure to wake at midnight with worse than
ever psychic lag, disorientation and fatigue.

In the garden, the few surviving magnolia flowers
fluttered in the gathering gloom, like handkerchiefs
signalling distress. Little shivers ran through the leafy
borders. Madly, the hydrangeas banged about. Over the

back, in Broomfield Road, other people's kitchens advertised themselves, as one after another the fluorescent strips flickered then blazed with blue light. Bedrooms, sitting-rooms, took on a warmer, more enticing glow.

When Alex arrived home, the pasta was already steeping, softening, like so much washing, with sticky wisps of steam curling off it. Bruised leaves of fresh basil on the chopping board, sliced and pinched into a tidy mound, seeping juices, gave off a pungent, aniseedy scent.

'Smells good,' he said to the distracted Kate, and helped himself to wine, slurping it appreciatively as he crossed to the stove to stir the sauce. The intervention was timely: scalding mixture spluttered as it touched the metal sides of the pan.

'Spaghetti,' Kate said.

'Ah, yes.'

She took a gulp of the poisonous wine. 'With tomato and ricotta,' she supplied, striking a note of ingratiation.

'Mmm. Lovely.'

She would now and then take a notion that a certain dish was his favourite, on no harder evidence than that he had once cleaned his plate of it. In truth, he did not much care for this way with spaghetti, which he found claggy and indigestible, and which, ever since Kate acquired the recipe from somebody, had become one of the staples here in Larkspur Road. But to tell her now, 'Well, actually, I really cannot stomach it', would be to run her through with words. He must not reject the food she set before him, for to do so, Alex sort of knew, would be taken as a rejection of her love. The choice, as he saw it, was to eat whatever she put in front of him with a semblance of enjoyment – or to leave home and make other arrangements.

He had realised over the years, though he hated to acknowledge it, that his mother was not the world's best cook. She was at once too heavy-handed and too nervous: she overdid the seasoning, added extra 'for good measure', and never knew quite what she might be starting when she set ingredients over a flame to fry.

Many of his likes and dislikes he had acquired in early life, when she had misinterpreted various foods for him. It had come to him as a revelation, at his friend Paul Mather's home at the age of twelve, that bacon did not have to shatter when you tried to cut it, and that liver wasn't meant to bounce.

On the other hand, Mrs Mather had been a frosty, unaccommodating woman, who had exacted from him, at the table, a few grudging, mumbled words of grace. She had been so very much on her dignity, she would never have run upstairs and down, or have gone about without her shoes the way Kate did. All in all, the boys had therefore agreed, rubbery liver, splintery bacon nothwithstanding, Paul had drawn the shorter straw.

'How was your day?' Kate asked him now.

'All right. Ordinary. Yours?'

'Well, not so bad.' She dumped her glass on the dresser, dangled her arms, swinging them back and forth. Her face was awry, pulled about by a funny non-smile. 'Your father's coming back to London, I am told.'

'So what?' He shrugged. 'Why should I care?'

'I just thought you might be interested.' She sounded oddly aggressive, almost surly.

'Well, I'm not. I couldn't be less so.'

'Then you're in a minority. Other people, it seems, are agog.'

'And who exactly are these "other people"? Ah, Elli, of course. I forgot you were having lunch with her. I suppose she's been bending your ear.'

'He's been offered a new job. Very high profile. Colossal salary, company car.'

'The best of luck to him, then. Kate, don't get on about it. It really doesn't matter any longer.'

'I know, I know.' She turned away, gnawed her knuckles, squeezed her eyes shut, and inexplicably remembered being at the seaside, in a tall building, mostly glass, with a hissing tea urn, and people in creaking mackintoshes, and a concrete floor awash. 'Take no notice of me, baby. I just get a bit ratty sometimes, still, when I think . . . What was that noise? Was it thunder? It must have been thunder.'

'It will be better after,' he said hopefully. 'Less oppressive.' The tensions in this house were becoming intolerable.

In less than a minute the rain filled up the gutters and came slopping over, splattering the flags beyond the window. Kate stood at the sink to drain the pasta. Something catastrophic – apocalyptic – seemed about to happen. 'Where is Naomi?' came her voice from a cloud of steam.

'She went out,' Alex responded levelly, 'to have her hair done.'

'Her . . .?' Kate turned to stare right into him. 'How do you know that?'

'I spoke to her today on the phone. I rang home because I thought I'd left my key on the . . . well, somewhere.'

'But you didn't?'

'No, I didn't. I had it all the time. In my back pocket.' He reached in there now, pulled it out, held it up as if in evidence. Exhibit A.

'So then she said she was going to the hairdresser's?'

'More or less that.'

Actually, it had been Naomi who had called *him*, almost speechless with hurt and distress. Her agent, Ariadne, had been on to her. There was just a possibility of some modelling work, it seemed. The word 'catalogue' had been mentioned. And, no, this was not great news. It was the ultimate humiliation. A calculated slight. 'You can see me in a flowery polyester housecoat, can you? In some fifteen-quid skirt from Freeman's? Or in old-lady thermals? How about that?' She had never in her life felt more insulted.

'Look, why don't you go out and cheer yourself up?' he had urged her, grinning like a fool in love (which he supposed he was). These days he found her histrionics, her *amour propre*, just adorable. 'Buy yourself something, huh? Cheer yourself up. A haircut? Well, your hair looks wonderful to me, but if you feel you need . . . What will it cost? *How* much? No, no, I'm sure it's worth every penny. Cheap at twice the price. I'll treat you, angel. Borrow my Access card. It's in the . . . Right. You want my PIN number?'

'How can she possibly afford to . . .?' Kate wondered aloud.

'Ah, well, of course, she and Nicky are old mates. He won't charge her, probably. Or just a token sum.'

'You seem to know an awful lot about her business.' Taking up two servers, Kate set about the squelching spaghetti, mulching in the tomato sauce, the melting cheese.

'She was in tears. I had to talk her round.' Alex crossed to the dresser, tugged open the cutlery drawer, raked noisily around among the jumbled knives and forks. 'We ought to get some dividers for in here. One of those trays with compartments.'

'We've managed without until now. And will she be joining us for supper? Should I be putting hers to keep warm?'

'How should I . . .? Look, what *is* this?'

'Only that, since she apparently confides in you –'

'Hey, get off my case, will you? It's not as if she tells me all her movements. Did she leave a note? She should have left you a note. But, now I remember, she did mention something about dropping in on Elli. Yes, I reckon that's where she'll be.'

Kate was pleased and not pleased. It was a break to have Naomi out of the way for the evening. On the other hand, why *this* evening, when she was right on the edge of herself, not best able to enjoy it? Then there was the woman's woeful lack of common courtesy. Slamming plates down on the table, she shared with Alex her impression of Naomi Markham, who apparently regarded this house as a hotel.

'Don't go on,' he begged her gently, bringing the knives and forks at last. He tilted his chair to unseat

Petal, took her place. 'She won't be here for that much longer.'

'She won't? Who says?'

'No one says. It's just my hunch.' He stared miserably at his lap, then bent at the waist to tickle the affronted Petal behind her ear, felt the blood run up his neck, filling his face, his ears, his temples. How was he ever going to confess to his mother their awful secret? Perhaps he should say now, up front, before Naomi came back. Perhaps he should come right out and tell Kate that he and she were going to . . .

'I'm sorry,' Kate told him with what passed for a laugh. 'I'm just a bit wound up. It was the mention of David, probably. Elli going on about him and his fat pay packet. I thought, well it's all right for some.'

'But it makes no difference what he does or what he earns,' said Alex reasonably, taking up his fork, 'any more than it makes a difference what other strangers do, or what they earn.' Then, ploughing the fork into the spaghetti sludge, drawing a breath, 'My favourite,' he told her heartily.

Through the loving eyes of Naomi Markham, the world seemed out of true. Walking dazedly in Bond Street, with the merest consciousness of her new hair, she looked askance at shop windows, and saw that clothes, however artfully cut and sewn, were only so much fabric. Oil paintings, antiques, jewellery were in the end just stuff.

There was a small, hard knot of disappointment in her chest, much as she had felt at the age of ten, when the coming of Christmas had brought, not delicious ripples of anticipation, but a dull apprehension of loss.

The condition of being suddenly, subtly grown up was, of course, irremediable. The child, with her new maturity, had accepted that. But this latest challenge to her disposition was another matter. Naomi could only hope that the more extreme effects – the unreality and misproportion – of the loving state would wear off with time. At the moment she was like a passenger on a heeling ship, for whom balance is a function of intense concentration, navigation one of wild guesswork or of reference to inconstant stars, and for whom perspective is all to pot.

Only weeks ago, these same expensive shops had seemed so beguiling. Pushing through their doors, she had had a deep, sustaining sense of repatriation, of being again where she truly belonged. But nothing, today, enticed her, and it wasn't even as if she had no money to spend. In her purse she had Alex's Access card, his flexible friend – less flexible certainly than Alan Neish's Gold Card, but still good, probably, for a bit of Romeo Gigli or Dolce e Gabbana, still good for a wad from the cash dispenser.

No, the problem was that she didn't feel like shopping. She simply wasn't up for it. She didn't want a new white vest top, a grey wool jacket or a quilted bag. She wanted Alex. She missed him. She longed to be with him, to kiss him. Longed, too, to unburden herself to someone. Should she tell Elli what was happening? No, she mustn't, for if she did she would surely live to regret it.

A Japanese tourist stepped aside for her and, as she

passed unnoticing, turned to watch her. From his hole in the road, a workman proposed marriage. Naomi carried on walking.

Finding herself on Oxford Street, she resisted the press of pedestrians which could have swept her all the way to Marble Arch, to stand for a moment by a stall piled high with uniform and unconducive oranges, bananas, grapes (when did these fruits cease to seem exotic?), waiting for some plan of action to suggest itself.

She took the rain, when it began, as a personal affront – you did not spend an afternoon being cut and blown dry by London's top stylist, only to have the weather piss all over you – and put out an arm to halt a cab.

On the ride to Hackney she closed her eyes, slid down in the seat, and gave herself over to eroticism, to images of Alex thrusting into her, of his eyes, the way they seemed to take her up, to take her into him. She felt great surges of concupiscence and was racked by shivers.

The driver, glancing in his rear-view mirror, saw only that the light and shade of the afternoon ran by turns over her face; he saw the shadow dance of waving leaves on her pale skin. In Bloomsbury he ventured a bit of chit-chat, tried her with the vagaries of the British summer, which seldom failed to exercise his passengers, but she offered no reply. Nor could she be enlisted to abominate the Old Street roundabout, to agree that the recent refurbishment was a bleeding abortion. She was similarly unmoved by the multiplicity of road works, by the fact that every street in the capital was apparently being dug up, for she was somewhere else, with Alex, in her mind, she was far, far away and up to all sorts.

Only as they sped past London Fields, with the windscreen wipers slapping, squelching back and forth, did she open her eyes, to focus dimly on the half-familiar geography, and to order him right, left, right.

With an uncomfortable mix of eagerness and trepidation, shielding her hair with her handbag, she half ran up the steep steps to Elli's door.

Briefly, Elli appeared in the front bay, wearing something very pink in crochet. In the instant before the porch enclosed her, Naomi saw her raise a hand, she saw her wave.

She had, then, an unexpected sense of elation, a sense of freedom, as though she had been discharged from hospital after long bed rest. Her knees, indeed, felt weak and shaky under her.

How constrained she had been at Larkspur Road, not only by unwritten house rules, or by her sense of being in the way, but by the discipline of keeping from her hostess her passionate affair with her hostess's son.

It was a kind of torture to have to love in secret, never to be able to discuss it. To talk of Alex to some third party would make the thing seem more believable and more possible. She needed to speak his name aloud, to link it with hers, to say 'Alex and I'.

She drew in a lot of clammy air, let it out in a rush. It was fresh and chill here in the shallow stone porch, with the rain coming down in sheets behind her. It was filthy and exhilarating. A sash window went up suddenly in a house across the road; defiantly music blared.

Muffy could be heard in Elli's hallway. The sound of his barking came and went as he shuttled up and down between the front door and the kitchen. Then there stood Elli herself, sparking with a dangerous energy like a lightning rod, saying 'So-o . . .' in her provocative manner.

'So,' responded Naomi curtly as she followed her inside.

'Wipe your feet, do. And you shut your face.' The latter instruction was for Muffy, whose bark drove him backwards in a series of small bounces.

Juin came barefoot from the kitchen with a towel around her neck. 'Oh,' she said, 'it's you.' Gathering up in her arms her threshing dog, she kissed him on his tangled head, and went rudely, pointedly upstairs.

'Take no notice of her,' Elli loudly counselled, 'it's her time of the month. I can always tell. It makes her more than usually odious. Well, doesn't it, Juin?' She swung on the newel post and sent a shout up after her daughter. 'You get frightfully premenstrual, don't you, darling? Now!' She rubbed her hands together with a papery sound. 'Come right on in, Markham, sit yourself down, have a glass or two of the blushful Hippocrene. Get rip-roaring drunk, why don't you, and sing lusty ballads long into the night? It's not as if you have to drive. It's not as if you even *can* drive. God forbid that *you* should ever get behind the wheel. You've had your hair done, I see. It will look better in a week. Does Kate know you're here? You ought to ring and tell her, otherwise she'll sulk and bear grudges.'

'Alex will tell her.' There, she'd said it! She'd said his name! Naomi sat down abruptly on the sofa, and folded her hands in her lap.

Alexander Garvey. An ordinary enough name it had sounded to her once, but now it was charged with great potency and meaning. She had managed to sound quite natural, she thought. There had been, perhaps, a little too much treble, a hint of a wobble, but not so much that anyone would notice.

'And is she feeding you all right? You're as thin as a stick.' Elli reached across to pinch Naomi speculatively on her upper arm.

'Well, yes. Oh, yes. She's been very kind. But I don't seem to have much appetite these days. Also, she lets the cats walk on the table and sniff the plates. That turns me off.'

'Revolting. Listen, now, I haven't shopped. I don't plan to cook. We'll send out for something a bit later. A pizza. Chinese. Whatever you fancy. First, though, we must catch up with the news. You start. Tell me everything you've been doing.'

'You don't want to know,' Naomi warned.

But, naturally, Elli *did*.

When Geraldine Garvey stepped out of the tub, it seemed half the bath water came with her. Was there some immutable law of physics, that the older one got, the more water would attach to one? She paddled about on the cork tile floor, pink and palpitating, wrapped in a fluffy towel, pondering it.

Wet without, it was, and wet within. The bloated clouds that were even now piling in on London had from late afternoon been passing overhead, relentlessly, with an apparent sense of destination, drenching the countryside as they went. The garden ingurgitated and gagged upon the puddles. The swimming pool was lapping over. The borders were awash. Any roses that were not clenched tight had been denuded of their petals, which floated in an earthy soup. The clematis had been half dragged off its trellis; it hung there in a dripping tangle. When Geraldine released the catch and eased open the misted latticed window, the bathroom vapours went visibly out, and a smell of sodden mud came invisibly in.

Wasn't this typical of a British summer, though? The heat, of which she'd so complained, she now peevishly desiderated. The cleansing storm was not, after all, to be welcomed. How could one hope to acclimatise to such inconstant weather? One, two, even three weeks it would take for the human body to complete the adaptive process. And it was change, of course, she reminded herself sniffily, that made one ill, that encouraged viruses to thrive and brought on colds and flu.

Here was the reason why so many British people chose to holiday in sunnier climes. Yet to venture overseas was to her mind grave folly, for there the temperatures were foreign, reckoned up in centigrade, and the water was not potable, and hygiene standards were questionable, and one might fall prey to all manner of exotic bugs.

Enamoured of the *idea* of the place, Geraldine had been just once to France. There, in a bar in Normandy, on asking in a discreet whisper for directions to the *toilette*, she had been humiliated by the *patron*, who had urged upon her across the counter, for all to see, a horrid, crêpey roll of lavatory paper. There too, on emerging from the airless little *cabinet* – she still shuddered at this recollection – she had almost walked slap-bang into a Frenchman relieving himself into a porcelain urinal.

Better England, she decided, and dear old Scotland, with their meteorological uncertainties, than an alien land with its alien mores.

Wheel splash on the drive, the munching sound of gravel under tyres, and the reek of damp exhaust told her that John was home. She ought to have been downstairs to greet him – this was more than mere wifely duty, it was ritual honoured over time – but she had had trouble with her daughter, she had lost an hour to pointless argument, and had been in pieces since.

Lucy had lately become tragic. She was more than ever given to extravagant gestures, to high-flown utterances, far-fetched schemes, incredible hyperbole and impetuosity. She tossed her head about, she threw herself around, recklessly insensible of furniture or self. All the chairs were on the move. There were ripples in the carpets. Doors flew open, crashed shut. Plates slipped to the floor and shattered. Pictures swung aslant on their hooks. Mysteriously, the Dresden shepherdess had lost an arm. Food enough to feed an army went missing from fridge and pantry. The handbasin in the cloakroom overflowed; a river ran under the door and down the hall. She had a new pal, Clemency, her best friend in the whole, wide world, upon whom she simply doted. (To her old friend, Sarah, she would never speak again for as long as she lived.) *When* could Clemency come to stay? *Why* must Juin come to Scotland? And anyway, why Scotland, when *everyone* these days went to Miami?

While other teenage girls outgrew their strength, becoming torpid and withdrawn, Lucy Gorst's strength seemed to have outgrown her; it took up its own space and went rampaging through the house ahead of her.

She was up in her room now, sulking. No one sulked more noisily than Lucy.

It was a measure of poor Geraldine's desperation that she had yesterday confided in Elli, even begging her for advice. Elaine must, after all, have been through it with Juin; she might have some wisdom to impart.

'I can't think what's come over her,' she'd sighed.

'It'll be sex,' Elli had diagnosed assuredly.

'But Lucy wouldn't . . .'

'Not actually, no. I mean, I dare say not. But you remember how it was when it first got into you? How fretful it made you? How you couldn't wait to get started?'

Geraldine Gorst could remember no such thing. Rather tersely, she had said as much.

'Well, *you*,' Elli had told her, 'always were too virtuous for this earth. Myself, as I remember, I was climbing the walls with frustration. Juin can't wait for Scotland, by the way. She talks of little else. She counts the days.'

'I wish Lucy felt the same. It's not good enough for her this year, it seems. She's on and on at me about Florida. "With my susceptibility to the heat," I tell her, "and with your delicate tum, it would be madness." '

'Geraldine, do you have to be so fucking precious?'

'Swearing, Elaine, I always think, betrays a limited vocabulary.'

'It's sheer valetudinarianism, you know that?'

'Val . . .?'

Now, 'What is valetudinarianism?' Geraldine asked her husband, whom she tracked down to the drawing-room, where he stood before the fireplace, fiddling with his tie.

'Sickliness, as I understand it,' he answered, frowning. 'Or an excessive preoccupation with health.'

'I see.'

'Why do you ask?'

'Oh, you know. I just wondered. It came up in conversation. I thought that was the meaning. I wasn't quite sure.'

'Some idiot,' he related, 'has driven his van straight through the plate-glass front of the Star of Bengal.'

'Drunk, perhaps?' Geraldine accepted a gin and tonic with a small, wan smile. I've earned this, the smile said.

'I have no idea,' he regretted, feeling that he had failed her somewhat. Routinely, dutifully, he would bring home to her these fishy tales; he fed them to her as a keeper feeds a seal, and snap, she would seize upon them. His own heart was not really in it. After twenty-five years of legal practice he was rarely surprised by the behaviour of others, he was past discountenancing human frailty, but he knew how she loved to deplore. And, for as long as she had a capacity for outrage, he was content to pander to it. It was something, at least, for them to talk about. It took the place of genuine dialogue.

'Any one hurt?' she demanded briskly. She liked to have casualty figures.

'I don't believe so.' It was not, after all, much of a story, lacking as it did some crucial element (drug-crazed driver, unroadworthy vehicle, commercial sabotage, vendetta), but he had nothing better this evening, no messy divorces, no neighbourly feuds to cause her to wonder aloud what the world was coming to.

'Of course, since they changed the traffic priorities . . .' she declared in triumph. 'For, didn't I say . . .?'

'You did.'

'I said it was an accident waiting to happen.'

'That's right.'

'I was in the high street myself today. I walked right past the Star of Bengal.' By the skin of her teeth, then, it might have been, that she had escaped serious injury.

'It happened just now. In the thick of the rush. Brought the traffic to a standstill. You can imagine.'

'And I'd no sooner got home than I had Lucy throwing another tantrum. Elli says it's sex.'

'What's sex?'

'Rather, it's puberty. Juin was the same, evidently. In fact, I'm not sure that she isn't still.'

'She's not a bad kid,' John moderated vaguely.

'Lucy?'

'No, Juin. I thought you said that Juin . . .'

'You'll change your tune, I fancy, when you're exposed to that one for a whole fortnight. When she's foisted upon us in Scotland, the full horror will come home to you.'

'Ah, yes, Scotland.' He stared meditatively into his glass. John Gorst was a thoroughly obliging chap. It was to please his parents that he'd studied law and joined the partnership of Gorst and Merridew. And it was to satisfy a general expectation that he'd married Geraldine Garvey. They had been introduced by mutual friends who, seeing no better possibilities for either, had talked them up, one to the other, and he had not cared to disappoint the matchmakers. Now, however, he was going to have to disoblige his wife.

'Hmm?' she queried suspiciously.

'I can drive you up there, stay the weekend, but after that I shall have to love you and leave you. The office can't spare me for two weeks. We simply have too much work on.'

Geraldine pulled a frightening face, her worst in living memory. Mostly, John found the look of her not displeasing. He liked her complex smile, the interplay of features, the way an upturn of her mouth plumped out her cheeks, dimpled her chin and crinkled the skin around her eyes. (His own face might, he had long felt, have been made up of spare parts, all working independently of one another. He could even waggle his ears, not just together but separately, a talent that had saved him, in his childhood, from some of the very worst school bullying.) She wasn't smiling now, though, and when her mouth turned down it took the rest of her face with it. 'You cannot,' she said, quivering with emotion, 'propose to leave me in sole charge of three children?'

'They're not exactly little kiddies,' he reasoned.

'No. Worse than that, they're adolescents.' Juin, she told herself. Lucy, Dominic. Truculence, recalcitrance, dumb insolence. 'I shan't be able to cope,' she wailed. 'You mustn't put upon me in that way.'

There were school fees to be found for the autumn term, when Lucy would need a whole new uniform if she grew another centimetre in any direction. The running of the house was a considerable expense. The Gorsts lived well, ate in safe, smart restaurants, gave dinner parties. And only through his efforts was any of this possible. John was tempted to remind her of it, but checked the impulse. Once she'd calmed down, she would figure it out for herself. Instead he said, 'I was thinking, maybe you should take someone. A chum. You could take Naomi. She has nothing better to do. Share the twin-bedded room with her.'

'Naomi? Good grief! She'd be like a fourth child. In any case, she'd never come. It's hardly her scene, is it?'

'Your mother, then? I'm sure she'd be glad of the break.'

'Well, maybe.' Geraldine, sighing, reflected on it. 'Maybe,' she said again.

In the room above, a small elephant was dancing a gavotte. Or a bulldozer was bulldozing. Or a poltergeist was wreaking havoc. The ceiling shook, the electric chandelier trembled. Geraldine and John raised their eyes heavenward. 'What have I just been telling you?' she said.

'Lock up your grandsons!' yelled Elli Sharpe, excessive as ever, bounding off the sofa. 'Naomi Markham's on the prowl.' She diminished the room with her long stride, to pause at the french windows and glare back at the sky. 'It's black as Newgate's knocker out there,' she reported, really just to let out a little emotion.

Naomi, wounded, offered no reply. Evening shadows gradually assimilated her: to Elli, from her vantage by the window, she seemed somewhat to dissolve.

'Well, well, well . . .' Elli shook her head incredulously. She was, frankly, gobsmacked. She was wearing on each hand a great variety of flamboyant rings, which she twisted in an agitated fashion. She must be psychic or something. She must be more perspicacious, even, than she knew. Except that she had never truly foreseen this. Oh, sure, she had taken great delight yesterday in needling Kate, in winding her up with talk of Naomi and Alex. But this had been just her fun, the mischievous confection of her imagination; she hadn't for one moment believed that propinquity, for all its power, would act upon the occupants at Larkspur Road.

'Tell me what you've been doing,' she had exhorted Naomi as she welcomed her into her home. And she had mentally set aside five minutes, at the maximum ten, for her old friend's self-pitying maunder, after which she had planned to give her, in return, the full Martin – salacious details, moral dilemma, resolution. He was an accomplished and inventive lover, she was to have confided. He was caring, considerate and, of course, crazy for her. But he had a wife . . . of sorts. He had a duty. And could she, Elli, with her hand on her heart, declare herself a feminist, while she dallied with a sister's husband? No, no, it must end! Before the summer was out, before Italy, she would lay the affair to rest.

Then, 'You don't want to know,' Naomi had cautioned, before launching upon this most hair-raising account of her recent exploits.

For heaven's sake, Alex was only . . . and Naomi was at least . . . In her febrile state, Elli could not furnish the precise figures, but twenty-odd years stood between them.

159

She scarcely knew how to respond, outwardly or in. No one was hotter for gossip than she, and here was a real scorcher, here was super-scandal, genuine shockerama. But, in a small part of herself, she was dismayed. And in a rather larger part of herself she was pig sick with jealousy. The news had set her back, somehow, as though Naomi had stolen a march on her.

For a few seconds, the space between them was fraught with silence. Then came that most heart-sinking of sounds, as Elaine Sharp drew a deep and fortifying breath. 'Now, you know,' she began, 'there is no one more broad-minded than I . . .'

If Naomi knew it, she chose not to say so. She cupped her chin in her hand and looked impenitent ('recusant' was the word Elli privately favoured, or 'perfectly bloody') as she waited for the inevitable but.

'But . . . ' Elli came back quickly to sit by her, to reason with her. She tipped forward on the sofa, resting her forearms on her knees, clasping her hands, striking an attitude of solicitude. Her face loomed large in Naomi's line of vision. 'But you knew him as a babe in arms. You dandled him on your knee.'

'No I didn't,' Naomi was stung at last into responding. And it was true, of course, for Naomi was never a dandler. While the other three, Geraldine, Elli, Kate, had gushed and cooed over the newborn Alex, 'their' first baby, passing him from hand to hand, she had held herself aloof and had looked resolutely elsewhere. She had always been at best indifferent to, and at worst repelled by, these tiny, needy creatures, maddened by their graspng hands and drooling, formless mouths.

Complacent young mothers, aglow with love and pride, pressing their offspring upon Ms Markham, persuaded absolutely of their transforming powers, would have them returned in short order. Prevailed upon to take charge for an instant of one such bundle of joy, she would grapple it unhappily, or dangle it at arm's length, with manifest discomfort and averted eyes.

She could honestly say that, until a few years ago, Alex Garvey had scarcely existed for her. He might have come into being at the age of nineteen, six-foot-something, muscular, hirsute, with size nine feet and thirty-two-inch inside leg, for all the earlier notice she had taken of him.

'You've changed your tune, haven't you?' she coldly accused Elli. 'When Bill Wyman married Mandy Smith, you said good luck to them. You wrote it in your stupid paper. I remember distinctly, you said age didn't matter. You said love was the bridge.'

Such acuity, from Naomi of all people, was disconcerting. 'Well,' Elli parried, 'I'm gratified to learn that you read my column with such close attention.'

'I don't as a rule. I can't be bothered with it. I just happened to pick up the *Globe* on that particular day. I thought, for friendship's sake, I ought to look and see what you were banging on about.'

Elli was nonplussed. Hoist, she told herself, with my own petard. It made her laugh, very sportingly, raucously, aloud.

'It isn't funny,' Naomi reproved her. 'Not to me it isn't. Because, you have to understand, I love him.'

Now she'll start to cry, thought Elli wearily.

Naomi began to cry.

She looked so lost and lorn and sort of pointlessly beautiful, so purely ornamental and delicate, that Elli was moved to take her hand. Naomi felt the bruising pressure of a half a dozen jewelled rings.

'I am only thinking,' Elli reasoned, 'that you're basically unsuited. You move in quite different circles. You know, in his way, darling boy though he is, Alex is terribly ordinary.'

'He isn't. He's actually quite *extraordinary*.' Naomi jabbed her elbow in an effort to retrieve her pincered hand, but Elli held fast. The two of them, with their gritted teeth, might have been trying to pull a peculiarly tenacious Christmas cracker.

'You were born into a different world,' Elli sermonised. 'Remember it? The Light Programme. Home and Colonial. Black and white telly. The test card. *Daily Herald*. Andy Pandy. *Reveille*. Threepenny halves. Jubbly. Skooby-Doo. Spend a penny. Press button A. Do not adjust your set.'

'I don't recall,' said Naomi woodenly, 'any of that.' She had, after all, been an introverted, unobservant and profoundly unhappy little girl. Why should she want to resort to memory of those days? She had put her past away with all childish things, and made no reference to it. 'I never heard of Home and Colonial. Nor, come to that, of anyone named Andy Pandy.'

'You have no seminal experiences in common. You wore flowers in your hair and protested against Vietnam. All right, all right, *you* personally didn't, you were too busy reading *Honey*, or trying on floppy hats and feather boas in Biba, but you are of that generation. These were

162

the influences that shaped you. Whereas Alex grew up to Thatcherism. To satellite television. Mass unemployment. Madonna. Ozone depletion. The poll tax riots.'

'Now, those things I *do* remember.' For Alex's sake, quite as much as for her own, for their precious relationship, she spoke up in furious advocacy. 'What are you trying to say, Elaine? What are you trying to do? To make out that I'm part of history? Well, I'm not. This is *my* time as much as it's his. I love Madonna. I've watched satellite telly. I know about the information super-highway. Don't look so astonished, I *do* know about it, Alex has explained it to me. And he needs me. And I need him. And I'm sure I shall find plenty to talk to him about besides Andy bloody Pandy, thank you very much.'

'I'm only saying . . .' Elli sighed. She relinquished her hold on Naomi's hand, which took flight like a bird. What *was* she saying, really? 'I'm only trying to warn you, it could be harder than you think.'

'How hard do you think I think it will be? Am I so simple that I need everything spelled out for me? Sure we'll have problems. But, then, who doesn't? There are no perfect partnerships. You just have to make more or less a go of it. And the thing is . . . what you have to understand is, I didn't plan this, and Alex didn't plan it. It just came upon us. And now we simply have to be together. Because we just can't be apart. I know you think I'm spoilt and selfish and useless. Yes you *do*, please don't deny it. But I did hope that you, of all people, who reckon to be so worldly, would have understood.'

Elli sucked for a while disconsolately upon her lower lip. Then, 'And what about Kate?' she enquired.

'What *about* Kate? Yes, I know she'll be upset. And angry.'

'Mortified, I'd say. And desolated. And consumed by rage. There'll be weeping and gnashing *chez* Garvey, mark my words.'

'Yes, right. All of that. But she'll get over it. And she can't hang on to her son for ever, can she? Because he's a big boy now.'

'I dare say she knows that. She will have prepared herself, I'm quite sure, to lose him to some nice girl of his own age.' For the first time, Elli remembered Juin. Her heart, which was not much given to smiting, smote her then. She was moved to pity for her daughter, who was secretly so desperately enamoured.

Naomi seemed not to have heard, or elected to ignore, this jibe. 'I can't bring myself to tell her, and I dread her finding out. But the longer we keep it from her, the worse she is going to feel.'

'Alex will have to do it,' Elli decided.

'Do you think so?'

'Well, don't you?'

'Yes, yes, absolutely.'

'Leave it to him. Let him take care of it.'

'Oh, I shall.' Relief overwhelmed Naomi. When she lay back, her blue eyes flicked shut like a doll's. I shall leave everything to Alex, she told herself over and over, her mantra.

'You and I, meanwhile,' said Elli, smiling, 'will put Plan A into operation.'

'What is Plan A?' queried Naomi, without opening her eyes.

164

'We crack open a bottle or two of vino, and send out for a pizza prontissimo.'

'I can't see the point of it,' said Trevor dismissively.

'But then *you*,' Juin reminded him, 'can't see the point of anything.' She sat on the top stair, hugging her knees, curling her shrimpy toes round the tread, gazing at him with her soulful, dark eyes as he dusted and polished his way to the bottom. He applied himself, this Friday morning, with more than usual vigour to the task. If he worked up the wood to an ice-rink finish, he reasoned, there was a chance that Elaine Sharpe would slip and come all the way down on her arse. ('Do not use on floors,' read a warning on the spray can, 'as the high gloss could be dangerous.') God willing, he would be around to witness collapse of stout party, though there were no sounds of life from her quarters, and the debris in the sitting-room – empty bottles, wine-stained glasses, overflowing ashtrays, pizza boxes, the unappetising remains of a takeaway – told him that she'd made a night of it, so might not emerge before noon. The place was a tip, as always. He could just imagine how she'd have gone on. 'Don't worry, leave that, leave everything. Trevor can clear up tomorrow. Why else do I pay the lazy little sod?'

Bitch! On second thoughts, he'd be thankful not to clap eyes on her today. By the time she showed her hideous face he should be gone, to college, to begin a gouache, a painting which, by its very ugliness and unmeaning, would make a powerful statement about futility and vainglory. He would call it 'The End of the World is

165

Nylon'. Or, 'Homage to Catatonia'. Or, better yet, if it turned out to be as grotesque on paper as in his mind's eye, simply, 'Elaine'.

'What I'm saying is . . .' He shook the aerosol, gave the stair a good blast of Mr Sheen, watched it effervescing, stooped and stuck his long nose almost into it, and inhaled deeply, appreciating the 'new pot-pourri fragrance', or indulging in the kind of intentional misuse against which the manufacturers further cautioned. 'What I want to know is, what's in it for any of us?'

'I should have thought that was obvious. There being no death as you understand it, just the four bardos of living, dying, after-death, and rebirth.'

'So we still have to die, am I right? There's no ducking out of it?'

'Yes, sure, but then we make another karmic connection and we're born again.'

'And what's the use of that? To come back as some other fucker?' To come back, he meant, without his essential Trevorness.

'In some other incarnation, yes, but with continuity of mind. Of the subtlest level of consciousness.'

'Look . . .' He straightened up, the better to take issue with her. A joint in his lower lumbar region clicked audibly. With his long back and poor posture, he would have trouble in middle age. 'You can't remember any of your past lives, can you?'

She squeezed her eyes shut. 'Sometimes I think I can. I have a sort of . . . afterimage.'

'And I suppose you were a handmaiden in the court of Cleopatra? Or chief lady-in-waiting to Marie Antoinette?'

'I couldn't say for sure. Maybe if I were hypnotised, regressed . . .'

'Because no one ever remembers, do they, being Joe Bloggs the pigswill man?'

'For all I know I might have been.'

'Exactly,' he replied in triumph. '*Exactly*. So might I if you're to be believed.'

'Well, not *me*, of course. It isn't I who have to be believed. These are the teachings of Prince Gautama Siddhartha, who we call Buddha, who attained enlightenment five centuries before the birth of Christ.'

'Yeah, yeah, and if this guy Gautama is to be believed, I could have been Joe Bloggs the swill man. Or you could have been. But Joe Bloggs is dead. And some day you'll be dead. And I'll be dead. And if I cannot live my next life as Trevor Pocock, I don't want to live it at all.'

'I can't imagine,' Juin deprecated, 'why you should want to live even one life as a Pocock. I should hate to have that name. Two rude words put together.'

'Pocock, my dear, is an old Wiltshire rendering of Peacock.'

'Then call yourself Peacock, why don't you?'

'But there's already an actor or someone, isn't there, who goes by that name?'

'I don't suppose too much confusion would arise. I don't imagine you'd get all his fan mail by mistake. Or he all yours.'

'Anyway, I'd sooner be a Pocock than a Titball.'

'There's no such name.' She barked in disbelief.

'Want to take a small bet? A hundred million pounds?'

'Maybe not. You could just be right. It's the sort of useless thing you might know.'

'I do. It's a corruption of Theobald. We had a Roger Titball in my class at school. We called him Breasticle to be polite.'

'He must have had a rough time.'

'Nah. Not as rough, at any rate, as poor old Smellie.'

'I don't doubt it. But, listen, I can't sit here all day trying to enlighten you.'

'We used to say "phew" whenever he came near. We'd go like this –' he made a fanning motion – 'or we'd hold our noses.'

'If you don't want to follow the spiritual path, that's up to you.'

'Needless to say, we called him Stinker.'

'Everything we think, everything we do and are, affects our karma.'

'In which case, I dare say I'm stuffed.'

'It's not too late for you, I'm sure. You can create change at any time. Hey, that's a gruesome zit you've got on your neck.'

'Thanks a lot.'

'I could squeeze it for you.'

'You lay off me.' He put up an arm defensively, but Juin made no move.

'It'll be your diet. Too many fry-ups. Not enough fruit and veg. Now, I really must get going. I have to revise my Chaucer. I'm learning the *Prologue* by heart so I'll be one up when we do it next year. I've got as far as the Monk. A man after your own heart. Listen to this, you'll like this bit. "What sholde he studie, and make himselven wood,

168

Upon a book in cloistre alwey to poure, Or swinken with his handes, and laboure." '

'Did they tell him that it makes you blind?'

'Huh?'

'To swinken with the hands. It makes you blind.'

'Do leave it out, Trev,' Juin sighed. 'For your information, "swinken" means "to work", an altogether foreign concept to you.'

'Look who's talking! I've never seen you do a stroke.'

'I do more than you realise.'

From behind Juin, through a door, came daylight, sluicing the landing carpet. Something went swishing by her, trailing a faint wake of Arpège. The bathroom door creaked and clicked shut.

'What was tha-at?' asked Trevor, awed. And belatedly, in a touching gesture of self-consciousness, he concealed behind his aching back the polish can and rag.

'Oh, her.' Juin wrinkled her nose. 'That's Naomi. An old, old friend of Mum's. They got shouting drunk together last night, so she slept over. If you take no notice of her, she'll probably go away.'

'She looks like a film star.'

'Well, she isn't. She isn't anything. She's just this really flaky character who goes about making a nuisance of herself.'

'She can be a nuisance to me any time.'

'Don't be such a total titball. She's forty if she's a day. Still, you're a bit of a flake yourself, aren't you? So the pair of you should have a lot in common.'

'Do I detect a cheeky hint of dislike?'

Juin clutched her ankles, put her face down between

169

her knees. 'I hate the sight of her,' she said into the warm folds of her skirt.

She had skulked up in her room all evening with Muffy, disdaining to join her mother and Naomi for supper. 'You're a snotty little madam,' Elli had accused her, bringing her *pizza marinara* on a tray. 'Now, say "That's tray *bien*, Mummy dearest." '

But, a grunted 'Ta' had been the best Juin could muster.

Trevor made an infuriating clicking sound with his tongue. 'That attitude is not going to do a lot for your karma, now is it?' he taunted her.

'You know what? Suddenly, I don't seem to care.' She stood up, descended gingerly, holding fast to the banister, eased past him and headed for the kitchen. 'I shall take Mum some strong, black coffee. Want me to make you one while I'm at it?'

'Chinese tea for me.'

'Oolong.'

'As the actress said to the bishop.'

'Cha for the char.'

'Oh, go swink yourself.'

'Is that you?' queried Elli feebly, five minutes later, hearing the scuff of door on carpet, the pad-pad of bare feet.

'Course it's me,' Juin told her. 'I'm off to school in a mo. Wake up and smell the coffee.'

'There's no need to shout.'

'I'm not shouting.' Clonk, a cup went down on the bedside cabinet. Screek, the curtains were drawn back. The room was flooded with unkindly light.

'Is it horribly sunny?'

'If you opened your eyes,' said Juin punishingly, 'you would see for yourself.'

'I can't. They won't open.'

'Of course they will.' Juin leaned her folded arms on the sill and peered down at the street. 'It's not a *bad* day,' she announced, 'but it's definitely gone off. It's all sort of wishy-washy. I reckon we've had our summer. You know, it's no wonder the poor old lime tree is on its last legs. The dog from number seventy-three does its business there every morning. Ugh! It's at it now. You should see it.'

'*Please*, Juin, don't do this.'

'Do what?'

'Don't make things worse for me. As it is, I'm not feeling exactly in the pink of health. I'm afraid I've been poisoned. That pizza was definitely off.'

'You've got a hangover, you mean. Serve you jolly well right.'

'It's not a hangover. I can tell the difference, can't I? You know, I *thought* the prawns smelt a bit suspect.'

'Well, it's a funny thing, isn't it, that *I* feel fine. Because I had the prawns as well, remember?'

'Ah, but you have an iron constitution; I don't. It's my mother's fault. She was always finicky about kitchen hygiene. She must have gone through gallons of bleach in a week. Never mind Parazone; paranoia, I'd call it. A speck of mould, and out went the cheese. Vegetables were washed within an inch of their lives. I had no chance, you see, to build up immunity as you're supposed to do in childhood. I was not allowed my peck of dirt.' She was a victim, it now seemed to her, of culpable negligence. Vengefully she cursed the hapless Sybil.

'Poor old Granny. She couldn't do anything right, could she?'

'Never you mind "poor old Granny". What about poor old me?'

'It'll wear off by lunchtime, I shouldn't wonder. Shall I get you a couple of aspirins? Some vitamin C?'

'In a minute.' With finger and thumb, Elli prised open one eye. 'The air hurts,' she grumbled.

'You *are* in a state.'

'How about that lazy little sod, the plug-ugly fellow who comes here and pretends to clean? Has he graced the house with his presence?'

'Trevor? He's having a cup of tea.'

'I don't pay him to sit around all day taking refreshment.'

'He's been very busy, actually. He's done the stairs already. He made a very thorough job of it.'

Juin turned from the window, perched on the sill and, bracing her arms, rocked back and forth on her hands, increasing Elli's feeling of disorientation. 'Will you pack that in?' she pleaded.

'Pack what in?'

'All that swaying about. You make my head spin.'

'Sorry.' Briefly, Juin sat quite still and sucked on her teeth. Then, 'Mu-um?' she weedled.

'Wha-at?' Elli mimicked. 'Hey, be a love, won't you, and pass me that mirror off the chest of drawers?'

'Okey-doke.' As Juin slid off the sill and reached for the mirror, she came over suddenly all existential. She contemplated the enigma of self, tried to imagine what it would mean to see, staring out of the silvered glass at one in unwavering self-love, the pellucid blue eyes of Naomi Markham; or to have the painted, plushy Elaine Sharpe tip one the wink of recognition; or, as it might be, to have returned to one each morning the image of a hand-maiden in the court of Cleopatra. And she was forced to concede the argument to Trevor: one was who one was, or one was nothing. What was to be gained by popping up in other guises down the centuries? That miraculous conflation of the physical and psychological known as a person was unique and aberrant, mortal and intractable. She would be Juin Sharpe until she died, and there would be an end of her.

Well, there were many worse things to be – not least, her own mother. Yet Elli, seeing reflected her own gussety face, still caked with yesterday's make-up, appeared only to be reassured. She even managed a brave smile for herself. Perhaps she was relieved to find she was still in once piece. Or else myopia was a marvellous condition.

'Is Naomi going to stay here, or what?' Juin demanded.

'She most certainly is not. There is a limit to my tolerance. Why?'

'Is she going back to Kate's, then?'

'For the time being.' Elli winced. And it was the return to full consciousness, more than the drumming in her skull, that pained her. How was she to explain?

'Only I had this idea . . .'

'Not now, Juin, huh? Won't it keep, whatever it is?'

'When you go to Italy, right?'

'What about it?'

'Naomi could come and stay here.'

'Oh, I dare say she'll have made other arrangements by then. She was telling me last night, she has something in prospect.'

'But if she doesn't, if her plans fall through, she can stay here.'

'I'm not sure she'd be up for babysitting you, my sweet. In any case, I thought you couldn't abide her?'

Juin shrugged. 'I could put up with her for a fortnight, at a pinch. I mean, if it came to a toss-up between her and Lucy Gorst. Between going to Scotland and staying in London. And it would be a great break for Kate and Alex.'

'Juin, darling.' Elli stared at her a moment, sallow-eyed. Then she patted the quilt beside her. 'Come and sit here, will you? There is something I want to tell you.'

Kate spent the afternoon at the Frobishers' in Putney, tending a motley congregation of terracotta tubs, old chimneypots, stone sinks and urns in their rear court-yard garden, before moving round to the front to replant the window-boxes which Janet Frobisher had been simply too remiss to water (their contents had put up a valiant struggle these past seven weeks; desiccated pelargonia still showed the odd, defiant red flag, but in vain). Kate quite liked Janet, a tall woman who, with her flat, pale hair and her penchant for washed-out Indian fabrics, gave the impression of having faded by several shades, like an exotic cushion left too long in the sun. She had a lazy eye which, wandering, compounded her air of distraction, and an assortment of children whose names she routinely, tranquilly interchanged. She was an undemanding, not to say a lax, employer.

At one point, as Kate dug in apple-blossom geraniums, Janet appeared at the window, to show her, wordlessly, two biscuit-coloured kittens, which squirmed in her hands. The women traded smiles through the glass – 'Perfectly adorable!' those smiles said – and Kate felt quite a pang, remembering how tiny Petal and Pushkin had once been. Janet held the kittens briefly, one against each cheek, then set them on the sofa-back, from where they mountaineered expertly down. Otherwise, Kate was alone with Radio 4 and her thoughts, which surfaced randomly, like wreckage from the ocean bed.

Gardening, she told herself, as she tamped the earth around the roots of trailing lobelia, was far harder, far more skilled work than people generally allowed. Non-gardeners, those with more significant calls upon their time, seemed pleased to think that you simply dug some holes and heeled the green stuff in. This, the least arduous, most rewarding part, was all they saw of a long process that began very early, at the plant market or nursery, and involved the humping around of sacks of soil, of flowerpots in polystyrene trays, the callousing of once-tender hands, laceration with whips and barbs, and a great deal of back-breaking spadework. To Janet Frobisher, for instance, glancing out, with half her mind on furry kittens, her task must appear a mere bagatelle.

Kate, in a fit of ruthless self-examination, admitted that there was obscure satisfaction to be had from being undervalued. Elli was right that she liked – no, not *liked*, but *needed* – to feel put-upon. There was something reassuring to her in the knowledge that she was due more than she was ever paid in earnings or esteem. It was like having equity in oneself, not to be mortgaged psychologically to the hilt.

Here, then, was the true nature of Naomi's destitution. It was about rather more than being for the present impecunious (although, goodness knows, that was for her a wretched state; it made her frail and tearful). One could stand being broke, just about, when one had secret reserves of self-belief, but Naomi had lived right out there on the limit of her worth; she had lived beyond it. She had not, since her childhood, been unappreciated. And now, impoverished of praise and adulation, looking inward, she found no vindication there.

I have done all right, Kate decided. I have managed well. Pushing her hair back with one forearm (did hair grow faster in summer than in winter, or was this just her fancy?), squinting up at the pearly sky, at a silver disc of sun, she wondered if, in managing, she had essayed too little, aspired too low.

Naomi at least had a story to tell; an account of her exploits would fill a book. Whereas, for the tale of Katharine Garvey, née Perkins, the reverse of a postage stamp ought to suffice.

What did she amount to, after all? She had been a 'good mother', whatever that meant, but the role was at an end. To say that, with Alex, she had accomplished something truly worthwhile, was to say, by implication, that her job was done. Could she have invested too heavily in it?

For the two decades that she had devoted to his

upbringing, she had sort of put herself to one side. There had been no sex for her, no romance, no personal development, no great intellectual challenge. She was as neglected, in her way, as this discarded pelargonium, a mess of parched leaves and snappy twigs, a horticultural travesty through which the vital sap no longer ran. She shook from the plant's roots a noisy shower of sun-baked earth. And in the moment of blinking the dust from her eyes and quelling a sneeze, she came as near to resenting Alex as she had ever come.

But, of course, the fault had not been his. No use to blame the baby born of the coupling of naïvety with arrogance. She had been responsible. She and David. And youth itself. And peer pressure.

David Garvey had been, by broad consensus, a great catch – and Kate had caught him, just as, in their time, she had caught chickenpox, measles, mumps. He had entered her, as undiscriminating as a virus, as careless of the consequence. And in one night the course of the next twenty-two years had been determined for her.

Now, suddenly, as it seemed, those next twenty-two years had become the past twenty-two years. It was as if her whole life had swung around. She felt like the central character in a stage play, upon whom the lights had dimmed, while the scenery revolved, and make-up and costume changes were invisibly effected. It was as though the lights had just come up again, and – no doubt to irritable coughing from the audience, to the bored rustle of barleysugar wrappers, the disaffected thud, thud, the flying up of fold-down seats – she stood revealed as older, greyer, in quite altered circumstances.

177

'Much later,' the programme would have it. And, 'In another part of the forest.'

It was time to let Alex go. That was his wish, she was more than ever sure of it. Deep down she knew that he stayed for her sake, not his own. And the past few weeks she'd felt the tug of his unutterable discontent, had seen his soft eyes fill with it from within, from way down in his gut, as if by some capillary action. But for her own sake, also, she must release him. She must create space for development, sex, romance and challenge.

Oh, crikey, what a terrifying prospect!

'That all looks very nice,' said Janet when she counted out Kate's money.

'You *will* take care of them this time, won't you?' Kate admonished her. 'Or they'll just die like the last lot.'

'Oh, yes. I'm sorry. One simply forgets . . . But I shall be diligent, I promise. You'll see. The next time you come . . . because you must come. Yes, to supper. To meet Paul. He would like to put a face to your name. He is always saying what wonders you perform.'

'That would be . . .' responded Kate doubtfully. Nice? She feared not. She had learned how a certain sort of married couple, bored half to death with each other, would make pets of single women. They sat you down and, with *faux* modesty, invited you to envy their homes, their ordered existence, their exalted oneness. They made much of the first-person plural, saying 'we' and 'us' and 'our', flaunting their coupledom to someone such as Kate, who was (poor love), and seemed destined to remain, a solitary 'I', a 'me'. Smiling indulgently at her, urging food upon her as if no one quite knew where her next meal would come from, they would talk of home improvements, of extensions, of foreign holidays, their hopes of moving some time to the country . . . She had been too often patronised in this fashion, not least by John and Geraldine, who had taken her up, and who had by and by, mercifully, set her down again.

Janet, however, having issued so vague an invitation, immediately, by sleight of hand, withdrew it. (Paul would perhaps not, on reflection, be so avid to sit down at table with the jobbing gardener.) 'But, of course,' she murmured, 'it's a long way for you to come. And I am sure you have a full diary.'

'Well, you know . . .' grinned Kate, stuffing banknotes into her jeans pocket, from where she might extricate them only with great difficulty. 'Deadhead them as I showed you,' she called over her shoulder as Janet saw her to her car. 'Don't just yank the tops off any old how; feel for the join.'

As she drove homeward, she opened the window a crack and let the wind take her mood. She relinquished her new resolve, her fine intentions, her determination to release poor Alex from commitment. With a sideways glance, she saw her purpose take flight over Wandsworth Common.

Instead, she decided that Alex must get out and about more. He was kicking his heels at home in Tooting. Very well. She had saved against such a crisis, she had money in the building society with which she would buy him a car.

By the time she turned into Larkspur Road, the thing had firmed up in her mind, almost to the make and model he should have (a Volkswagen Beetle, she fancied for him, well engineered, reliable but not too fast or flash, not dangerous).

She parked with her usual inexpertise, bumping on and off the steep kerb, then hauled herself out on to the pavement.

The girl with the dishevelled dog who waited at her gate might have stepped out of a painting, the work of some outrageous sentimentalist, so *distraite* did she appear. With her affectingly thin arms, her wide eyes, her shabby cotton dress, she was the epitome of a street urchin. Staring from the pages of a newspaper, she would have compelled charity. But she was no urchin, certainly. She was only . . .

'Why, Juin,' said Kate kindly, 'how lovely! Have you been waiting long? I've been working, you see. In Putney. And I didn't expect . . . If you had rung, I could have told you. I'm seldom home before six.' Concern exerted itself upon her face, drawing her features together. Through narrowed eyes she peered at Juin. Hay fever, she wondered. Or had the girl been crying? If so, then no prize for guessing why. She must have fallen out with her impossible mother.

Swelling slightly with conceit, with the satisfaction of being, by any measure, a better parent, Kate prepared to take Juin, metaphorically, to her bosom. She would sit her down and pour her Coke and say 'Right, come on, tell your Auntie Katie all about it.' She would be the voice of tolerance and sweet reason as she made a case for Elli, who was so hard-working, so talented, so driven, and whose heart was surely in the right place, however selfish or thoughtless or contemptuous she might sometimes seem.

Juin stooped and swept her dog up in her arms, he a bundle of yelps and wags. She hugged him defensively to her, jigged him about, then stood a moment rigid, summoning courage, commanding her emotions, which could be seen all on the loose behind her eyes. She threw back her head and regarded Kate with something like defiance. When finally she spoke, her tone was almost accusatory.

'Kate,' she said, in a hoarse and shaken voice, 'I think you should be told.'

'Told what?' Involuntarily, Kate stepped back, as if to be out of the range of an explosion. She blinked at Juin uncomprehendingly. For the first time it occurred to her that the child might be unhinged.

'I think you should know,' Juin continued. She nipped her lip to stop it trembling, drew a shuddering breath. 'You should know what's been going on,' she finished in a rush, 'under your very roof. Under your nose. I think you have a right to know what Naomi is doing.'

CHAPTER

5

Kate joined the quick-in-and-out queue at her local Sainsbury's, the brisk line of cash-paying customers with humble hand-baskets and no life to speak of. Not for her a capacious supermarket trolley, precariously piled with fancy groceries, freighted with boisterous infants in baseball caps. She was single and, finally, very much alone. The basket's handles cut into her bare arm. And it was for the purchase of dull, essential items (washing-up liquid, toilet rolls, cat food, instant coffee), not for more celebratory fare (goat cheese, capers, sun-dried tomatoes or delicious Frascati), that she suffered this indignity.

Depressed people, she told herself, should never visit supermarkets. In her present state – not, actually, depressed, but right outside herself, exposed – this advice seemed almost Confucian in its wisdom.

The press of humanity in the store had reduced her to a tearful wreck. She had hovered, fuming, excluded from shelf and chill cabinet, around which whole families held conferences: she had awaited, gibbering with impatience, the outcome of their deliberations over one tin of beans and its identical twin, this pint of half-fat milk and that. She had hissed and glowered at erratic drivers who slewed their wire vehicles in her path and cluttered all the aisles. At the same time, her own disequilibrium had run her up against hard edges, she had skewered herself on corners. Somewhere between the desserts section and frozen pastries, she had lost it altogether. With jellies, custards, tinned rice puddings rearing up in front of her, 'I can't go on!' she had said aloud, and for a whole minute she really *couldn't*.

Now she shut her eyes, heard children make their shrill demands, heard 'I want *whine* gums, I want *whine* gums.' And she wondered if there was a way to tell if you were about to have a nervous breakdown.

It was three weeks since her world had fallen so completely to pieces. Three weeks since Juin Sharpe, with good or ill intent, or perhaps not really understanding what she did, had arrived to tell her that which she had wanted least of all on earth to hear.

Naomi and Alex. Alex and Naomi. In her head, their names, in the manner of like poles, repelled. And, in the same way, cringing consciousness and hideous truth would fly apart (the word 'unthinkable' had never seemed more apt).

'You're lying!' she had screamed, out there in the street for all to hear (the Wiltons, climbing from their Subaru, had turned as one in disapproval), while Juin, holding hard to an overwrought Muffy, his eyes showing white, had shrunk abjectly from her, trusting herself to the privet hedge.

Then, 'I shan't believe it,' she'd declared, 'until I hear it for myself from Alex.'

And from Alex she had heard it.

She had been deceived by her friend, deceived by her

son. Even her own house, it had seemed to her, by concealing in its recesses the furtive lovers, by accommodating them in hole and corner, hushing up their antics, keeping secrets, had colluded with them against her. And she had banged vindictively about it, up and down, in and out, stamping on stairs, slamming doors, pounding with her fist upon perfidious plastered walls.

'You cannot . . .' Naomi had informed her – and the injustice of this, above all, the ridiculous, insulting imagery, the sheer bloody impertinence, came back time and time again to Kate and stole her breath – 'You cannot tie him to your apron strings for ever.'

Kate had been always, like a good Girl Guide, in an advanced state of preparedness, forethinking all the usual evil dispensations (illness, accident, death), she had been teed up for ordinary, everyday disaster, but she had made no provision whatever for this most ghastly of contingencies. A drugs habit she could have envisaged for Alex, sooner than a Naomi habit. A weakness for alcohol, any day, rather than a weakness for Ms Markham. She might even, she decided – no, she definitely *would* – have preferred to learn that he was gay. Her son's attachment to this striking female was as terrible as it was incomprehensible.

'We were afraid you'd take it badly,' Elli had informed her, thus smartly aligning herself with the conspirators. To have known of this *affaire de coeur* a full twenty-four hours before poor old Kate had given her a tremendous fillip: she had lambasted Juin for her indiscretion, she had torn the foolish girl off a strip, before making loud and unmelodious enquiry, on her way upstairs to depilate her bikini line, as to who put the bop in the whop, di-bop, di-bop, who the bam in the bam-a-lam-a ding-dong. Or words to that effect.

'It's not the tragedy you make it out to be, Kate,' she had counselled. 'This is a fling, no more than that. It will run its course, you wait and see.'

'You just don't understand, do you?' Kate had bitterly reproached her.

'So, what's to understand?'

But Kate could not have explained, even had she been of a mind to try, quite how much had been lost here. Not just the physical companionship – the propinquity – of her adult son, who was staying with Naomi ('shacked up', as Elli Sharpe would have it) in a borrowed studio flat; but all his past, in which she had prefigured for him such a different future. Hopes, dreams, ambitions must now, in hindsight, be recast. Memory had been debased. And Alex was a stranger.

From the moment he was born, she had had the odd flash of unrecognition. He might have been lying in his cot gazing up at the electric light, or running, laughing, knock-kneed after a ball, or bent in concentration, with his whole self poured into his face, over an Airfix model at the table. And she would think, Who are you? *What* are you? How can you *be*? A similar thing could happen when you wrote 'fascinate', or 'flattery', or 'February', and it started out of the page at you, and you thought, *Is* there such a word? It was, for her, the questioning of something long taken for granted. No, it was more than that, because Alex had been Kate's miracle, and, inevitably, from time to time, she was visited by a sense of the miraculous.

But it had been a new and alien Alex who had confronted her that night. He had shown her rich anger and cold defiance unseen in him, unguessed at, until now. He had stood very tall and turned a look of pure dislike upon her. Then he had deserted her.

She had always expected one day to wave him off, to see him dwindle down some wide, straight, charted road. But his departure had been so sudden and so absolute, with nothing of sweet sorrow: he had appeared to turn a corner and immediately to pass from her sight.

So, for your information, Elaine Sharpe, it *was*, for Kate, the tragedy she made it out to be. It was every bit as tragic as she said. *That* was what there was to understand.

Only Geraldine had responded with appropriate dismay. 'What, *your* Alex?' she had queried, breathless with agitation, huffing down the phone. '*Our* Naomi? But it's . . .'

'Yes, isn't it? Unspeakable.'

There must be something (Geraldine would be thinking) in the Garvey genes, with her philandering brother, her oversexed nephew, both gone to the bad, and her son set to follow them imminently.

'I could cheerfully kill her,' Kate had confided, and she had meant it (oh, except the 'cheerfully').

Three weeks. Twenty-one days. Five-hundred-odd hours. And she could no more countenance the relationship this Friday evening than she could have done at the moment of appalling revelation.

She told herself she should have known – then told

herself she *had* known. Better this than to have been a dupe. Either she had picked up, at some subliminal level, the intimacy expressed in the casual brush of hand on hand, the guilt in two colliding glances; or, recollecting these trifles, she reinterpreted them.

'Go,' she had ordered, 'go, go, get out.' And upon Naomi, only, this eviction notice had been served. But, naturally, dutifully (selective, that is, of duty, since loyalty to both women would have been, to both, disloyal), Alex had gone too.

'Kate, Kate,' he had begged her from the door, briefly restored to himself, the old Alex, *her* Alex, 'I would not for anything upset you. Only that . . .' Only that I love her, had gone mercifully unsaid, but his whole posture had proclaimed it. Uxoriousness, he had demonstrated then, the sheer – to Kate, obscene – devotion of a man for his woman.

Now they spoke daily, desultorily, mother and son, on the telephone. He would not visit unless with Naomi. And Kate, with the 'apron strings' calumny still zinging in her brain, would not accommodate the pair of them. She could not, she warned, be responsible for her actions upon seeing them together. Oh, she was being unreasonable, was she? Well, she would show him unreason!

Meanwhile, life went on. And the rubber belt conveyed to the bored checkout operator such bits and pieces as got used up in the process. She still drank coffee, washed the cup, nipped off to the loo. Pushkin and Petal had still to be fed; they would not be overlooked.

'That's eleven pounds, seventy-two,' said the operator.

'Oh.' Kate reached for her bag, which ought to have swung, a reassuring weight, from her shoulder, and found nothing. 'I . . .' All of her being seemed to bunch around her heart. She might have been a rose, blush crimson, tightly furled at the centre, loose and floppy at the edges. 'I must have left it in the car,' she confessed in desperation. And she told herself, I'm falling apart, that's what. I'm on the verge.

So a supervisor was summoned, and her purchases, in their carrier-bags, suddenly so pathetic, were put to the side against her return. She must not feel the least embarrassed. People did this sort of thing all the time. (This according to the uniformed assistant, who must enjoy these *divertissements*; but the shoppers behind her, shuffling their feet and muttering, would have her know otherwise.)

Distressed and panting, she ran across the car park, to where she'd left the Fiat, away from the congested area near the automatic doors, by the far perimeter fence.

There were glass fragments, like fake gems, a pretty scattering on the tarmac on the near side of the car. The window had been staved in; her bag snatched from the front passenger seat where she had, in her confusion, left it. In the bag were her door keys, her credit cards, cash to last her for the week. In it her wallet with the darlingest pictures of Alex which she always carried. And her cleaning ticket. And some crumpled tissues, and the bill from the garden centre for the Johnsons' dianthus.

Her despair was overwhelming. She sat down right there in the dust and wept.

Some people came, irresistibly drawn; others, repulsed by such loss of control, scurried away. To Kate, they were so many legs, so many feet. 'What happened?' a pair of tan moccasins asked a pair of denim espadrilles. Someone (probably the polished brogues) dialled 999 on his mobile.

A consoling hand came down on Kate's shoulder.

'Has much been taken?'

'Everything,' she could have told them, had she words to do so. '*Everything*.'

'Is there someone we can call? Your husband? A friend?'

The woman in the espadrilles, owner of the consoling hand, dipped at the knees. She descended springily; her kind face bobbed about in front of Kate.

'My son,' she murmured. 'Oh, no, best not him.' Then, against – or in the absence of – her better judgement, she offered up the name of Elli Sharpe.

Geraldine Gorst petted her hair unmindfully, the way you might a small and not particularly endearing dog, and, as the clocks around the house gave out their disparate versions of the hour, she caught her breath and bit her lip to button in exasperation.

A sudden wind came through the glass doors, bright with evening sunlight, bullying the curtains. It snatched John's papers, one by one, in quick succession, from the table, and swirled them in the air. A wedding photo-

189

graph, gilt-framed, on the sideboard, folding up, fell comically flat.

'Give Lucy another shout, will you?' Geraldine implored, as John went in pursuit of his documents. 'What *can* that girl be doing?' They were due at Tilston village hall at seven-thirty for the Tilston Players' production of *The Yeomen of the Guard*. She had conceived it as a family outing, had bought four tickets, fancying that they'd make an impressive and cohesive group. ('Here are the Gorsts,' people would be sure to say, nudging one another, as they made their entrance.) But Dominic had scorned the enterprise, he'd said to count him out (this was probably no bad thing, Geraldine had decided, renegotiating the fantasy, for there was the fear that he might heckle); he had declared, indeed, that Gilbert and Sullivan sucked. Then Lucy had said, well, all right, she was up for it, so long as Jacintha could come too. Who? Clemency Chapman? Get outta here! Clemency Chapman could rot in hell. There, she'd said it! Clemency Chapman and Sarah Brooke could go boil their silly heads.

Promptly, John, the unforgiven, went into the hall to call his daughter. He was thankful to step, however fleetingly, outside the circle of opprobrium. His wife was miffed with him, and when Geraldine was miffed, you knew about it. Scotland, his proposed defection, the consequent, inequitable burden upon her, formed a core around which all her resentments were agglomerated. And there was to be no let-up in hostilities. A dedicated woman, implacable, she would give herself over utterly to her cause, relinquishing it only for some new exigency. She must take a notion that the bathroom wanted decorating, or the kitchen refitting, she must apperceive a need for a whole new wardrobe, before the Scotland question could be laid to rest. An interim, a breathing space, between one grievance and another, he knew better than to hope for.

'Is she on her way?' Geraldine demanded, as John, still clutching his sheaf of papers, returned.

'Yes, yes.' For, although his daughter had not favoured him with a response, there had been a kind of bracing of the silence, he had sensed something being taken up, and knew, at least, that she had heard him.

'We have to collect young Jacintha. That's ten minutes out of our way. Such a nuisance. I do think her people might . . . but then, I suppose, we did offer. At this rate, we won't be there until after curtain-up. Oh, it really is too bad!' She saw their little party stealing, sheepish, into the small brick hall, where blinds drawn down at high windows would exclude the day. She visualised the stage, the focus, a vibrant rectangle of light, within which members of the local amateur dramatics group would appear, at once strange and strangely familiar, in theatrical disguise. Ripples of annoyance would run up and down the row, as stacking chairs scraped on lino, as they struggled over unseen knees and stamped on unseen toes. 'Sorry, sorry, do excuse me, so sorry . . .' 'Who *are* those latecomers?' 'Need you ask?' She had a good mind to call off the excursion, which was ruined before it had begun. And she could have shed hot tears of petulance.

'We'll make it,' said John unconcernedly, being little

interested in his local standing, in the high esteem of his neighbours, and much of the same mind as Dominic where the lyrics of Sir William Schwenck Gilbert, the music of Arthur Seymour Sullivan were concerned. The worst of it was that they got inside your head and maddened you: all weekend he would surely drive himself crazy, singing of a merryman, moping mum, who would sip no sup, and crave no crumb, as he sighed for the love of a ladye. Still, better that, he told himself – this man of dark and secret humour – than three little girls from school are we, filled to the brim with girlish glee. Better that than dicky-birds and willow, titwillow, titwillow . . .

'You know, I don't much care for this Jacintha Ainsley,' Geraldine confided. 'She's a saucy little madam, if you ask me.'

'Pert as a schoolgirl well can be.'

'I beg your pardon?'

'Nothing, nothing.'

'She backchats one terribly. Her parents, from what I hear, are very *laissez-faire*. They sound altogether too modern.' For the word was out that the Ainsleys had 'theories'. 'Lucy is picking up some unappealing habits. You notice, she has started to speak in this absurd . . .' She wanted the word 'argot', it was there to be used, she knew; but did one pronounce it 'got' as in faggot, or 'go' as in *escargot*? 'This absurd lingo,' she settled for. 'I do so detest slang, don't you? The debasement of the Queen's English.' She passed her fingertips across her brow and juggled her features fractiously. She was, she told herself, fagged out. She could do with a snifter. But how went the enemy? Five past seven. Ten quid she'd coughed up for this little jamboree. Well, frankly, they'd do better to stay in and watch the box.

John snapped open his briefcase and slid the papers into it. No hope, this evening, of reading through them. 'Have you had any word from Eleanor?' he nerved himself to enquire. If Geraldine's mother could just give a firm yes or no to the question of the holiday . . . But, of course, that was not Eleanor Garvey's way. She went in for attenuation; she liked to have people constantly strung out or standing by. She would threaten a visit, often, he suspected, simply to keep them on their mettle. There would be a frenzy of housework. Bags of laundry and dry-cleaning would be generated. Copperfields would gleam with ardent expectation. Geraldine would lay in stocks of food, the best that money could buy. Lucy and Dominic would be drilled in good behaviour – on what were and were not appropriate topics to discuss at table. Then, at the last minute, Eleanor would ring to cancel, pleading the sniffles, a frozen shoulder, a subsequent engagement.

'Not as yet,' said Geraldine with asperity.

Dangerous, he realised, to have touched upon the subject. He went quietly to close the glass door, to pull it to, against the boisterous breeze. Dominic was on the lawn, kicking a football with surprising proficiency (such discipline in one so wayward was unlooked-for). The ball seemed to attach itself, first to left then to right toe, to balance featly, in defiance of the tug of gravity. In his silk shorts and singlet top, the youth looked sun-burnished, blond and beautifully wrought. Strange to think that here was his son, his heir, his progeny. Dominic Gorst was so much a Garvey, John found it hard to credit that he'd had a hand – well, not a *hand* exactly, but a . . . you know – in his procreation. John's true son, his very heir, would have been a weedier, wheezier proposition.

He'll put that thing through the greenhouse roof, he predicted privately, helplessly. Another ancient pane, thin and flawed and shivery, seemed doomed to shatter. But it did not occur to him to bang on the window or to shout a fatherly reproof. He had years ago despaired of holding sway with his children.

Occasionally Lucy, bossy child, would try to borrow his authority, she would come to him for some mandate to compel her beastly brother ('Daddy says you mustn't'). Or she would invoke his terrible wrath ('Just don't blame me if Daddy catches you'). But Dominic, innately disregarding, would be unmoved unless to mirth.

Geraldine did her utmost to control the pair of them. John respected this in her, he admired her tenacity, her stick-at-it-ability. But, for himself, he knew when he was beaten.

'And what of Kate?' he asked, with his eyes still on Dominic, but with his musings elsewhere. He held himself very still, very square. Geraldine must answer to the back of his head.

'Ah, well, you know . . .'

'Bearing up, would you suppose?'

'All things considered. She's pruned the ceanothus.'

'Poor Kate. She was always so devoted.'

'More than was healthy, wouldn't you think?'

'I wouldn't know. How should I?'

'Whether or not, though, it's a bad business.'

'It is.'

For once his reprehension was real. They both, for different reasons, felt it. John could not have given two hoots, frankly, what Alex Garvey did. Alex Garvey could take care of himself. But he thought the world of Kate, always had done. This was how Geraldine glibly represented it – 'John thinks the world of Kate' – and, while detesting the patronage that this implied, he sought no other form of words to account for it. Powerful things, words, as he knew from his work. Manipulative tools. And yet, inadequate. Language was fine for identifying the concrete: it enabled one to call a spade a spade. But when it came to the abstract, it wasn't up to the job. It was a system of crude calibration: with broad regard for irregularities, it graduated emotions. It gave you no end of ways to misdescribe what you were feeling.

This might not trouble a woman such as Geraldine, who took the Humpty Dumpty approach – when *she* used a word, it meant what she wanted it to mean; no more, no less. But, for himself, he found the available vocabulary far too imprecise. So many concepts – relativity, infinity, antimatter, nuclear fusion, Bucherer's experiment, de Broglie's postulate, Schroedinger's theory – could only really be expressed and understood numerically. If he were to set down what he truly felt about Kate Garvey, it might have read:

$$\frac{d\sigma_L}{d\Omega_L} = \frac{d\sigma_C}{d\Omega_C} \frac{[1 + (m_1/m_2)^2 + 2\,(m_1/m_2)\cos\theta_C]^{3/2}}{1 + (m_1/m_2)\cos\theta_C}$$

Or whatever.

'It was bound to happen,' continued Geraldine, 'as Elli points out, with the lot of them living . . .' She couldn't quite bring herself to say 'cheek by jowl', a perfectly harmless expression, which nonetheless conjured a not very pleasing picture. 'I mean, on top of one another as they were.'

Alex, at any rate, on top of Naomi, thought John. Or, for all he knew – and he didn't claim to know much, he was no Lothario – the other way about. 'She should have come here,' he said. 'We have the room.'

'I simply couldn't have tolerated . . . I mean, *Naomi*.'

'I take your point.'

'There is no denying, though, that she's very striking, even now. Very alluring. One can quite see how a headstrong young man . . .'

Striking? Alluring? John supposed she was. But Naomi Markham had always seemed to him so glossy and so two-dimensional, she might have been snipped from the pages of a fashion magazine. Turning at last from the window, he offered therefore in reply the merest shrug.

'Here I am,' announced Lucy, presenting herself defensively at this, the last possible moment. There was no time for her mother to pack her off upstairs again, with orders to remove the make-up which she had so heavily misapplied, of which green eyeshadow was the least successful feature.

'Greetings, earthlings,' said Dominic, tugging open the french windows and shimmering in on the draught. 'How's it hanging? Hey, Lucy, you poor saddo, what's with the greasepaint? I thought you were going to watch a panto, not to play the dame.'

'It's light opera, if you must know,' Lucy haughtily informed him. 'Ugh, don't come near me, you're sweating like a pig.'

'Dominic,' scolded Geraldine faintly, reaching for her handbag. 'Lucy.'

'Come along,' said a weary John, sparing not a glance for his family as he made for the door.

He was the original merryman, moping mum, whose soul was sad, and whose glance was glum. And he sighed for the love of a ladye.

Juin and Muffy had been out pooper-scooping. Here was the arrangement: he pooped, she scooped. She had never taken lightly her responsibilities as a dog owner, and now that Muffy was her one friend on the entire planet, the only creature this side of Alpha Centauri who cared a fig for her, she was more than ever mindful of her duty to him.

She walked the legs off him, round and round the streets of Hackney, Shoreditch, De Beauvoir Town, mentally reciting Chaucer, or turning over and over in her mind the events of recent weeks.

With the standoff in the weather, which refused to commit itself either way, there was a feeling of time, too, standing almost still. The sky seemed merely to be hovering. Cars, with their stereos blaring, were boxes of meaningless noise. There was a faint smell of decay, as if London were slowly, inexorably rotting. Without wishing to wax too metaphysical, Juin thought that London smelt the way she felt.

She wasn't speaking to Elli. Things had been said, following her visit to Kate, which no decent, caring mother would say to a daughter.

Juin would admit that she had been a bit out of order . . . probably. But she had meant well. She had been genuine in the conviction that Kate should be told what Alex was up to – and that, once apprised of it, she could intercede. She would tell him, 'Stop this nonsense, now,' and, like a good boy, he would stop it. She had felt morally outraged that Elaine should know of these sexual shenanigans – which meant that any minute half the world would know – while Kate was kept in ignorance. And not for one nanosecond had it occurred to her that Alex would up and go with drippy, droopy Naomi. So she certainly didn't deserve to be called a . . . what was it? A stirring shitbag? A shit-stirring bag? She didn't deserve to be called a bloody blabbermouth or a manipulative little toad. Well, *did* she?

So she was shunning Elli, refusing to communicate – which had the effect, only, of providing the woman with more air time, more silences to fill with her own *aperçus*. 'What's your problem?' Elli had demanded when she first sensed a certain frost. 'Cat got your tongue?' Since when, she had given no sign of noticing that she was being cut.

Strained relations at home were nothing new, of course; there was a long tradition of feuding at Schloss Sharpe. By and by, both Elli and Juin would relent; a more agreeable disharmony would spring up again between them, it would come back like the thorny growth of roses. But would Kate ever talk to her again?

Would she forgive her? (Kate's screams and accusations still rang in her ears; she still started up in panic at the memory in the dark hours of the night.) And would she, Juin, ever be able to hear the name Alex Garvey without the sensation of being punched with extreme violence in the pit of the stomach? Then, how could she abide the forfeiture of her fondest dream?

Juin's passion for Alex seemed always to have been inside her. It had undergone no sea change in her adolescence, there had been no sexual awakening, for it had ever, in its way, been sexual, it had been from the first a girl–boy thing. And just as Elli Sharpe had grown up in the certitude – common among small girls of her generation, but in none more pertinacious – that she would one day marry Prince Charles and be Queen, so Juin had grown up with the confidence that she would marry Alex and be Mrs Garvey.

Thus, every time he favoured her with his undifferentiated smile, when he was so very polite, so politely impartial, when his easy charm was bestowed without preference, when he neglected to mark her out, when his eyes took her in but failed to hold her, when he was simply, sweetly, everybody's Alex, she had died a little more from disillusionment.

Still, for as long as he'd been everybody's Alex . . . Juin, turned the corner and headed homeward, with Muffy barking, harking after bitches. For as long as he'd been anybody's, she told herself, there had been the chance that she could make him hers. Only now that he was Naomi's must she finally relinquish hope.

Not that the affair would last, she reflected, yanking

the lead to bring her frolicky, bollocky dog to heel. It would be over in six weeks, if Elli's confident predictions came to pass. Alex would emerge from the experience sadder and wiser. 'I've been a complete fool,' he would declare, as he sought the solace of resilient young flesh, the comfort of a pair of loving arms. (If you wanted something hard enough, Juin was almost persuaded, if you willed it in your every waking moment, you could make it happen . . . couldn't you?)

But here was the question: had something very precious gone beyond repair? Alex Garvey had repudiated Juin Sharpe's dream. He had reneged on a solemn, binding pact to which he had never knowingly been party. She had been forced to question her faith in him and in their mutual destiny. Besides which, she wasn't altogether sure if she wanted Naomi Markham's cast-offs.

They had been lectured at school on the subject of safe sex, they had heard about the 'pool of infection'. When you went to bed with someone, ran the wisdom, you went to bed with everyone they'd ever been to bed with. You hacked into a kind of viral super-highway. So to sleep with Alex Garvey would be, in a sense, to sleep with Naomi Markham, which was not something that Juin Sharpe would bust a gut to do. And it wouldn't just be Naomi since, presumably, by extension, you'd be sleeping with everyone she'd ever slept with, and with everyone *they'd* ever slept with, lovers too numerous to mention. It really didn't bear contemplation.

As Juin, slightly breathless, broached the steps to her front door, she heard from within the trill of the telephone and, lest it be the call upon which her future would depend, the one to determine the course of her life, she fumbled in a fever of impatience with the key.

Muffy, picking up on her panic as she crossed the threshold, ran excitedly between her legs and around them, binding her ankles with his lead. 'Oh, stop, *stop*,' she wailed, hobbling. She set the pooper-scoop down, extricated herself, and blundered through the hall to snatch up the extension in the sitting-room

'Hello, 4260.'

'Juin Sharpe?' enquired someone smooth and male.

'Yes, this is Juin.'

'Dominic Gorst here.'

'Hello, Dominic Gorst,' she responded, sitting down heavily, sort of dumping herself on a chair, abandoning herself to disappointment (although what she had expected, what desired, the reason for the racing of her pulses, she could not have articulated).

'You have a very pleasing telephone voice.'

'I do?'

'You'll make some lucky man a wonderful secretary.'

'Thanks, you chauvinist git. But I'm planning to be an airline pilot.'

'Not tempted by journalism, then? By the Street of Shame? You don't propose to follow in Elli Sharpe's illustrious footsteps?'

'Not at all. Good gracious, no!' Slumping, she shaded her eyes with her free hand. If I took after my mother, she told herself fervently, I'd top myself. No I wouldn't. If I took after my mother, I suppose I'd be pleased as punch at being me.

'Nice work if you can get it,' persisted Dominic, whom Juin had long held in healthy disregard (arrogant, she considered him, and leering). 'I mean, to be paid good money for your weekly right-wing rantings.'

'My mum's not right-wing,' Juin reflexively retorted. 'She's maybe not as left of sensible as she used to be, but she definitely has socialist leanings. She was deeply into the class struggle when she was our age, you realise? She stole a policeman's helmet or something. She almost joined the Angry Brigade.'

'Ah, yes.' Laughter ran in Dominic's voice. 'My mama, you know, is a life member of the Not Angry But Terribly, Terribly Hurt Brigade.'

'Dominic, you're a total nerd. Look, why are you ringing me?'

'Well, it's like this. The mere mortals have gone out for the evening. They got all gussied up and went off to the op-rah. So, finding I was all alone, I tiptoed to the telephone.'

'To make nuisance calls? Is this a nuisance call? One of those funny ones you read about in newspapers?'

'You've got it. This is how it goes: you tell me what colour knickers you're wearing, while I do some heavy breathing.'

She considered it a moment, then 'Paisley,' she said, for she could think of nothing less arousing – except, perhaps, string.

'Very sexy. Hey, tell me, Juin, are you looking forward to our hols in haggis country?'

'Not a great deal, to be honest.' Juin, who had never ventured north of Birmingham, had a highly simplistic image of Scotland, lifted straight from the lid of a shortbread tin. Bagpipes, she visualised, and tartan, and heather . . .

'It'll be great,' he promised her, and for a second, there, he was in earnest. He loved the west coast, the isolation and the beauty of it, which miraculously charged his spirit: not just his lungs but his heart and mind seemed to fill up with the Scottish air. He had some unhealthy preoccupations, but was basically superbly fit, and he gloried in his physical being. The cold, rough sea was his element. It made his blood sing.

'If you say so.'

'I do. And it occurred to me that, you know, while we're up there, you and I might get it on.'

With some difficulty (for they were tightly laced), Juin kicked off her shabby plimsolls, hooking heel under instep and pushing. She found she was smiling and didn't know why, unless at his sheer preposterousness. 'Can't be done. I'm spoken for. I already have a boyf.'

'You do? What's his name?'

'Joe Bloggs.'

'What does he do?'

'Oh, he's in swill.'

'Steady job.'

'Yeah, well . . . there's never any shortage.'

'Do you seriously want to be a pilot?'

'Absolutely,' insisted she, who had never so much as thought of it until this minute.

'I quite fancy the print, myself. To be an ace reporter like the great David Garvey.'

'Oof!' reacted Juin at mention of the Garvey name.

'The worst news is that my grandmother might be coming with us to Waverley.'

'No, no, no, Dominic. The worst part of it – quite the worst part – is that I have to share with Lucy. Because, you know, we don't get on.'

'Then share with me by all means,' he offered expansively. 'I'm a lot more fun than my snitch of a sister.'

'On the whole, I'd settle for Lucy. *Even* Lucy.'

'She's coming to keep us in order, you understand? My sweet, white-haired old granny, that is.'

'From what I hear, she'll have her work cut out,' Juin coolly admonished him.

Her experience of Eleanor Garvey was, after all, minimal. She had no way of knowing – Dominic generously allowed – what a blight, what a pustule the woman would be. 'It's my dad's fault,' he grumbled. 'He's pleading pressure at the office. He's to stay here at home, alone and loyally patering.'

'What a bore for him,' murmured Juin, peeling a yellow Post-it note from the glass tabletop, 'to have no break, no proper holiday.' Her mother – the note informed her in Elli's rounded, confident hand – had gone round to Tooting. Kate was having a crisis. Her bag had been snatched. She was hysterical. Urgent mopping-up operation. Juin to make her own catering arrangements. Plenty of food in freezer. Salami and stuff in fridge. Not to wait up. Not to sulk. A full stop was represented by a smiley face. *Comme ça*   .

'Well, yes, I suppose it will be,' replied Dominic, surprised by her into seeing the situation from another point of view. 'Anyway, what do you reckon, Juin? Shall we have fun and games? A Highland fling? Will I get to toss my caber?'

'I doubt that you could get it up,' she riposted. And, biting down hard on a smile, she replaced the receiver.

Muffy was on the rampage with his lead in tow. She slapped her thigh and he came exuberantly to her. 'Cheeky so-and-so, that Dominic,' she confided to him, slipping the metal clasp and releasing him. 'So uncouth. No manners. Still, he's not such a dork as his sister, I suppose.'

Her insides suddenly, urgently, signalled hunger. She realised she'd eaten nothing but a slice of toast all day. Salami, Elli had proposed for supper. Yeeeeuck. Elaine Sharpe categorised food according to her personal taste. Those things which she liked were good; those which she disliked, bad. And anyone who protested that he or she didn't much care for the 'good' things was assumed to be posturing. Or, in the case of Juin, 'showing off'.

She wasn't showing off, however, when she stood before the mirror and arranged her face, tweaking her mouth at the corners, trying for a happier, more optimistic expression. I've been so miserable, she told herself, and was briefly moved to pity for her own condition. Tears threatened.

But all at once and inexplicably she was cheered. Hope crept back like warmth into cold fingers, it tingled under her skin. And with it came an intimation that somehow, *somehow*, everything would be all right. Even the most profound unhappiness would pass.

Her GCSE grades would be good. She'd stay on to

advanced level. Then she'd go to training school and learn to fly.

In the meantime, though, she was starving. She would go and buy some fish and chips.

The Bangladeshi waiter wore a dazzling white jacket with gold buttons, gold braid epaulettes. A new uniform. 'It's Navy style,' he said with sweet, shy deprecation, offering menus and, as he did so, covertly admiring his own starched cuff. The whole place had been refurbished: dated flock wallpaper and plush had been stripped out; cool creams and greens and rattan belatedly imported. A ceiling fan, like a giant blender, stirred the spicy air. But this was, for all its fresh ambition, a standard high street curry house.

That's it then, Naomi told herself, inclining blindly over the menu to hide her chagrin. We're really, really poor.

'Let's go out for dinner?' Alex had suggested, phoning from his studio that afternoon, sounding very upbeat. 'My treat' (as though it might be anyone's but his).

'Lovely,' she had reacted, her mind skittering off. San Lorenzo, she had thought. Or Daphne's? The Caprice? The Ivy? Quaglino's? (Would they get a table at Quag's?) She had a small, uncertain appetite, easily discouraged, and scant interest in food, but she could eat the atmosphere in these places, she could dine off style. She would wear her Alberta Ferretti silk tunic dress, her last extravagant purchase before the money supply was cut off, she would put her hair up with small combs. It would be so good, so good, to be there in the swim again.

'I'll be home around seven-thirty,' Alex had promised. And, 'Love you,' he had assured her, for his colleagues to hear or not to hear – what should he care? – before ringing off.

She had spent a full half-hour considering her few clothes, which were hung about the flat, from shelf and picture rail, under polythene, there being no proper place to store them. The flat's owner, someone named Guy, an aid worker, an old schoolfriend of Alex's, was abroad. He must have travelled light, to judge by the number of sweatshirts, trousers, jackets, which he'd left behind to occupy the available spaces, and which Naomi resented as a landlord might a lot of sitting tenants.

I have barely a stitch to wear, she had thought. Which, in her terms, she truly hadn't.

As she went to take a shower, she had reflected on the change in . . . no, the intensification of Alex. Having made such a dramatic commitment to her, he seemed to be pitching everything into the two of them. He was the same guy he had always been, but more so. He showed greater tenderness, deeper love. He smiled more readily, laughed more humorously, held tighter, fucked harder. And, underneath it, she had sensed – untested until now – a streak of pure, unalloyed purpose. He had firmed up before her eyes. There was this much of David in him after all.

She was good for Alex Garvey, then, she had concluded, as she stepped under the ineffectual spray, a mere piddle, too light to make lather (half an hour, it would take, to rinse out the shampoo, to run the scented unguents off her limbs, her breasts, her back). She could congratulate herself on bringing out in him this adamantine quality, hitherto repressed.

'We'll go to the Viceroy,' he'd announced, as he came through the door of their borrowed apartment three hours later, warm and flushed from his bike ride. The wheels of the cycle – a second-hand model, which he had bought to save on travel expenses – whirred merrily as he propelled it through to park it on the small roof terrace. 'They do a tremendous chicken tikka.'

At the sight of him in his black Lycra biker's gear, so close-fitting as to be almost rude, she had crossed the room to welcome him, placing a hand in the small of his back. 'Oh, I had the idea that –'

Alex was the least tentative kisser she had ever met. He overwhelmed her at times when he covered her mouth and just went for her. Perhaps fortunately, she had not had the chance or the breath to share with him her far more costly plans for the night.

Now, Naomi's sleek, clean hair took up tandoor smoke (turning in her sleep tonight, burying her face in the pillow, she would smell chilli, cumin, cardamom, and would dream confusing, foreign dreams). The fine vapours from spluttering dishes wafting by her settled invisibly on her silk tunic and sank in. She felt ineffably stupid and overdressed. Worse, she had the oddest sensation that she was being kippered: she would emerge from here the colour of one of those tandoori chicken pieces that sizzled past her ear.

But, 'You never looked more lovely,' Alex murmured, and – as she laid aside the menu with a sigh of perplexity, as he took hold of her wrist, turned her hand over, and

208

stared into her palm, frowning, perhaps in an effort to read the lines, to know her destiny – maybe she never had.

I'm lost to myself, he decided, awed, when she raised her fulgent eyes to gaze at him. She has me absolutely.

It was true, as she perceived, that he had found within himself new courage and determination. But it was she who had sprung him from the trap. He would still be back there, otherwise, with dear, devoted Kate; he would still be watching out for her, still waiting for his moment, marking time till his life might begin.

The realisation that life had at last begun, so unexpectedly and with such a hoo-ha, was a daunting one. He felt like a man who, jumping aboard a departing train, hearing its shrill whistle as it gathers speed, wonders where on earth the thing is bound.

Mixed in with his excitement was a terrible compunction. It racked him to recall the disarray in which the pair of them had left home, the way they had bundled into a minicab with whatever they could carry. (The jangling of coat-hangers, the squeal of suitcases on concrete, grated even now upon his memory.) It was one thing, with tempers running high, to storm off into the night; another to sustain a posture of wounded self-righteousness.

He knew how his mother, endlessly repining, would wander around the house. The wardrobe mirror would show her, in its own mean and biased way, as she dithered in the doorway, his bedroom ransacked: drawers hauled from the chest, the bed unmade. He felt such fondness for her, and such dreadful pain.

She would, however, be fine. She would come round. He must hang on to that knowlege, and to the belief in his own integrity. Time could prove to Kate how true and how consistent was his love for Naomi Markham. Time would make it all seem possible. And time would win her over, at last, to their cause.

'Would you . . .?' he ventured in the hushed, respectful, restaurant-going voice he'd learned from Kate (no word of their conversation, however anodyne, must reach the ears of diners at the neighbouring tables).

'Yes, Alex?' She smiled at this apparent intimacy.

'Would you like a couple of poppadums?'

She laughed, as he signed to the waiter, and felt suddenly light-headed, free. How much more fun to be here than among the poseurs at boring old Quaglino's! 'Whatever you want,' she responded. 'You order, hmm? Because I'm not, you know, a connoisseur of Indian cooking.'

'A lager? No, *wine*. Will you have some wine? You see, we have to celebrate. It's all come good. The agent has been back in touch. The vendors have accepted my offer. They want to press ahead, to complete quickly. We'll be moving soon to Chafford Road.'

'That's great.'

'You're not pleased?' Suspicious, he pressed her.

'I am. I'm thrilled. Yes, truly, Alex, I'm delighted.'

'A place of our own.'

'Of course.'

From verdant St John's Wood and a veritable mansion, via a Tooting semi, to a long and narrow living space in Chafford Road. Why wouldn't she be thrilled?

He regarded her darkly. 'You swore to me, Naomi, it wouldn't bother you that we'd be skint.'

'It doesn't. Not in my heart of hearts.' She picked up a fork and idly pronged the tablecloth. 'Forgive me, baby,' she pleaded. 'I long to be with you, to make a home for you.'

Was this what she meant to do? To make a home? It seemed to neither of them, at that instant, a remotely appropriate use of her time. She'll have to find something to fulfil her, Alex determined. But of what was she capable?

Uncomfortably, ashamed of his disloyal turn of mind, he reviewed her options, which seemed to him to be woefully few. She was no better or worse placed, he figured, than the average spoilt young Sloane who must hold down some little job until she either married or came into her inheritance. How did those girls scratch a living, whose only talents were for looking good and being social?

They worked as nannies, some of them, but that would never do for Naomi Markham. Or they managed art galleries, took buyers' money, put little red stickers on the paintings to indicate that they were sold. They hung about looking bored behind the counters of smart boutiques and Italian kitchen shops. Or they called themselves interior designers. Well, frankly, he could not imagine her in any of those situations.

Naomi had actually made no plans for what remained of the summer, beyond sitting out when the weather permitted, to acquire a suntan. Least of all was she truly into home-making. But she noticed his preoccupation, and half guessed the reason for it. 'I shall be able to help, of course,' she volunteered simply, 'when I get some modelling assignments.'

He, who had been trying so hard to envisage for her a second career, realised with a pang that, in her mind, the first was still extant, still viable.

'Yes, so you will.' He smiled at her with aching tenderness. Naomi was so organically feminine. This was somewhat against the prevailing fashion, it flew in the face of feminism, but there had always been, would always be, such women. They couldn't help themselves. It was as if they had some extra chromosomal component, an additional X.

Naomi would never shout, snore, belch, fart, perceptibly sweat, whistle for a taxi, engage in contact sports, drink at the bar or tell a ribald joke. She would never actively commission sex, although, by the demure downcasting of her eyes, she might invite a man to do so. Her legs would not carry her very far; her bicep strength was lamentable. Squeamish, she would shudder at the sight of spiders, scream at an imagined mouse, cover her eyes to shield herself from the horror of a violent movie. Her tears were seldom far below the surface. She could no more emulate the likes of spiky, flamboyant Elaine Sharpe, say, than a lily could emulate gorse.

I'll find some way for her, Alex silently vowed. I'll find the way out. He would steer her gently, firmly, to a more fulfilling existence. He did not reckon to support her indefinitely, to keep her at home, to infantilise her. As far as possible he would emancipate her. He knew it would not be easy, but he had unshakeable faith in her innate worth, he was confident of the outcome.

'I spoke to Kate today,' he confided.

Naomi reached for the poppadum basket, and with her long, restless fingers snapped a piece off one of the thin, crisp discs. 'How is she?'

'Oh, fine. She was on her way out. To Sainsbury's.' He had drawn encouragement from this; he liked to think of Kate taking care of herself, perhaps indulging a fancy for goat cheese or sun-dried tomatoes, treating herself to a nice bottle of wine.

'Did she . . .?'

'Mention you? No, not as such.'

Beneath her high cheekbones she had beguiling hollows. Pressing finger and thumb into them, he could turn her face up to his and thereby engage not just her look but her complete attention. He was moved to do this just as the waiter arrived at his elbow.

'Do you know what you would like, sir?'

'Thank you,' said Alex distractedly. Yes, he knew what he would like.

'She's put some kind of spell on him,' said Kate, who, her common sense having so conspicuously failed her, seemed resolved to make no further calls upon it. She sat on the floor, to which she was naturally drawn, jammed up against the sofa arm, abjectly hugging herself.

'You know,' scolded Elaine Sharpe, as she eased open the window to let out the dregs of the afternoon, to let in the unrefreshing evening, 'you talk out of your arse at times.' She paced the room, back and forth, paused by the hearth, took up Eleanor Garvey from the mantel-piece, considered her slightingly for barely a second, then traded her for a raffia elephant. 'Naomi's a gorgeous, mature woman, that's the sum and substance of it. And Alex is a normal, red-blooded, heterosexual male (for which species, much thanks). The guy's infatuated. Can you blame him? And Naomi's flattered by his attentions, it's gone to her head. So be a bit rational, will you? Show some understanding. And, while you're at it, get a grip on this house. You're just letting it go. It's a sty. These roses are as dead as mutton. Then, here, look . . .' She ran her finger along the shelf, would have Kate see how begrimed was its tip.

'Some of us,' retorted Kate, 'must do our own house-work when we can find the time. Not having the benefit of a domestic slave.'

'Trevor, you mean? He's a liability. He just sucks up one's valuables with the vacuum-cleaner and greases the stairs.'

'So why do you keep him on?'

'I'm not sure that I shall. I may sack him any minute. Employ a little woman, like Geraldine's Mrs Mopp.'

'Mrs du Slack,' said Kate tartly, 'is hardly a "little woman", as you would have it.'

No. But Elaine, who had been using "little" only to cut such people down to size, to place them socially, could not be bothered to explain. 'You need a holiday,' she declared instead. 'You're very pasty.'

'I *had* a holiday. We went to . . .' Brittany, she remembered. At Whitsun. She had gone with Alex. The weather had been kind. They'd sat on the front as a salt wind came off the sea, squinting into the light, eating mussels and *frites*, drinking pale French beer. Her thighs had burned in the deceptively beneficent sun. It seemed a lifetime ago.

'You heard that I am off to Italy, did you? To Tuscany? With a crowd of the big bananas from the paper?'

'Oh, yes, you did tell me. More than once. You're dumping Juin on Geraldine, as I recollect.'

'Not *dumping*. She's just longing to go with them. *She* needs a change of scene, too. You know, all this Alex business has really got to her.'

'Got to *her*?' Kate laughed then, mirthlessly, acrimoniously.

'She's smitten, you see. She carries a torch for your boy. And it's no good your blaming my Juin for anything. No use to kill the messenger. She came here in good faith, the silly tart. She imagined she was doing you a favour.'

'Some favour! If only I had never found out . . .'

'Ignorance is bliss, you mean?'

'Yes, I rather think it might be.'

'The whole affair would have run its course, is that it? Alex could have bonked Naomi's brains out, while you went your own sweet way, gathering rosebuds, communing with our feathered friends, with small furry animals. And my name's Pollyanna.'

'I don't see why –'

'You're an obdurate woman, Katharine Perkins as was. And an intolerant one.'

'You think I should give them my blessing?'

'I think you should be more laid back. And play a

215

shrewder game. It isn't as if she's run off with your husband.'

Kate made a prayerbook of her hands, sent up an entreaty for patience and restraint. 'She could have *had* my husband,' she responded tonelessly. 'Why not? Everybody else has. But what she's doing is far, far worse. This I can never forgive.'

'Tush. You're being silly.' With David on her mind, now, Elli turned to the mirror above the fireplace and made a routine assessment of her neck, her chest, her clavicles. (You couldn't beat a good clavicle.) Her eyes, in the glass, appraised her. Not quite *everyone*, Kate Garvey, she thought. *I* haven't had your husband. Not yet. 'Right, you run along and wash your face,' she chided, as you might an eight-year-old, all at once brisk. 'It's blotchy and awful. I'll fix us a snack while you're gone.'

High-handed bitch, Kate told herself, but she went anyway, obediently, upstairs. She ran water into the basin, dabbled her hands, confirming in the mirror the truth of Elli's words: blotchy and awful she looked.

Did she give a stuff? Not really. Why should she? Nobody else seemed to.

But, hang on, that wasn't fair. Surely Elli, in her crass way, did. For hadn't she come straight over, at Kate's request, all the way from east London, picked her up in the car park, furnished her with wads of tissues, paid for her shopping, subsumed it in a greater, more triumphal trolley-load?

She had driven Kate slowly home, forbearing to beep her horn, to drive at people's bumpers, to hurry the dawdlers in her usual style. She had found the spare front door key under the upturned flowerpot, excoriated her friend for her lack of security (Kate must count herself lucky that she'd not been murdered in her bed). She had cancelled her credit cards, called in a locksmith to change the locks lest the thief, possessed of both latchkey and address, decided to call in here. She had returned to the scene of the crime with Kate and spare car key; summoned a vehicle glass specialist to replace the car window; she had stumped up the money for the lot.

She had put wine in the ice-box to chill; put chilled moussaka in the oven to heat. She had forced upon Kate a cup of warm milk laced with brandy, then, purely to keep her company, had knocked back a drop of the hard stuff herself.

She had called down all manner of curses upon the scumbags who had done her chum this rotten turn; they must consider themselves damned for all eternity. She was even now downstairs, singing at the top of her voice, comparing herself lyrically, implausibly, to a virgin, touched for the very first time, and tossing salad in an evil garlic dressing. So praise the Lord, actually, thank God for Elaine Sharpe.

'Better?' Elli enquired, when Kate presented herself in the kitchen ten minutes later, much calmer, meek and scrubbed, in a clean T-shirt and denim skirt.

'Yes.'

'Then have a slurp of this Sancerre, there's my girl. And don't dare . . .' Elli slapped away the hand that hovered over the salad bowl. 'Don't pick.'

'But suddenly I'm quite hungry. Having had no appetite for days and days.'

'You should look after the inner woman. Keep her fed and watered, that's my advice. Stay her with flagons, comfort her with apples, I would. Because, frankly, you don't impress anyone by wasting away to a mere shadow.'

'It's not a matter of impressing.'

'Here, then. Try these olives. There you go. The black ones are best. I had one just now. It had all the flavour of a fullback's jockstrap.'

'*Please.*' Kate, revolted, spat an olive into her palm.

'An acquired taste, I suppose. And has Alex been in touch?'

'Oh, daily,' revealed Kate with undisguised bitterness. 'He's most conscientious.'

'Poor, darling boy. I imagine you're being very punishing.'

'I don't mean to,' Kate confessed, chancing a green olive, which, mercifully, had about it a faint taste of lemon, and no hint of an athletic support. 'I tell myself, "Be nice". Then I hear his voice, and all this badness wells up in me.'

'You're not going to cry, are you? I can't be doing with you if you are. I've no truck with self-pity. And you've used up my Kleenex with your snivelling.'

'No, I'm not. I'm cried out. In a funny way, being robbed like that was kind of –'

'Cathartic?'

'Mmm.'

'Well, that's something.'

Kate, scooping Pushkin off the kitchen floor, sat down and nursed him on her lap, pressing her cheek against his fuzzy head. The cat seemed to humour her for a minute as it summoned its strength, then struggled out of her clutches. 'What am I to *do*, though, Ell?'

'In regard to what?' With strong teeth, Elli grated the purple-brown flesh from an olive stone. 'Cor, poky!'

'With regard to myself. And Alex and Naomi. Am I meant to be civilised? Have them round for dinner? Go with Naomi to John Lewis to choose curtains? Am I expected to behave to them as if they were simply sweethearts?'

'For the moment, my precious Katie, I should do sweet fuck all. Hey, this Sancerre is a pert little number. For shame! You've not touched your glass. Try it, why don't you? It'll make your shoes shine. No, seriously, for the time being I shouldn't do anything. Except maybe get your own life together. And give Naomi a good slap if she makes any mother-in-law cracks.'

Elli lit a fag and at once ground it out in the ashtray. She tugged open the oven door, stooped to peer inside. Her blond hair lifted in a thermal current, and when she straightened she was flushed with heat. 'It's Hellenic in there,' she reported. 'Ancient grease. Have you not heard of ammonia? Hey, I say. Knock, knock.'

'Who's there?' supplied Kate a shade reluctantly.

'Ammonia.'

'Go on then. Ammonia who?'

'Ammonia bird in a gilded cage. Moussaka's burning nicely. I love it when the topping's crusty. No, as I was telling you, you should sort yourself out. Look upon this as an opportunity. You've done the child-rearing bit. You're on your own now. You're shot of your responsibilties, free to do as you wish. Goodness knows, I can't wait to get Juin out from under my feet.'

'Poor Juin.'

'So-o, "poor Juin", is it now? A few moments ago, you hadn't a kind word to say about her.'

'Oh, I know I was mad with her, but I still think she's a sweetie.'

'A sweetie, indeed? I shouldn't go that far. She's boot-faced, to be truthful. And, though I'm fond of her and all that . . . I mean, I worship the ground she walks on, but she doesn't half cramp my style.'

Kate gazed at her old pal consideringly. She must have left home in a rush. She seemed to be in her undies – for surely one was meant to wear something over this sort of camisole top? How she might conduct herself when there were no checks or restraints upon her, no daughter to find fault with her, did not bear contemplation.

'Do you think he'll come back?'

'If I were you, I'm not sure that I should *have* him back.'

'I didn't exactly . . .' Kate had had in mind something more notional, more emotional than geographical. She had meant, would Alex come back in spirit?

'You could let his room out. Take in lodgers.'

'I wouldn't dream of it.'

'It could be a way of meeting Mr Right.'

'Elaine, *you* know, and *I* know, that there is no such animal.'

'The more reason, then, to make your own life, and to have your own fun. Now, will you get off your bottom, Lady Garvey, and get some plates out for us?'

'I'm not being much help, am I? Sorry.'

'Listen, I don't want your help. Only do one thing for me.' Elli leant her two hands on the table, propped herself, stared into Kate's face.

'Anything. I'd do anything. You've been so kind to me today. I just want to say . . . I honestly do . . . I shan't forget.'

'Agh, hush your mouth. I want you to promise me one thing.'

'What's that?'

'Give my Juin a ring, huh? Kiss and make up. Because she's eating her heart out, the pitiful cow.'

CHAPTER

6

The incidence of tummy trouble among visitors to the Mediterranean was twenty times higher than in those who stayed at home. The British tourist in southern Europe faced a significantly increased danger of gastro-intestinal infections, including typhoid and paratyphoid fever. A fatal outcome was not unknown.

'Oh, *really*,' protested Kate, listening with half an ear to this catalogue of possible disasters, as she unwound convolvulus from around the bushy Margaret Merrill. How relentless, how ineradicable was this parasite! And how insipidly pretty its bloodless bell flowers! It put her in mind of . . . someone who should be nameless. 'Italy is not exactly a Third World country, you know.'

'Be that as it may . . .' said Geraldine, whose flimsy shadow wavered around the lawn and borders after her industrious gardener, running up the roses, and away to nothing in the more assertive shade of the boundary wall. 'This is what I read. The facts as they were printed.'

Kate had arrived to find her sister-in-law on the terrace, at a wrought-iron table under a fringed umbrella, with the burden of summer heavy upon her (she was not, it had to be remembered, a great one for the heat). This, Kate had told herself, must be the much-vaunted new patio set; for no other reason would the woman have been outdoors in the hard morning sun.

Geraldine was very big on sets, she went in for co-ordinates. The works of Dickens, in matching red and gold livery, graced the bookcase in her sitting-room. Little tables truckled under larger ones of identical design. The saucepans in her kitchen were of the same expensive range; egg slice, slotted spoon, ladle and the like had family affinity. Such accoutrements of a lifestyle, and the lifestyle itself, were to her one and indivisible. As a small child she had committed to paper, in yellow crayon, her earnest desire for a 'princess set'; she had sent it up the chimney to Father Christmas, and but for his failure to deliver, she would certainly have *been* a princess.

To Kate, who had no two possessions alike (aside, that is, from shoes and socks), and no lifestyle as such, this was a source of both fascination and depression. She thought she would die before she bought the whole of Mantovani in a box.

The instant she had stepped out on to the terrace, declaring herself as she did so, Geraldine had heaved herself up, to follow her about, chatting. She seemed to Kate to be an extraordinarily inactive person, to do almost nothing from one day's end to the next. She was usually to be found ensconced in a chair, but she somehow managed to convey the impression that she had just this second taken the weight of her feet, being quite overcome by her exertions.

Geraldine's own perception, her sense of industry, had to do with the emotional energy she expended on the slightest task, for she went about everything with a quite disproportionate consciousness, exhausting herself with irrelevant concerns, ever mindful of pitfalls, confused by choice, avid for value, and above all preoccupied with the impression she would make. An easier person than Geraldine Gorst would have found Geraldine Gorst's an easier life.

With the trip to Scotland still nearly three weeks away, she was deeply into preparation, as much psychological as practical. She had made numerous dispositions, endless plans upon which she could not, until the last minute, act. No use, for instance, for obvious reasons, to top up the petrol in the Rover, or to pack the children's toothbrushes: these things must wait, and the waiting made her twitchy. Lists, she had compiled. Lists of lists. What she could not effect at once, she could at least scheme about. And there must be no eventuality which she did not foresee. She made herself almost ill, at times, with her busying brain.

When she had come, by chance, the other evening, upon a magazine article about the hazards of travel, she had seized on it with alacrity, terribly bucked to think that other people's holidays were more fraught even than her own. It was, indeed, with a tinge of disappointment that she learned that bilharzia, dengue and yellow fever were not a problem in mainland Europe, that malaria, too, was a disease of the tropics, while the venomous stonefish, which artfully impersonated a lump of rock, confined its antics to the Indian and Pacific Oceans.

'In any case . . .' Kate sat back on her heels as she

reeled in, hand over hand, long ropes of weed, moved in spite of herself to admiration for its snap and vitality. 'In point of fact, Geraldine, I don't suppose Elli will go within a mile of the sea. It's a country farmhouse she'll be staying in.'

But it was not only, apparently, the Med itself, bacterial stew though it might be, that accounted for so much diarrhoea. Nor was it just the shellfish they dredged out of it. Rice was implicated, and tap water also; ice cubes, salads, fresh fruit, unpasteurised cheese . . .

'Well, I shouldn't worry too much,' Kate decided, taking the view that any self-respecting protozoon, confronted by the Sharpe interior, would make its excuses and leave ('rude health' might best describe the woman's natural condition). 'I fancy our Elaine will survive.'

'I have no doubt of it,' responded Geraldine tersely, nettled by Kate's flippant tone. 'I am simply saying that she should be sure to take along her Imodium.'

'Alka Seltzer, rather. That would be more what the doctor would order. For the morning after the night before, if you take my meaning.'

Geraldine sniffed peevishly and dabbed at her nose with the corner of a lacy hankie. And she mentally excused Kate, she reminded herself, with an effort, in mitigation, that the girl was still a bit unbalanced, her mind disordered by this shocking business between Naomi and Alexander. What might be happening on that front? One hardly liked to ask. 'And how are you, Kate, *in yourself*?' she contented herself with enquiring.

'In myself?' Kate, with a look of intense concentration, mashing her lip, yanked at the bindweed, which tightened like a tourniquet around her hand – her fingers blenched – and would not yield at the root. 'I'm fine, I guess.'

Which, in some respects, she was. She was better, at least, than she had been. For a time after Alex left, she had seemed to draw down upon herself all manner of misfortunes, of which the smashing of her car window and the theft of her handbag had been neither the first nor the last. Bad karma or what?

The bag had never been found, as she had known it wouldn't. It was gone for ever, with all its precious contents. And, though she had new door locks, it nonetheless disquieted her to think that somewhere, someone – axiomatically, not a very nice someone – knew who she was and where to come looking for her.

The insurance companies had offered numbers of reasons why they had no duty to pay out on her various claims. Her attention had been drawn to this clause and that. They referred, in communication, to the 'risk address'. Twenty-eight Larkspur Road, then, was officially at risk.

And a letter had come about victim support: Kate Garvey was officially a victim.

Those nice people in Swansea, envisaging her sudden death, sent with her new driving licence an invitation to donate her vital organs.

After which, as was to be expected, the boiler had packed up. The first plumber had overcharged and botched the job. And the second plumber, when he finally materialised, had charged even more to put it only half right. (Once bitten, Kate had told herself resignedly, twice bitten.)

Elli had rung – doubtless on the kindest impulse – to commend to her a certain introduction agency, famously discreet, of which people spoke very highly. She could obviously not vouch for it herself, but she did know it had had some notable successes. And there was no need for Kate to be defensive. It was not, of course, just life's pathetic misfits who had use for such a service; it did not exist only for social pariahs. The widowed and divorced; high-powered company executives too busy to make romantic attachments; solitary types such as Kate herself, perfectly presentable, marriageable propositions, all might have their relationships brokered for them. (Oh, you bet, Elli would consult one herself like a shot if she weren't up to her ears already in eligible men.)

But the hurts, insults and vexations had become fewer; and the underlying pain, though always there, was more easily borne. Lately Kate's anger had found expression mainly in her dreams, when, horribly wronged, and with the whole world against her, she would shout herself hoarse (waking limp and ragged, with a backwash of tears, she would wonder if she'd cried aloud).

Reaching up for a rose bough, she pulled a fat bloom down over her face, and, as though it were an oxygen mask, breathed deeply of its honeyed scent. Then she sneezed, said 'Bless me', and 'Excuse me', before confiding to Geraldine with a hint of mockery, 'Elli's on at me to marry again – if only I can find a man who'll have me.'

'Ah, well, you should. Yes, you really should. You

were never for David, or he for you. That was a mistake. But you were both so young. And there is sure to be someone out there . . .' Geraldine's hand described a broad compass: the four corners of the earth were somehow implied. 'There is someone for everyone, they say.'

'Well, I'm not so sure about that. And I shan't go out of my way, I don't think, to meet anyone. It's sort of interesting, being on one's own. I mean, I've been alone before, for short spells. When Alex went skiing with those Malpas people, and when he went to Germany with the school. But then I always had the confidence that he'd be back. It was a finite aloneness. A chance, simply, to dust his room. Now, suddenly . . . you know what I mean? I see no end to it.'

'Ah, yes, I do see . . .' But Geraldine's interest, of foggy intensity at its most focused, had already begun to disperse (a kind of brilliant blankness shone through). 'I'll make us some . . .' she murmured.

'Tea?'

'Yes, tea.' And she turned to go indoors, trailing her shadow, a poor, attenuated, insubstantial thing, behind her.

'You had problems, I suppose, with Alex?' she ventured, as Kate appeared at the back door five minutes later. 'When he was at that "difficult age"?'

Not so as you'd have noticed, Kate told herself. He was always bright, wildly popular, broadly reliable. He'd had dozens of friends, and a capacity also to lose himself in books or to amuse himself with solitary pursuits. He had excelled at all things athletic and artistic. He had grown effortlessly into his adult body, his adult sexuality, as animals do, without, somehow, ever going through an awkward stage. So, no, she had had no problems. There had been no 'difficult age'. But, kindly forbearing, she made no comment, merely inclined her head as she went to scrub her hands at the sink. And she found herself wishing, as she soaped off the dirt, that her troubles with her boy had come at the appointed time, not now, so much later, when the textbooks could offer neither comfort nor counsel.

'It's Dominic, you see. I find him . . . He gives me great concern. He shows an unnatural obsession with S-E-X.'

'At seventeen, Geraldine,' said Kate, sighing over her own desolation, 'I should have said an obsession with sex was the most natural thing on earth.'

'But, you see, he talks of little else.'

'Who is this little Else? Oh, no, Geraldine, I'm sorry. Take no notice of me. But you have to appreciate –'

'It's like an addiction. There is such a thing, apparently. It can be treated. There are special clinics.'

'Nonsense,' scoffed Kate, remembering the days when so-called 'special clinics' dealt with unmentionable diseases. She remembered how David . . . How she'd had to go and sit there in a dismal waiting-room, with a lot of other shamefaced women, under a poster warning about gonorrhoea. 'You read too many alarmist magazines,' she added bleakly.

'Also . . .' Geraldine had no words to convey her sense of impotence, the feeling that all those years of assiduous parenting, the money spent on education, had been for naught. Her upturned palms, the spread of her hands, however, spoke of utter futility. Kate, reaching for the roll of paper towels, shifted inwardly from self-absorption to compassion for this daffy human being.

There was a little girl in Geraldine who showed herself occasionally, in petulance or distress. Her face would crumple, and all her pretensions, all artifice would fall away, but for the transparent artifice of a child who would be Mummy's darling. It was a disconcerting spectacle, from which Kate's attention fled. She gazed in suppressed panic around her at the fitted kitchen, designed to recall rusticity, though with none of the inconvenience that the rustic life entails. 'I am honestly convinced,' she offered distantly, 'that it's a phase. He'll grow out of it, you'll find.'

'John gives me no backing. He won't intervene. He lets it all wash over him. It drives me mad.'

'Perhaps he feels, the less said . . .' Kate got up and went to stand by Geraldine, edged her over, and, as the kettle came to a hectic boil, poured water into the teapot. 'He may take the view that you encourage Dominic into devilry by making so much of his pranks.'

Privately, though, she blamed Geraldine for her husband's uninvolvement. She had marginalised him for so much of their married life; she could not now complain if he had come to like it on the margins.

'Mother is to join us in Scotland, did I tell you?' Geraldine, gathering herself, regaining her composure, adopted a polite, conversational tone.

'You didn't.' Kate set the tray and carried it to the kitchen table. She felt only detestation for frightful Eleanor Garvey, she could think of no one she would less care to spend a fortnight with. And Geraldine's simper, her gratified tone, said much of the thrall in which mother held daughter still. 'You must be happy about that,' she offered through a battery of clenched teeth.

'Well, I'm sure she needs the break.'

'I'm sure she does.'

'And she can help me to keep order.' Geraldine had no sense of fun, the concept quite eluded her, but she affected now a note of gay banter. 'She can help me to manage the under-eighteens.'

'You'll be glad of that.'

The big woman sat down with a little puff, she fanned her face. 'Is it warm enough for you, this weather, Kate? Perhaps we should water the lawn.'

'Perhaps "we" should.'

'And after Scotland, of course, we'll have David back in our midst. That's something to look forward to.'

When Kate raised her cup to her lips, the tea scalded her tongue. Her eyes smarted. 'Oh, yes,' she concurred with heavy irony, 'something to look forward to indeed.'

'You'll be sorry later on, you know,' said Mrs Flowers, 'that you never dressed pretty.'

'Just one sugar, isn't it?' said Juin evenly, for she had made it her business, in her ten days here, to learn everyone's preferences for tea or coffee, sweet or not, weak, strong or 'as it comes'. She accepted the criticism good-humouredly, as it was meant. Mabel Flowers had been young in the era of guinea gown shops, georgette and rayon, silk hosiery, French knickers, chinchilla stoles and dinky hats. She had worked as a machinist, dressed in the new ready-to-wear, while hankering after the designs of Hartnell, Molyneux, Jean Patou. She could not be expected to comprehend Juin in her biker boots and black T-shirt, which bore the mystifying legend 'Kurt Cobain RIP'; Juin with her cropped hair now bleached blonde at its fringes, and with (since Saturday) a gold sleeper through her nose. Mabel Flowers could not know that, to the modern teenager, this look was . . . not pretty, of course (who needed pretty?), but definitely sussed. So, for the girl's sake, as she saw it, she offered this timely advice. And, in response, for Mrs Flowers's sake, sensitive to her feelings, Juin merely smiled acceptingly.

'How's your knee, Mrs Salter?' she asked then, moving on to the next old lady with slight but unfeigned solicitude. 'Not so swollen? And you're a very white coffee, milk and a splash, no sugar, right?'

Was it such a strange thing for her to do, to help out here for her pocket money? Her schoolfriends plainly thought so. Sales assistants, they wanted to be, running customers' swipe cards through the cash registers at Hennes, Oasis, River Island, bagging up their purchases with a studied insouciance that was itself communication of a kind, a reciprocal cool, among their peer group. A retirement home – or 'twilight home' as Elli would insist on calling it – was not for them. No way!

In her prediction that they would not let Juin through the door for fear that she would scare the inmates – the spectre of heart attack and accident had been raised, and of pacemakers going haywire – Elli had been wide of the mark. The matron, Mrs Southgate, a strong effectual woman with a brusque manner and disciplined hair, had put down a smile before it could take hold of her handsome features, had bent over her desktop, shuffled papers, and had simply enquired of this gamine as to how soon she might start. She must have discerned, then, behind the bolshie presentation, sympathy and patience rare in one of Juin's generation. Or else, as seemed to be the case, she was desperately short-handed, owing to the scarcity of these estimable human qualities.

Whoever had named the place Downside House had had no sense of irony. The majestic sweep of the South Downs was being recalled here, *rus in urbe* suggested – but, while *urbe* was everywhere in evidence, *rus* was meanly represented by a small front lawn, a few square metres of mown grass which surrounded the hard standing for cars, and by a couple of trees which seemed not to aspire beyond the sapling state. Downside was a modern, purpose-built brick structure, with rails around the walls, and ramps for wheelchairs. Depressing? Not really, once you were accustomed to it. It reminded Juin of nowhere so much as school, and school was tolerable, she could hack it.

On her first day, Peggy Southgate had sorted out for her a suitable overall – 'Slip of a thing, aren't you?' she had said, holding against her, with a look of hard appraisal, pinning to her shoulders with her two hands, the smallest of these drab garments – and had delivered herself of a terse lecture. 'Some of our residents have been through two world wars. They have brought up families, often in quite desperate circumstances. They have led valuable, interesting lives. Respect their dignity always. And never forget, when you're very frail, one fall changes everything.'

This admonishment had been well received. Better, anyway, than the brown and apricot overall, at which Juin had drawn a firm line. And for once, martinet though she was in these matters, Mrs Southgate had turned a blind eye, since the girl was proving to be a natural. The fact was that Juin had time for the elderly. Not a lot, but as much as it took. She did not avoid their society, as people do who are in dread of being like them. She was sufficiently far from them in age, and remote from their condition, to feel that she would never be so stricken in years. Or, if the same fate should befall her, she would at least have had a long, long interim in which to make the necessary adjustments.

It did not occur to her that, for these women, to wake in the morning to the knowledge that they were seventy, eighty, ninety, was almost as profoundly shocking and as baffling as it would have been for her. Age is the cruellest trick life plays on us; it is a gross insult to the ageless self. Juin had yet to understand this, or to appreciate that she and they stood at an equal distance – which is to say, but a step – from death. Yet the sympathy was there in some measure, and the patience.

Her duties were not, then, arduous to her, as they might have been were she more fey. There was nothing, really, in seeing Mrs Salter safe on and off the loo, or in cutting up food for the Misses Chitty and Armitage.

'I don't know how you stand it,' Elli had taunted her, 'running round after a lot of crumblies.'

'You'll be a crumbly yourself one day,' Juin had retorted, and it was no strain to envisage this outcome for her mother, at least.

'Not if Trevor has his way, I won't. He'll be the death of me, that boy.'

'You should keep in mind,' Juin had told her piously, 'that these women have been through two wars. They've brought up families in all sorts of difficult circumstances. They've led full lives. You should hear the stories they can tell.'

'And *you* should keep in mind, jewel of my womb, that I am your mother. You should be a bit less hoity, not to say toity.'

The women's pasts were, indeed, to Juin, like vivid fictions. Now she parked her tea trolley, appropriated Mrs Salter's footstool, perched at her side and attended to her reminiscenses of the old East End, her memories of the Blitz, so deeply absorbed that she picked up and ate, unnoticing, from a plate, the chewy crusts of bread to which someone's teeth had evidently not been equal.

Vera Salter came from Bromley-by-Bow, she was a true cockney, and might not, therefore, be heard to utter, 'Cor, blimey, mate, mind your backs, get off me barrow, and stone the bleeding crows'. Her bright, darting eyes, her lined complexion, contributed to an impression of fierce concentration, and nothing, it seemed, escaped her notice.

Mabel Flowers, by contrast, had a smooth, serene face and eyes of such pale hue that they appeared, in her more vague moments, to be almost achromatic. It was as if time had scribbled all over Vera, while partially erasing her friend. The two were inseparable, if argumentative, and spent each teatime, as today, in bickering retrospection. Disagreement united them and kept them going.

'Four coupons for a petticoat or a pair of camiknicks,' said Mabel Flowers, musing upon wartime privations. 'Three for corsets. Seven for a frock. No embroidery, no ornamental stitching, no cloth wasted on wide sleeves or pleats or deep hems.'

'I should have thought,' said Juin, 'you could have done without the corsets.'

'Oh, no, my dear, you'd not have been seen dead without your foundation garments.'

'But you never needed coupons for braces,' Vera Salter recalled. 'Nor for hats, clogs, suspenders –'

'Much good suspenders were to us! We couldn't get the nylons. You remember liquid stockings, Vera? Leg dye, that was.'

'Cold tea, we used. In the bath. Tin bath out the back. You, Miss Raggedy Anne, don't know you're born. You could have your pick of little dresses, nice skirts and tops . . .'

'What is this, then,' demanded Downside's newest care assistant wryly, 'national Have A Go At Juin Day?'

'You'll not get the young men chasing after you while you walk about like something the cat dragged in.'

'I'm not sure,' confessed Juin, frowning, 'that I *want* the young men after me. I'm not sure that men aren't more trouble than they're worth.' Absenting herself mentally from these women's company, she allowed her mind and her gaze to wander.

One entire wall of Downside's lounge was of glass, so

that passers-by could take a moment out of their busy round to peer in at the occupants, to congratulate themselves on not being of their number. The décor was dismal. Orange, theoretically the colour of flamboyance and camaraderie, and green, which is said to create a mood of harmony and hope, were rendered here to almost opposite effect. Where did council workers lay their hands on such paints? In what great vat were theymixed? Where, come to that, had they found the blue for the bathroom, a shade like no other? If you wanted a blue to evoke depression – never mind to promote it – it would be just the job. It mirrored very nicely, Juin told herself, her own state of mind.

A call from Kate had cheered her, though not hugely. 'I'm sorry I flew off the handle,' Kate had told her, 'it was unfair of me to take it out on you.' But she had sounded so listless, she had been so unpropitiating, that Juin had taken somewhat cold comfort from the brief exchange. And the real awfulness, with Alex and Naomi now, she had heard, snug in a new home, was a source to Juin, as to Kate, of unrelieved anguish.

'. . . wear glamour bands,' Mabel Flowers was saying.

'What were they?' said Juin, returned to herself.

'Them scarves, you know,' supplied Vera Salter, 'twisted round the head and tied in a roll at the front.' She made, with her hands, a rolling motion, tied a glamorous band. 'You had to cover your hair in case it got caught in the machinery. You would hear of women being literally scalped. Like what happened to you, so far as I can see.'

'You lay off me.' Juin ran a hand over her bristling head. 'This, I'll have you know, is the height of fashion.'

'The height of silliosity, more like,' Vera scoffed. 'No, you make yourself more presentable and find yourself a nice fellow. One with a bit of go in him.'

Alex had go in him, Juin told herself. And, having go, he'd gone.

'My Ed was a good man,' Vera persisted, 'a decent man, but he never had no go.'

'I'm only sixteen,' Juin protested mildly. 'There's plenty of time.'

'By sixteen I was spoken for,' reported Vera with satisfaction. 'I had my first child at seventeen.'

'The first of how many?'

'Eight in all. Five lived, three I buried.'

'That's terrible,' said Juin, appalled. And it crossed her mind that Ed could not have been wholly deficient in the Go department.

'It was God's will,' said Vera flatly. A confirmed atheist, she nevertheless liked to have someone to blame.

'But *why* did they die?'

'Because they did in them days,' Vera responded shortly. Her face, darkening, appeared more than ever cross-hatched as she dwelt for a few seconds on the two boys (one stillborn, one lost to diphtheria) and the girl (so premature, so tiny), who lived even now in her consciousness. 'We were very poor,' she said in a matter-of-fact way. 'You really can't imagine.'

'So where are they now? The ones that lived?'

'Ah.' Vera raised a hand, let it waver in the air in an apparent search for purpose. 'They're round and about,' she said, with an air of resignation. 'They come and see me when they can. Christmas, birthdays. Never miss. They're really very good.'

And I think *I've* got problems, Juin scolded herself, resolving to be more positive in all things, to count her blessings.

'So how long will we have the pleasure of your company?' asked Mabel Flowers, for they saw them come at Downside, these youthful helpers, and they saw them go.

'I'm off on holiday at the end of the month,' Juin explained. 'After that, I'll be back at school.'

'Going somewhere nice, are you?'

'To Scotland.' This without enthusiasm.

'I'd have loved to see Scotland,' Mabel Flowers sighed, and her eyes took on that curious lightness. 'Still, too late for that now.'

'Perhaps I'll do weekends in term time,' Juin said quickly, fearing that her emotions were overloading. 'If Mrs Southgate still wants me.'

'She'll want you. You're a nice lass, for all that you dress like the dog's breakfast.'

Juin was deeply, strangely gratified. 'That's not what my mother tells me,' she reported gruffly. 'About my being nice, I mean. But she's with you about the dog's breakfast bit.'

'Well, maybe your mother don't know it all,' offered Vera consolingly.

'Oh, no.' Juin, clasping her knees, rocked back on the stool (orange, the colour of alienation, green, the colour of hope deferred, flashed before her eyes). 'Oh, no, Mrs

Salter. If you read the *Globe* you'd know: my mother knows absolutely everything.'

'It's only Elli,' said Elaine Sharpe, with a satirical stress on the 'only'. She stood on the doorstep laden and smiling, confident of a welcome. She seldom went anywhere empty-handed; she liked to bring provisions, against there being none – which, with Naomi Markham as quartermaster here at Chafford Road, seemed almost a given. Prudent, she had come bearing Bombay mix, Kettle Chips, wine, more wine, a bottle of Jim Beam for when the wine ran out. And something else. 'House-warming present,' she announced, offering the non-plussed Naomi a package, expertly wrapped by the sales-woman. Elli herself had no time for such frippery, no patience with patterned paper that would not stay folded, or with Sellotape, which stuck to nothing so effectively as to itself. If God had meant us to make parcels, she always maintained, She'd have given us three hands. She would never say no to gift wrapping, though, which made a thing seem that much more meant. 'Now, aren't you going to ask me in?'

'Oh, yes, of course.'

'Well, then.' When Naomi merely stood about in confusion, Elli thrust her purchases into her arms and shooed her with the backs of her hands. 'Come on, put yourself about a bit, show some old-fashioned hos-pitality.'

Recovering herself, Naomi, who was unused to receiv-ing callers, led her friend down the narrow hallway and into the bedroom. This would have seemed more eccentric, a more odd place to entertain visitors, had the room not given on to a minute rear garden. Double doors stood open, benign sunlight flooded in.

'This'll do,' decided Elli, kicking off her spiky shoes, stretching out at once on the bed and yawning self-indulgently. A radio played soft and eminently forgettable music. She made none of her usual impact, somehow, on the drowsy atmosphere here. There was that feeling of having walked in upon a sleeper, who, stirring, smiling, dreamt sweetly on.

'It's very heavy.' Naomi stood at the foot of the bed, weighing Elli's gift in her hand. She was dressed unfussily in simple shift, a pair of plain canvas shoes; her hair, parted at the crown, was looped back with a length of blue ribbon, and her make-up was infinitely subtle. Such simplicity suited her. Or else it was an effect of happiness, for she seemed to have shed years. 'What is it?' she wondered aloud.

'You'll never guess.'

And Naomi never would have. Even when the packaging was stripped away, she was scarcely the wiser.

'Don't tell me you already have one,' Elli chafed her.

'But what *is* it?' Naomi queried again, frowning in perplexity, turning the moulded terracotta object this way and that.

'It's a chicken brick.' Ellie's tone was one of immense satisfaction. A more desirable item, she conveyed, might not be found in all of London.

'A . . .?'

'Chicken brick.'

'And what is it for, actually?'

'To be truthful . . .' Elli rolled on to her side, propped herself on one elbow and studied the thing keenly. She knew about chickens. She knew about bricks. But the function of a chicken brick seemed to her, to say the least, arcane. 'To be honest, I've never had use for one myself. But I was rather taken by the look of it. It spoke to me. I felt that every home should have one. You could just put it on a shelf, if you liked. As a talking point. Or . . .'

'I could keep eggs in it, perhaps,' suggested Naomi helpfully.

'Yes, yes. *Or* – and this is just an idea – you *could* roast a chicken in it.'

'What would I have to do exactly?' Naomi placed the brick, with care, on the top of the chest of drawers beside a pile of Alex's shirts, into which she had this morning ironed copious salt tears and unwanted creases, as she wept at her own ineptitude.

'First you heat up the oven, right?'

'To what setting? Gas, this is.'

'How should I know what setting? Is my name Escoffier? Hey, listen now. Take this one invaluable tip from me. It simplifies matters no end if you cook everything at the same temperature. I can personally vouch for regulo six: it seems to hold good for all foods. Except meringues.'

'*Meringues*?'

'Don't ask. I once went mad and threw together a Pavlova. Big mistake. My only culinary failure. Ever.'

'I don't suppose I shall want to –'

'Better not, eh? So-o . . . set the oven to mark six.

242

When it's hot as stink – you can test it with your elbow to make sure – put chicken inside brick, replace lid, slide brick into oven, leave to stew in own juices for one to two hours.'

'And then?'

'Take brick from oven. Inspect contents. Retch violently. Throw chicken and brick in dustbin and send virile young lover out for Chinese takeaway. Ah, so! How is the dear boy, by the way?'

'Alex?'

'Well, who else? Yes, Alex. How many other dear boys do we know? Is our society stiff with them? Because I can't say I've noticed. Perhaps you have a string of them at your beck and call?'

'No, there's just Alex. He's fine.'

Naomi assumed a dazed, besotted expression, upon which Elli could not look with equanimity. The woman's eyes were set extraordinarily wide. This lent her, in Elli's view, the look of a ninny, it hinted at congenital stupidity. Pinching the bridge of her nose, she felt her own eyes, reassuringly placed, one just left, one just right of the Sharpe proboscis (no intellectual weakness there!). And she consoled herself that, while she was not possessed of Naomi's excelling beauty, she had, by way of compensation, a bumper brain. She still felt, deep down, that she had suffered some kind of serious reverse when her friend got it on with Alex Garvey. (Perhaps she, too, should find herself a nice toy boy?) Hence the self-justification, the squaring away.

'And you're settling in all right?' Now Elli looked around her at the airy, sparsely furnished room (the bed, the chest of drawers, was all it had to offer): 'So, this is where it happens, eh? The *love nest*.'

'I'm settled, yes.' Naomi elected to ignore the jibe.

'Tell me do, and tell me true, did he carry you across the threshold?'

'Mind your own business.'

Naomi's gaze wandered over the ceiling and into corners. 'Do you like the flat, Elli?'

'Oh, very *bijou*.'

'You mean small? But I don't care.' She thrust her chin out in defiance. Her hair escaped from its ribbon tie and fell about her face. 'It's quite big enough for the two of us.' She sat abruptly on the foot of the bed, picked a wisp of down off the quilt and flicked it on to the floor. She had no way of explaining to Elli – and was disinclined to try – just what the flat represented to her. This was the first place in her whole life that she could call her own. Not that she had contributed a penny to its acquisition, not that she maintained herself within it, but the sense of being a kept woman, which had constrained and alienated her in St John's Wood and elsewhere, driving her from room to room in an aimless quest for the indefinable, was not present with Alex. Deliberately, determinedly, he had enfranchised her.

Seeing how she sat there, so reflective, reposeful, Elli realised with a slight shock that this was certainly no mere aberration. The unimaginable was happening: Naomi Markham was putting down roots.

'You're completely serious, then, you and Alex?'

'Oh, yes,' responded Naomi assuredly.

'In that case, I think you ought to show me round,

don't you? If you're going to hang on in for more than a fortnight. Let me take a shufti before we pop a cork or two and talk about old times.'

'All right, come on.' Naomi slid off the bed decisively. 'Though there's not much to see at the moment,' she confessed.

Bare boards made much of their footsteps. When Elli, clattering about the front room, passed favourable comment upon it, it threw her words straight back at her.

'It will be better,' said Naomi mildly, 'when we get some curtains up, some carpet down. It will be better when we can afford to furnish it.' Leaning against the fireplace she seemed almost to caress it. 'They do places out all in white these days,' she explained with great seriousness. 'Neutral colours sell better, apparently. People like to put their own stamp on their home. We shall want to do that as soon as we can afford to, naturally.'

'Naturally,' responded Elli faintly. This woman was priceless! Where had she been all her life? A visitor from the planet Zog would be more *au fait* with the workings of British society in the Nineties than she was.

'Not that we're completely broke. And I'm bound to get some good assignment myself, any day. It has to be something a bit special, that's what's taking the time. I could have catalogue work tomorrow, but that would be a disastrous career move. Anyway, fortunately the mortgage isn't that steep. We have a special rate, you know, as first-time buyers.'

This, then, was what Alex had done for her. In every way he had involved her. The flat, the mortgage, were in joint names. He had explained to her the formalities, shared with her his anxieties, discussed each decision, deferred always to her judgement. For that, she could live with bare boards, with white walls, with old sticks of furniture. She would not just live with them, indeed, but would love them. The flat would not be designed around her, as in the past, by highly paid experts, without reference to her tastes and preferences. And she could walk into the kitchen without feeling she intruded in another woman's domain.

'All my life,' she said, and the echo, the resonance, lent a peculiar power, a stirring quality to the utterance, 'I have been bought off. My mother, Uncle Huw, they paid a lot of money to have me off their hands. Riding lessons. Ballet and tap. Elocution. Modelling school. And you know what I did? Because, I suppose, I knew no better. I went straight for the kind of men who would treat me the same. They would pay for my haircuts, my facials, my clothes, and to keep a roof over my head. They would like to be seen about town with me. But they never really let me into their lives. *That* is why they never lasted, those so-called relationships.'

'Yes, I do see,' allowed Elli, impressed by this analysis, and convinced by it. She had never credited Naomi with such acute perception.

'Whereas with Alex,' Naomi continued, hugging herself, addressing her words to the wall above the fireplace, 'it's about sharing. And caring.'

This, however, was a banality too far for Elli. 'Enough with the hearts and flowers. Direct me to the lavatory,' she commanded. 'I'm dying for a pee.'

The bathroom was a windowless cell, contrived by the developer from borrowed spaces. When you stepped inside and tugged the light switch, an extractor fan set up a relentless drone. On a tiled shelf, Naomi's cleansers, moisturisers and lotions crowded in with Alex's shaver and comb. There was something so intimate about this airless space that Elli felt almost shifty, and, pausing only to check her reflection, forbearing to unscrew jars and bottles, to dip into the revitalising creme, she hurried out.

Naomi was by now in the garden. She had brought tumblers, a corkscrew, had spread out a towel on what passed for a lawn, and was kneeling upon it. Even when she sat back on her haunches, her thighs appeared lean. 'These are nice, aren't they?' she queried, holding a tumbler at arm's length for inspection, twirling it so it should catch the sun's rays. 'Just seventy-five pence from the Conran Shop. You see how I'm learning to economise.'

'Have you ever noticed . . .?' Elli asked her, touring the borders, in which grew a few sad plant remnants. She reached to give the heeling, creosoted fence an experimental shove, then, 'Have you noticed what silly little feet Geraldine has?' she demanded.

'Geraldine? Her feet? No, I can't say I have.'

'You wouldn't think they'd support her. Not in a high wind. I hate small feet, don't you? I think long, thin ones are the ideal. Like yours and mine.'

Naomi, who obsessed on physical perfection, had nevertheless given not a moment's thought to this particular aspect. 'Aren't people's feet, generally, in scale with the rest of them?' she wondered aloud. 'Ooh, I can't budge this. Will you do it?'

'Give it here, you wimp.'

Obediently, Naomi handed the bottle up to Elli, who clamped it between her knees and drew the cork proficiently. '*Voilà*. Here we go. No, the whole point about Geraldine . . .' She dropped down beside Naomi. 'This is precisely what I'm saying. That her feet *aren't* in scale.'

'Well, if you say not.'

'Unless it's just that she's fat. They might simply *appear* small in comparison to her great girth.' Elli undid a button, slackened her waistband. 'Phwaw, that's better. This skirt was cutting me in half. Pour us a drink, then, girlie.'

'This garden could be nice, couldn't it?' said Naomi, as she complied.

'*Could* be. You should get Kate to fix it for you. If she can ever bring herself to come here, that is.'

'I do wish she would, for Alex's sake mainly. It's most unfair of her, I think, to behave in this way. And the things she's said about me, you would not believe.'

'Hey, hey, hey, you can't blame her, can you? I should say the same about you, no doubt, if you had shafted me the way you've shafted her. I mean, Naomi Markham, with friends like you, who needs enemas?'

'Sometimes I think I shall never forgive her.'

'*You* forgive *her*?' Elli choked in disbelief, she honked and spluttered as wine burned its way down inside her nose and issued from her nostrils.

'But then I think, if we could get her over here, show her that it's working . . . I could invite her for a meal, couldn't I? I must learn to cook, Elaine. To cook *properly*. Nice dinners for Alex.'

'I can't see the need, quite frankly. What's wrong with ready meals? Frozen ones or chilled. There's such a vast choice – whatever you fancy.'

'I'm not being ungrateful,' persisted Naomi, flying in the face of truth like a wasp against a window, unable to see it when she hit up against it, 'but the food at Kate's was unspeakable.'

'Poor Kate's no Fanny Cradock,' Elli agreed. 'Oh, come on, Naomi, you can't tell me you don't remember Fanny and Johnny.'

Naomi, though, flopped out on her back, flung an arm across her face, and would have it that the names rang not the faintest bell with her.

'You're unbelievable,' Elli reacted. Then, reclining on the towel, she spent a good half-hour in retrospective vein. She mentioned skiffle, and Chelsea Girl, and Maidenform bras; she evoked the grand old days when AA men would salute association members, and lorry drivers were truly knights of the road.

If she was bent, though, on reminding Naomi how very many years she'd been around – perhaps on forcing her to confess to middle age – it was a waste of her breath. 'Don't keep going over ancient history,' was all Naomi would say, sitting up, hugging her knees, resting her chin upon them. 'Myself, I like to live in the moment.'

'Only because you lack the imagination to live anywhere else.'

'That's not true. It *isn't*.' Naomi brought her shoulders up to her ears.

'So what do you reckon will happen with Kate?' she asked presently.

'Oh, she'll get more and more dotty, for sure. She'll end up a barmy old recluse with a house full of cats. I've tried to persuade her to get out and about, perhaps to meet a man before it's too late, but she isn't having any of it. She'll be like her mother, who, you will recall, was absolutely dotty.'

'No, I seem to recollect she was rather nice.' Naomi's mind strained after a fugitive image of Pam's kind, worried face.

'But then, you have, as we know, a very faulty memory. Or difficulties with retrieval, should I say, because it's all in there somewhere, it has to be. No, I'm afraid poor Kate will be as cranky as Pam was. She's already showing signs. Geraldine was telling me only today – because, you know, she had her over there this morning – that her behaviour is distinctly odd. She'd be laughing like a hyena one minute, cross as two sticks the next. Not stable, not stable at all.'

'We can't be to blame for that. Alex and I. Not entirely.'

'Dear heavens, no! She was always inclined to hysteria. Between you and me, Naomi, the problem with Kate –'

'Shut up,' Naomi told her rudely.

Elli was about to protest – no one, but *no one*, spoke thus to Elaine Sharpe – when she realised that Naomi was looking not at her but beyond her. Following the direction of her gaze, she saw Alex Garvey, framed in the doorway, looking down on them.

'Alex. You're early.' In an enchanting gesture, Naomi

put up her arms, as a baby does who wants to be lifted. 'How lovely. Do come out and join us. Elli's here, as you see. And she's brought us a wonderful house-warming present.'

'Elli.' Alex spared her a casual, not unfriendly nod. She was surprised to find him little changed; in her imagination Naomi had wrought some sort of transformation, not entirely to be desired. The smile was the same: tolerant, knowing. And weeks of heavy sex had not worn him to a shadow. If anything, he was in better shape than ever, suntanned, sinewy, relaxed.

'I just popped in,' she told him loftily, 'to give your place the once-over.'

'And does it meet with your approval?'

'It will do you for now, I reckon.'

In an instant he was at Naomi's side, gathering her up in an effusive embrace.

'Don't mind me, I'm sure,' said Elli, disgruntled, and for once she felt ever so slightly awkward, unsure of her presence.

'No, we don't mind you, Elli.' He sat down matily between them and swigged from her glass.

'Guess,' insisted Naomi. 'Go on Alex, guess what Elli's bought us.'

'I simply haven't a clue.'

'A chicken brick,' she told him grandly, knowledge-ably. 'D'you know what that is, Alex? A brick for cooking chicken. You just put it in the oven, apparently. For an hour. At regulo six.'

His work done for another day, John Gorst felt a powerful disinclination to go home. So averse was he to the idea, that he could not stir, but sat there, leaden, dog-earing a buff folder, until Pat the cleaner put her head around the door at half-past six and clucked reprovingly. All work and no play, she cautioned, would make Jack a dull boy.

John, sliding the Pettifer file into the drawer and locking it away, suggested in reply that some kind of damage limitation was the best that might be hoped for at this stage.

'Go on with you!' Pat chuckled, and pulling the door decisively to, she left him to make good his departure.

Clasping his hands behind his head, he rocked back in his chair, yawning, enjoying the stretch in his midriff as his shirt escaped the cincture of his trousers. And he gave consideration to work in progress, to the messy and degrading unpicking of the Pettifer marriage. With nothing to entertain his eye but the blank, white ceiling, his mind filled with a motion picture of Jean-Anne Pettifer, who leaned towards him, clutching the desk rim, seeming to strive to drive her fingers through the veneered wood. She was a thin woman with stringy hair and perhaps the meanest face he'd ever seen (mouth, chin, eyelids, all had been skimped, while her range of expressions was narrow in the extreme). Three weeks ago she had instructed him thus: 'I want you to make him pay through the nose. Destitute the bastard. Take him to the sodding cleaners.' Which said, she had sat back – had lounged, you might say – and, with monstrous arrogance, staring not at him but beyond him, at the Gorst and Merridew car park behind his right shoulder, she had treated him to a long and largely irrelevant discourse on the failures of Graham Pettifer, his sins of omission and commission, beginning with his woeful inability to wire a plug or hang a shelf, and building to a small but unforgivable sexual indiscretion.

From time to time taking up his pen, making desultory notes, John had felt himself drawn to the hapless Graham, who had assumed in his imagination a kind of martyred dignity. The fellow had, in the event, however, disappointed him, responding, via his solicitors, with denials, accusations and vindictive counter-claims (in the offices of Lomax, Lloyd and Munday, on the other side of town, Mike Munday had no doubt been treated to a corresponding stream of vituperation).

Must people be so niggardly and so squalid? *His* Graham Pettifer, the one who had enjoyed the brief and glorious existence of a mayfly in John's fancy, would have made more noble or more paradoxical reply. He would certainly, for instance, have renounced his ownership of every brick and every stick they'd held in common. Probably he'd have gone further: he would have had her keep not merely the hi-fi but his treasured Muddy Waters albums; not just the dinner service but his mother's twelve apostle spoons. He would have dropped into her lap the keys to the Cavalier, packed a small case with a change of clothing, and left town on a bus to begin life anew. Sadly, however, the real Graham Pettifer had no such pluck or dash.

The present adversarial system did, of course, make for unseemly divorce, it set spouse against spouse. The law required disputatious couples to engage in bouts of moral mud-wrestling. But change was being urged, to a cheaper, expedient no-fault procedure, based on conciliation. Thinking on this, John was bound to wonder what some well-meaning conciliator, drawn maybe from the ranks of middle-class do-gooders, would make of the confrontational Jean-Anne and Graham. To arbitrate between two snarling pit bull terriers was, on the whole, to be preferred.

Pat was singing in the front office, a menacing tra-la, signalling her intention to barge in again at any moment (*she* had a home to go to, if no one else had).

The firm of Gorst and Merridew was right on the high street; its glass front door gave on to the narrow pavement. The partners traded from old shop premises, but vertical blinds in the window spoke of suitable discretion, while a sign promised first-class confidential legal advice to families and businesses, it boasted expertise in residential and commercial conveyancing, matrimonial matters, personal injuries claims, employment and civil disputes, wills and probate. Joss Merridew, by far the more flamboyant half of the Gorst and Merridew double act, had an office upstairs, from where he might look lovingly down upon the Pontiac Firebird that he had chosen instead of a family. John Gorst, below, had immediate access to the back door and the car park.

Stirred at last by the imminence of Pat (he heard the clang of a waste bin, the whisper of a black plastic sack on synthetic fibre carpet), he got up and made a hasty exit. The concrete out here was breaking up; its hardcore innards were exposed. Weeds ate at the fabric of the surrounding brick wall. A supermarket trolley had somehow found its way in. They should think of having the small square of ground resurfaced, John told himself, then at once set the notion aside.

He eased into the Rover, sat at the wheel with the driver's door open, waiting for the engine to warm and for the interior to cool. Such ennui he felt today, such a drabness of spirit. It must, he supposed, be an effect of the atmosphere, for it was very close, the town sweltered as under a close-fitting lid. When Pat, in his office, waved good night, he could scarcely lift his hand to make answering gesture.

The egress, over cobbles, through an alley between his office and Garner's the soft furnishing shop, seemed more strait than ever. To right and left, walls slipped by, inches from the car's metal flanks. There was no chance of emerging at the appropriate angle – or of seeing oncoming traffic until the bonnet of the Rover was right in amongst it. The sheer awkwardness of the manoeuvre was tiresome in the extreme; the idea that he must continue to make it until he retired was insupportable; while the aggression of the motorists who bore down upon him, hooting him, shouting at him (had he heard 'silly old fucker'?), did nothing whatever for his humour.

He was headed out of town when he remembered – and here was a likely reason for his present despondency – that the Peacheys and the Hugh-Joneses were expected tonight. It was this that had been nudging up against his resistant consciousness. A barbecue, Geraldine had promised them, weather permitting. And though the sky was milky it could muster not one serious cloud, so there was little hope that rain would stop play.

John did not care for barbecues. The food that came off

them was too often red-raw at the middle, though charred on the outside; it was carcinogenic and not the least gastronomic. But that was not his principal objection. Nor did he hate, above all, the palaver, the feats of skewersmanship he would be called upon to perform over hot coals. No, what he most abominated was the blue and white butcher's apron that she would knot around his waist, and the paper chef's hat with which his wife would crown him.

Stealing a glance at his watch, he saw that it was nearly seven. The Peacheys, Tim and Jessica, the Hugh-Joneses, Owen and Val, would be at Copperfields before him if he didn't put his foot down, their voices would rise, and their laughter ring, as they knocked back aperitifs in the warm and chlorine-scented air around the pool.

What was it about this county that it failed to give him more than superficial pleasure? Surrey? Sorry. Its trees were proper trees with old, gnarled trunks beneath great, leafy canopies. The grass was green and lush. The hedgerows, recently shorn, showed forth willowherb, figwort, foxgloves, blackberries . . . In springtime, the woodland was awash with bluebells and pink purslane, it seemed magically to trap the sunlight in its lofty vaults.

Yet the landscape had none of the majesty of mountainous Cumbria, or the melancholy of the fenlands, flat for ever, or the restless energy of the sea. And everywhere, in clearings, had sprung up houses like his own, which made a mock of heritage. Houses in whose manicured gardens, at this very moment, the occupants might be lighting barbecues, they might be sporting paper chef hats and blue and white striped butch——

Only now, finally, did the full horror of his situation dawn upon him. It hit him with such force, indeed, that he swerved into a shallow ditch and braked to a bucking halt. For had not Geraldine, this morning, at breakfast, asked him to call in at Layton's in his lunch break? 'Yes, yes,' he had consented, giving her a scant half of his attention, while with the other half he had wondered how to temper the demands of the frightful Mrs Pettifer, to introduce into the proceedings a modicum of reason. He had taken and pocketed a list of meat products especially suited to incineration. He must buy a good two pounds of Mr Layton's hand-made pork and sage sausages, a dozen of his prime beef hamburgers, lamb shish kebabs . . . 'You won't forget?' she had actually pressed him. And, 'No, of course not,' he had vowed.

What to do? He slammed the car into first gear, revved hard, powered out of the gulley – the wheels, spinning wildly, wrenching at the undergrowth, sent up clouds of dust – and went blinding along in a funk, though he could not have said what precisely he feared. What, after all, was the worst she could do to him? Belittle him before their guests? He was man enough to handle that, wasn't he?

No, he wasn't. And this was not the worst of it, for while Geraldine was no Jean-Anne, in that she never spat or swore or set about him with a copper-bottomed frying pan, while she controlled her temper always, seeming to sit down hard and in no small discomfort upon it, she did make hostages of all his little transgressions; she held them, perhaps for months, in a controlling way, against him. And things were dicey enough, frankly, with his withdrawal from the Scottish fixture; he needed a second charge to answer like he needed a hole in the head.

For a few exhilarating moments he felt he might do as Graham Pettifer – *his* Graham Pettifer – would have done. He'd turn the car around and drive as far and as fast as possible. He would assume an alias, a false identity (family, friends, his business contacts would not hear of him again). You did read, from time to time, of people who did this. The scheme had about it a beautiful simplicity. You just cut loose.

But then there rose up before him, like a revelation, notice of a filling-station. He knew that he was saved, he need not after all grow a beard or flee the country, and as he pulled on to the forecourt he could have wept with relief. BP for barbecue parties! Because it had not escaped his attention, when he'd nipped in here for petrol in the past, that the place comprised a sort of shop affair, which sold almost anything you could wish for, from paddling pools to Cornish pasties, pot plants to Pepsi-Cola.

Killing the engine, he went hurriedly inside, followed his nose to the chill cabinet, and found two packs of pork chipolatas. Better still, in the deep freeze he found chicken portions (rock hard, but they would thaw out, surely?), and packets of beefy-looking items that went by the promising name of Steak House Grills. Layton's, purveyors of fine meats, might offer better quality, but, hell, what was the difference? One carbonised burger must be much like another.

'Will these be all right for barbecuing?' he nevertheless enquired of the assistant as he piled the purchases up by the cash till.

'Oh, yes, very good,' she told him indifferently, sparing him not a glance as she rang up the prices. She would, he suspected, have given the same assurance had he set before her paddling pool, pot plant and Pepsi. And, as she turned to take the notes he offered, she seemed to see right through him.

Ten past seven. Their little group would already have forgathered. Fragrant gin would be poured over clinking ice cubes. In his absence, some stout fellow – Owen, John decided, one could count on Owen – would volunteer to lay and light the fire, while Geraldine, watching restively for his arrival, straining after the sound of tyres on gravel, would offer half-formed apologies for him, she would say how hard, how *very* hard he . . . She would murmur that he must have been delayed by . . .

With the goodies beside him on the front passenger seat, he sped off in the direction of home. He would strip the wrappings off, discard the boxes, present as fresh these manufactured foods, and bluff it out.

If they all got a bit tipsy, he could get the stuff past them; they'd say, 'How simply delicious!' and 'I dote on Layton's, don't you?' What he must do, then, instead of going hell for leather, was to stop off for a pint at the golf club, he must give them an extra half-hour in which to mellow.

No one at the club gave any sign of recognising him, no fellow member got up to slap him on the back and buy him drinks, no one sought his society. He perched on a

259

stool and, because he was invisible to bar staff, tapped on the counter with a pound coin.

The young woman who served him was got up in terrifying fashion. She reminded him, in style, of Elli's girl, except that there was something quite endearing, quite enchanting about Juin. She was, despite her presentation, really very pretty. He wouldn't . . . how had Dominic put it? Very neatly, as he remembered. Ah, yes: he wouldn't kick her out of bed.

He knocked back a large Bell's and felt calmer. Whisky was balm to his insides, it was just the job. He had had a close call, but he had come through it. He took up a coin and tap-tap-tapped it. For his enterprise, he would award himself another double.

At nine o'clock, the Gorsts' guests started on the salads. Geraldine had telephoned the office, she had telephoned the local police. She could only say, apologetically, how hard, how very hard John . . . She said he must have been delayed by . . .

At nine-thirty, as the night enfolded them, as husbands were sent to the cars to fetch cardigans, they heard the scrunch of tyres on gravel.

A minute passed, two minutes, three, before John Gorst appeared around the side of the house. His tie was pulled awry, and he clutched in his arms a flimsy carrier-bag, striped red and white, which conspicuously lacked the Layton's logo.

Geraldine could not help herself. She tried, and she failed. 'John,' she said, aghast, 'where have you been? We're starving, here.' Then, as the full dreadfulness of the situation was borne in upon her, 'And look at you. I do believe you're drunk!'

CHAPTER

7

Elli dreamt she had her own business, selling fascinating conversations. That is, she produced, on a computer, scripts for two voices, lively exchanges of ideas, shot through with wit and wisdom. Really stupid people, total wallies, could sit across a table from each other and, with constant reference to their print-outs, engage in cut-and-thrust far beyond their intellectual capabilities. For this they paid happily through the nose. It proved quite a moneyspinner.

She came out of most of her dreams as if out of a cinema, impressed by their artistic and erotic quality. This morning, she fancied that here was an idea of such brilliance, it could not fail to make her fortune. Only when she ran through possible subject headings – politics, religion, theatre, the monarchy, existentialism, dialectical materialism, angling and field sports, the meaning of life – did it occur to her that she might still be in the bustling, bright-lit foyer of the subconscious, in theta mode, dreaming, albeit lucidly, and that she had yet to emerge fully into the real world. Angling and field sports, for fuck's sake!

She lay with her eyes closed, wreathed in the teasing, twining scents of Italy, of the ancient stone walls that enclosed her, of aching timbers, fermenting apricots, and the citronella candle she had burned to drive out mosquitoes (in vain, for she had slapped about all night, after one particularly persistent blighter that kept bombilating past her ear). Through her eyelids, she could see ripples of early sunlight. From hilltop to hilltop, campanile spoke to campanile, groaning church bells, long past pensionable age, tolled the hour of nine.

I'm luxuriating, she told herself. I am in Tuscany, on my holiday, and I am happy to the depths of my being.

But she wasn't. Frankly she felt rather groggy. On this Monday, their third morning at Il Poggio, she was crapulous and cranky, sated with wine, glutted with the beauty of the place. *Dolce far niente*, the sweetness of doing nothing, was not for Elaine Sharpe, who twitched with irritation at too much enforced idleness. She had supposed it would be very larky, hanging out with like-minded people, but the meeting of like minds here was as the meeting of cymbals, it was more in the nature of a crash. And, boy, did these people talk shop! She had never thought to be so bored with the notion of newspapers. She was missing home, she was missing Juin. A small part of her even missed her regular run-ins with the hapless Trevor. What was more, she told herself, her mouth tasted worse than a fiddler's armpit.

She and Patti had flown into Pisa in delirious high spirits on Friday afternoon, loudly pitying the poor, ill-favoured saps back at Globe Tower, who had not the good fortune to be with them. They had picked up a hire car from the airport, and driven to the farmhouse, stopping only to stock up at Esselunga with vast quantities of cheese, pasta, tomatoes, onions and fresh basil, on the way. Elli still had not warmed to her companion, however, nor fathomed why Patti had invited her along on the jaunt.

Covertly, from behind dark glasses, as La Henderson steered the Fiat Tipo in and out of various hairy traffic situations, she had enumerated her flaws and infelicities. Blonde divorcee Patti Henderson, 49 (as the *Globe* would have had it), was burdened with the sort of half-baked complexion that a tan would do nothing to improve; the strewing of freckles on nose and cheeks seemed faintly preposterous in a woman of her age (she ought, Elli privately considered, to have grown out of them long since); her mouth was somehow too pliant, her face collapsing in on itself. Was Elli being harsh in these judgements? Over-critical? Uncharitable? She had thought not.

In any case, all this must be set against a small, compact body which looked good in clothes and – Elli must now ruefully admit – not half bad out of them.

A mile of mud track, deeply rutted, turning back and back on itself in disorientating fashion, had led them through wooded fields, where horses grazed in a torment of flies, up the hillside and at last to Poggio nel Vento. 'Can't you get this fixed?' Elli had complained, as the wheels dropped into yet another crater and her head banged against the passenger window. But, 'Cost a fortune,' Patti had dismissed the proposition. 'You can't imagine. Anyway, it's better left alone, it discourages intruders. Oh, look. Do look. Here's Paolo, come to meet us. He's the farmer, you know, who keeps an eye on things for me. Goodie! He'll have brought the wine and olive oil! We make our own, did I tell you?'

'You do?'

'Well, not me personally, of course,' Patti disclaimed with a merry laugh. A busy executive, she could not be expected to, figuratively speaking, tread the grapes herself, ha, ha. By the time of the *vendemmia*, that frantic week when the vines must be picked clean, she would be back in England.

'*Ciao, principessa*,' the genial Paolo had greeted her, holding her by the elbows like an awkward dance partner.

'*Ciao, Paolo. Come vai?*'

Bloody show-off, Elli had told herself darkly, as she waited to be introduced.

'Now, Paolo, this is my friend, *la mia amica*, Elaine Sharpe. *Da Londra.*'

'*Piacere.*' Paolo, who was a handsome sixty, with nice, crinkled eyes in a deeply tanned face, had looked her over with unguarded approval as he shook her by the hand (a man of taste and discrimination, Elli had decided).

'Come and have a nose around the place,' Patti had urged her then, taking her elbow, drawing her indoors. 'It's a typical *casa colonica*. Henry and I bought it with my inheritance and his redundo from the *Mirror*. It was part of my divorce settlement. He gets a share of the lettings income, such as it is. As you see, it's nothing fancy. The effect is very bucolic, very *rustico*, if you know what I mean, but I think you're going to like it.'

So Elli had trailed behind her from room to room. She

265

had found the ground floor faintly oppressive, built as it was to exclude the punishing sun, but it would not have been politic to say so, and as they traipsed upstairs, where shimmering light and air stole in through open shutters, she had uttered sincere expressions of delight.

'This is your room,' Patti had announced. 'It's quite the nicest of the guest bedrooms, so you're most frightfully honoured. And there's a bathroom next door. Let's freshen up, both of us, and we can meet downstairs in . . . how long do you need? Twenty minutes? We'll meet downstairs and try the *vino della casa*. What do you say?'

Well, what *would* Elli say? She'd said 'Great!'

At the end of that afternoon, Simon and Tina Tulley had drawn up in a storm of dust and quarrelsome humour, having motored down through France. Navigational difficulties had led to tiffs, tiffs to bitter accusations, legal separation had been threatened on both sides, and what had been conceived as a romantic journey had apparently turned into a nightmare. Then, with the appearance next day of Mike Braithwaite from the picture desk, and Seamus Hicks, sports reporter, their little party had been complete. Or nearly. Only one further member was expected – was awaited, indeed, by some, with barely concealed impatience.

The 'boys', perhaps supposing that they'd been asked along to squire the single women, uncertain of their situation, wanting for a role, had been set to uncork bottles and to stoke the pizza oven, which they did with a curmudgeonly lack of grace.

Now, lying on this unfamiliar, lumpy mattress, in her canopied bed, Elli heard the rhythmic crunch of footsteps on gravel. She opened her eyes and gazed a moment at the chestnut-beamed ceiling, before swinging herself up. Her bare feet found the small rectangle of rug which rucked on the rough-hewn, red-painted brick floor that Patti called *cotto*. Blinking, she reached for her contact-lens case, spat on each lens in turn and stuck them in her eyes.

She had a corner room, with windows set deep into the thick stone fabric of the building. One window looked up over serried ranks of vines and silvered olive trees to a precarious hill village. In the evening, when the village church stood in silhouette against the sunset, and the cypresses toiled in solemn procession to the summit, as the bells tolled seven, eight, nine, it framed the scene like a perfect oil painting. The other window, through which she now thrust her head, leaning her arms on the cold marble sill, offered a view across the plain, bathed in blue morning haze, to distant Lucca. At night, the perfect little walled city flaunted itself in rings of electric lamplight, but in the early mist, through the blear of her lenses, she could barely make it out.

Down there in the centre, according to her guidebook, was a cathedral which had its beginnings in the twelfth century, and which housed in its left transept Jacopo della Quercia's tomb of Ilaria del Carretto. There was the Palazzo Guinigi, from whose tall, square towers a giant holm oak sprouted incongruously; the Romanesque church of San Frediano; Palazzo Mansi with its baroque *piano nobile*; the ornate gardens of Palazzo Pfanner . . .

It was good to know of these attractions, but one didn't need actually to schlepp around them. They had stood for hundreds of years already; they would await with chill indifference a later visit. Besides, having come so close to them, having read about them, however cursorily, one almost felt one *had* seen them; they were numbered among one's mental souvenirs.

Elaine amused herself for a while, imagining how it would be, were she here with her true friends, the old gang, Naomi, Geraldine, Kate. Geraldine, having first located a sympathetic pharmacist and mimed for him some acutely distressing ailment, would be sure to insist on 'doing' the sights, she would attach herself to a tour guide and go tip-tapping after him over time-worn flags on her tiny feet, listening to a tape-recorded English translation as she peered earnestly at carvings of the life of St Regolo or through incense smoke, up into the rafters of some dark and echoey church. Kate would want to explore, too, on her own if need be: doggedly, with a street plan to hand, she would trudge the narrow thoroughfares in baggy shorts and noisome plimsolls, bright-eyed and flushed with anxiety, her shoulders red with sunburn, chafed by the strap of her bag. Naomi and Elli could meanwhile hang out at some pavement café, sipping Bellinis – what *were* Bellinis, by the way? – admiring the tight little bums of the Italian youths, and no doubt attracting admiration in their turn. It would all seem more vibrant, and so much more pleasurable, if she could share it with people closer, dearer to her.

Glancing down at the terrace beneath the window, Elli saw that Patti was there. The crunchy footsteps had been hers, then. She had dragged a plastic chair up to the balustrade, and sat with her feet propped, among tubs of trailing pink geraniums and miniature lemon trees, nursing a cup of coffee, gazing out at the horizon as wraiths of mist rose up from the valley. She looked cool and rather chic in a dress of pale linen with straps that crossed at the back. But, from above, Elli noted that the woman's roots were growing out, her hair was in urgent need of a retouch.

Her mood of gloom and introspection magically evaporated. She snapped on some Lycra sportswear, lime green and black, then made haste down the solid stairway to the sunless kitchen. There she found hot coffee in the aluminium espresso jug on the gas hob, and tipped the lot into a mug.

In the twin sinks, beakers, salad bowls, plates, a pasta pan awaited a volunteer. The game was to see who would be first to crack; or who hold out against it longest. Just as, in every group, a natural leader is supposed eventually to emerge, so, in theory, should a natural washer-up. But if there was one in their midst, he or she had yet to stand up and be counted. Now, if Kate were here . . . thought Elli for the second time that morning, with the benign contempt which equated in a curious way to affection. With a quick backwards glance, disowning the workload, she went to join the executive editor on the terrace.

The two, with a brief exchange of greetings, sat side by side, their faces offered to the sky, eyes closed against the gradually intensifying glare.

'Blissful, huh?' queried Patti, who, Elli had learned, might be a generous hostess, might keep a good table and ply the company with wine, but sought constant recompense in compliments.

'Mmm,' she conceded off-handedly. No one, but *no one*, told Elaine Sharpe what to say. She did not supply flattery to order. What was she, a parrot, that she should make such meaningless noises on demand? Besides, breathtaking views were all very well, but what could you *do* with them? The more you stared at them, the more they returned you to yourself and desolated you. Reach out for them though you might, you could never quite get a hold of them, you couldn't climb inside them or hug them to you. Then your eyes would smart, and all sorts of unwelcome thoughts about mortality and such would steal in on you. So, withholding her appreciation, she merely remarked with satisfaction, 'Conference this morning. Look-ahead meeting.'

'For those who can't escape it,' Patti, complacent, sighing, confirmed.

They lapsed into a lethargic, not wholly uncompanionable silence, until, ten minutes later, Patti queried, 'If you had just one wish, what would it be? World peace, do you suppose? Or no more cellulite?'

'It's a tough one.' Elli crimped her brow, grimaced as she pondered it, and surreptitiously she stole a glance at Ms Henderson's thigh, or at the small portion of it that was revealed beneath the draped linen.

'No contest in the end, though?' Patti pressed her.

And Elli, reluctant, said she supposed there wasn't.

There followed another moment's silence, as each dwelt on her regret. Shame, they told themselves, about world peace.

Every so often a hazelnut would dissever itself from a nearby tree, skip through the branches and drop on to the grass. A pair of wolfish, yellow-eyed farm dogs made short rushes at the women, to butt them with wet noses. 'Yeeagh!' protested Elli as they trotted, panting, off again. The shaggy lawn was full, she saw, of dog turds, and of ripe hazelnuts smooth as pebbles.

'Yet they say there's no such thing,' said Patti eventually.

'As what?' wondered Elli, sunk in reverie. 'A free lunch?'

'No, cellulite. They would have us believe that it doesn't exist. But we have the evidence of our eyes, don't we?'

'Yes, I believe I have seen the phenomenon. On somebody.'

The capricious wind, changing direction, fanning their faces, brought them, in place of apricots, a sharp, abrasive waft of swimming pool. 'We ought to have a dip,' said Patti vaguely.

'We ought.' But the two women shifted in their seats, only in pursuit of greater comfort. The lads could do their swimming for them, diving competitively, cutting through the water, bombing each other, whooping, declaring how refreshing, how invigorating was that first cold shock to the system.

'The trouble with swimming,' Elli mused, 'is that it means getting wet.'

'That's the worst of it.'

'And one's hair . . .'

'Quite.'

'Not to mention –'

'One's mascara, yes.'

'If they could just invent a dry swimming pool. Some other medium to swim in. Some form of jelly, perhaps? Now, the man who did that –'

'Or the woman.'

'Or the woman, indeed, could make himself, *her*self, a bundle. D'you know, last night I dreamt –'

'You went to Manderley again?'

'Not exactly, no, I dreamt that . . .' But Elli could not somehow bring herself to confide the quaint and unaccountable workings of her subconscious.

'Good morning, campers.' An amorphous shadow in the sitting-room thickened in the doorway. It took shape as Simon Tulley, who, smiling broadly, appeared horribly stuffed with himself. The Tulleys were finding their way already, insidiously, under Elli's skin. They were obviously working all hours to repair their marriage, which on Friday night had looked to be in tatters. In the hot afternoons, heaving with lunch, and with a sly ostentation, they would absent themselves, announcing that they were slipping upstairs for a 'siesta'.

A shag, more like, Elli would tell herself. Smug bastards! Of all four-legged animals, she cared least for the married couple, a prodigious feeder, that had two heads, the better to congratulate itself, and was always to be found in your most comfortable chairs, licking and grooming itself like a cat. How much more gripping it would have been to stand by and watch as this relationship came unstuck. She loathed the Tulleys' mutuality, the way they looked out for one another, each passing the salad first to the other, or filling the other's glass before handing the wine jug down the table. And the idea of a pair so long together, still having sex with one another quite repelled her. If they were any sort of people they would get it on with outsiders, while seeking within marriage more cerebral relations.

'Sleep all right?' asked Patti sweetly, winningly, as well she might of the deputy editor of the *Inquirer* who, rumour had it, was being courted by management for some very senior hiring-and-firing role at the *Globe*.

'Not a wink,' he responded, laughing meaningfully. He was a tall man, borderline fat (biceps, triceps, pectorals struggled to assert themselves through layers of padding), with a baby softness about the cheeks, and deceptively soulful brown eyes, out of which he was continually brushing a lock of fine hair. In his vest top and knee-length shorts, he had something of the lager lout about him, and he was, indeed, famous in the business for his bully-boy tactics.

Tina was tall and slim, with dark hair almost to her waist, which she threw about a great deal and wore caught up with plastic grips, with velvet rosettes, and – lately – adorned with wilting sprays of oleander. She cultivated the look of a flamenco dancer, and had developed an exaggerated, sway-hipped walk which made Elli want to shout with sheer derision. Tina and Patti had worked together in the past, on *Mia* magazine, they went way, way back and loved to hash over old times in an excluding fashion.

'Any plans for today?' Simon wanted to know.

'Maybe we should have lunch out,' offered Elli, mindful of the crockery crisis (unless they infest a local restaurant, someone would have to clear the sink, to free up a few plates and glasses, before the day was out).

No one, however, took up the suggestion. It was too soon to make plans.

Instead, 'Who's being Elli Sharpe,' Simon asked her – and did she detect a faint note of sarcasm? – 'while Elli Sharpe is being the life and soul of this party?'

'You won't have heard of her,' revealed Elli, signalling her indifference with a yawn. 'Some little pipsqueak from features,' she added confidingly. 'Barely out of school. Wants to be a journalist when she grows up.' She'd had no say in the choice of her stand-in, whose function, as she saw it, was merely to fill space till she returned. (A small italic footnote would reassure her public: she was on holiday, but she would be back.)

'Dawn Hancock,' supplied Patti more helpfully.

Hancock's half-hour, Elli reflected wryly. This Dawn could enjoy thirty minutes of fame, which was twice as long as Andy Warhol had predicted for the nobodies of this world, and was doubtless thirty minutes more than the girl merited.

But Simon was nodding as if the name actually signified something. 'Won the talent prize in *Mia* a couple of years ago, as I don't need to remind you, Patti. Tina speaks very highly of her.'

'Oh, yes, I am aware.' Simpering, Patti smoothed her skirt over her knees. 'I brought her to the paper. She's sort of a protégée of mine.'

Elli stared very hard through slitty eyes at the sun, which seemed to be inordinately slow, today, to climb over the yard-arm. Her thoughts turned to the fridge, where the home-grown yellow wine was chilling, and she wondered at what time one could decently propose a draught of the rank yet strangely moreish vintage. Checking her watch she saw that it was not quite ten. Just nine o'clock in England. She had better sit tight.

Presently, they would all stagger up to the poolside, then someone was sure to summon refreshment. These were her kind of people, after all. She was among her own.

Odd, though, that she made better sense of them at home in London; she saw the point of them more there. At the office, or around town, in the Groucho Club, at glitzy press preview nights and other media bashes, they belonged. Here, against this foreign background, they appeared mysteriously alien. And they had such poor mouths. They all drew fat salaries, they were well paid on any scale, they were wealthy, yet they seemed to see themselves, variously, as hard-up and hard-done-by. She, who had been brought up in something like penury, and who these days considered herself rich as Croesus, would listen to their plaints appalled, uncomprehending.

'So when does Garvey make his entrance?' Simon queried.

'David? In a couple of days. He'll phone me with an ETA, and I'll drive over to pick him up in the Tipo.'

'I look forward to seeing the old reprobate. We are, after all, to be close colleagues.'

'Yes, I look forward to it, too,' agreed Patti, and with an ingenuous, girlish gesture she took up the hem of her skirt and flurried it. '*I* look forward to seeing him very much.'

Elli turned away. She put up a hand like an open door to screen her face. She had to. She simply could not watch. Nor dared she show her pained reaction. She looked as she had looked in her Class War period, when a policeman's horse had stood on her toe (an event now misremembered as the day she hauled one of those lackeys of Capitalism clean out of the saddle). Her mouth opened wider, wider in a silent scream.

Then, turning back, smiling coolly, she said with a kind of charged nonchalance, 'David Garvey? Ah, yes. I know the family well. His sister, and his former wife, the mother of his son, are my best friends.'

Juin Sharpe was happier than she had thought she could ever be again. She had a deep, abstruse sense of contentment, an unfathomable calm that even the infantile Lucy, with whom she must share a bedroom, could not disturb. She felt as she had done as a little girl when, convalescing from one of the more virulent childhood illnesses, weak but no longer desperately poorly, she had seen a softer, more caring side to her mother – albeit strictly temporary, conditional upon her running a temperature and looking pinched. She had a sense of spiritual nurture. She felt as if she had survived a long ordeal, and that now some superhuman agency was ministering to her soul, nursing her back to psychological health.

She would probably never love again for as long as she lived. She would certainly never marry. She would devote herself instead to good works; in a quiet and unassuming way she would serve her fellows. Her existence would not, after all, be for nothing. And, in the meantime, against her expectations, she was rather enjoying her holiday.

They had set off in the Rover very early on Friday, Juin wedged in the back between Lucy and Dominic, with Muffy swaying on her lap (first her left thigh, then her right, would be imprinted with the pressure of a rubbery paw). At Newport Pagnell, where they'd stopped for coffee and what Geraldine called 'a bite', Dominic had chivalrously offered to change places with her, and they had travelled thus, with Muffy excitedly misting the window, all the way to Knutsford. There Dominic, pleading cramp, had swapped with a very grudging Lucy, and they had pressed on as far as Forton services, where Geraldine, declaring she could stand no more of her children's incessant bickering, or of Muffy slavering down her neck, had ordered Juin into the front, and placed herself, like a great bulwark, between her troublesome offspring.

This, then, was family, a four-square arrangement, strange to someone such as Juin, who was used to an altogether more fluid set-up.

In Lancashire, the traffic had begun to thin. In Cumbria it had strung out ever looser. And as they crossed the border into Scotland, Juin had understood for the first time what was meant by 'the open road'.

She had been unprepared for the beauty of the scenery (those shortbread tins had really undersold the country), or for the luminous quality of the light, so slow to die at the end of the northern day. Nor had she for one instant envisaged such an enchanting destination.

Waverley was a slate-roofed, whitewashed house, which stood with a sort of stubborn dignity, quite alone on the clifftop, with its own rugged, graduated path running down to the deserted beach. A low wall, yellow with lichen, marked out the property boundaries, but little otherwise distinguished its garden from the surrounding acres of spongy turf, sea campion, scurvy grass and thrift. A squeaking gate, twice as tall as the wall, its green paint splintering, made a pointless statement about territory. Beyond it, a shell rockery had at some time been begun and soon abandoned. Nothing had been planted here in decades, but there must have drifted in over the years the seeds of other people's plantings. Thus tree mallow. Thus, too, perhaps, great cabbage-looking, leathery foliage. In a brick lean-to, rotting deckchairs, shreds of canvas on rickety wood frames, were home to colonies of tiny spiders.

The interior of the house was sparsely furnished, with austere wooden pieces built to withstand the depredations of the paying guests. Waxed floorboards, scrubbed quarry tiles, and plain, hard-wearing fabrics set the tone. In the kitchen and the old-fashioned scullery, in a semi-basement, there was the dank, sly smell of mushrooms. But the seaward windows, if you stood off from them, seemed filled with nothing but sky.

Juin, sleepless, at night, would listen as the tide came and went, as the waves sighed over the shore and wrapped themselves around the cliff foot, before the ocean gathered them back in.

I shall send a postcard to Downside, she resolved this Monday morning, lying with the sheet drawn up to her chin. She would stroll along the coast road to the village post office and general store, to choose from the wire rack a suitably pleasing representation of this particular corner of paradise. She would sit on the bench in front of the shop, pen a friendly message, care of Mrs Southgate, and pop it in the pillar box. She only wished there was a way to take something of Waverley back with her to share it with her ladies, Mabel Flowers and Vera Salter, Miss Chitty and Miss Armitage . . .

Hearing in the kitchen below a low murmur of voices, the resonant clang of a cast-iron pan on the Rayburn, its echo in the chimney all up the metal flue, she supposed she must stir herself. The Gorsts sat down to breakfast together, a novelty which Juin would learn in time to enjoy. So often at home she ate with a plate balanced on her knee, with no one but Muffy and the television for company. Soon, frying bacon made itself known to her, it came in whispering temptation, and she renewed her solemn vow to resist it.

Perverse, Elli had called Juin's decision, reached on the very eve of her departure, to become a vegetarian (not a morsel of meat would pass her lips from that day forth). 'You're just being awkward,' she'd accused. 'Am I to worry about you every waking minute in Italy, for fear you're being a trial to Geraldine? How very typical, how thoroughly selfish of you!' But the resolution had not been so lightly taken, and was consistent with Juin's new philosophy. For how could she be sure she would not herself, in spite of her best efforts, her proposed good works, come back next time as a Tamworth, or a Middle White, or a Gloucester Old Spot, to be salted and sliced into so many rashers? Meanwhile, given their attitudes, there was surely more than an outside chance that Elli, say, or Trevor, or whoever, would be reincarnated as an Aberdeen Angus and end up portioned and packaged in polystyrene in a supermarket chiller.

Anyway, Geraldine's disfavour, on hearing over supper on Friday that Juin had forsworn animal products, was as nothing compared with her distaste for the gold sleeper in the girl's nostril. Something in the nature of a Gloucester Old Spot she had evoked. Pigs, she had said witheringly, wore rings through their noses. Pigs, and primitive peoples who could not be expected to know better.

'My next piercing,' Juin had announced, unabashed, helping herself to a slice of bread, 'is going to be through my belly-button. When I can afford it.'

'I should like to see that,' had been Dominic's response.

Oh, Dominic Gorst was a pain! He really got on her tits sometimes, with his never-ending kidding around.

Throwing back the sheet, Juin slithered out of bed and went to the window, to stand there in her nightie on the sun-warmed bare boards, in a pool of pale light.

On the beach, way below, she saw Dominic cavorting with Muffy, the pair of them appearing scarcely earth-bound – they might be capable, perhaps, of short, ungainly flight.

As she watched, Dominic sprinted into the sea, sending up a diffusion of watery sparks, diving into the breakers – she almost gasped to imagine the icy clutch of the water – while Muffy, delirious, hounded the mischievous wavelets off the sand.

Seeing her dog so waggy, so barky, she felt choked with emotion. She prised Lucy's Garfield, her hideous stuffed cat, off the window, and held his suckered feet over her swollen heart.

'Juin?' asked a voice behind her, thick with sleep.

'Oh, Lucy!' Smartly, Juin passed off her faint embarrassment as irritation. 'Stupid soft toys. You're too old for them,' she scorned, turning abruptly, discarding ghastly Garfield, dashing him to the floor.

'He's my mascot, if you must know,' Lucy retorted hotly. Her hair was hooked behind her ears, her face looked sort of blurred, and one cheek bore the criss-cross pattern of a creased pillowcase, creating the illusion that she was on the brink of tears.

Juin, affected by the sight of her, at once regretted her outburst. 'Fair enough,' she allowed.

Stooping, she retrieved the orange-striped cat, dusted him gratuitously and tossed him to Lucy, who caught him and bestowed upon his head a perfunctory, proprietorial kiss. 'He brings me luck,' she explained glibly.

'I see.'

'Juin?'

'Yes, Lucy.'

'What is French kissing, exactly?'

'We-ell . . . It's a kind of snogging, I suppose, when a guy pushes his tongue into your mouth. And vice versa.'

'Is that all?'

'That's all. What else should there be? Though it's more than it sounds, in a way. I say . . .' Juin assumed a bossy, big-sister attitude. She took upon herself responsibility. 'I trust you're not thinking of trying it.

Because, you know, you're far too young for that sort of thing. I doubt that you have the maturity to handle it.'

'Oh, no,' Lucy was quick to assure her.

'No?'

'No.' Lucy drew the sheet up right over her face and sighed gustily into it. The cotton fabric billowed, then, settling, moulded itself to her features. 'I just needed to know, you see,' she confided through it. 'Because a couple of the girls at school were going on about it. And they said, "Oh, *she* won't have a clue what we're talking about." Meaning me. So I said of course I knew, I'd done it loads of times. But I'm not sure if they believed me.'

'Ah, right.'

'And what's a love bite?' Lucy threw back the sheet. She leaned half out of bed after information.

'What it says, more or less. If you ever see somebody with a mark on her neck, like a bruise, that will probably be one. They're made by sort of biting and sucking. They say you can get rid of them by combing them. Otherwise, you can disguise them with make-up. Or wear a scarf.'

'Have you ever had one?'

'Maybe.'

'Does it hurt?'

'Not so as you'd notice when you're carried away.'

'You don't mind me asking, do you? Only I can't consult my mum about it.'

'You should try consulting *my* mum,' Juin told her drily. 'She'd give you chapter and verse. All you ever wanted to know about sex but were afraid to ask.'

'And have you ever gone . . . all the way?'

'Mind your own business,' Juin snapped, and crossing

hand over hand, taking her nightie by the hem, she inverted it over her head.

Cripes, thought Lucy, with a *frisson* of horror, transfixed by the sight of small, hard breasts, a tiny waist, a neat, dark triangle of pubic hair, I hope she's not a lesbian! It occurred to her that Juin looked a bit like . . . well, *one of those*.

'Are you going to lie there all day?' Juin chivvied her. 'We'll be late for breakfast.'

'Yes. No. I'm sorry if I said the wrong thing just now.'

'No worries.'

'I feel such a fool sometimes. So naïve. Because we have sex education lessons, they've told us how babies are conceived, how not to get AIDS, but they don't even mention all the really important stuff. And Sarah Brooke and Jacintha Ainsley put on such airs, as if they were a cut above, because they've both got boyfriends, and Sarah Brooke is going steady.'

'If I were you,' Juin told her kindly, lightly, truthfully, 'I should tell Sarah Brooke and Jacintha Ainsley to take a flying fuck. Now, any more questions?'

'No.'

'Good. Because –' Juin wrapped herself sarong-fashion in a towel, rolling it, securing it above her left breast – 'I want to go to the bathroom.'

She was halfway through the door when she heard 'Except . . .'

'Yes, Lucy?'

'Except, I just wondered . . .' Lucy ventured. 'What's a flying fuck?'

*

283

Dominic Gorst lay breathless, panting from his swim and from his scramble up the cliff steps, with his head among the stalky wild cabbages, the shells of the aborted rockery, just inside the little garden wall, and felt the blessing of the sun upon him. Through half-closed eyes he watched the papery flight of a dozen tiny skipper butterflies. He had a keen sense of his own physique, bronzed and fit. He loved himself mightily at that moment. And his lascivious smile ran almost into his ears as he remembered how, there in the window right above him, for a tantalising few seconds, Juin Sharpe had appeared to him, absolutely starkers. Juin Sharpe who, with her slight, white, boyish, eminently bonkable body, was going, if he had his way, to make his holiday for him.

Vegetarianism? Faddy nonsense. The little madam was simply showing off. Eleanor Garvey said as much as she stood over the stove and jabbed with a fork at the crimping bacon. She had arrived on Saturday, under her own steam, in her Mercedes cabriolet. She wore a pair of stiff white shorts with an Aertex top. Her dyed hair, which she called *rousse*, was held back with a wide, elasticated band, so tightly that it seemed to drag on the skin at her temples, and at the outer corners of her eyes. She did very well for seventy, so everybody told her, and there was this assumption, somehow, in her carriage. Yet, it might have been more true to say that seventy did well for her. It was as if she had been building all her life to it; she had reached the acme of self-assurance, she fancied herself unassailable. She looked, thought Dominic – who was making it his project to assail her –

like a founder member of the Women's League of Health and Beauty (health division).

'She's taking a principled stand,' he said smoothly, sauntering through the back door, damp and glistening, with his fringe plastered to his brow. 'We should respect it.'

For reply, Eleanor made the same repressive tssssing noise she made at people's cats and dogs if they were foolish enough to venture near her.

'It's a bit of a nuisance,' put in Geraldine, doing a fine demolition job with a blunt breadknife on a cottage loaf, 'to be asked to cater for special needs.' Having lost control of the kitchen to her mother, she betrayed her upset by her querulous undertone, and she dabbed at her brow with the back of one limp wrist.

'But you're *not* being asked to,' Dominic reminded her. 'She'll just eat veg, she said. And potatoes, rice, whatever. Take her at her word, why don't you? She can be responsible for her own nutrition. She'll survive.'

'To go home skinny as a rake. Then I shall have Elli on my back, accusing me of starving her foolish daughter, if you please!' Geraldine anticipated this injustice with powerful indignation. 'It's not fair. It really isn't.'

'It's just for two weeks. She won't waste away. And it's her choice, isn't it?'

'Dominic, I do believe you take the girl's part simply to antagonise me. Now, please put some clothes on. I won't have you sit down to breakfast half undressed.'

'Throw us that T-shirt, then, will you? From the back of the chair. That's the one.'

'She'll have an egg, at least. A fresh farm egg,' declared Eleanor emphatically, breaking one into the pan.

'No she won't,' contradicted Dominic with equal emphasis. 'She's made that clear – not even eggs.'

'Then I dare say,' Eleanor sniffed, 'you can manage two of them, a growing boy like you.'

'No. One egg for me.'

'Hello,' said Juin meekly, peering round the door at them. 'Where's Muffy?'

Dominic indicated, with a sideways jerk of the head, the scullery door. 'Out there drying off. He . . . well, let's just say he's no rose garden. In high heaven, even as we speak, celestial noses must be twitching.'

'That's my boy!' she smiled adoringly and came right on in.

'Yes, he pongs something terrible. Why do you call him Muffy?'

'Well, it's Muffin, really, of course.' Juin drew out a chair and sat primly beside Dominic with her hands on her knees. Not that she would have chosen to sit next to him. Who, given the option, would put herself within groping range of such a randy devil? But, in the short time she'd been here – for such were the arcane workings of this thing called family – it had somehow been designated 'her' place. Geraldine and Lucy would station themselves opposite, and Eleanor would take the seat at the head of the table which would have been John's. 'Muffin the Mule,' she added incomprehensibly.

'I was just saying, Juin,' Eleanor turned from the stove to threaten her with the spatula, 'that you will have an egg.'

'No, just bread and marmalade, thanks very much.'

'Tsssss. And where is my lazy lump of a grand-daughter?'

'Lucy's on her way.'

'Then we shall start without her. She'll have no one but herself to blame if there's nothing left. Not that it would hurt her to miss breakfast. She's becoming quite a lump. We can no longer speak of "puppy fat", I fear.'

'She won't be a mo,' promised Juin. And then, protectively, 'You shouldn't get on to her about weight. You'll give her a complex. That's where eating disorders start. Should I pour the tea or something, to be useful? Who wants a cup?'

Eleanor Garvey handed round plates of bacon, egg and fried tomatoes. Juin would have loved tomatoes. She retained Dominic's plate for a second, held it under her nose and considered them wistfully, before relinquishing it to him, supposing that they must be part of the breakfast package, the bacon-and-egg deal, which you took or you left.

'I expect,' said Eleanor in a provoking way, sitting down and snatching up her cutlery, 'that Dominic can't wait to get his first car?'

'I guess I shall have to,' said Dominic indifferently, 'since I have no means of affording one. Would you like these tomatoes, Juin? I don't go for them myself.'

'Perhaps you are hoping that your grandad will buy one for you?' His grandmother affected a bantering tone, but the light in her eye was more hard gleam than twinkle.

'It hadn't occurred to me, to be honest.'

'Just as well. Because we are not, after all, made of money. Young people today expect, don't they, to have whatever they want, *whenever*? Instant gratification, hmm?'

'Oh, I can wait for things – when I must,' Dominic assured her, with an oblique smirk at Juin, who started visibly when she felt his fingers, under cover of the gingham tablecloth, brush her bare thigh. 'So long as those things are worth waiting for.'

'I must say, I'm glad to hear it. Work hard, that's the way, and you'll be able to afford the luxuries. I dare say you're ambitious to become a journalist like your uncle?'

'I don't think so.' Dominic dismissed the notion. 'I'm more interested in computer sciences.'

'David has a lap-top, he tells me. Please pass the pepper. And you, young lady. What do you propose to do with yourself when you leave school?'

Juin thought she disliked being called young lady more even than a stirring shitbag of a blabbermouth toad. She shut her eyes for an instant and had a vision of the teeming, boiling sea. 'I shall be a marine biologist,' she responded smartly, setting aside for the moment her more philanthropic aspirations, and washing the lie down with a swig of tea.

'Oh, my *dear*!' Eleanor laughed nastily and raised a tweezed eyebrow. Marine biology was not a field for girlies, she conveyed.

'Like Rachel Carson,' prompted Dominic.

'What say?' demanded Eleanor.

'Rachel Carson. She was a marine biologist in Maryland. A great environmentalist. She studied the way pesticides ended up in our rivers and oceans. She was responsible for the banning of DDT in the States.'

'Well, la-di-da.' Eleanor, ruffled, speared her fried egg

288

so the yolk ran. 'I thought we were here for a quiet breakfast, not to play *Mastermind*.'

'But environmental issues really matter, Granny. The future of the planet is in our hands.'

'Tssss. This planet was around for a good many years before you were born, my lad.'

'About four and a half billion, would you say?'

'And, never fear, it will be around for a good many years after you're gone.'

'They say it all started with a big bang. That must have been quite a bang, eh, Juin?'

Eleanor made a tidy little mouth. She warned her daughter with a frown. Nothing must be made of this. Neither of them must rise to it. Such fourth-form humour was on no account to be acknowledged.

'Oh dear,' said Geraldine, distractedly, to herself.

Juin and Dominic lay on the beach, side by side like a pair of kippers, propped on their elbows, with their toes pointing out to sea, Juin dressed in a tiny black bikini.

He said lazily, affably, 'I suppose a blow job is out of the question?'

She said, 'You suppose right.'

'Well, I merely ask.' He rolled away from her, on to his back, flung his arms wide. 'No harm in asking, is there?'

'Except that a smack in the mouth might offend.'

'Don't be like that, now, Juin.'

'I'm not being like anything,' she assured him, which in fact she wasn't, she was being like nothing but herself. Then, 'It was funny,' she said, rather loudly, distinctly, changing the subject, 'your knowing about that woman.'

'What woman?' He sat up abruptly, shoved his hand under his nose, made the tortured face of someone who is about to sneeze – then didn't.

'Ruth Carson, was it?'

'Rachel Carson. Well,' he deprecated with unfeigned modesty, for it was only the truth, 'one does pick up the odd scrap. It's serendipity or something. One happens upon a piece of info, and pockets it in case it comes in useful.'

'It settled your grandmother's hash.'

'For the time being. Ohmygod.' The sneeze, which had been there all along, awaiting its moment, came through him like an express train.

'Bless you,' offered Juin routinely. 'You know, I don't think I like her very much.'

'Like her? You're not supposed to *like* her. She was not put on this earth to be liked. She was sent to try us. And as for settling her hash, don't kid yourself that it will stay settled. Constant vigilance, we need, around her. Never give her an inch, that's my advice. Have you got a tissue on you?'

'No.'

'Never mind. It's not an emergency.' He sniffed experimentally, wrinkled his nose, came down beside her, propped himself on his elbows once again.

'I bet you'd not refuse me if I were my sainted cousin?' he remarked after a minute, with an uncharacteristic trace of bitterness, goading her, or himself. 'You'd be all over me, then, like a suntan.'

'Who?' she demanded angrily, burrowing her fingers

in the gritty sand to prevent herself from tearing into him, or from thumping him hard on the back.

'Why, the esteemed Alex Garvey. Because I seem to have heard that you carry a torch for him.'

'Oh, you seem to, do you? And who precisely seems to be your source in the matter?'

'I had it from my mother, who had it from yours. That is, I chanced to overhear –'

'She wouldn't,' Juin protested, screwing up her eyes, feeling suddenly hollowed. 'She wouldn't say such a thing. And if she did, she was lying. What would *she* know, anyway? No one in their right mind confides in my mother.'

'Then you don't have the hots for him?'

'For Alex?' she dispatched the suggestion, sent it on its way with a snort. 'I hadn't given it any thought. He's all right, I suppose. At least he has manners.'

'He also has Naomi Markham.'

'So he does,' conceded Juin wearily, and now she put her face down in the sand. It was all coming back, the pain, the disappointment. Her heart ached and ached.

'Tell me, then. What has he got that I haven't? Apart from manners, I mean.'

'Where should I start?'

'Because I am, underneath, you know, a perfectly beezer sort of bloke.'

'I shall take your word for it.'

But Alex, she thought, is never brash or coarse. He doesn't swagger about. He's beautiful and humorous and sensitive and strong. If I look into his eyes, I am utterly lost. How could I have believed that I was over him? I'm afraid I shall die for love of him.

'Mind you,' offered Dominic, sensing her desolation, concerned that he had gone too far, setting aside his own self-interest, 'I have a feeling your mother was a bit bevvied up at the time. In her cups.'

'When is she ever out of them?'

'So it could have been the drink talking?'

'That's what it will have been, then. The drink.'

'Hey, but you should have seen my old man the other week, lit up like a Christmas tree.' He laughed aloud at the memory.

'What, *John*?' she replied dully. 'John *drunk*? I don't believe you.'

'No word of a lie. He came home pissed as a pudding, danced in the moonlight with a garland of pork sausages round his neck. Went up several notches in *my* estimation, but Mama was less than pleased with his performance. She said she'd never live it down.'

'Dominic?'

'Juin, old thing?'

'I was wondering . . .' He was, after all, a boy, a man, although of a very different cast from Alex Garvey. Perhaps, then, he could explain to her the inexplicable. 'What do *you* reckon to Naomi Markham?'

But, 'Naomi?' was all he said, in his unserious manner. 'I shouldn't kick her out of bed, I'll tell you that. I mean, she's one tast—— Oh, look. Ay-oop. Here comes goosey Lucy. Couldn't you just ravage me a bit, Juin Sharpe? Try to have your evil way with me? I have my reputation to consider.'

*

The serial small cups of black coffee he had swigged, the sandwiches – dainty triangles of cucumber and smoked salmon – of which he'd made short work, had done nothing to settle his mind or his stomach. He sat sprawled in the VIP lounge, waiting, waiting, yawning wolfishly, spreading his long legs, in the grip of numbers of emotions, some more agreeable than others.

He felt muzzy for lack of sleep. He was sorry, although not *that* sorry, about Kirstin, who had had a radiant smile for everyone last evening – in all corners of the room she had been witty and social, laughter had sprung up around her like so many fountains among the palm fronds, she had never looked more vital or more beautiful – then had sobbed all night in the bathroom, trumpeting her sorrows into shreds of tissue, and in the early hours, recriminating bitterly, had thrown punches. He was still a little drunk on champagne and adulation, following his quite spectacular send-off, but his hangover had more to do with bruised ribs and drowned sensibilities than with those particular excesses.

He had dragged himself from his bed at eight, and in less than four hours he would touch down in London, where late afternoon would feel like midday. Funny old business, time.

Around the globe, nations basked in the delusions of sunrise and sunset. But David Garvey knew better: he knew that the earth was a wonky sphere, pirouetting madly around an indifferent yellow dwarf star; he knew that the sun neither rose nor set, that these were merely

293

reassuring fictions for a human race enslaved to circadian rhythms.

From single-cell organisms up, all life danced to the sun's tune. Mindless protoplasm went spiralling after the light. Cockroaches got busy after dark. In a solar eclipse birds fell in confusion from the blackened sky. And here was the funny part: the sun couldn't give a bugger. It was, in this sense, a planet after his own heart, for around David Garvey spiralled, scuttled, plummeted that life form known as Woman.

He liked to think of night and day as choices that one made (both were there to be had whenever; they might be visited, like restaurants, at a price). But he supposed he could not rationalise jet lag out of existence, and it was with some despondency that he anticipated the disengagement of environmental cues and biological function, the persistent sleep disturbance, bad dreams, bone-weariness, moodiness, loss of appetite that were such a feature of an eastward journey, and might be his lot for several days.

Also – tell no one this – he was scared shitless. But that was fine, it was half the fun of flying. Thus with delicious dread he waited to be bing-bonged. He always insisted upon Concorde, so swift, so prestigious, for he believed in making his employers pay. On the last flight out, cramped under a blanket in the deserted back row, he and a bored brunette with androgynous body and long, lascivious upper lip, the daughter of an oil billionaire, had joined the Mach Two Club, he had made her come at twice the speed of sound.

But the take-off was better, even, than sex. That great

silver speedbird thundering down the runway, the engine roar, the sudden exhilarating boost as it hurtled skyward. . . . This was the most exciting thing he knew. Planes were fine by him on the way up; it was in the coming down that it could all go so horribly wrong.

His thoughts turned more comfortably to home in Notting Hill, to an elegant, book-lined, first-floor flat, in a tall, white house, which gazed narcissistically through sash windows at its mirror image across a garden square. In this flat, he felt sure, at his desk under the window, on peaceful Sunday afternoons, The Novel would at last come into being.

A few days there to readjust, a week or so in Italy, in the company of that hellhag Henderson (he used the term with affection; he thought well enough of the silly cow) and of assorted gargoyles from the national press, blots, all of them, on the Fleet Street escutcheon, and he would feel like a new man.

Or, David being David, like a new woman.

Aboard the plane, where he was ministered to by stewardesses of long experience with deeply etched smiles, he took from his pocket, to amuse himself, a letter from his sister. She looked forward to seeing him, she counted the hours. John, too, and the children, Lucy, Dominic, were beside themselves. In September he must spend a weekend. Meanwhile, she ought to warn him of hypoxia, a grave condition afflicting heavy drinkers who indulged their habit while airborne. In its mild form, hypoxia mimicked intoxication, it was characterised by feelings of euphoria, mental impairment and poor co-ordination. The lips, nail beds and earlobes might then all turn blue and oxygen would have to be administered.

Well, there had been little wrong, as he recalled, with his mental processes last time aboard, or with his co-ordination. His nose and earlobes had been pinker than pink. The billionaire's daughter would surely drink to that!

So he bit into a friable caviare canapé, and when vintage champagne was offered, never mind hypoxia, he didn't say no.

Naomi Markham had been doing it by the book. Well, she had to, really. There was no question of improvising, since cooking was to her an esoteric business, a recipe was as mystical, as powerful as a magic spell, and without a colour picture she had simply no idea how things might turn out.

When she slipped her hands into the heat-proof gloves, squatted before the oven and drew the dish towards her on the metal shelf, she felt just like a housewife in a television commercial. But whereas in commercials, smiling, competent housewives with not a hair out of place, offered to camera their culinary and orthodontic triumphs, she would not have cared to share with the nation her Catalonian macaroni or her pained grimace. She was sure it was wrong – but *how* wrong, and why wrong, she could not tell. It looked very dry, very stuck-on, somehow, with none of the plumpness or gloss that the photograph promised.

I can't do *anything*, she told herself, defeated. I can't *do* anything. I am completely and utterly useless.

And where was Alex? Trust him to be late, when she had gone to such trouble. She supposed he must be in the pub. Now and then, after work, he would go with his partner for a swift pint and a chat in the Angel. It was a small satisfaction at the end of the day, which she knew she should not begrudge him. Grudges, however, came not from the head but from the pit of oneself, from somewhere not altogether nice or worthy, they rose up uninvited, insisting.

She was hot and flustered from her efforts, stifled by the weather. Although the window stood open, there was no resuscitating breeze, no exchange of air, no kiss of life between garden and house, no stirring in the leaves, which just hung there limp on the twig.

Nowhere more than in the domestic situation did her lack of self-confidence show itself. She made constant reference to instructions on cans, packages, detergent boxes, aerosols and squeezy bottles, she followed menu plans to the letter, deferred in all matters to a higher authority, measured everything as indicated, a spoonful here, a capful there, approaching each new task with profound misgivings, trusting not at all to instinct. Prescribed water temperatures, the precise size of carrot dice preoccupied her. Was she the only person ever to have used an actual matchstick as a guide when slicing courgettes into julienne?

Then, when nothing quite worked as it was supposed to work, when the sink blossomed with suds, and dresses shrank to doll proportions, and soufflés went splat, she reproached herself, not for being too slavish, or for want of nous, but for her failure to follow, in some minute detail, the stated directions.

All this had so paralysing an effect upon her that the mere making of a pot of tea became a protracted and nerve-racking process. Thus, Catalonian macaroni had been no small endeavour.

She took a tablespoon from the drawer, broke through the blackened *gratin* crust, which belched out aromatic steam, and dug around among the pasta tubes. Some were baked hard, but at the bottom of the dish she found a sloppy mess. It wasn't fair to blame Alex, whose lateness hadn't been a factor, but she blamed him anyway. She rehearsed the gentle chiding with which she meant to greet him, the words of mild reproof which could not be called 'nagging' (a certain placability, a forgiving would be implicit in her tone). He would tell her, then, that he was sorry. Denouncing himself as an inconsiderate brute, he would bundle her in his arms and offer consolations. Simply to hear these sentiments expressed, to have him make up to her in this way, to put himself in the wrong would soothe her.

In rather too many of Naomi's inner dialogues, people were heard to grovel and abase themselves, confessing to the dreadful wrong they'd done her. If she had a single message for the world, it was: 'Apologise!' But the people who truly owed her – her father, her mother, Uncle Huw – were not given to contrition, and it was left to the nice guys such as Alex to try to make amends.

Despairing of the macaroni, and of her young lover, who should have been there when she needed him, she went and ran herself a bath, scented it with lemon oil, swept up her hair and pinned it randomly, then lowered herself gratefully into the warm water.

There Alex found her, half an hour later, by which time she had taken on the stupefied aspect of an overtired child who has been too long in front of the television. Despite the ceaseless whining of the fan, the tiny bathroom was awash with steam, which, condensing, ran in rivulets down the cold, hard, tiled and mirrored surfaces. 'What happened to you?' she asked groggily, clutching at her hair, which was escaping in tendrils from its grip and clip restraints. 'Did you go drinking with Peter, or what?'

The expression 'to go drinking' irritated him, perhaps irrationally, for it seemed to make alcohol too much his motive. He had not, in any case, been to the pub.

'Nothing happened to me,' he said shortly, and, sitting down heavily on the side of the bath, he dabbled his hands in a manner which she, in turn, resented. She would have welcomed the whole of him in there with her, she would have smiled as he stripped off his shirt, his jeans, would have eased over, brought her knees up to accommodate him, but there was something impersonal, even lavatorial about this distracted rinsing. Then, though he looked at her, his eyes made insultingly little of her, as if his thoughts were quite elsewhere. And the rogue phrase suggested itself to her: 'He is washing his hands of me.'

'What's the matter?' she asked anxiously, chasing an elusive bar of soap which darted from her grasp. 'What kept you?' Then, before she could check the words or disguise the sentiment behind them, she added with no hint of placability, 'I made a meal, but I'm afraid it's spoiled.'

'I went to Tooting.' He stood up and showed her his broad back, his faded blue shirt blousing from his narrow waistband. With his fingertips he made a window in the misted mirror: an unfamiliar Alex Garvey glared in through it at the two of them.

Naomi slid down in the tub as if to conceal more of herself, to submerge her knees, her breasts, all the islands of flesh and bone. 'How was Kate?' she asked meekly.

'She wasn't there,' said the cold, cross Alex in the glass before he faded.

'Will you hand me a towel? Thank you, darling.'

Swathed, covered, she felt able to stand up to him, and, when he turned again to face her, addressed herself to his shirt pocket, 'What, then?' she wanted to know.

'Then . . .' He put one arm about her and, careless of her dampness, drew her to him. The buttons of his shirt pressed into her cheek. She heard the shuddery progress in and out of his breath. 'I thought I would say hello, and while I was there, pick up a few more of my things.'

'But she wasn't in. So-o . . . ?' Naomi queried, tweaking, fussing at his sleeve.

'She was out. No problem. I would see her another time. And I had my key, after all. I could let myself in. Except . . .'

'Mmm?'

'Well, except, Naomi, she's only gone and changed the locks.'

'She *hasn't*?' A cheap stunt, Naomi thought this. A

low, miserable, vengeful gesture. And her mind ran on to the day when Kate would repent ('I was so wrong, I was jealous, please don't hold it against me, tell me we can still be friends').

'It's just not like her, you see. Well, you know as well as I do, it isn't in her nature to . . . I'm afraid she has been affected rather badly – worse even than I had supposed – by you and me.'

'So what are you saying?' she demanded of his breathing, buttoned shirt front. 'You want to go back home to Mummy?' And she spun herself angrily out of his embrace.

After a minute he followed her into the bedroom, where she stood about, at a loss, half dressed – or, half undressed, as it appeared to him – tearful, dishevelled, *en déshabillé*. And if, for one moment there, he hadn't loved her, he loved her now the more. 'Come here, silly,' he said to her with tenderness.

'Leave me alone,' she protested weakly, fumbling with a fastening on a blouse the colour of jade which, stealing something of her pallor, made her paler yet. She had the pellucid quality of something merely imagined; he felt if he reached for her his grasp might close on thin air.

'Let me.' He made a beckoning motion, curling his fingers repeatedly into his palm. 'Come.'

All the resistance she could marshal did not amount to any sort of stand. When he caught her wrist, tugged it and, liking the substance of it, tugged again, she wilted on to the bed. It seemed to her – but this must be illusion – that the light dimmed suddenly; corners seemed blurred, hard edges indistinct. Even his features, always so strong, seemed to lose something of their definition. 'It was never going to be easy,' he told her, showing her his whole self in his face as he insinuated a hand, determinedly, not indecorously, under the jade silk fabric to caress her small, unfettered breast.

'I know. Of course I know.' She closed her eyes and rolled her head first this way then that. Her wet hair whipped about her shoulders in pretty coils.

When she lay back, revealing her long waist, he swooped to kiss her just below her ribs until she stretched and bowed her back with pleasure. 'I shall never stop wanting you,' he said with certainty. And he sort of creaked down on to her, his muscles jibbing with the fear of extinguishing her, so much an airy notion did he still feel her to be.

'Nor I you,' she responded ardently.

'Then kiss me. Kiss me properly.' But his mind was straying, he was full of hurt, he made love without his habitual langour, urgently, absently, so that she felt cheated in a fashion.

'I wish you wouldn't cry so much. You make me feel hopeless.'

'I don't mean to, Alex. I can't help it. It's all going wrong.'

'No it isn't,' he told her patiently, knowing nothing of Catalonian macaroni, or of what it betokened.

'It's not your fault,' she responded bleakly. 'It's me.' And she thought, No, it's Kate. *She* has done this. Who would have thought . . .? But, after all, how very clever she is.

*

In the dry heat of the greenhouse, Kate worked methodically, unhurriedly, oblivious of time. She wore a sleeveless white blouse with rickrack trim, an Oxfam shop find, over denim shorts (a pair of jeans, sheared off and fraying above her knees). Her feet on the beaten earth floor were bare and dusty. Her wayward hair, for want of cutting, reached nearly to her shoulders.

All up the sides and under the pitched roof of this aged and neglected glass-and-timber structure, vines had made a tortuous journey; they dripped with fat agglomerations of blue-black Alicante grapes, the fruits wizened and wadded, filmed with powdery mildew, giving off a faint raisin aroma.

Tomato plants, bursting out of rotting straw bales, were cropping heavily, though their leaves were touched with yellow mould. Elsewhere, mottled foliage hinted at the presence of red spider mite, and at her less than rigorous greenhouse management.

The dozen or more ripe tomatoes which she had picked, sat fat and scarlet in a seed tray on the wooden workbench beside a seeping bag of fertiliser and a forgotten glass of lemon barley, warm as tea and full of twiggy debris. Beneath the bench, embedded in the soil border, her transistor radio was tuned to *The Archers*: among the weeds and broken flowerpots, the residents of Ambridge, country folk, went about their everyday business unheeded; the doings of Mrs Antrobus were really no concern of Kate's.

There was in the air that too-sweet smell of incipient decay, a first sign, she thought, with a twinge of regret, that the year was on the turn.

Humming tunelessly, she trawled a watering can through a tank of rainwater green with slime, refreshed the weigela cuttings she was rooting, then wiped her clammy palms on her flanks. I'm pottering, she told herself contentedly. It was a pleasure to be here at Copperfields, to work indisturbed in this near-derelict glasshouse – one fierce wind could dismantle it – dabbling in nature, propagating.

She achieved so much more without Geraldine around to interefere. It was a relief not to have her trailing after her, for ever prattling about features (as in 'This lavatera makes a nice feature'), or about infection, finding more and more tasks for Kate to begin before those in hand were halfway finished, that she should be worthy of her hire.

This was for Kate a private place, where no one but she ever came. Closed in with the plants and their parasites, she had a strong sense of those long-ago days when, it was said, an abbey stood on the site, as though a little bit of history had somehow been encapsulated. And, for sure, something vital of the past survived in ancient soil and root stocks.

So lost was she in her own musings, so involved with her cuttings, that she heard yet did not hear the passing of a car, the growl of the engine, the spray of tiny pebbles at the curve of the drive.

Presently John appeared on the lawn, looked about him, saw her and came over. He stood before her, peering in at her, jiggling at the handle ineffectually. He often had trouble with doors: he pushed when he should pull, he got into difficulties going in and out of shops.

People on the other side would laugh at his ineptitude. Kate didn't laugh, though. She simply smiled vaguely and raised a trowel in greeting, but made no move to help him, resenting this intrusion.

Picking up a flowerpot, she saw nestled in it something that revolted her, a fat, curled grub almost the size of her thumb.

The doorknob was wrested from John's grasp, and Kate came flying out, making faces, going 'Yeeeugh!', to lob the offending creature, flowerpot and all, into a patch of dock and nettles.

'What was it?' he asked in mild consternation.

'A creepy-crawly of some sort.' She shuddered and hugged herself. 'I don't normally mind them. I mean, one gets used to them. But this was a monster. I'm not sure what sort. Perhaps a cockchafer.'

'Would that be the same as a prick-teaser?' he wondered aloud.

'No. Different animal.' She laughed in surprise (for who would have thought this of John?). She looked at him anew then, she saw him differently, this tall, thin man with a widow's peak, a stoop of anxiety and soft, intelligent gaze. Only for lack of self-assurance was he not attractive. But, with no sense of his own attraction, how could he feel self-assured? It was, as Geraldine would have said, a vicious circle.

'It's late, you know, Katie,' he told her, sounding solicitous (mentally, she played on the word; she said 'solicitors').

'What's late? What time?' She made as if to check her watch, which she had left indoors beside the kitchen sink (a sort of phantom wristwatch showed out white against her sunburned wrist).

'Well, you know, it must be pushing seven-thirty.'

'Oh, good gracious.' She had meant to leave at six. But then, what did it matter? She had nothing to rush home for. No one waited anxiously for her return.

'I wondered if you'd like a drink?'

'Well, yes, I would. That would be lovely. In a minute. As soon as I finish up here.'

She looked so strong, so resourceful. There was nothing soppy about her. He loved her blunt fingers, her black and bitten nails, her aura of very female warmth, the sheen of sweat on her upper lip, the pale down on her limbs. The flush in her cheeks, meanwhile, suggested to him, however spuriously, sexual arousal.

Taking off his jacket he hung it over the corner of the door. Without it, he felt braver. He flexed his shoulders, drew himself up – his stoop disappeared – and coughed sheepishly.

'As a child,' he said, 'I wore National Health specs with pink wire frames, and with a square of pink sticking plaster over one eye to correct a strabismus. A squint, that is. I was boss-eyed. I was also – still am – too thin. And pigeon-chested. I don't seem to be able to build muscle. I was excused games because of asthma. My mother wrote to the headmaster, d'you see? She explained that I was delicate. They called me Specky – among other things. I was not, as you may imagine, popular.

'I never had much success with women. I married Geraldine because she told me to. My children despise me – or, at least, my son does. I blotted my copybook the other week, came home pie-eyed. But I have been, otherwise, for all this time, an unexceptionable if unexciting husband.

'I am not artistic, or good with my hands. I am tone deaf. I dare say I should make a woefully inadequate lover. Rude am I in my speech, and little bless'd with the soft phrase of peace. But I have adored you for as long as I have known you. It has taken me more than twenty years to find the nerve to tell you this. Will you, now, please, for God's sake, come to bed with me?'

Well, what could Kate say? She said yes.

CHAPTER

8

'This is silly,' Kate sighed.

'Don't say that.' Kneeling before her, bobbing about on the spongy mattress, he picked up her foot, studied the sole, which was indelibly black at ball and heel, pushed his face into the pink instep and grazed it with his teeth. Silliness was a very Geraldine concept. Her world was thronged with silly people. The queue for her derogation went three times round the block. Among the multitudes who got the raspberry from her were the sort who bought their toilet rolls in twos and not in economic dozens; who partied all night so were fit for nothing in the morning; who filled up with bread in restaurants then had no room for pudding; who voted Labour and who dabbled in the occult. Silly people were those who did as Geraldine did not.

A balding, middle-aged man making love to his sister-in-law would represent, in her book, the very apotheosis of silliness – but he would prefer that Kate did not remind him of it.

She hadn't meant 'silly', though, of course. It was just a kind of catch-all word for whatever had got into them these past ten days. 'Reckless' would have better met the case. And 'self-destructive'. Not to mention 'morally indefensible'. She could not plead, as Elli had of Ruth Curran, that Geraldine was 'no angel' (not, at any rate, meaning by it what Elli had meant). Still, 'You know it is,' she insisted, and, as he replaced her foot on the bed, pairing it neatly with the other, she flopped back on the pillow, flung her arms wide and looked all washed up (here, she proclaimed by the gesture, was a good woman *manquée*).

It was surprisingly easy, somehow, and liberating, to admit that one was wholly in the wrong. It involved no contortions of reason, no rich sophistry or strained self-justification. 'This thing,' she told him, sending up the affair, 'is bigger than both of us.'

'Oh,' John glanced with mock-modesty down at his erect penis, the long, thin organ of a long, thin man, 'I wouldn't say that.'

Kate put a hand to her mouth and giggled. Love had sort of plumped her out; she appeared physically squashy and satisfied. He marvelled at the constitution of her, at her compact body, her tiny waist. He adored the texture of her uncompliant hair, the fluting of her lip, her dimpled cheeks in which the fires of emotion flared. She took on a set expression when she was concentrating, or, as he now knew, when moved by powerful passions. People occasionally thought her dislikeable, they saw in her something inexorable that wasn't really there. It would have amazed her to know how, as she stood about and introspected, total strangers, misreading her, took against her. But John read her right; he knew her thoroughly.

For his part, he seemed to her to be transfigured. She

wondered if this was a matter merely of perception. Perhaps only *she* saw a shift in style, a new jaunty presentation, or how handsome he had become. But, no, she was sure he was visibly altered. There had been, until last week, something unresolved in his demeanour, as if he had yet to decide who he was (some kind of declaration was to be hoped for). It was odd that a man in his forties, very probably more than halfway through his life, should have been in such flux. In Kate's experience, after a certain age nothing was negotiable. A person could not be different, only more and more the same. As John himself had said, however, he was a late developer. And suddenly, miraculously, in giving expression to his feeling for her, he had been realised.

He had a high, intelligent forehead, a long, thin nose, a humorous mouth and an almost noble profile. If others had always overlooked him, or forgotten him, it was because of the way he had withheld himself, choosing for his own ends to be null and void. If he'd grown his hair to his collar and dressed with a hint of flamboyance, he would have passed for an actor of the sort one saw from time to time on television (shop assistants, barmaids, nudging each other, would whisper, 'Isn't that . . .?' and 'Wasn't he in . . .?' before, primping their hair, they bustled up to him). He wore glasses for driving, and now and again to impress a client (it was with a very earnest, bespectacled professional that Jean-Anne Pettifer had done business). Without them he had a visionary's cloudy stare which tantalised Kate. Now, he favoured the small bedroom with his vague attention, peering into the woolly shadows, thinking how very Kate it was.

He had not been for years to Larkspur Road, and was entranced by all he found there. A very particular kind of chaos this woman generated, which had a logic, an order of its own. He liked to think that, if he'd been shown around the place and challenged to guess the nature, gender, disposition of its occupant, he would have had her to a T.

'This is it,' she had told him last week, when she led him through the door. And, tramping over a huddle of mackintoshes which the ugly, horned hall stand had shrugged off at her feet, she had led him into a front room full of amber evening light. 'Excuse the clutter,' she had begged, moving bits of it about with an air of futility, finding no resting place for anything.

'Leave it,' he'd implored, 'leave it all as it is.' And he had gazed appreciatively around at the miscegenation, the mixed marriages of furniture and fabrics. 'You obviously have an eye.'

'An *eye*?'

'A feel. For colour and so forth.'

'Ah.' She had snatched a raffia elephant from the mantelpiece and huffed the dust off it, to settle where it would.

'Those roses are past their best.'

'Yes, I must throw them out,' she had agreed. And, clearing her throat of dust, blinking away tears, she had picked up the vase of crackly blooms, glanced about her helplessly, then returned it to its customary station.

'Now, what is this? A portrait of the fiendish Eleanor?'

'Yes. Your mother-in-law. And mine.'

'Why do you keep her there?'

'Well, I don't know, really. She used, of course, to visit. She expected to see herself. And after she stopped calling – when she went off us so absolutely – it would have seemed awfully rude to take her down.'

'I wouldn't give her house room. Not if it were up to me.'

'Look, shall we have a drink?' She had brought for him, from the kitchen, a bottle of wine, and a screwdriver. 'Could you just push the cork in? I don't know what happened to the doodah. The corkscrew. I haven't seen it since. . . This was a present, you know, from Janet. She's a client. She brought it from a trip to Hampshire. Country Wine. Oh, dear. It says nettle and ginger. Will we like that? I can't imagine it. Though it is twelve per cent alcohol by volume.'

'Here, Kate.' He had taken bottle and screwdriver from her, set both aside, drawn her to him and, when she turned her face up, kissed her very gently. 'We don't need it, do we?'

'I wanted to show you, you see, some hospitality.'

'Then show me,' he had said, 'your bedroom.'

So her little house had become their refuge. Once, only, they had made love in Geraldine's home, in Geraldine's bed, on and under the marital duvet. And, sitting at the dressing-table afterwards, seeing strands of Geraldine's hair in the matching brush and comb, seeing the very tweezers with which the woman travestied her eyebrows, seeing her own ruined self in the bevelled mirror, Kate had decided: never again.

So, every morning, John had driven over, he had spent his nights with her, leaving at dawn, to be sure to reach

Copperfields before Molly du Slack did (Molly, on her arrival, would find him breakfasting on toast and coffee). He and Kate had fallen into sweet routine, so pleasing to them both, and so surprising, neither could quite believe that it was happening. And if it was silly, as he supposed it must be, it was the most delicious silliness he had ever known.

'The thing is,' she persisted bravely, doomily, 'we're sunk.'

'We are?'

'Yes. It's all up with us. We've had our time.'

'No.' In the half-light her face defied scrutiny. He could only make out with clarity a moist lip, the tip of her nose, her bright eyes (was it with tears that they shone so?).

Next door, the Wiltons moved about. They heard through the wall the sound of something dropping, breaking, the thud of a boot on a wood floor, the judder of air locked in an iron pipe, the singing in the tanks in the roof space. 'He works on the railways,' offered Kate simply, by way of explanation.

'But we mustn't end. We've barely begun.'

'I know, John, but it has to be over, hasn't it? Because, tonight . . .'

Because tonight he must leave work promptly and drive all the way to Scotland. And tomorrow he must bring the family back to Copperfields.

'But I have to see you. And you have to see me. Or what has this been *for*?'

'I'm not sure,' she responded frankly. 'It was just a chance, maybe, to have that little time together. Because

313

you will never leave Geraldine.' She was telling, not asking him this.

'Won't I? I don't know. I have to think.' He subsided next to her with an insupportable heaviness of spirit. 'I could just tell her, couldn't I? And make the necessary dispositions. She could have the house – I shouldn't want it – and much of what I earn.' He would, in other words, make the sort of sacrifices that Graham Pettifer would not.

'You will never leave Geraldine,' Kate said again, firmly. 'Because she would be mortified. It would do her in. And neither you nor I could live with that. I mean, being the people we are.'

By his silence he seemed to concede this.

'In any case . . .' Kate rolled away from him, hung her head over the side of the bed, and looked at Petal, who was sleeping, balled up, pneumatic, whistling softly through her tiny nostrils, on a pile of work clothes. 'In any case, you love her.'

John called to mind a large, pink woman in a large, pink nightie. He couldn't, for a moment, get a fix on her. 'Do I?' he wondered aloud. Then he gave himself the answer, 'I suppose so.'

'I'm your children's aunt,' Kate went on dully, unrelenting, addressing her words to the floor. 'And you are Alex's uncle. And Geraldine has been good to me – in her fashion. And we have friends in common. Then, can you imagine . . .' Another giggle escaped her, the sound flew out, of appalled amusement. 'Can you imagine what Eleanor would make of it? Can you picture the scene?'

'I suppose, for that alone, it might be worth it,' John agreed.

'Now you must get up.' Kate rolled back and clung to his arm, squeezing, probing bone beneath the flesh. She kissed his shoulder, nudged it with her chin, considered the perfect sculpture of an ear. 'Ah, yes, it's over.'

'No, Kate. I shall still see you.'

'How? When?' She became at once demanding, interrogatory. After all, this was what she wanted, reassurances, affirmations, promises, promises.

'Soon,' he vowed. 'Very soon. I shall ring you when I can,' he reassured her. And, 'I love you,' he affirmed. 'Now I must go.'

If someone would lay down an H she could spell out 'historic'. She would then earn, on top of her word total, a bonus of fifty points for using all her letters. If, however, she could build on to an L, she could have 'clitoris' and thus – according to the rules of Smutty Scrabble, devised by a certain prurient party at Il Poggio – double an already astronomic score. In this game, the explicitly sexual, scatological, obscene and profane were rewarded. And, while there had been lively debate over 'snog' (which, by consensus, simply wasn't rude enough), and over the alternative 'snot' (which was borderline at best), with tempers at times running very high, 'clitoris' must be incontrovertibly a winner.

The idea of a walkover, of vanquishing her madly competitive friends and colleagues, was peculiarly piquant. It served as a welcome distraction from that other contest, which had come to depress and fatigue Elli, and at which both players seemed set to fail (a no-score draw was forecast).

Settling in her chair, easing away from the table, uttering little groaning noises, making a subterfuge of stiffness, she allowed her gaze to run out through the double doors, which stood open on to the terrace. The morning, which had dawned reluctant, was gathering in around the house. Great slate-grey clouds bunched on the gloomy hillsides. The valley was lost in mist. Air rushed through the house and banged about upstairs. Along the balustrade, the pelargonia appeared shockingly pink, they quivered ominously.

How typical, they had all agreed, that on this, their last day, rain should threaten. And board games – or bored games, as Elli thought of them, in the grip as she was of ennui – had seemed the only answer.

'Whose turn is it?' demanded Patti crisply, her gaze confluent with Elli's, ebbing, unstoppable, on to the terrace. For each of them, a rear view of a folding canvas chair, the top of David Garvey's head, his elbows jutting east and west, was as irresistible as it was unrewarding. (Car crashes had the same unwholesome fascination, and inspired the same gut-wrenching response.) He had been so moody in his time here, and so inaccessible. He had held himself aloof and – with the excuse of jet lag no longer credible – confessed himself, if not actually depressed, then out of sorts. The louring sky must feel itself out-loured by him now.

'It's Seamus to go,' said Tina, who stood behind Simon, draped over his shoulder, watching. Every few minutes she would advance a fuchsia fingernail and, sliding the letter tiles about, reveal to him some naughty word, or whisper in his ear to make him smirk. She must have washed her hair this morning; it was very full, redolent of what hairdressers call 'products'; when she tossed it, it made an irritating swishing sound. The combined scents of conditioners, thickeners and lacquers cloyed.

'No, it's not,' said Seamus, 'it's Elli.'

'It isn't me. I've been.'

'Concentrate, can't you?' Patti snapped at him. 'Tina, be a love, while you're on your feet, and fix some drinks for us. Mike should be back any second with the lunch.'

'What's a Bellini?' Elli idly enquired.

'Nothing very saucy, so far as I'm aware,' said Simon.

'Oh, no, I didn't suppose . . . It just occurred to me to wonder.'

'White peach juice and champagne . . . or something,' offered Patti. The 'or something', Elli suspected, would be disingenuous.

They focused now with palpable hostility upon the game. For once, Elli felt no quickening of pleasure at the prospect of wine. Two weeks here had sated her and, anyway, she was almost faint with fearful anticipation. They'd be sick as parrots, the lot of them, if she achieved so decisive, so spectacular a victory; they would take it in bad part.

'How do you spell goolies?' Seamus muttered.

'Not like that, anyway,' Tina informed him, passing behind him, trailing a finger across his shoulders, tweaking his ear as she snooped at his letters. On her way into the kitchen, she flicked a switch; the overhead lamp shed its indifference upon them, disclosing nothing new and giving no cheer.

The house seemed to be in a cold sweat; everything was clammy to the touch. The group listened in uncompanionable silence as Tina opened then closed the fridge. Elli pictured, for an instant, the chill interior, a bleak still life of leftovers, the dregs of a fortnight – cheese, tomato, wilted salad, with perhaps a tub of pesto. 'Slam it,' shouted Patti. They heard the fridge door once more open, then thud shut, heard the ring of glass on glass as Tina set a tray.

'And bring olives,' Patti called to her.

'Bring olives, *please*,' Tina coolly admonished.

'Yes, olives, and those little salty biscuits. *Please*. Come on, Hicks, do *something*. We're tired of waiting.' Patti tugged at her knuckles until they cracked. 'Or change your letters if you're stuck.'

'He's not stuck,' Tina assured them all, returning, smiling, sassy, with the reverberant tray, her heels going clickety-clack on the brick floor. 'There are things he can do.'

'Hey, look here, Tina, maybe you want to play for me. I mean, if you're so bloody clever.' Seamus had a blandly handsome face, devoid of real character, a blank wall upon which contumely was momentarily scrawled.

'I'm not saying I'm clever, Seamus. I just happened to spot something, *en passant*. A fresh eye, you know, will see things differently.'

'Well, don't tell me, OK? I shall do my own thing, thanks.'

Something about Seamus's look, however, was more than Patti Henderson could tolerate. 'No, do tell him,

Tina,' she begged. 'Some of us have a plane to catch tomorrow.'

'Right. I was only thinking, Seamus, you can do 'glues'. Put as S on 'lag' and you'll have 'slag', which must be worth a double.'

'Certainly it is,' offered Elli magnanimously, calculating that, so long as neither Patti nor Simon queered her pitch, she would have the L upon which she had been counting.

Only, then, 'I don't want to play any more, to be honest,' said Patti.

And, 'I'm with you,' said Simon. 'This is tedious beyond belief.'

'I should have been able to think a good deal straighter,' Seamus grumbled, 'if other people hadn't interfered.'

'You shouldn't be so slow, then,' Patti scolded him. 'Were there any nuts?' she asked of Tina.

'Oh, nuts!' exclaimed Simon, throwing in his letters with an air of detachment. 'I could have put nuts.'

'This is a bloody stupid game,' grumbled Elli. 'Who thought of it, anyway?'

'You did,' the others chorused.

She stood and went through a stretching routine, raised her arms above her head, then folded them across her face, sort of hanging them from the elbows. 'I think,' she said, 'I'll get a breath of air.'

David Garvey's dullness of spirit had only so much to do with the unpersonable company in which he found himself. The megrims, which he indulged as he would all his other moods and drives and fancies – for it was his way to humour himself, it was how he got through – were inspired by grim reflection. Scarcely conscious of the cold and damp which seeped through his white cotton shirt, unaware that the weather was piling it on, he kept his eye trained resolutely inward.

He had become, with each passing year, more sexually compelling. He had no need of a mirror to tell him so, when women of all ages and complexions, from flat-chested heiresses not yet out of college, to ambitious, busty blondes of his own generation, made unambiguous eyes at him and rubbed themselves, metaphorically, up against him. It had never been for reassurance that he sought his image in the glass; rather, to treat his ego. Why, then, did he feel, suddenly, so discomposed, so threatened?

Twenty-something years ago, in the back of his mind he had made a small accommodation for a boy child, he had made mental space for him to grow from mewling infancy, through gawky adolescence, to some sort of unassuming adulthood. He had forked out, over time, for bigger blazers, bigger shirts and shoes; he had sent, at longer intervals, bigger cheques. But he had somehow failed to make that final imaginative leap, to envisage a son as tall as him and inch for inch as sexy.

Alex, then, had confounded him. Because it seemed the guy was through that awkward, wet-dreams stage, and had moved in on his very territory. David felt himself in an odd way usurped. Far from masturbating over photos of Madonna, like some blasted Oedipus Garvey Junior was actually putting it about with women twice his age. He was, indeed, living with Naomi Markham. And Naomi Markham was probably, it now occurred to Garvey Senior, the most beautiful woman to walk this earth. He had always meant to hit on her and – still wanting for the time and opportunity – until last week had hoped that he might yet. In general he favoured younger flesh, but for someone so exceptional he was prepared to make exception.

She had been, when he first met her, so elusive, gliding out of rooms as he stalked into them, sliding into fast sports cars, blowing farewell kisses at her flatmates as she was whisked away to Paris by wealthy pop stars, restaurateurs, entrepreneurs. She had been into money in those days, into extravagant display. He supposed she must have changed crucially, she must have revised her values, for he doubted that Alex had a pot to piss in. The whole business turned him up. He could make no sense of it. Meanwhile, Naomi burned in his brain like a candle, night and day.

News of the outrageous affair he had had from his father, Jack, in Gloucestershire, and by telephone from Geraldine in Scotland – the former in tones of wry amusement, the latter in that peculiar, carrying whisper by which his sister always broadcast scandal (in restaurants and other public places, or at cocktail parties, private Garvey business would be thus confided to the farthest corners; all around the room, heads would turn, necks would crane).

So, forget circadian rhythms; it was the larger cycle known as life that was getting to David now. It wasn't years that aged you, he decided; it was other people.

More than ever he regretted the issue with which his brief marriage had been blessed.

In short, if he was honest, he was jealous. He could not rest for envy of a younger and – for all he knew – more virile man.

When Elli Sharpe emerged to join him, clearing her throat of the damp fug, he spared her barely half a glance.

'What's eating you?' she asked him with her usual directness, waving a tumbler under his nose.

The wine was yellow-white and faintly *pétillant*: when he snatched it from her and raised it to his lips, the breeze blew a sort of alcoholic spindrift in his face. 'I'm just dandy,' he said, though he gave no indication of it.

'You should have joined the game.'

'But it's for four players maximum.'

'I don't see why.'

'That's just the way it works. Logistics.'

She dragged a chair over and sat right by him, inappropriately close. 'How long have I known you, Garvey?'

'Too long.'

'Long enough, at any rate, to recognise when you're not yourself. Come on, 'fess up. What's eating you?'

'Of course I'm myself. Who else should I be? I'm fine, Elaine. Just, maybe, missing the States. You know, missing that special buzz.'

'Well, I'm sorry we're not buzzing here for you,' she told him flippantly, folding her arms across her stomach. She was wearing a yellow halter top, into which she looked to have been scooped like strawberry ice cream. 'I say, check out the sky. I reckon it's going to chuck it down any minute.'

'Rain?' With tired eyes he registered the weather. 'I expect so.'

'Not much to do on a dismal day like this.'

'Not a lot, no.'

'One might as well have stayed in bed.'

'One might.'

Short of declaring outright that she would like to have her evil way with him – 'Let's do the business,' she might have proposed, game as she was to open the negotitions, had he been more approachable – she could scarcely have been more explicit. But he declined to take a cue.

'Well, goodness, gracious, you're a great ball of fire, I must say,' she reproached him. 'I don't know why you bothered to come here if you won't join in the fun.' It would almost have been more endurable if Patti had got in ahead of her. Elli would have been most horribly miffed, of course, if La Henderson's archness, the aggressive vivacity which set her teeth on edge, had cut it with him; but the fact that he manifestly preferred no one – that he would sooner sleep alone than sleep with her – was quite exquisitely insulting. If she had been one iota less assured of her feminine charms, it might have given her a hang-up.

'This stuff is like gnat's piss,' he complained, feeling unreasonably that white wine was a woman's drink. 'Is there no red left?'

'I haven't a clue. It was Tina poured it. I'm up to here with it myself.' She chopped angrily at her forehead with the side of her hand.

'You're not drinking?'

'Not just now. Like I say, I've had enough to last me.'

'Oh, go on, fetch yourself one, Elli. I hardly know you without a glass in your hand.'

'You hardly know me, full stop. Hey, I wonder how Kate is. Did you make contact at all when you were in London?'

'No. Oh, hell, no. We hardly speak these days.'

'She took it very hard, you realise, when Alex. . .?'

'Ah, yes, Alex.'

'I must say, I would never have believed it of him.'

'Not the type, eh?'

'Well, he's a hunk, of course, like his father. But the quiet sort. One might even say a mother's boy. More solid than you, David, if you don't mind my saying. More dependable.'

'Is that so?' David brightened visibly.

Seeing the first flicker of animation, Elli proceeded to fan it alight. 'It was a matter, you see, of propinquity. There they were, he and Naomi, snug as bugs under the same roof. And I guess inevitably they got together. But it's a completely off-the-wall relationship. It cannot last.'

'Not?'

'I mean to say, they couldn't be less . . . Now, had it been *you*, you shocking reprobate, I could have understood it. But Alex is a horse of another colour. He should marry a nice girl and settle down. My Juin, as a matter of fact, is more than a bit keen. It's my private wish –' she heeled towards him in a confiding manner – 'that he'll come to his senses and settle down with Juin.'

David fingered his glass meditatively. He creaked about in the canvas chair. Turning to Elli he bestowed on her a smile. 'This plonk is all right, I guess, when you get the taste for it.'

'Yes, I guess it is. On second thoughts, I may join you.'

'Any chance, do you think, that the sun will come out later?'

'You never can tell, David,' said Elli with a rush of elation. 'You simply never can tell.'

Molly du Slack had not come up the river on a bicycle. Or down with the last shower. She was not, in other words, born yesterday. She could distinguish, for instance, a bed that had been slept in from one that had not – especially when it was one of 'her' beds. She would tuck in the corners nice and tight, shake out the double duvet, making waves upon the air, before allowing it to settle, with a faint sigh, just so. She would plump and smooth the pillows, rearrange the valance. No man could pass a night, however peacefully, among such starchy polyester, no man could sprawl across the sheet, snuggle under the duvet, lay his head upon the pillow, then restore all to perfection.

In any case, it wasn't just the bed. Arriving at Copperfields each morning, she had heard the tick and flinch of shrinking metal, she had seen the emanation of warmth from the bonnet of the Rover. There was a different atmosphere entirely around a car that had been left to stand for hours, and one that had only minutes ago arrived. Even the tyre marks on the gravel spoke to her of new disturbance, she might catch a lingering wraith of exhaust smoke, see gashes of fresh earth, while the rooks in the beeches, raucous, told a tale.

This morning, as on so many mornings, when she stepped into the pristine kitchen she had found John putting up his paper, breakfasting behind a screen of newsprint, pretending a keen interest in the stories of the day. The atmosphere had been thick with the guilty aroma of coffee just brewed. Ay-ay, she had told herself, there's something funny going on here.

Still, 'Nice enough for you today?' she had asked as she buttoned the cuffs of her overall, and, glancing through the window, she'd approved the weather, her behaviour so natural, no one would have guessed she smelt a rat.

She would not, of course, say anything to anyone. Wild horses would not drag this secret from her. Her lips were sealed. (Thinking on it now, she set them firm, she made an astringent little mouth in unconscious re-hearsal, against those very wild horses). When Geraldine came to ask her on Monday, as she surely would, if all had been well, she'd say yes, thank you very much, just fine and dandy. Her employers' private life was no concern of hers. But this much she would admit to herself: such goings-on she would never have seen in the Robbies' era. And she couldn't help but wonder what old man Gorst was playing at.

The place meanwhile gave her more than usual satis-faction. She had put such a gloss on it while the family had been away. A new pin she invoked by way of simile. There was this much to say for an errant husband, out every night: he didn't make an awful lot of mess.

The sitting-room, especially, pleased her with its deep sense of stillness and order. In glass cabinet doors, against a rich background of leather-bound literary classics, it appeared inverted, deeper yet, and stiller and more ordered. On little lacy runners, on dark polished surfaces, a pair of candlesticks, a porcelain shepherd and shepherdess stood for mutuality. The curtains hung in regular pleats.

Come the hour, the ormolu mantel clock found itself in sweet accord with the carriage clock, which had had no quarrel with the casement clock since Molly du Slack had set them right. The impression this created in the otherwise silent house was, strangely, one of timelessness: into some sort of void the chimes seemed to fall; there was a sense that nothing happened here.

Yet time had passed, two weeks elapsed, and tomorrow Copperfields would be overrun once more, which was to be regretted in a way.

Picking up from the sideboard the picture postcard addressed to His Lordship, Molly read that Geraldine and the kids had been having a very lovely time. Well, in this, she thought dourly, they were not alone. Someone else had been having a very lovely time. Better, certainly, than he should.

Trevor Pocock reached for the remote control, flipped idly through the television channels, then peeled himself off the sofa and padded through to the kitchen in a desultory search for lunch. The freezer offered something called a Healthy Option, which disqualified itself on name alone. A rootle around among the frosty, smoking packages, however, threw up hamburgers and a bag of crinkly chips. Beef products were, if you could believe the nutrition police, deeply suspect. Well, if he caught BSE, if he started acting like a mad cow, he could blame it on the burger. What was Elli Sharpe's excuse?

He would fix himself a snack, he resolved, then roll up his sleeves and set to with a will. Wielding mop and bucket, he would leave the place perfectly spick, not to say span. This was a labour at which Hercules himself might have drawn the line. Mucking out the Augean Stables was one thing, scrubbing the grimy rim from the bath and swabbing the lino quite another; while to take possession of the girdle of Hippolyta, and to bring Cerberus from the infernal region, would seem a mere bagatelle beside the job of clawing the fluff and socks and pants out from under the bed. But for Trevor there might be no release. In his two weeks of squatting here, he had been something other than a treasure. He had, indeed, he was forced to confess, been rather less than scrupulous. He looked around him with considerable chagrin, and a pigsty he invoked by way of simile. Unless he wrought a lightning transformation, he could whistle for the reward of a few measly quid.

'When I get back,' Elli had warned him with her usual unpleasantness, 'I shall expect to find this house spotless, do you understand? I shall want to see my face in it.'

At this, Trevor had naturally expressed some surprise, he had replied that there was no accounting for it.

Now he poured some oil into the chip pan and set it on the gas hob. While it heated, he slipped upstairs to scritch-scratch round the bath with a scourer. He dragged the soiled and rumpled sheets off Elli's bed and chucked them down the stairs for later machine washing. Next he attached himself to the vacuum and went cruising up and down the landing, whistling, wondering at how little impact he was making.

When the telephone rang he took the call in the bedroom, supine on the bare mattress, staring at the ceiling. 'I told you not to ring me at the office,' he reproved the girl, Nicola. (They had met at a rave. He had told her he was chief executive of an environmental cleansing operation, at which she had said, 'Cor', and had quite understandably dropped her knickers.) Then, with a smile spread right across his face, and with a hand thrust down the front of his jeans, he started to talk dirty to her (not about grimy bathtubs, either; not about Augean Stables).

Down in the kitchen, on the gas hob, meanwhile, the oil for the chips was heating nicely.

Naomi was crying again. That great sump of misery inside her seemed never to be drained. As she waited in the window for the hire car to arrive, she fielded tears with the blue-veined underside of her thin wrist, rubbing at her cheeks with the heel of her hand so they took on a deceiving brightness.

In and out of people's lives she went, by cab. When Alex came home tonight he would find her gone. A brief note would explain: she was undone. This was what he wanted, she was sure of it. Last night, for the first time, they had quarrelled, for the first time turned their backs in anger, lain there frigid, unloving and unloved. Hard words had been spoken. Hurtful things said. And she could find nowhere inside herself to put that hurt. Nor had she any way to deal with censure.

She was too damaged, too insecure, to take criticism. It made her feel damned to hell, it destroyed her. And she had the problem of the lonely only child who has never learned the art of robust argument. At school she had made no clinging friendships of the kind that are positively enlivened by spats, by the sick thrill of hostilities, the heart-stopping business of cutting one another, the melodrama of a showdown and blubbery rapture of reconciliation. No classmate had ever linked an arm through Naomi Markham's and, drawing her aside, sought her views on sex or whispered darkest secrets in her ear. She had not been unpopular, exactly, but her air of inadvertence, her inattention to the social mores, and her look of being somehow elsewhere, had not inspired devotion. A falling-out is simply not a possibility if one has not first fallen in.

Alex, finding fault with her, had seemed only to bully. She could not see that love had anything to do with it. She gave no thought to the substance of his argument (that she was indolent, undirected, overdependent, inert); he might have had no higher purpose than to wound her.

Her doomed search for unconditional love, which had led her after so long to Alex Garvey and to such unexpected happiness, must now, she told herself, resume. Somewhere she must find the man in whose eyes she was perfect. She had fancied that she fulfilled for Alex some womanly ideal. Finding this was not the case, she suffered terrible disaffection. 'For *you*,' he had insisted, slapping his brow with the flat of his hand, 'for *your* sake, you impossible creature, I am saying this.' His cruelty was, she had been asked to accept, kindly meant. But she would not, could not, believe it.

She put her arm to the glass pane and leaned her forehead against it. She was stiff and aching, having slept only fitfully, holding herself taut, flinching from him if they chanced to touch. Dawn had come on remorselessly. Thin daylight, sinking shafts into her consciousness, she had welcomed as the suicidal person, absolute for death, welcomes the reviving slap, the shake, the poison kiss of life. She had sensed his eyes upon her, watching, speculative. The envelope of bedding had been opened, closed – she had been exposed for an instant to a different quality of air – as he eased out of it. Rationing herself to one shallow breath every few seconds, she had stayed stone still while with clumsy surreptitiousness he had prepared to leave for work. Would he speak to her? Offer abject apologies? Would he take her hand, entreat her to forgive him? For only by so doing could he transfuse her with new hope and save them from this cataclysm.

Every sound she knew so well, from the scratch of fingernails on laundered denim, to the singing of a metal comb in tousled hair; from the barely audible heaving noise he uttered as he doubled at the waist to tie his trainers, to the running of a shoelace through a metal eyelet. She had been that horribly attuned.

A voice in her head had urged her to sit up and face him, to offer herself, to make some appeal to compassion, but a more repressive voice had told her no.

The slam of the front door, sending shocks through the walls, had seemed so finally decisive. That, she had told herself desolately, was that.

'Fallen out with your toy boy, have you?' her father had jibed on the telephone. And, 'I am an old man,' he had told her, 'set in my ways. We would have nothing now in common. Besides, you are too much your mother's daughter. You would try my patience. I should take not the least pleasure in your society. Irena and Huw are your best bet, what?'

He had not, however, said she mustn't come. And who else would have her? Elli was in Italy until tomorrow. Geraldine was in Scotland. And she could hardly go to Kate.

So, when the white Ford saloon drew up outside, as the driver sounded his horn, she tottered on to the front step, with gestures of helplessness pressed him into porter service, had him stow her luggage in the boot, then ordered him to Pimlico.

'Two weeks,' grumbled Dominic, 'and not so much as a kiss. I must say, I'm disappointed in you, Ju-ju. I had you down for a sport.'

'Then I'm sorry to disappoint you.'

He went ahead of her along the swishing grass verge, brandishing a stick, now and then taking swipes at the undergrowth, sending up showers of leaves and flower-heads. Around him a devoted Muffy fawned. 'Don't be so destructive,' Juin chided.

The guy had a very uppity way of walking, rising on the balls of his feet and virtually throwing his legs. Juin, tramping along in a wake of words, a stream of provoca-tion, confabulation and banter, could only wonder anew at his energy and self-possession. She felt frankly a bit heartsick at the thought of going home. On Monday she'd be back to the old routine, back to school. She'd be in the thick of life again, and in the thick of disappointment. She didn't want to go. She loved it on this rugged coast. As soon as she was able, she would return, to inhabit a very basic cottage among wind-bent grasses on some remote headland. In her mind she saw a smoking chimney, saw a solitary light burning in the black of night. She saw herself reclusive, withdrawn, deeply strange and fascinating. (Rumours would spring up about her. It would be said of her that, crossed in love, she had quite lost her mind.)

The day was warm but pearly grey, as if disputatious weather forces had come to a tenuous agreement. Rain was not threatened, but might come in suddenly off the sea. The road, which gave out sour wafts of tarmac, took them past a copse where the breeze made silvery sounds in the leaf canopy. They followed its downward curve and their goal came into view. Dominic's stride lengthened. Juin, shrugging, let space open up between them. She wasn't going to break her neck to keep pace with him.

On the pub forecourt he waited for her, stood leaning against a tree. His legs, in shorts, appeared powerful and sinewy, furred with golden hair. 'Chop chop,' he urged her, 'shape up. Look sharp, Sharpe. We haven't got all day. If we're not back for lunch in half an hour, they'll send a search party. They worry that you're not safe in my hands.'

'See this?' she said, so used now to his unstoppable sexual badinage that she barely noticed it. And she held out an arm, a mere stick of a limb, on which a ladybird had settled. 'Aren't they weird? I haven't seen one for ages. Years. I'd forgotten they existed. Where have they all gone? What's happened to them? Do they bite? I'm never sure.'

'No, but they can tickle you to death.'

'Oh, *you*,' she sighed, despairing of him. 'Why is it called a ladybird, d'you suppose? It doesn't look especially female. Not like a butterfly.'

'Ladybird implies 'bird of Our Lady'. A tribute to the work they do in eating all the sodding aphids.'

'How come you know *everything*?' she queried, sighing, resentful, for it seemed there was no subject on earth upon which he could not expatiate.

'Well, you did ask. I'm just naturally brilliant, I guess,' he responded, spreading his hands, rolling back his rapacious lips, showing strong, white teeth.

'Your grandmother says –'

'Ah, my grandmother. What will she do for a face, I wonder, when the monkey wants its arse back?'

'That's very disrespectful.'

'Respect has to be earned, Juin, don't you reckon? Like I didn't respect my old man till he came home pixilated as a newt. That pernicious old witch would have to do something pretty spectacular to have an ounce of regard from me. She would have, at the very least, to do a streak at Ascot with a smoke bracket up her bottom.'

'*Anyway*,' persisted Juin, suppressing a laugh, 'your grandmother says you get it from your uncle. Your aptitude for learning. She says you're just like David was at that age.'

'It is tedious in the extreme, as you can perhaps imagine, constantly to be compared to someone – especially when that someone is a jerk of the first water.'

'Is David a jerk?' Her eyebrows went up in genuine surprise. 'That's not what my mum tells me. She thinks he's a genius.'

'She probably wants to have his love child. Most women do. I should be happy to take after him to that degree only.'

'What a gruesome thought. At her age.' Juin crooked her arm, brought it in front of her face, and squinted at the ladybird.

'Stranger things have happened. Come on now, let's get that drink, shall we?'

'Hang about.' With some seriousness, with a childish belief in magic incantation, she addressed the spotted beetle. 'Ladybird, ladybird, fly away home. Your house is on fire – Ooh, look, there she goes. I wonder where her house is.'

'Or his. In a dry hole in some tree. That's where they spend the winter. Hibernating. Sleeping over. Now, for pity's sake, move it.'

The Flowers of the Forest was a tall, double-fronted brick house with narrow, disapproving bay windows. It was done up, not so much with bad taste, as with no taste, and with a kind of reverence for function. Quite a feature was made of Formica.

Beside the mean accommodation, the extensive car park seemed a sort of folly. One wondered how the occupants of several dozen vehicles could hope to crowd inside. No such problem today, however: the place was quite deserted, with an air of having gone beyond despair. A child's swing, derelict, on the grassy bank behind, lent something especially poignant to the scene. Passing trade – motor cars, coaches – would not be welcome here. The licensees would content themselves with local custom.

To the right of a small entrance lobby a door stood open on to the dining-room (a blackboard menu could be seen, and a tray of squeezy plastic sauce bottles; the smell of frying food did not entice). Dominic put his head in, withdrew it hastily and rolled his eyes at her. 'Stoved howtowdie with clapshot,' he reported. 'Wee drappit eggs wi' skirlie and bashed neeps.'

'Oh, do *stop*,' she pleaded, seizing his elbow and digging her nails in as hard as she could. 'It's cod and chips, gammon and chips, lasagne . . . a lot of dead flesh and fries. *I* can read as well as you.'

'It's a special promotional menu.'

'Nonsense. Hey, hey . . .' Feeling constrained un-accountably, she dropped her voice to a whisper. 'I was hoping to buy a haggis for my mum. I suppose it's too late now. I shan't find one.'

'What the hell would she want with a haggis? There's dead flesh, *if* you like. Big bladder of suet.'

'Don't speak of my mother in that way.'

'I'm talking, as you well know, of the noble haggis, great chieftain o' the puddin' race. Like a giant condom stuffed with offal. Come to think of it, it should be right up her alley.'

'I just thought it would be novel.'

'So would painting your face red, pouring custard on

336

your hair, topping up with cream and trifling with my affections. Now, will you walk this way.'

The bar to the left, which called itself a 'saloon', was marginally less uninviting than the dining-room, an imbalance which the landlady, a thin and ferrety woman, seemed bent upon redressing. Having presumably heard their conference without, she fixed the two of them, as they approached, with a sceptical stare, swabbing the counter-top all the while with small, circular motions. Her expression would have done credit to Eleanor Garvey. The monkey could keep his arse, thought Dominic, for here was the real thing. Still, 'Good afternoon,' he said pleasantly. 'I should like a pint of lager. And my friend will have a half of bitter shandy.'

'What age is she?' With a curt inclination of the head, the woman indicated Juin.

'I'm nineteen,' Juin spoke up for herself. 'And I do understand English. It's my first language, as a matter of fact. I've been speaking it since the age of two.'

The bunched cloth described three more wet and futile circles. Hush my mouth, thought Juin, now she won't serve us. But then, with no further discussion, and although still with an air of disbelieving, the woman thrust a glass under the lager tap and pulled a grudging pint. 'Will you want to see the bill of fare? Rolls and sandwiches only are served in here. Hot food and salads in the dining-room. Where, of course,' their hostess added with a gleam of triumph, 'dogs are not permitted.'

'No, no,' said Dominic, 'we've just dropped in to quench our thirst. We've been humping all morning, you see. Mmm.' He took up his beer, drank deeply and

337

sighed appreciatively as he had seen 'real' men do in television commercials. 'Sacks of coal,' he added.

'Oh, yes?'

'Yes. We're taking them to Newcastle.'

Leaving Juin to pay – for she was flush with pocket money, pressed upon her by a guilty and not ungenerous Elli – he carried the drinks to a corner table where he sat beneath a dismal trio of hunting prints. Through thin net curtains, the vestigial sunlight could not pass.

'How d'you like this carpet?' he enquired when Juin joined him, draining the change from her hand into her pocket, plonking herself down beside him. 'Such a practical design. If some old drunk threw up on it, it wouldn't even show.'

'Dominic,' she reproved him, 'do you have to talk such bullshit? And why must you wind people up all the time?'

'I can't seem to help it. It's inborn.'

'Perhaps you get it from David Garvey.'

'Perhaps I don't. He's not that way at all. He never kids around. The guy is *serious*.'

'And you don't want to be a writer like him?'

'I don't want to be a writer like anyone. I want to be a kissogram delivery boy.'

'There you go again, talking shit. Tell me what you *truly* want to do.'

He took another long draught of beer, set the glass down in front of him, looked at it consideringly, moved it an inch one way, two inches the other. 'I want to be an actor,' he said finally, and for the first time she saw diffidence there, she saw modesty.

338

'Crikey! Honestly?'

'Yes, honestly.'

'Does your mum know? Or your dad?'

'No one knows. Only you.'

'Then I'm flattered,' she said, but too flippantly.

He made a dismissive motion with his hand, gestured that she'd blown it, she might expect no further confidences from him. 'Keep it to yourself,' he told her warningly. 'If that lot get wind of it they'll try to talk me out of it. My mother will, at any rate.'

'Yes, all right. And what would your mum say if she knew we were here?'

'She'd say . . .' He sat back and, closing his eyes, went into maternal mode, querulous, helpless, with trembling lip and with something dangerous held in; he became Geraldine to the life. 'I would have expected no better from Dominic, but I had hoped that you, Juin, would have had more sense than to . . . I mean, what am I to tell your . . . Oh, this is simply too bad of the pair of you.'

'That's awful.' Juin dropped her head and giggled. She picked up her shandy and took a sip. She was going through a kind of drinking adolescence; she had outgrown sweet fizz, but had yet to acquire a taste for alcohol. 'And *this* is awful, too.' So saying, she disappeared momentarily under the table with the glass and let Muffy lap at it.

Dominic downed the last third of his pint. He tipped back his head and seemed, like a bird, to open his throat. 'We'd better make tracks,' he declared.

The landlady rather pointedly neglected to wish them

a very good day, she did not thank them for their custom, or beg them to call again. Indeed, as they crossed the threshold, Juin, with a backward glance, saw the woman swabbing their table with grim determination, as if to expunge them entirely from memory. It was no wonder, she told herself, that the car park was empty.

But it wasn't. For, stationed at the top of a ramp, in a playsuit, a sort of all-in-one affair with divided skirt in confectionery colours, was a pink-faced, hot and bothered Lucy.

'Look who it isn't,' muttered Dominic crossly. 'I thought we'd shaken her off.'

'Evidently not,' responded Juin, feeling mean and low and wholly reprehensible. Lucy had been so avid to know where they were going, and they so determined that she should not. It would perhaps have been safer to tell her the truth and to swear her to secrecy. It would certainly have been kinder, less excluding. There was such hurt in her face, such uglifying petulance; Juin saw, with compunction, why the poor kid was forever being teased at school, she saw why her friendships failed.

'Sorry,' she offered humbly.

Dominic, however, was more punishing. 'You insufferable little sneak,' he challenged his sister. 'What the hell do you think you're doing? What right have you to follow us everywhere?'

'It's a free country, isn't it? I have as much right to be here as you do. Look, look . . .' Lucy, wild-eyed, preposterous, waved a hand about. 'What does it say up there? "Free house".'

'The thing is, Lucy,' offered Juin, anxious to make

peace, 'you're too young to go drinking. It's just not allowed.'

'So are you. *You're* too young.'

'But in your case it's more obvious.' Juin, unable to meet the younger girl's eye, was transfixed by her pudgy knees, pads of skin, wrinkled and twitchy. She thought she had never seen such outraged knees.

'I could have had a Coke. We could have sat outside, the three of us, and had a Coke. You can't tell me that's against the law.' Lucy, charmed by this imagined treat, then felt that she'd been cheated of it. A sob was wrenched from her, and she bunged her mouth with her fist. 'You're both hateful,' she flung at them as the tears flowed. 'I'm not surprised at Dominic, but I had thought that you, Juin –'

The look that passed between them then, amused, complicit, further incensed the girl. 'I suppose you fancy him, do you?' she accused, stamping her foot. 'I suppose you want to go out with him. And French kiss him. And do flying fucks with him. I suppose you think he's God's gift, is that it, Juin Sharpe? Because, if so, I can't say much for your taste.'

Juin swayed back in surprise and blinked at her. 'Oh, no,' she said definitely, shaking her head. 'Oh, no, Lucy, I really, really don't.'

And she quite believed she really, really didn't.

The big bouquet, cellophone-wrapped, was a cliché, of course. Alex would not normally have chosen to 'say it with flowers', which seemed to him at best an exercise in equivocation, and at worst thoroughly dishonest. Actual words were more costly – you might have to pay for them for ever – and, unlike cut flowers, they would not wither away. Then, wasn't the phrase 'floral tribute' the most depressing in the English language?

Besides, there was at Chafford Road no vase, since the two of them were barely embarked upon the whole-hogging process of acquisition that is married – or quasi-married – life. Naomi had come to him with a designer wardrobe, but with few other possessions. She might have stepped out of a painting, clean out of her background. And at Tooting everything – all the stuff – was Kate's.

Still, any old jar would do at a pinch. And these daisy affairs with jolly faces had seemed to express with more than usual honesty what he was feeling. They said 'I love you', but larkily, optimistically, with no shade of desperation. They hadn't the abjectness or cant of lilies, nor were they anal and uptight in the manner of bud roses. Nothing about them said, hypocritically, 'sorry'.

Oh, sure, he regretted hurting her. It tore at him to see her wrecked. But relationships must be fundamentally honest. This was a conviction informed not by high-minded principle, but by innate straightforwardness. What use to pussyfoot around each other, never confessing what one truly felt? Deceit did everybody in, as he had learned through his deceit of Kate. And he had done nothing more unkind than to appeal to Naomi's reason.

This morning he had slammed out in a dark and brooding temper. The world had seemed a place without pity, from which their little flat offered no refuge. His head had filled with traffic roar, it had fogged up with uncatalysed car fumes and funereal notions. He had watched people doing what people do – a harassed woman slapped a screaming child; at a pavement table, outside a café, a black man in a hat addressed himself primly to breakfast; a young woman, her dark hair swinging, gave Alex fleetingly the eye – and he had ached for each of them. He had seen, then, starkly, that for every human being life was an intensely personal tragedy – that there weren't any happy endings, merely happy episodes. No amount of screaming, slapping, breakfasting or flirting would stave off the inevitable. There was nowhere to hide from it. You could hold very tight to a hand, as Kate had held to Pam's, but death would wrench a person from you, you could not stop the going of them. Mortality was a cruel and unusual punishment: how was it to be endured?

Much of his bleak mood had been down to Naomi, and yet was not her fault. It had not been about her irresolution or her apparent unfitness for work of any kind. He loved her with all her weakness. She could have anything within his gift – only he could not give meaning to her existence. But she had behind her twenty years of reckless spending – and, reckless, had spent those twenty years. Time, once forfeited, could never be redeemed. So he had grieved for what had gone, which was lost for ever to both of them. And he had foreseen for her an empty future, so much shorter than it might have been, devoid of everything but himself.

Or else air pollution, low blood sugar, fitful sleep, confusing dreams, and the depleting of emotional energies had brought him low. Whatever the reason, as the day had warmed up, he had warmed with it. He had consumed a bacon sandwich and a *cappuccino*, and had been restored to sunny humour. He had come around to the idea that everything would work out one way or another. Even mortality had commended itself to him (he could not, indeed, think of a more satisfactory scheme). His love of life, like a fire before which chillier mortals warmed themselves, had leapt again into flickering brightness.

So he had the flowers. He had love in his heart. And, as he emerged from the suffocating clutches of the under-ground and waded out into the evening rush-hour traffic, he had confidence that he would find her waiting for him at home.

Throughout the day, at intervals, he had tried to call her. And although she had not picked up the phone – his own voice had advised him, obstructively, that neither he nor Naomi could take the call, it had exhorted him to speak after the beep – he had had a powerful sense that she was there, perhaps sitting very still, listening as he talked of love on to the tape. A telephone ringing in an unpeopled space makes a very different sound, some-how, from one that finds an audience. His intuition had failed to tell him, though, that his voice had found her sobbing, packing, standing in the window watching for the cab.

His first apprehension of something badly amiss came as he turned into Chafford Road. And it grew in him with every step. His usual loose gait would not serve him now; be braced up, bent towards his destination with a concentrated gaze. When he unlocked and pushed open his front door, a great waft of emptiness came past him, he felt an escaping silence, as if something of Naomi, left behind her in error, had gone out in a huff. 'Hi,' he called hopefully, but his voice ran away from him into some distant corner. There came no answering call. And no one emerged into the passageway.

In the kitchen he found her note. 'Oh, for heaven's sake!' he muttered with impatience. If flowers were a cliché, how much more so was this frantic scribble, an incoherent catalogue of self-loathing, self-justification, apology, reproach. (It was all her fault. No it wasn't. She was to blame. He was to blame. Or no one was.) Her going, she had written at the end – a piece of empty rhetoric – was 'for the best'. With what an attitude of sacrifice must she have closed the door upon their love!

Alex dumped the flowers in the sink, he gave them a good drink. He took a beer from the fridge, prised off the fluted metal cap, drank from the bottle. In an effort to suppress his panic, he worked at a show of outward calm, but his hand shook uncontrollably, the bottle chinked against his teeth, and all the while, in his brain, his thoughts unspooled.

Where had she gone? She didn't say. Not to Kate's this time, for sure. Not to Elli's or Geraldine's, since both were away. She might have stepped again into that background of which he knew so little, and been subtly reabsorbed. Her history, which was part of her, was deeply mysterious to him. He was intrigued by it, he was jealous of it. He had stolen her from it, and now it had snatched her back and secreted her from him.

She had parents, of whom she preferred not to speak. At the mere mention of them, her face would change; hurt would show through her thin skin, anguish would work at her mouth, at her eyes. She had had strings of lovers, each one, by her accounting, some sort of louse. To which of these unlikely characters would she turn in her despair?

He was at a loss. He sat down heavily on the floor, with his back against the oven door, his feet against a wall cupboard, and tried to make a plan. But the best he could come up with for the moment was a resolution.

Wherever she was, this beloved stranger, he would find her. He would bring her home.

The first clap of thunder made them all a bit skittish. Tina gave an excited little scream, put her hands up to her face and dragged at the loose skin under her eyes to reveal red rims. Patti giggled nervously and primped her hair. Seamus and Simon guffawed, they punched each other on the shoulder, poured themselves large shots of rotgut grappa and swaggered up and down the sitting-room, looking like the very devil, breathing fire. It was, they were agreed, the loudest thunder ever; it was surely the end of the world.

Elli, glancing out through the double doors as the rain came slapping in, saw coruscating lightning – for the blink of an eye, the hilltop villages stood out against a contused sky, making a final appeal to her affections, then the dark reclaimed them.

Mike, out at the sink – for he was firmly established, at the last, as kitchen porter – was heard to drop a plate in fright, and to curse as it shattered on the brick floor.

'Having a smashing time?' called Simon to him heartily.

'All breakages to be paid for on departure,' Patti intoned, then uttered a tinkling laugh to show that this was just her fun.

In the kitchen a dustpan choked on shards of china swept into its maw.

'I think we can forget our trip into town,' Patti pronounced, with a strange mix of gloom and satisfaction, putting her fingers together, steepling them, resting her chin upon them. 'The track will be washed away.' And she smiled unendearingly at them by turns, as though she took some small delight in disappointing each of them personally. In fact, she was feeling slightly proprietorial, and in a perverse way proud of her Italy, her mountains, her thunderstorm. No half-measures here!

'Oh no,' said Simon bullishly, his rubber soles squealing on the tiles, 'we can't be beaten by the weather. The minute this eases off we should set out. We are, let us not forget, British to the core. With a tow-row-row, and a row-row-row, and that kind of rot.'

'Where's David?' Patti enquired of no one in particular, in a tired voice that suggested she no longer much cared.

'He went,' responded Seamus vaguely, 'to take a shower.'

Elli wandered to the sideboard and picked up her camera, she weighed in her hand this deceiving apparatus, which contained thirty-six fictions, tightly reeled. Into her lens the group had smiled as they had not smiled face to face. Heads had been thrown back, teeth bared, glasses waved aloft. Arms had encircled waists, legs had kicked hilariously, cheek had pressed cheek; a high old time would be seen to have been had by all.

Something of the ineffable beauty of the landscape might also have been captured, miniaturised, made accessible. She had stolen a fragment of the country's soul to show about among her friends. And, in her choice of subject, a feeling for it, a keen aesthetic sense would be implied.

Back in London, with the trading of snapshots ('There's you by the pool', 'Remember this little *ristorante*?', 'What a hoot!'), shared memories would be manufactured. Casually, the photos would be handed round the office; colleagues would be offered vicarious delight. Already, among the six of them (the seventh of their number, David, so standoffish, did not deign to be included), there was a new mood of confederacy, a closing of ranks. There was an unspoken agreement to put a travel agent's gloss upon the holiday, to reinvent the past two weeks, to represent themselves as solid. So much would they trump it up that, long before next year, they would believe it, they would be desperate to be included, to do it all again.

More bizarre, though, was a genuine feeling of amity, a tenous and belated bonding. So they had not been one big, happy family? So what? The less drawn they had been, one to another, the more they now seemed to want to make amends. There was insecurity in the air; each of them was anxious, for the moment, to be liked.

It's the storm, thought Elli. It's making us cranky.

'*Tacconi* with hare sauce for me, I think,' pronounced

348

Simon, the glutton, who had been salivating over the guidebook. 'Then spit-roasted goat.'

And, 'I'll have risotto,' said Seamus, quite as if there were a waiter at his shoulder with pad and pencil poised. 'Then guinea fowl, perhaps.'

'Piggy-wiggies,' Tina chided them, wagging a finger at them.

'Will I do as I am?' Elli wanted to know, revealing her shaved underarms, twirling in front of them, inviting them to appraise her in white halter top and miniskirt.

'Good enough to eat,' replied Seamus, but in the tone of one who, having lost all appetite, is at pains to reassure his hostess.

'Not too skimpy?'

'Well, yes, actually, since you ask,' Patti put in. 'This is a very smart restaurant, you realise? The best in Lucca.'

'Then,' conceded Elli, regarding her narrowly, wondering at the woman's glib assertions of best, 'I shall nip up to my room and slip into something more appropriate.'

What was it with the Europeans, that they could not produce a decent shower? David, who was used to those great, whooshy, gushy American jobs that beat hell out of you and left you winded, felt wildly impatient with the ineffectual dribble at Il Poggio. Water issued from the shower-head in a kind of plait and wouldn't mix: skeins of it, icy cold and boiling hot, stung his back; it felt gritty on his skin, was salty in his mouth, and would not lather. For a minute he almost wished himself back in his Washington apartment, where he might emerge gasping, exhilarated, from his ablutions, into Kirstin's libidinous embrace.

There wasn't even a proper tray, just a tiled receptacle with mouldy grouting and a clogged drain hole at its centre. Spray ran off a plastic curtain and escaped the confines of the cubicle. He paddled in a scurfy puddle, and would walk dirt from his feet all across the bathroom floor. It felt somehow a squalid exericise, from which he would emerge no cleaner.

Despairing of the temperature controls, as of the pressure, he worked shampoo into his thick, unruly hair. Enclosed as he was on three sides by tiled walls, and with the curtain drawn, he did not see the bathroom door open. But, at the instant that the lights went out, and as a great groan went up in the sitting-room below, someone eased around the curtain to join him in the blackness.

With a practised and impartial touch, he cupped the pliant breast that fell so ripely into his hand, he palpated it assessingly. For a delicious instant he had hoped this might be Tina. She was an insufferably silly cow, ridiculously coy and mannered. It would have spiced matters up no end, however, to think her husband was downstairs.

But no. Elli it was who, true to her promise to slip into something, had been driven by impulse to slip in here. 'Power cut,' she diagnosed cheerfully.

'So it would seem.'

She scathed his soapy stomach with her nails and seized hard upon an awesome penis which, in a wearily dutiful way, had consented to stand. The rumours were true, then? Or, if anything, had undersold him.

'Not much you can do in a power cut,' she ventured.

'Not a lot,' he allowed.

'Just, you know . . . this and that.'

'This, that and the other.'

He drew a deep breath and, as if to consolidate the dark, he closed his eyes before he kissed her, running his fingertips speculatively over her hip. Her damp skin felt squelchy, rubbery.

'Mmm,' she murmured, moving right against him, inviting him to take a proper hold. And she congratulated herself on her enterprise in bringing this about. Why had she waited so long? She should have done this years ago. Uh-uh.

'We old bachelors,' said Geoffrey Markham, 'are creatures of habit.' He sprawled in his buttoned leather armchair, with his feet, in embroidered slippers, propped on the fender as though before a warming fire, and with a tumbler of single malt whisky on a small inlaid table to hand.

Naomi, sitting back on her haunches, found that the empty fireplace drew her, she stared into its yawning grate as if mesmerised by burning coals, she saw flickering pictures in the very nothingness. 'Technically,' she reminded him, spreading her skirt about her like a flower, smoothing the fabric over her knees, 'I suppose you're not a bachelor. Having once been married, I mean. That makes you a divorcé.'

'I am a happily unmarried man. I bless the day that Irena left.'

'Taking me with her.'

'Taking you with her, yes. What would I have done with a daughter? How should I have brought you up? Talked to you of women's things? A girl is her mother's affair.'

'It would have been different if I'd been a boy?'

'Perhaps, yes, practically speaking. But you weren't. You were a whey-faced little character with jug ears. I believe you were a changeling. The fairies took my own adorable child and left you in her place. There was some jiggery-pokery along the line.'

'You're suggesting I'm not even yours?'

He brought up one shoulder in a maddening half-shrug. It was, he seemed to say, a possibility.

'You've been no kind of father,' she reproached him bitterly. 'You have given me nothing all my life. Now you would even deny me legitimacy.'

'Ungrateful child! You haven't a filling in your head. So who do you thank for that?'

'Ah, my teeth, yes.'

'Who was it taught you to brush correctly? To massage your gums? And to floss? Who warned you against the evils of plaque, hm, hm?'

She did not care for his taunting tone. 'You know,' she said softly, tweaking at her hem, 'I don't think you're a very nice man.'

'I dare say not.' He let his head roll against the wing of the armchair and momentarily closed his eyes, so she saw that he was profoundly tired. He wore a quilted smoking jacket with food stains on the lapels. When his hand, smooth and manicured, set off in search of whisky, it went out of control, to fasten at last, and with difficulty, on the leaded crystal glass. She supposed he must be really very old. Maybe, also, he was very ill.

'Will you leave me some money in your will?' she questioned boldly.

'I shall have to see. But I've made no plans to die. I am sorry if this disappoints you.'

'Not especially. But I should like to think, if anything were to happen to you –'

'That you'd be rich beyond the dreams of avarice? Well, I don't know. I shall have to see. Would it be a kindness, after all, to pander to your venal nature? Ought I to encourage your improvidence?'

'Or else give me something now. Make me a gift, and we'll call it quits.' She cast around her, conjecturing wildly. The depth of the carpet, the bunchy folds of curtain, the mellow gleam of wood, the glint of ornaments, the sheer substantiality of everything suggested worth. 'Give me that.' She fixed upon a Minton vase. 'Or that.' A bronze lion proposed itself. 'Or that.' A gilt and ebony cabinet caught her eye.

'They stay where they are, for my lifetime at least. After that . . . well, you will have to wait and see.'

'You know, Father, I truly think I hate you.'

'Be that as it may . . .' His glass found his lips at last. He swigged the whisky, coughed, and said, 'I told you not to come here.'

'No you didn't. You didn't say. Not in so many words. And, believe me, I would not have, if I'd had anywhere else on earth to go.'

'How about Irena?'

'She's in the Maldives with Uncle Huw.'

'She bleeds him white, I imagine,' he remarked with satisfaction. 'So what is behind it, huh, your sudden flight? Fall out, did you, with the gigolo?'

'Alex is not . . . *not* a gigolo. He's sweet and kind and decent – unlike some.'

'So why did you hoof it over here?'

She looked down sharply at her hands resting on her lap. 'It was for the best,' she said dully, obstinately. If she could offer herself no better explanation, what hope had she of explaining all to this most unsympathetic of listeners? 'It was what he wanted. Or, if he didn't, it was what he would come to want. I couldn't bear to stay around and wait for it to fall apart.'

'Dear girl, don't tell me that you are, withal, a romantic?'

'I suppose I must be.'

'Head full of airy nothings? I say, be a sport, pour me another scotch. Have one yourself if you must. Have a small one. I cannot abide a woman who drinks.'

'So you won't help me out?' she pressed him, getting slowly to her feet and going to the bureau, to the tantalus. She picked up a decanter and held it consideringly to the light. 'You could change my life in an instant, but you won't.'

'Some small token, maybe, if and when I pass on. As I say, you will have to wait and see.'

'You're a monster. You give me no promises and no security.'

'I worked all my life, Naomi, drilling and filling the crowned heads of Europe. Dukes, Earls, captains of industry have teeth chock-full of amalgam, thanks to me. I have pulled the molar of many a marquis. I have earned these few comforts for my dotage.'

'And who will you dote on, Daddy? Who will there be to care for you, now you've driven us all away?'

'I shall employ a young nurse,' he said with vigour, 'to wheel me about. If she's pretty, I shall probably marry her and settle a fortune upon her. You, meanwhile, Miss, should find yourself a job.'

All the fight, the little feist she had, went out of her. She set the decanter down with a thud. Over and over in her head she had turned the thought of employment. If not modelling, there must be something she could do, that she would enjoy, that would fulfil her. She had considered working with children or animals, had pictured the gratitude in their limpid eyes, but quite what her function would be she could not envisage, and she did not, anyway, care for things that slavered.

'You know,' she said, gripping the edge of the bureau, regarding herself in the gilt-framed mirror above, 'that is just what *he* says. You are sounding just like Alex.'

On the twenty-third floor of Globe Tower that Friday evening, a meeting of top brass was in progress, convened by Gus Maclean, the editorial director and proprietor's henchman, who liked to test the loyalty of his senior editorial staff by demanding that they, at short notice, and with good grace, cancel dinner dates, miss school concerts, forfeit opera seats, call off secret assignations, disappoint partners, parents, children, let down loved ones (for everyone around that table, there would be recriminations later on, there would be hell to pay).

First on the agenda tonight was a discussion of Dawn Hancock, a talented writer and commentator who, in the proprietor's view, had brought new life to the paper these past two weeks with her witty, sassy *aperçus*. She was young, she was hungry, but above all she was . . . er, with it. She had been languishing too long in the backwater of features. She would be a tremendous asset to the *Globe* as a front-rank columnist, and must be offered a lucrative writer's contract immediately.

'A breath of fresh air,' declared Maclean, sniffing, dabbing at his nose and at the corners of his mouth with his knuckle. It was not a summer cold he had, but a nervous tic, an intensely annoying and distracting habit: his audience, riveted by the dab-dab-dabbing, would attend to his words with only half a mind. He seemed to have a fantasy that he was constantly oozing something nasty, which in a sense, of course, he was. It lent him, furthermore, a furtive air, which was not the least misplaced.

His basically handsome face was subject to grotesque distortions, pulled about by the strain of being a petty, snaky, pusillanimous, twisted, devious, vain, concupiscent sychophant and thoroughly bad egg (' "Hello," he lied,' as the running gag went among the staff).

Ron Housego, the paper's editor, notionally in charge of editorial, put his head down, clasping his hands over his balding pate, and lifted bloodshot, bloodhound eyes to his superior. 'But,' he argued, as though Maclean needed reminding, 'we have Elli Sharpe. She's the voice of the *Globe*.'

'Well, of course. And her contribution has been . . . That is, over the years she has given. . . She is, however, well past her sell-by date, Ron, as you must agree.'

Ron didn't. Not for one second. Dawn Hancock, in his estimation, could not hold a candle to Elli Sharpe. Dawn was shallow, callow, ludicrously overconfident. Her perceptions were snide, childish, paltry, priggish, and lacked any context beyond her own prejudices. She had scant experience of the world, a tenuous grasp of moral issues, she was an uncultured, untravelled, apolitical iconoclast, with a yah-boo-sucks attitude to major issues, a howling snobbishness, and unforgivable contempt for anyone who was not young, slim, beautiful, rich and fashionable.

Irrational, Elli might be at times, inconsistent often, outspoken always, but there was a fine, shrewd mind at work there, a strong egalitarian streak, and sympathy for the underdog. She also had a command of language, of syntax, which the younger woman lacked. He would say as much, he would resist this latest trespass by the proprietor upon his patch.

'Umm . . .' he ventured manfully, reaching for the water jug.

'The idea of fashion clamps,' enthused Maclean, slapping the conference table with his palm. 'Immobilising anyone in a velour tracksuit or an anorak. Towing away men in shiny suits and nylon shirts. Impounding their Hush Puppies. Great sport!'

'Well, if you think . . .' came back Ron, smart as paint, pouring a glass of water and taking a swig.

'Fat people should pay double on public transport.

How right! Because she's only saying, isn't she, what the rest of us believe?'

'You use public transport a lot?' enquired Laurie Martin, from the Review section. She was due to retire at the end of the year, so had nothing to lose (except – Maclean reflected nastily – about four stones).

'Indeed I do,' he assured her smoothly. 'How else would I get to New York?'

'Well, I didn't quite mean . . . I was thinking more of the number nine bus.'

'Let me get this straight.' Ron Housego picked up his pencil and drew in a slow, controlled, pensive way on his notepad, a tight coil design. 'You are asking me to sack Elli Sharpe?'

'Oh, no. Good heavens no.' Maclean waved aside the proposition. 'How long has she been with us? She has given many years of loyal service.'

'It would,' Laurie Martin translated wryly, 'cost the company a fortune if they had to pay her off.' And she fixed Ron Housego with her hardest stare, challenging him to stand up for the old guard.

Ron, however, being principal among the old guard, and all too aware of his own vulnerability, merely sank six inches in the chair; his whole body telescoped.

'There are ways and ways,' Maclean told him meaningfully. 'We are looking to you to be creative. Ingenuity, yes? Perhaps a reshuffle? Find a new role for Elli Sharpe. For the time being, they can alternate, hmm?' Up went his knuckle to his nose, back and forth, back and forth he dashed it under his nostrils. 'They can do the column turn and turn about. Patti Henderson will have a brief to keep an eye on Dawn. The girl is, after all, a novice, she will need a little guidance from a more experienced journalist.'

Inclining his head, Ron implied acquiescence, even as he silently responded: You don't know our Elli, mate. If she goes, she'll go kicking and screaming. You watch her, huh? You brace yourself. Because she's a better man than you are, Gunga Din.

Trevor Pocock lay in his hospital bed, staring at the ceiling, at white nothingness. Had it not been for that disease-ridden lime tree, he might not have made good his escape.

Smoke killed, they had said. He was lucky to be alive, they had said. To which he had responded, hoarsely, that this was a matter for deep philosophical debate. And, of course, they had failed to take Elli Sharpe into the reckoning.

Elli, he thought, turning his poor, pitted face into the pillow, would not be best pleased. She would, indeed, go ballistic.

CHAPTER

9

'If you must know,' said Kate, 'it's John.' She was in a weak, confiding mood – a symptom of the flu for which, according to Elli, she had only herself to blame, since she had certainly 'let it in'. Her face felt bloated, with too much going on behind it. Her eyes and nose streamed. She heard ringing in her ears. Her throat rasped when she swallowed. Her limbs were leaden. Every few minutes a great wave of heat would rush up inside her; she had a panicky sensation of boiling over. And all this was, apparently, optional. She had elected to suffer so.

'Wooo,' responded Elli, fanning herself, then patting her chest in an agitated fashion, miming the battering of her heart. 'I'm not sure I want to hear this. I'm all for a bit of extramarital – I mean, given that there are no eligible single men for us women in the prime of life – but this is something else. Frankly, I'm appalled. I can't think what's got into the pair of you. However did you come to . . .? Because two more unlikely protagonists I never met. And how, while we're on the subject, can you square it with that exacting conscience of yours? There are husbands, Kate Garvey, and there are husbands. There are the husbands of strangers, or of mere nodding acquaintances, who, as far as I'm concerned, are up for grabs; and there are the husbands of friends, with whom we do not get involved.'

'Ruth Curran is your friend,' Kate reminded her, sitting down heavily on the margin of the lawn and picking at a scab on her arm. 'Or she was.'

'Not in the same degree as Geraldine is yours. And Geraldine is also, of course, though one tends to forget it, your sister-in-law. What a mess! *I* don't know. I'm out of the country for two short weeks, and chaos is come again.'

'As for squaring it with my conscience, I can't. I'm simply riddled with guilt. I never dreamt that I'd fall into such a situation.'

'Oh-ho! I like "fall". A complete denial of volition. As if you had no responsibility for anything.'

'Well, that's the way it feels, to be honest, however silly it may sound to you.'

'It's a wonder you can look her in the face. Will you go on doing her garden for her? Shagging her old man on one hand, pruning her petunias on the other?'

'One doesn't prune petunias.'

'Will you go on dead-heading her dahlias, drinking tea at her table, being paid good coin?'

'I may not. She is always hinting that I'm too expensive.'

'And you're smitten? Truly? But that's incredible. I can see I shall have to revise my opinion of our Johnno. I've always surmised that he hadn't a good fuck in him.'

'Then you surmise wrongly,' responded Kate with dismaying coyness. Another hot flush, this time of sheer embarrassment, swept through her. 'Of course,' she

361

added humbly, 'I can't claim to be an expert in these matters, having no one to compare him with but David.'

'But that was so long ago,' said Elli, sounding suddenly, unaccountably, very cross indeed, as though the full impact of Kate's revelation had only this second hit her. 'I doubt that you can even remember it.'

'My first sexual experience. My *only* sexual experience until now. With the father of my child. I'm hardly likely to have forgotten.'

'So, tell. How *do* they compare? Surely John can't measure up to David? He's world champion – or so his reputation has it.'

'I shouldn't dream of telling you, Elli. I shouldn't dream of discussing it. You can be bloody impertinent at times.'

'Be like that, then, po-face. Anyway, the point is, what are you going to do?'

'I haven't a clue.' Kate gave a miserable shrug. She prospected up her sleeve for a soggy tissue and snuffled into it self-pityingly. 'All those years, when Alex was a boy, I put my own needs aside. I didn't tend them. Now they're running rampant. We could make one another so happy, you see. So much happier than we are now.' A perfect life, she and John had conjured for themselves, the kind of blissful, leisured, companionable, pure, free existence that is possible in an imagined world.

'And devastate Geraldine in the process?'

'Er . . .' Kate shoved the balled, wet tissue back up her cuff, and shook her head. Her eyes were watering again. 'That's what I say to him. That we could never . . . But I don't think she loves him, do you? Not properly.'

'Sure she does, in her own sweet way. More, actually, than she realises. But it would be the loss of face, the damage to her standing with the golfing, gin-and-tonic set that would destroy her, the poor silly. No, Kate, it's not on. Have your fling, if you must, but have a care. Now, please, burden me no further with your troubles. I have enough of my own, thanks very much.'

'I do have to hand it to you, Elli,' Kate confessed, as Petal came crashing out of the bushes and rolled about on the path beside her in a fit of pussycat ecstasy, delighting, perhaps, in the absence of Muffy, who had gone with Juin on the long trek across town to Downside, bearing gifts of shortbread for her old ladies. 'You are awfully resilient.'

'Resilient? I should think I have to be. My friends are all quite loopy. They're in and out of bed with the most unsuitable people. First Naomi with Alex. Now you with . . . Then, as if that weren't enough, there's some snotty little upstart after my job. And my cleaner has burnt my house down.'

'We-ell . . .' Kate, always so reasonable, extenuated, 'not *down*, exactly.'

'Out, then. It's a burnt-out shell. The stairs are gone. There's soot up the walls. You can stand in the kitchen and see daylight through the roof. When I get my hands on Trevor Pocock I shall . . .' Closing her eyes she took on a look of such intense excogitation that by the power of thought alone, it seemed, some dreadful retribution might be visited upon him. Seeing Elli's hard, impervious face, Kate guessed that a range of truly terrifying reprisals was under review.

'Poor chap,' she was moved to sympathise, as she spread her toes and considered the white spaces between them. 'He must be mortified.'

'Mortified? He'll be *cruc*ified if I have my way.'

'It would have been an accident, wouldn't it? It's not as if he'd have started it on purpose.'

'Don't bet on it. It's precisely the sort of stunt that idle little sod would pull to get out of cleaning the cooker. Anyway, accident or no, my home is reduced to rubble.' Elli, who had bagged the only deckchair ('guest's privilege'), yawned and stretched her legs, she pointed her toes, put her bare feet apart and together, apart and together, in the air, banging her heels. She had been back from Italy for just a week. The two women were sitting in the garden in Tooting on Saturday morning, turning to good account the sun's brief benefaction, for the black September shadows would soon drive them indoors. Rear windows, watching them from all directions, were full of trees and sky, of wheeling birds, and of each other; the outside world was turned back by the glass. There was a sharper edge to the air now than there had been all summer, and a piquant smell about it. Bonfire smoke and papery cinders drifted on a breath of wind from behind a distant garden wall; the scent of dry leaves burning was a powerful portent of autumn.

Elli was in extraordinarily good spirits for someone upon whom adversity had so comprehensively dumped. She had been distraught, she had almost – *almost* – wept to find her home gutted. But then she, being essentially a pragmatist, unsentimental, had been cheered to think how she would make a killing on the insurance. The place would be rebuilt to a higher standard. She would have a new kitchen, new carpets, new everything.

On the work front, also, now that she had steadied herself, she found cause for optimism. She would continue to write for the *Globe*, to draw a fat salary, to charge to the company hefty expenses, she would see off that Hancock character – 'the hopeless Dawn', she had dubbed the young pretender, refusing to regard her as a serious threat – or she would plead constructive dismissal and command a redundancy payment of legendary proportions. She was in, she liked to think, an unassailable position.

Homeless as she was for the time being, she had considered putting up in a hotel, or renting somewhere. But then she'd had a brainwave: she and Juin would come to Tooting, they would stay with Kate and 'cheer her up', they would be company for her, and solace.

Incipient flu, it must have been, that had caused Kate to appear less than thrilled at the proposal. (A gruff 'All right' had been her best effort.) 'I shall go in and make us some coffee,' she said blearily, now, before being seized by such paralysing apathy that she could not stir. 'I shall go in a minute,' she revised. She rather hoped Elli would volunteer; Elli didn't.

She was a better and a worse guest than Naomi. She didn't waft about or anything, she didn't drip off the sofa all day, but her shoes were everywhere, with their vicious, spiky heels sticking up, and she was very interfering. She had retuned the radio to a particularly crass pop station. She had put the kitchen clock right, in defiance of Kate's protests that – never mind the illogi-cality – she liked to have it five minutes fast. When the phone rang she would make a grab for it, on the clear assumption that the call must be for her – which, annoyingly, invariably it was.

Now, in answer to a summons from the doorbell, she was up on her feet and in through the back door in a decided fashion, before Kate could gather her wits. 'Stay there. I'll get it.'

'Make yourself at home, do,' Kate mouthed at her friend's back. 'Treat the place as though it were your own.'

A brief interview on the front step must have ensued; it was moments before Elli marched out through the back door and, with a heralding gesture, her arms flung wide, announced, 'You have a visitor.'

It was Alex, and he looked just awful. That, at any rate, was his mother's shocked perception; Elli, for her part, saw nothing much amiss. It was not that he had shaved with inattention, if at all; or that he wore his oldest sweatshirt and had made no effort to subdue his hair. There was worse dishevelment within. He managed for Kate a ragged smile which merely discomposed his features. Naomi, Kate told herself with such violent dislike that it shook her, must be driving him crazy with her demands.

'Why did you change the lock?' he asked, but vaguely, not accusingly; her answer – whatever answer – he would meet with indifference.

'My bag was taken from my car. My keys.'

'Oh.'

She stood and went on tiptoe to embrace him, but he brushed her distractedly off him, and told them, 'Naomi's gone.'

'What do you mean, "gone"?' Kate quizzed him, with wild, unworthy hope, which she had not the cunning to disguise (seeing it, Alex turned from her, dismissing her utterly; she was not with him, therefore she was against him).

'Gone where?' queried Elli, back in her deckchair, blinking up at him. And she, of course, had the guile to show concern; she crimped her brow in sympathy, slapped a hand over her mouth and palmed a smile, she put into it that telltale sign of glee.

'That's just it. I don't have a clue. We had a row, you see. A bust-up. Nothing very serious – or so I thought. Then she walked out. Left a goodbye note. And I haven't heard a word from her since.'

'She must be somewhere,' ventured Kate fatuously, in a doomed effort to redeem herself.

'With her mother, maybe?' mused Elli. 'In Oxford. Or Cambridge, is it?'

'She wouldn't be with Alan, would she?' wondered Kate, earning herself, from her son, still colder disregard.

'We must try her father first. Geoffrey Markham. He's sure to be in the directory.' Elli, heaving herself out of the complaining chair, talking cheery non sequiturs, took charge. 'You take the weight off your feet, Alex, darling, and I'll go call. Best I do it, in case she's lying low, avoiding you. She does go in for such dramatics, doesn't she? Mind what you're doing, though. Two and a half thousand people a year need hospital treatment for injuries caused by garden furniture. Pinched fingers, mainly. Pinched right off, so Geraldine informs me. She read it in a magazine. Well, she would, wouldn't she? My house burnt down, by the way, Alex – maybe you heard? – so Juin and I have imposed ourselves on Kate.' Her tone was warm and conversational: such a delightful imposition she made this sound.

Left alone, Kate and Alex had nothing to say. She hung her arms down by her sides like a little girl and looked lost. His dark eyes took in and just as soon discarded her. He was so beautiful and so remote, with something magnificent in his bearing. He was not her boy any more, he was every whit a man. She feared she might die of hurt over him. She longed to tell him, 'I'm having an affair. It will end in tears for me too. We are both being such fools.' Instead, she blew her nose again, and cleared her throat.

When the sun dropped behind the distant rooftops, in the small square of garden it was all at once grey.

Presently, they heard a ting as the telephone receiver went down. 'She *was* there,' Elli's voice preceded her from the kitchen. She sounded brisk and businesslike, completely at grips. 'She stayed with him until this morning. Cleared out not an hour ago. He doesn't know where she's gone, and by the sound of it he doesn't give a damn. So what I suggest, you gorgeous hunk, is that I make some coffee, then we'll put our heads together, hmm? And think what we do next.'

The leaded windows of Copperfields, open just a squint, let in the scents of mown grass and petrol smoke. John,

368

aboard the ride-on mower, made a bumpy circuit of the lawn. With wearying predictability, the noise came and went, came and went. At each new approach, the listeners grew tense, they gritted their teeth; breathing was suspended, conversation set aside.

When at last the mowing stopped, the silence settled only slowly on the garden; sound soaked away into freshly watered beds. And for a while it seemed there was nothing, anyway, to be said. Geraldine poked a finger in her ringing ear, and remembered reading something interesting about 'Strimmer rash', a sort of dermatitis caused by harmful substances in plants. She lacked, however, the energy to raise the topic. She had not the heart, at this moment, for playing hostess.

In a minute, John, with a slight but perceptible stoop, as if he carried on his shoulders something weighty, trudged right by the sitting-room, offering its two uncompanionable occupants a view of his profile. He had the taut look of an ascetic, perhaps a religious celibate, which did not impress itself upon Naomi. She did not see, in that glimpse of the man, the nobility that Kate saw; but, then, she saw nothing very much outside the scope of her self-absorption. Unconsciously, she ran her thumb and finger up and down the sherry schooner she'd been nursing.

'You know,' said Geraldine, finally finding in herself the snap to speak her mind, 'it wasn't going to work. These irregular arrangements never do.' Her tone was assured, even scolding, for was there not a wealth of empirical evidence? (One had only to read the newspapers.) And should not Naomi, at her age, have known better?

She moved to the sideboard, creating her own commotion, a big, womanly pother. Her dress, of some diaphanous material, unintelligibly patterned in pale lilac and grey, a controlled explosion of colour, shaped without regard to the human female form, lent her a diffuse aspect; one could not tell where she began or ended.

Naomi offered no reply. Indignation gripped her throat so tightly that her face was washed with pink and she could not utter. She wanted to say that *of course* it might have worked. That all manner of 'irregular arrangements' succeeded. But the fact was – and here bloody Geraldine had her – that it hadn't. It had failed. It was over.

'My nephew,' Geraldine continued, by the use of the possessive pronoun claiming Alex, making him very particularly hers, 'is a suggestible young man.'

She thinks I seduced him, Naomi told herself. She honestly believes it was all down to me.

'I do wish . . .' murmured Geraldine, refilling her own sherry glass with an unsteady hand (an alcoholic glug, the amber liquid made). 'That is, I think you might have . . .'

She did wish that Naomi had telephoned first. She thought she might have *asked* before turning up here. However intolerable the situation at her father's (and it did sound grim, it sounded desolating), she might have given them a few days' notice.

Not that there wasn't space for her, or food. The large,

accommodating house had three guest bedrooms, and the Gorsts always kept a good table. But, today of all days, Naomi was unwelcome. David was expected at any moment for lunch. He was to stay the weekend. David was Alex's father. Alex had been Naomi's, er, boyfriend. Therefore, it would be awkward.

Geraldine was very alive to awkwardness, she watched for it, and where she found it she enlarged it by her efforts to make light of it, whipping up vague social unease into a veritable froth of anxiety. People oblivious of their predicament would have it brought by her, irresistibly, to their notice. She would sit, today, at the end of the table, palpably not saying something. Then, should the unmentionable be mentioned, she would loudly change the subject, offer brussels sprouts with ostentation, remark that of course they were not at the best till the first frost got to them, and probably send her wine glass flying as she handed dishes.

Her children, in their different ways, had a particular talent for setting her off. Lucy, through sheer ineptitude, unerringly, would put her foot in it (whatever 'it' might be), while Dominic, mischievous, danced around it.

He came into the room now, blowing a fanfare through his cupped hand. And, 'Oh, hi,' he greeted Naomi, eyeing her frankly, speculatively, in a manner that discomfited her. Too plainly, from his look, he had on his mind her affair with Alex; he was thinking of sex, and all sorts; he was enumerating for himself her considerable charms, probably giving her marks out of ten. Then, 'How does a fellow get a drink around here?' he demanded.

His likeness to his cousin – more nuance, really; a not-quite-the-sameness of certain features; an indefinable family resemblance – gave her quite excruciating pain. When she absent-mindedly sipped her sherry, the glass bumped off her trembling lip.

'Dominic,' said his mother in a strained voice, 'you are *not* going to sit down to lunch dressed like that.'

'No?' He checked himself out, one arm, then the other; he glanced down at his front, then, twisting, peered over his shoulder, as if to determine of what arcane dress rule he was in contravention. The fact that he was wearing old jeans with the knees out, and was naked from the waist up but for a string of beads which hung down his bronzed chest almost to his navel, the fact that he appeared so thoroughly dissolute, with his sun-streaked hair falling in his eyes, gave a lie to this elaborate show of bemusement. 'Just as you wish,' he responded, finally, in that amenable manner which was itself a tease.

'Cover up, at least.' Geraldine sat down hard on a fiddle-back chair against the wall.

'Can I get a beer, first?'

'No, first you change. Put a shirt on, do. And find Lucy for me. And call your father in. Tell him I said to wash his hands. David will be here at any second.'

'Will there be fingernail inspection?'

'Oh . . .' Geraldine put her hand up to the bridge of her nose, she pinched it hard, pressed her fingers into the corners of her eyes and sighed her exhaustion at him. 'You tire me out,' she told him feelingly, 'you really do.'

'Sorry,' offered Dominic. He went out of the room, closing the door quietly. Then he opened it again, put his head around it, winked saucily at Naomi, and withdrew.

Mabel Flowers sat at the window with her hands on her knees and gazed out. Useless, those hands had become; idle. Once they had been needed for so many things, they had been always busy. There had been power in their touch, to bring reassurance, comfort, delight. But no longer. Trembling, they would set off on a short, fraught journey with a cup of tea, or make crumbs of a slice of dry 'farmhouse' fruit cake. Drumming on the silencing fabric of her shirt, they would seem to pick out a tune. Morning and night they fumbled with zip fasteners, buttons, hooks and eyes. With practised mutuality they soaped and rinsed each other; they washed her 'bits and bobs'. And that was about it, really.

Her head was to one side, and she had a patient, waiting air about her. Those faded eyes, trained upon the distance, might have been watching for something or someone to appear over the horizon. The corners of her mouth turned up, and yet she did not smile.

'I'm sorry,' tendered Juin softly, going down on her knees beside the old woman, resting her cheek against her arm, noticing, irrelevantly, the intricate knit of her cardigan, an ultimately pointless intrigue of K3 and P2. She picked at the pilling on the bouclé sleeve.

Mabel said nothing, but lifted a finger, a signal of sorts. Perhaps she did not trust herself to speak. Or was there nothing, in the end, to say?

'At least she didn't suffer,' Juin persisted. But such a

platitude this sounded. And beside, how could one know?

Stroke? The word had two such opposite meanings. A stroke was something sweetly soothing, a caress. Or it was fell, it was a death blow.

Vera Salter had been subject to the latter. Last week, this was, some time on Tuesday night; it had been morning before anyone knew of it, too late to do anything, if indeed there had been anything to be done. Three days Vera had lain in a coma. Mabel, always by her side, had watched her slip away. 'Slip away' was, at least, how Peggy Southgate expressed it. To Juin it seemed that life, having scribbled all over Vera, had finally obliterated her.

She wished she hadn't come today to Downside. She felt unequal to it. The coping skills of Mrs Southgate, the brisk efficiency which had so impressed her in the past, seemed cold-blooded to her now. The place smelt, as usual, of cleaning fluids – polish, disinfectant – and of an early, ungastronomic lunch. A vase of Michaelmas daisies, untidy, indeterminately mauve, graced the entrance hall. The helpers called in loud voices to each other; they chivvied and cajoled the inmates; they were very brisk – no mourning, no hushed tones here, and no empty beds (a new arrival slept in Vera's now).

'Did you get my postcard?' Juin pressed Mabel for an answer.

Another listless lifting of the fingers – or was it just a twitch? – gave her her reply.

'Scotland was so beautiful. I had simply no idea. I must tell you all about it when I'm next here.'

Privately, Juin felt she would never come again. Elli had been right, of course. She was not up to this sort of thing. She didn't have in her either the quality of care or that of uncare, of infinite sympathy or of cheery fatalism that would make it possible. She could not see God's will at work among the residents the way the matron seemed to. She saw only decay.

Sitting back on her haunches, she allowed her gaze to go gently alongside Mabel's, to keep company with it as far as the lawn, with those few municipal-looking trees at its margins, and with tall, frondy pampas grass, a horticulturalist's conceit, peculiarly unpleasing, in a circle of soil at its precise centre. She hoped, by her nearness, to bring some small comfort, but had no means of judging if she did.

In a minute she would make a dash for the office, she'd collect Muffy and embark on the long journey 'home' to Tooting. Kate, at any rate, she reassured herself, would understand her feelings (she pictured that snubby face, creased with concern for her). Juin was a good deal less sanguine than Elli about their burnt-out house. It was the only home she'd ever known, and its loss, however temporary or remediable, made her insecure. The long minicab ride to and from school was tedious beyond words. She felt funny at Larkspur Road, where Alex so conspicuously wasn't, and yet where at any heart-stopping moment he might be. She felt odd and out of place. But to be close to Kate again, to find that things really were just fine between them, went a long way to compensate her.

Loosening her grip on the arm of Mabel's chair, she

began the process of disengagement, got to her feet, then, with murmured promises, swooping, dropped a kiss on the woman's white head. Her legs were weak, she felt shaken as she made good her escape.

'Come back soon, do, Raggedy Anne,' she thought she heard. But when she turned abruptly at the door, Mabel still sat motionless.

Ten minutes later, heading for the tube, with Muffy misbehaving at the full extent of his lead, she was overtaken in a rush by the desire to talk to someone young and vital who would make her laugh, and maybe vex her just a little, also. She wanted someone to restore her faith in a life worth living.

So she dug in her pocket for coins, scooped Muffy up under her arm, recoiled from the slaver of his tongue, dived into a phone box and dialled the number.

Dominic Gorst sat across from the man whose like he was widely held to be, and felt only intense loathing. He despises us, he told himself. How very dull and bourgeois we appear to him! He measures himself all the time against us. And just look how mother craves his approval!

If it came down to taking sides – and he was disposed to think that it did – he must sacrifice his own cool, blow his credibility, align himself with his parents, rather than play up to the condescending outsider, to share in his scorn for Gorst values, powerful though the temptation was to do so.

To this end, he comported himself with a rare and conscious decorum, which had Geraldine seriously rattled. In Dominic, such impeccable behaviour seemed perverse. She feared some elaborate prank, and could scarcely attend to her brother's views on Hillary Clinton, or to his amusing anecdotes of that small world circumscribed by the DC Beltway, for sending darting glances down the table at her son, catching him one minute in the act of offering bread, the next paying gallant court to a silent and distracted Naomi. And what – she was bound to ask herself – was the boy's game?

David, it must be said, could not give much thought to La Clinton, either. But then, he didn't need to, since his Washington spiel was endlessly rehearsed, his White House stories had been tried and tested on numerous more demanding audiences. His mind was thus free to wander around Geraldine, her home, her lifestyle, her constrained existence. Upstairs and down it went, making its assessments. And everywhere it barked itself on an ineluctable Englishness which had him wincing, screwing up his eyes. Could she not be more exotic? More original? More worthy of him? Her life appeared to him to be composed of vast areas of disappointment, and a very few small satisfactions, strung out like fairy lights, which preoccupied her disproportionately.

Her children displeased him above all – the girl with her gracelessness, her brutish expressions, her air of petulance; the youth with his apparent complaisance, his conforming attitudes, and with, confusingly, the roguish look of someone laughing up his sleeve. This was family. All sorts of affinities and similarities were assumed. Yet these Gorsts were not – they *could* not be – his people.

When, beckoning with her two hands, curling her

fingers into her palms, Geraldine called in the empty soup plates – chilled cucumber and mint, from a recipe, she had said, deprecating her efforts, crediting *Good Housekeeping* – David stood up as if to help to clear them. In so doing, he sought himself in the mirror above the long sideboard, where waited a green salad, fresh fruit, cheeses under a plastic cloche, crackers in a barrel; he found a tall, lean, wolfish man, blessed with uncommon sex appeal, he found the nearest thing he knew to God.

'*You* sit down, David,' Geraldine exhorted him, emphasising his guest status, and she turned her gaze on Lucy, silently commanding her. The child, however, sat there, stolid, oblivious (what a flump, David thought), and, unnervingly, it was Dominic who sprang to his feet, came round to collect the stacked plates, and whisked them away to the kitchen.

David, with an acquiescing gesture, then, lowered himself once more into his chair, planted his elbows on the table, made a tree of his big hands, put his chin down into it, and turned the full beam of his curiosity upon Naomi opposite.

She had not, in his memory, ever been more desirable. As she sat there with her head bowed, some quality of sadness and of childlike vulnerability aroused in him a howling want of her.

How had she given him the slip for so long? And how had she so cheated time? All the years that had flowed through her seemed only to have refreshed her. Her eyes were clear, blue, ineffably soulful; her skin was the texture of rose petals, white, with the faintest flush. He itched to wind his fingers in her floppy hair, to haul her head back on her frail neck, to graze her pale throat with his teeth.

No one would guess that this woman was . . . what? Forty-two? Geraldine, of course, had always been forty, she'd been born that way. He recalled her as a little girl, off to Sunday school in white lacy gloves, with a pillbox hat clamped to her bobbing curls, a patent hangbag swinging from her arm in a decisively middle-aged fashion. The rest of them had achieved forty, or had had forty thrust upon them. John Gorst's hair had receded; John, himself, indeed, appeared to be in some form of recession, he was more than ever difficult to reach. Elli Sharpe had smoked, drunk, screwed her way to aggress-ive maturity (David shuddered rather at the memory of her stifling embrace). Kate's face, always crimped by worry, was sure by now to be riddled with frown lines. And he, too, though he wore it with style, might be seen to be in middle life. Alone among them, Naomi Markham retained an air of tender youth. And she was still susceptible, it seemed, to youthful crushes.

He was seized by the violent desire to drive Alex out of her. Silently he raged against the boy who trespassed on a more adult preserve. Some little flibbertigibbet, that great oaf should content himself with; a popsy. He must leave the foxy babes for the real men.

Salmon mayonnaise was set before him with a flourish. And, 'How is Kate?' the devil in David drove him to enquire. This brought them all, he was aware, within one remove of Alex, and he kept Naomi in his sights to see if she would squirm.

Ooh, *awkward*. The question touched off feverish

activity. Geraldine's fingers fluttered around her throat, they fretted at her pearls as colour surged in her plump cheeks.

John, coughing, lunged across the table, offering salad indiscriminately, and sent his wine glass flying.

'She keeps the gardens beautifully as you can see,' Geraldine responded finally, pinkly, with a wave in the direction of the window. Then, 'I believe she's well,' she added as an afterthought. 'Yes, I would say she's keeping very well. Apart from having, you know, a touch of influenza.'

Naomi, at the death of this conversation, with an audible sigh, strove to make less of the food on her plate, compressing it with knife and fork. Tactlessly tactful, she drew attention to her extreme disrelish; she failed to notice that she held the other five transfixed.

Her appetite, at its best a compromise between the will to live and a vague inclination not to bother, had quite deserted her. And her sleep patterns were increasingly disturbed. Every night last week she had gone early to bed, falling into a deep and druggy slumber, only to start up, two, three hours later, gripped by panic, to lie peering into agitated darkness. Then, in the daytime, morning or afternoon, she would bump her cheek down on her arm and doze wherever she sat, always dreaming that she was wakeful, watchful.

She was in serious trouble now. She was in dire distress. In that great, gloomy house in Pimlico she had discovered her childhood, still there where she had left it, intact. Behind doors and in drawers her past had lurked. It had waited around corners, at the bend of the stairs, and in shadowy recesses, to jump her. For seven days she had suffered a succession of psychic shocks, she had been assailed by memories as mystifying and disturbing as intimations of the future.

Going out through the big front door, passing callers come to keep appointments with the young Australian dentist who now leased the ground-floor surgery, picking up on these patients' sickly apprehension, she had fancied some sixth sense must tell them what a truly terrible house this was. And it was not Irena's tantrums – appalling though they had been – that she so vividly recalled.

Terrible things, Geoffrey Markham had done to her, terrible nothings, for which he could not be prosecuted, and with which she might never confront him (to do so would be to hear again his odious, dismissing laugh, which drove her to the edge of reason). He would never be punished, unless by his conscience – which seemed unlikely – for that insidious campaign of humiliation and demoralisation that he had waged against his only daughter.

First, hearing *Parsifal* played again at volume, her mind had flooded with images of this man leaning over her, peering at her perfect molars – 'Open wide' – with his free hand all the while up her skirt, stroking with a spidery softness the inner aspect of her clammy thigh.

Then, as she lay in her old room, in her old bed, staring at the door, she had fantasised that it stood suddenly wide – she almost heard the squeak of hinges – to reveal him, framed there in a wedge of hallway, staring at her, wordless, with a leer upon his face that mortified her strangely (in the draught from the long, vaulted corridor, a mobile of fantastical birds, swinging madly, clacking, had thrown shadows all about the ceiling).

The scent of Turkish cigarettes, a curl of blue smoke, had evoked for her the time he tipped his ash into her glass of milk in a manner that, to an innocent, had been as meaning and as sullying as it was incomprehensible.

One evening, bidding him a cool 'Sleep well', she had recollected all those other hideous 'goodnights', she had seen again Geoffrey sitting on the bed and scratch-scratch-scratching at her starchy pillow with a menacing detachment, with immaculate, clipped nails.

Not to sexual abuse so much as to some sinister, infinitely subtle controlling ploys had she been subjected. And the nameless guilt, the shame she had experienced then, she experienced again today.

That's what happened, she told herself, toying with a slab of salmon, coral flesh on whiskery bone. And, distantly, as she introspected, she heard the ringing of the telephone, heard Dominic go out to answer it. No wonder I'm so screwy, she decided. Then, in a defeated way, writing herself off, I'm absolutely fucked, she concluded.

'Can I take Uncle David to see Topper after lunch?' pleaded Lucy. 'Topper,' she explained, turning to David with a kind of grotesque coquetry, a clumsy flirtatiousness, 'is a pony. He belongs to my best friend Jocasta.'

Dear Lord, David groaned inwardly, she has a crush on me! 'Will we all go,' he suggested smartly, 'for the fresh air?'

'Oh, I don't think Naomi is into horses.'

Hearing her name (Lucy, she seemed to think, had spoken to her), Naomi raised her eyes, she fluttered the long lashes that had reposed upon her cheeks. And she glimpsed for a fleeting second, with a pang of recognition, across from her, resting on the table, on the damask cloth, the hands of Alex Garvey. (This much, only, her darling had from his father: fine, strong fingers, a powerful grasp.) And her heart was wrung.

'Hey, Juin, how're you doin'?' cried Dominic heartily, anglicising her name, subordinating pronunciation to rhyme. 'How are you, my June? Still bursting out all over?'

'Not exactly,' Juin told him gruffly, and she burst, instead, into tears.

'Whoa, whoa, whoa,' he pleaded with her, 'don't take on. What's up? What's happened? Tell your Uncle Dom about it. Situate the facts. Has somebody hurt you? Name names.'

'It's . . .' blubbered Juin helplessly down the line. There was a long pause, a sound of snuffling. Then, 'It's Vera,' she essayed again. 'Vera Salter. You remember I told you? One of my old ladies.'

'The East Ender?'

'That was her.'

'*Was*? So she died? Then I'm sorry.'

'Why should you be? You didn't even know her.' Her tone was truculent. If he dared to say anything about a 'good innings', to suggest that this was God's will or whatever, she would let him have the full force of her rage.

However, 'You made her live for me, Juin, with your talk of her,' he told her with evident sincerity. 'No, I mean it. Truly you did. And in any case, I should be sad for you. And about . . . you know, another little light gone out.'

Patient, he waited for her hiccuping sobs to abate. And he bit hard down on his tongue, lest some stupid, inappropriate joke escape him, as was apt to happen in times of stress.

'Sorry,' she told him finally, dully, composed.

'You have been through it, haven't you, Ju-ju, since we came back from the holiday of a lifetime?'

'It hasn't been great, I admit.'

'Do cheer up, chicken. Try not to take the worries of the world upon yourself. Tell me, how did the haggis go down with Elli?'

'She didn't say much about it, being a bit distracted, I suppose, with the small matter of our house going up in flames.'

'You should have told her it's traditional on Burns night.'

There, it was out! The inevitable joke, and a lame one at that. He waited sheepishly for her to hang up on him – serve him right if she did – but to his relief she laughed. 'You, Dominic,' she told him, 'are like the brother I never had.'

'But you could have had me. Don't say you weren't asked. In fact, the invitation still stands, for the nonce. Closes December 31.'

'So I have until then to decide?'

'If you need it. I say, guess what. We have a full house

here. The great David Garvey has honoured us with a visit. Lucy's going all goosey, and Mother's in a dither.' But he's only interested in Naomi, of course, he reflected cynically. 'Oh, and Juin,' he felt obliged to add (she would hear of it soon enough from someone, he reasoned), 'Naomi's with us, too. She's split with Alex.'

There was a moment's hesitation, the catching of a breath, and then, 'I've got to go,' she said abruptly, 'my money's just about to run –'

'Have you ever noticed,' said Elli, shaking a Stuyvesant from the pack, 'what absurdly small feet Geraldine has?'

'I can't say I have,' Kate responded, in a tired, detached tone, with a sideways look at Alex. Any mention of Geraldine, in the circumstances, seemed to her unwarranted. She regretted already, having told Elli about John, for she was sure to harp on, to return to the subject again and again, to torment her.

'Well, she does.' Elli snapped her lighter, bunched her face around the cigarette and sucked the flame. 'Naomi agrees. She's spotted it too. Take a look next time you're over there pricking out her polyanthus. And those preposterous pumps she wears. I mean, I will defend to the death a woman's right to shoes, but there are limits. Incy-wincy buckles. Kitten heels. They make me want to smack her.'

'I shall go there,' Alex announced. He strode to the piano, banged the lid open, put his knee up on the stool and ran a finger down the keyboard. Sonorous, ominous, out of tune, the notes, colliding, ran around the room. 'I shall speak to her. If this is really it, then she can tell me to my face.'

'I shouldn't go just yet, darling,' Elli counselled, seeking an ashtray and settling for a plant pot. It had been her idea to ring Copperfields, to see if Naomi had fetched up *chez* Gorst. She had called on a pretext and confirmed it, learning also, for her pains, that David Garvey was in temporary residence. To hear his name had put her badly out of countenance. Having given him one on holiday, she felt that he owed her, at the very least, a decent dinner, but she'd had no word from him. 'Give her twenty-four hours.' This sound advice she offered, against her secret wish to urge Alex out of there. If Juin returned, as she might at any minute, to find him in this dark and brooding state, so obviously in love and half demented, it could set her right back, then she'd be hell to live with. 'Softly, softly, catchee Markham. The last thing you want to do is to startle her. She'll run like a hare from any kind of scene. You know what she's like (well, you should do). Gutless, basically. And I say that with affection, I speak as her good friend.'

'Wait a day or so, you mean? You may have a point.'

'Not so much of the "may have". I'm not always right, my lad,' she tapped the side of her nose with her forefinger, 'but I'm never wrong.'

'No?'

'No. Now, I wonder what's becoame of that daughter of mine. She should have been back hours ago. She was working in this twilight home, as you probably heard, Alex. And she's gone back on a visit. How long can you spend with a bunch of old crumblies? I ask you.'

'I think it speaks very well of her that she cares for those old people,' offered Kate, keen to give the girl a glowing reference, to commend her to her son. She sat down on the sofa, snatched up a cushion, hugged it to her chest, rocked back and forth. 'It shows a lot of character.'

'Oh, she has *character* all right,' Elli confirmed – and character, it seemed, was not entirely to be desired.

'We always said she was a nice girl, didn't we, Al?'

Alex slammed the piano lid. He asked, 'Who? What, Juin? Oh, yeah, sure. Sweet.' And his indifference, Kate told herself, was universal; he cared for nothing and no one at this minute but bloody Naomi Markham. He had been bewitched.

Up went the piano lid again. He picked out doh, ray, me, fah, doh, ray, me fah. 'Oh, stop it, do,' pleaded Kate, and put her hand up to her temple. She wanted to go to her room, to lie down on the bed, to close her eyes, close out the world, and make some sort of mental communion with John. If she had scant patience with her son's obsession it was only because she was similarly obsessed. And if his cause was hopeless, as it well might be, then how much more hopeless was her own!

'Hey-ho,' said Elli, sighing, and she spoke for all of them. For each of them there was someone at Copperfields. Or not.

Naomi, feeling drowsy, warm and scented from the bath, dragged her suitcase on to the bed, snapped the catches and lifted the lid. Her own face she saw first, swimming up at her from the depths of watery jade silk and frothing lace. Reaching in, she took the silver mirror that had been Irena's – its antique glass, in curlicue frame, had suffered all the woman's moods – and set it on the chest of drawers, on an embroidered runner. Then, riffling through her clothes, she found, by touch, among soft folds of tussore, moire, cashmere and linen, the branched candlestick and oriental snuff bottle that might, with luck, be worth a hundred pounds or so. She set the candlestick beside the mirror, and the snuff bottle in front of it so that it seemed to have a twin. The general effect was of an altar or a shrine.

She had chosen items which could be readily sequestered; she had helped herself from her father's house to these valuable, eminently portable souvenirs. It would be a while before he missed them – if, indeed, he ever did. No ghosting on the wallpaper, no faded square or oblong, no screw hole, rawl plug, picture hook, dint in the carpet pile, yawning gap or mark on polished wood was there to bring to mind a missing *objet*. These were things of little consequence, neutral, non-participatory, which merely sat about. The place would not look the poorer for lack of them; it would function just the same. And if, after some time, he should discover the loss, what would he do about it? Probably nothing. Such petty larceny, she shrewdly guessed, would appeal to the bitter cynic in him. He would have the small satisfaction of knowing that she was, as he had always told her, lost to shame.

For herself, she had no qualms about the theft. Her father was a monster. Long before she knew the word, he had made her believe herself a whore, he had degraded her. He had raised the spectre of sex, merely to over-master her. She had been tyrannised by the long, black shadow of something that she could not understand, and had been sickened to her soul. He should make resititution, and since he would not, she might take what was owed to her. This was justice of a sort, it was due recompense.

Good, she thought, as the mirror flashed at her a quick smile of congratulation. Then, turning from it, she began the protracted nightly ritual of preparing for sleep.

Sitting on the bed, she cleansed and toned her skin, she brushed her hair until it crackled. She performed some facial exercises said to improve muscle tone, she tapped about with her fingertips to stimulate the circulation until the blood fizzed in her veins. Only then did she strip off her robe, cast it on to a chair, run her hands caressingly down her flanks, slide naked between the sheets and reach to switch on the dark.

She felt tired half to death and heartbroken. The nightmare week had plundered her emotions, it had depleted her already scant reserves of inner strength. But here, at least, among the most ordinary of ordinary people, she was safe. In this placid room, with its fresh gloss paint, its floral frieze, its matching duvet cover and curtains, nothing untoward had ever happened or ever would. Her head sank into downy pillows, and she sank into profound unconsciousness, went at once too deep for dreams.

Alex came to her an hour later: he stood by the bed in a shaft of moonlight, a familiar silhouette. She smiled with sweet relief and, sighing, moved over to admit him. 'You

389

came back,' she said, or thought she said, without quite
knowing what she meant by it. He, alone, could make
the hurt and self-hate go away.

He shoved in beside her, this tall, strong man, and,
rolling on top of her, with rough ardour, forced his
mouth on hers. He wound his fingers in her hair and
yanked her head about. Such tough stuff both excited
and confused her. She had never known him so insist-
ent. His penis, wedged between them, bruised her
thigh. Shifting beneath him, she encouraged it into her,
murmuring, imploring, incoherent.

Then, as is possible in dreams, she knew that this was
not entirely Alex – that it was at least partly David
Garvey. The two, like Box and Cox – Box and Cocks,
punned a voice, a shade hysterical, inside her spinning
head – were on to her, turn and turn about.

'Now I have you,' said David, for of course it was he.
And, of course, there was no Alex. She *knew* there was no
Alex. She had woken too late, however: she was by now
quite unravelled, unable to protest. She performed a
desperate form of backstroke, threw first one arm, then
the other up over her head, she seized the iron bedhead,
bowed her back and moaned, despairing of herself.

'You're mine now,' he told her, in a determining way
that made her shudder. She would be his, he managed to
convey, or she'd be nobody's.

At eight o'clock on Sunday morning, Alex arrived. He
swung in through the double gates of Copperfields,
dismounting as he did so, dispatched his whirring bike
into the rhododendrons – a flock of small brown birds

390

went up in an indignant flap – and trudged purposefully the length of the drive.

No one was about but Dominic, playing solo tennis in the soft September sunshine against the flank wall of the house. He'd had half an ear cocked for his mother, who had absolutely forbidden ball games near her parterre, and hearing footsteps, alert to trouble, he came round at once, pre-emptively, to meet his cousin, if possible to deflect him. Alex, tearing at a gnashing Velcro strap, whipped off a cycling glove, and solemnly the pair of them shook hands.

The two youths, despite their similarity, were striking in their differences. A stranger, seeing them together, would sooner have contrasted than compared them.

In Alex, five years older, three inches taller, manhood had been fully furnished. Beside him Dominic was, after all, still a boy. Alex was more powerfully constructed, darker, unshaven, and, in the morning light, faintly haggard. His eyes were flinty with purpose. The cycle ride had primed his pulses; he was almost visibly throbbing. There were fresh sweat patches on his white T-shirt, and a lock of hair clove to his forehead, but his grip was hard and dry.

Dominic's brown hair was streaked with gold. His eyes were versicolour, tricksy, changeful; they would not stay still, but seemed to Alex intent upon evasion. Slim and fleet, with an insolent mien, he did not have – nor ever would – his cousin's presence. Whereas Alex had the aura of a film star, Dominic would have been more at home in some shambolic tiro rock band of the sort that make the headlines more for their shenanigans offstage, and for unseasoned sex appeal, than for any musical ability.

'Yo,' said Dominic, disingenuous, 'what brings you here at this hour? Long time no see, huh?' Privately, he thought, Oh, shit! He thought, Alex, you poor bloody bastard!

'I've come to see Naomi,' Alex told him shortly, stepping back from the gravel on to the grass, making a shade with his arm, to scan the house as if in hope that her face might appear at one of the windows. And such was his composure, his pride and dignity, that it was not possible really to pity him, dupe though he might be; the pathos simply would not stick.

'Ah, right. Sure,' Dominic prevaricated. 'She did pitch up here yesterday, but I think she's still in bed.' With David, he might then have added. Naomi was in bed with David. Because he'd heard them last night, he was convinced of it, going at it like the proverbial clappers. And, while he wasn't one to judge, he couldn't help but feel this was a rotten show on Naomi's part. Like, what a complete cow!

'I shall go to her,' Alex told him peremptorily, 'if you'll just show me where . . .' He was, frankly, anxious to confront her, before his nerve or his adrenalin failed him. That this showed itself as arrogance was probably no bad thing.

'Er . . . look.' Motioning with his head, with a jerk of the chin, for Alex to follow, Dominic led him across a spongy lawn cobwebbed with silver, iridescent with dew, to the rear terrace. He gestured to him to sit on a rustic patio chair. The garden, bathed in a warm, wet autumnal haze, exuded scents of leaf mould and of dying roses. 'Want some coffee?' he offered.

'No thanks. I just need to have a word with her. Please tell me where to find her.' Why did Dominic appear so shifty, so embarrassed? There was no question, surely, of impropriety, when he and Naomi had been lovers? No sense in which he did not have a right to call on her?

'Listen, Al,' Dominic ad-libbed, 'let me explain the posish, will you? Allow me to situate the facts. Because, you know, my dear old mother takes a dim view of . . . Well, she does not, to put it mildly, smile upon your latest *affaire de coeur*. The word "outrageous" has been mentioned. "Shocking", also. I cannot guarantee that, if she catches you together, she won't chuck a bucket of cold water over you. I can't promise that she won't go ape. No, I have a better plan. I shall ease indoors and bring Naomi out here to you. You can slip away to some quiet corner and hold your conference undisturbed. How does that sound?'

Alex waved his ungloved hand dismissively, signalled that it made no odds to him.

'Right-ho,' responded Dominic, though he did not go at once upon this mission. He stood sheepishly about, scuffing his shoes on the stone flags. 'Sure you don't want that coffee?'

'Quite sure, thanks.'

'Ah, well. Right-ho,' repeated Dominic, before the house gulped him in through the open french windows.

He shot upstairs, glancing apprehensively to right and left – there was a wakefulness about the place now; at any minute people might start issuing from their sleeping quarters, asking questions – and rapped gently yet imperatively upon Naomi's door. There ensued an urgent, whispered conversation, then she opened up a crack, she put her face to it and stared at him. She appeared to him, not smug as he'd expected, not deliriously fucked, but oddly blank and utterly bewildered. 'There's, uhm, someone here to see you,' he advised her, and he cleared his throat.

'Who?' Startled, she blinked at him, as if he'd shone a torch into her eyes.

'It's Alex. He wants a chat. Will you come down?'

'Tell him to sod off.' David, behind Naomi, unseen, issued this cold command, and there was no knowing if by 'him' he meant Dominic himself, or Alex.

'I can't see him, Dominic,' pleaded Naomi, turning and turning the doorknob, clicking the latch. 'You say to him, will you, that I just *can't*? Say it's no good. He should never have come here. Do you understand?'

'Yes,' Dominic replied with a contemptuous twitch of the lip, 'it is all very inconvenient, isn't it? I quite see how you're fixed.'

'Do you?' She slumped against the door, swaying so it closed, opened (momentarily, a naked David, standing by the far wall, undeservedly well endowed and with a monumental hard-on, was disclosed to him).

'As you wish.' He turned smartly and took himself downstairs, through the dining-room, back on to the terrace. 'She says you shouldn't have come here,' he informed Alex, with the merest tremor in his voice, more than ever evading his cousin's eye. 'I mean, sorry and all that, but she's adamant.'

'Will you tell her, Dom,' Alex replied, with frightening control (only a barely perceptible tic in his cheek betrayed emotion), 'that if she wants me to leave she must say so herself? Tell her she must come down here and face me. I shan't give up until she does.'

'You're the boss,' reacted Dominic, shrugging, making silent comment upon the unwisdom of the plan. Off upstairs he went again. 'Naomi, listen, please. He says he wants to hear it from you. If you won't come down, then he won't leave. I think perhaps you ought –'

'Go on then,' he heard David bark at her, 'go see that stubborn bugger. Kiss him off and have done. Put him wise – or else I shall.'

Naomi, clamping a hand to her mouth to stifle a sob, shot out of the bedroom and past Dominic in a silken flurry. At the top of the stairs she hesitated, threw a glance of entreaty, a wordless exhortation over her shoulder, then plunged to her doom.

She appeared to Alex, only fleetingly, on the threshold. The dining-room curtains, red and gold brocade, lent the aspect of a stage, which did justice to her brief, theatrical performance. 'Go away,' was all she said, and all she could say.

Alex saw, but did not comprehend, her suffering. He thought, perplexedly, Have I done this to you? But *how* have I? That she wished him anywhere but here was evident to him.

Impaled on his gaze like a butterfly on a pin, she fluttered, trembling for several agonising seconds. Then, abruptly, he stood, and saying nothing more, turned and walked away.

David Garvey, watching from the bedroom window with arms folded, afforded himself a small smile of satisfaction. Meet, he considered this. A fitting end to an unfitting relationship.

So that, he told himself, is that.

CHAPTER

10

No sun, no moon, no morn, no noon. No dawn, no dusk, no proper time of day. No warmth, no cheerfulness, no healthful ease. No something something something. Er, no bees. No fruits, no flowers, no leaves, no birds. November.

Naomi, with something furtive in her manner, slipping out of her rented Knightsbridge flat on to the shared landing, at noon on a dreary Tuesday, strained after the lines of a poem, half learned in her far-off schooldays, and since then half forgotten.

No social life, she reflected darkly, no friends, no cheery ring of phone. No sex, no laughs, no love. No good alone. No brain, no sense, no future tense. No hope. Know nothing. Naomi.

When she pressed the button to call the lift she heard, somewhere above her, the discreet cough of the machinery, then the rattling of air in the shaft, the respiratory tract, the wheezy chest of this smart apartment building, which otherwise showed little sign of life.

In the long corridor, the silence was profound. Plush carpet expropriated every footfall; no vibration of floor could be felt through the dense beige pile. If people lurked behind the solid, locked and bolted doors to either hand, they could not be heard to do so. Peep-holes, like prying eyes, stared glassily out. Thin shadows gathered in round scalloped shades, from which grew up the wall pale, peachy blooms of lamplight. In this windowless place there was, indeed, no dawn or dusk or proper time of day.

The handsome mansion block was home to some intensely private people. The other residents, like Naomi, maintained a determinedly low profile. Casual callers, at whatever hour, must breach the secure front entrance, then account for themselves to a sceptical hall porter. There were few comings, few goings. Naomi could put her eye to her own peep-hole, to see delivery boys, worryingly distorted, ballooning at her on the mat, with groceries, cut flowers, dry cleaning, for she shopped these days, and commanded services, mostly by telephone, she bought by credit card, and generally hung out. Otherwise, she had no visitors; no one except her agent had her number; she had effectively disappeared.

She was a woman of some substance. With careful husbanding of her bank accounts she could survive perhaps two years before she'd need to earn. Her mother's mirror, repository of all Irena's vile humours, putting on its bravest face, had fetched eight hundred pounds at auction; the branched candlestick, a singularly ugly artefact, had been knocked down for five. But it had been that tiny Chinese snuff bottle, not two inches tall, pocketed by her only on an impulse, that had caught the expert's eye. 'Very *nice*,' he had said in an understanding way, as Naomi, with her head on one side, had tried and failed to see in it what he saw. Then, for this perfect, hand-painted porcelain piece, from the Imperial Palace workshop in eighteenth-century Peking (as the auctioneer had had it), a collector of oriental arts had paid almost a hundred thousand pounds.

What she had regarded as an act of pilfering had thus assumed the proportions of audacious crime: she had ripped off her old man for a cool hundred grand. It made her woozy, even now, to think of it. She felt guilt and pride in equal measure, but mostly she felt grateful for the money.

This, though, was not the reason why she'd vanished. If her father ever should discover the theft, if he had even an inkling of the object's worth, if he summoned the police, if she were prosecuted, she would swear the snuff bottle had been a gift from him to her.

She was in hiding, not from the law, but from David Garvey, from the feelings of revulsion that the very name aroused, from reminders of her own perfidy and folly. She was in hiding, really, truly, if she could but confess it, from herself.

She had leased for six months, through an agency, the home of one Mrs Nichols, a widow, who was said to be travelling abroad. She lived now as she imagined Mrs Nichols lived, quietly and alone. Nothing in the apartment jarred her femininity, nor was there anything about it to outrage good taste. She slept in an enormous bed beneath an antique cashmere covering. She walked barefoot on Turkish rugs. When she drew back billowing taffeta curtains, the daylight found a drawing-room done out in cream and gold, with ample armchairs, panelled doors, Venetian glass chandelier, and whole walls of books, well thumbed, many with their spines broken, with fussy annotations in their margins.

More and more Naomi pretended to *be* Mrs Nichols, whose personal effects were locked away in a box room, but whose wedding portrait, on a lacquer table, showed a comely, homely, eminently sensible bride.

The late Mr Nichols had been discriminating in his choice of wife. Mrs Nichols, Mrs *M.* Nichols (Mary? Marjorie? Maeve?) was so plainly not the sort of person who would – as it might be – run off with a lover half her age. She was manifestly not the type who, sleep-fuddled and frail, would submit to sex with her young lover's father, skewer herself upon his prick and, sobbing, beg him to fill, if he could, the hole in her being. (Mrs Nichols, you could bet, didn't *have* a hole in her being.)

Only someone as flawed as Naomi would put herself in moral hock to the likes of David Garvey, a man so utterly convinced of the suasion of his sexuality that a 'no' would drive him to a disbelieving frenzy, and might at any time be horribly revenged.

Was she being paranoid? She fancied not. Perhaps she exaggerated to herself the man's propensity for evil; he was an arrogant, self-seeking shit, but nothing worse. It was not true, however, as she had tried to reassure herself, that he had not half the power to do her harm as she had to be hurt. Because he could tell at any time: moved by umbrage or envy, sheer spite or a simple wish to brag, he could broadcast the shocking truth about her, he could say 'Been there, done that.' Then Kate might hear. And Alex. And if Alex heard, she thought she would expire.

David had come to her a second time, that Sunday night – had found her sitting at the window, unmoving, cold as death. Did she want him? She *must* want him? Her shrug as, rocking back and forth, she nursed like a dead baby her remorse had said it didn't matter any longer either way.

If she had only recriminated, shouted, stamped her foot, thrown punches, he could probably have handled it. But such had been her apathy, she would have given in to him without a murmur. Well, David Garvey had had no way of handling *that*. And the taste of this, the rejection to end all rejections, must even now be setting his teeth on edge.

The following morning she had begged a lift to town with John. 'Lend me five hundred pounds,' she'd importuned him, laying a hand upon his arm, tweaking his sleeve. 'I'll repay you when I'm on my feet again.' She had sensed in him, for all those years, but never before tested, a peculiar largeness, a liberal spirit. She had thought he might dash off a cheque, while sparing her his questions – as he had done. 'Best you don't mention this to Geraldine,' was all he'd said.

She had booked into the Dorchester, stayed a fortnight, presuming on room service, in a mood of suppressed panic running up an astronomical bill, until her luck should change – which, incredibly, and beyond her wildest expectations, her luck had.

So, a very little had been accomplished – and a great deal sacrificed. She had quite blown herself out. 'Well done, Miss Markham,' she said as the lift car arrived and she stepped in, addressing her reflection in caramelised glass, opening her wool coat, smoothing the tartan Ferragamo miniskirt which she wore with a black body, heavy-duty black tights and black stiletto ankle boots. And, as she pulled her belt in a notch at her diminished waist, 'You screwed up real good,' she told herself.

'Off out somewhere?' asked Douglas, the hall porter, as she brushed past a potted palm and swept through the marbled foyer. This question, too fatuous to merit a response, she pointedly left hanging, in the faint hope of discouraging him. Douglas was one of those men who oppress with jest; he would have his little joke, he liked to tease the girlies, and was fun the way that polio is fun. Her fashionable clothes were always good for a quip ('Are you wearing spots,' he'd say, 'or is my liver playing me up?'). 'In your kilt, too?' he ventured now, provokingly.

'Yes, Douglas, in my kilt.' If he asked her, as she guessed he meant to do, what she was wearing under it, she resolved that she would have him fired. But, maybe thinking better of it, he merely tipped his hat satirically and ushered her on to the street.

The car awaited her as promised: a chauffeured white Mercedes. 'Come to lunch,' Ariadne had enjoined her. 'Some people want to meet you. It's important. Look your best.'

For Naomi Markham to look other than her best had never been an option. This instruction had served, therefore, merely to confuse her – dress up, she would have better understood, dress down, look smart, look cool, look drop-dead gorgeous – and she had changed perhaps a dozen times before opting for plaid.

Well, her driver, at any rate, approved: he endorsed her choice with a glance over his shoulder as she slid into the rear seat. Less presumptuous than Douglas, more prosaic, with hammy humility, a studied air of knowing his place, engaging first gear and drawing away, he passed comment on the weather and the weight of London traffic.

'Yes,' said Naomi, and closed her eyes.

Warmth from the heater came up in ripples. She felt utterly torpid. Here I am, she thought, being whisked off to the Halcyon for a glamour lunch. I have money for clothes, for cars and holidays if I want them. I can do whatever I decide without reference to anyone. My career might not, after all, be over (lunch with Ariadne was no idle undertaking: Ariadne never lunched for pleasure). And I'm as miserable as sin itself.

She had a flashback, then, to a moment of pure happiness. She saw herself on the bed with Alex, curled around him, wearing his T-shirt and a pair of fluffy socks, sharing a take-out pizza with him from its box. No money could every buy the love and intimacy she had forfeited. And she could not even explain to herself why she had done it, why blown it all to bits.

I should give anything in the world, she told herself, to turn the clock back. But that is something none of us can do.

When Elli, coming in, closed her front door, the whole house got to hear of it, although it was her bedroom up above that took the brunt. She stood in the hall and sniffed disconsolately at the all-new reek of paint, plaster and sour, sawn timbers. Somehow the place felt like nobody's home, least of all her own.

In the inhospitable sitting-room, bare boards reported on her irritable pacing. Sun and wind through the branches of the sickly lime tree made agitated patterns up the wall. The brightness of pristine redecoration pained her eyes. Nextdoor a child blew some reedy unmusic through a recorder; a spin-drier booted someone's socks and pants around. On a plank bridge between two stepladders were ranged pots of satin emulsion, a radio, a fleecy roller. The labourers – as they laughably described themselves – must be at the café taking their break.

She stood for a moment gazing out on to the street, at a skip piled with lath and plaster, charred wood, the burnt-out fabric and the character of the place. Then she marched to the rear window to take stock of the garden, which dramatically recalled a building site. She would have the decorators clear their mess up, when they deigned to do a hand's turn. Why did no one take pride in a job any more?

She was as cross as two sticks. She had had a simply bloody week so far, and it wasn't even halfway through. Last night, at the Groucho Club, she had run into David Garvey, all over a sofa, with his long legs stuck inconsiderately out. Seeing her, he had raised an indolent hand in a gesture that had scarcely counted as a wave – if he'd thumbed his nose at her she could not have felt more slighted – before turning his attentions to a voluptuous redhead, whose palm he had affected to read (a good time in bed with a tall, handsome stranger, an all-night bonking marathon had no doubt been foretold to her).

Elli might have a love 'em and leave 'em approach, a knockabout attitude to sex, but such public repudiation, when she had been so game for a rematch, had not pleased her one little bit.

Then, this morning, on the walk from the subterranean car park across the riverfront to Globe Tower, cutting quite a dash in new spike-heeled thigh boots, and with the breeze bringing perkily to life the pink poodle-fur of her jacket, she had been greeted by a gang of oiks, chanting at her the proposition that she get her tits out for the lads. Not content with this insult, as she drew nearer, they had added to it injury, expressing very vocal second thoughts ('Keep your tits in for the lads'). If the glass did not tell an altogether happier story, she might have been persuaded she was losing her good looks.

Arriving at her work station in a fury, she had found the insufferable Dawn Hancock there instated, with a polystyrene cup of *cappuccino* and a slice of toast in greaseproof on the desk in front of her. 'But it's *my* week,' Elli had protested, with a momentary, uncharacteristic loss of her composure, a telltale trembling of the lower lip (she blamed premenstrual syndrome, hormone hell, for this), 'and it's *my* desk. I had it first.'

The hopeless Dawn had a round face, as pretty as it was to Elli unappealing (a custard pie, the older woman felt, was called for here). She had a niminy-piminy manner, deceptive sweetpea colouring, and the kind of unfounded confidence that would carry her straight to the top. 'But, Elli,' she had responded, irreproachably polite, yet with an air of long suffering and a big heave of her chest, rattling away at the keys as she spoke, peering into her computer screen at the miraculous skeins of thought, 'I'm working on a major feature for tomorrow's edition. I'm arguing that the Rolling Stones should just fade away. The great grand-daddies of rock are frankly an embarrassment. Stone age music is irrelevant. Perhaps you'll read it for me when I've finished? I should value your opinion. You are of their era, after all. Yes, I do realise you have to file your copy, but it's first come, first served here, remember? And Patti's asked me specially for the piece.'

'This is intolerable,' Elli had reacted, bursting in on Patti Henderson to demand that she intercede.

'Elli, kindly knock,' Patti had reproved her, 'then wait till I say "enter". And don't impose upon my friendship in this unprofessional manner. What is the problem, anyway? Why don't you file from home? You always did.'

True, Elli had allowed, but that was in the good old, far off, palmy days, those piping times when she had actually *had* a home. Her house, though it was habitable once more, was not entirely functioning. Her study had yet to be refurbished and equipped.

Finally, from Patti, she had been forced to endure a lecture on the need to set a fresh tone for the *Globe*, to strike a younger posture (this from a woman who would not see forty-nine-and-three-quarters again). She must have sussed, thought Elli, that she'd had it off with David that last evening in Italy, she must be mad as a wet hen with wounded pride (for how else to explain her changed demeanour?).

In the highest of dudgeon, having failed to oust a sub-editor who had insisted that he was busy with the op-ed page, Elli had sneaked into the seat of the religious affairs correspondent, who was up on his feet somewhere, pontificating, she had rattled off her column at top speed and slammed out of the office.

'Bitch,' she muttered as she glowered at her garden, and the epithet described Dawn as nicely as it did Patti. Then, 'Who the fuck . . .?' she queried as the doorbell rang.

'It's me,' said the spotty youth in hooded sweatshirt whom she found on the step, shuffling his feet, looking sheepish (as well he might), and he held in front of him, as if to shield him, a large piece of card or board wrapped in brown paper.

'Self-evidently,' she responded acidly. 'So the arsonist returns to the scene of the crime!'

'Don't be like that, Elli. I didn't mean to do it. It was an accident, you know. Could have happened to anyone. And I was lucky to escape with my life.'

'That's what *you* think. Why have you come here, you bloody pyromaniac?'

'Just to tell you that I'm sorry. And to give you something.' Ominously, he weighed the brown paper package in his hands. 'Can I come in?'

'All right, if you must,' she relented, leading the way, privately quite thankful for the company, 'but no playing with matches, you hear?'

In the front room, she sat down inelegantly on a roll of

carpet and folded her arms across her chest. 'I suppose you're going to plead for your old job back. Well, don't even think about it. And don't ask for a reference, will you? Because I couldn't, in all conscience, could I, give you one?'

'Oh, no, that's fine, I don't want it back.'

'And why not? I was good to you, wasn't I? I was a fair employer.'

'You paid me, if that's what you mean. But I have no wish to work for you again – although it's kind of you to suggest it. No, I'm very well suited. I clean for some people called Maclean.'

'And you haven't torched their place yet? Such restraint!'

'It was a one-off, Elli, the fire. I don't make a habit of . . . Now, look, this is my present to you. By way of an apology.' He stripped the wrapping from a painting so garish that she caught her breath and briefly hid her eyes. 'It's very . . . abstract,' was all that she could think to say.

'You like it, then?'

'It's execrable.'

'Thank you,' he replied, with a modest inclination of the head. 'I must admit I'm rather pleased with it myself. I call it –' he put his fist up to his mouth and cleared his throat – ' "Mere anarchy is loosed upon the world".'

'Use a brush, did you? Or squeeze the paint straight from the tube? What is it supposed to be, actually?'

'What does it look like? What can *you* see in it?'

'Llamas in pyjamas, coming down the stairs.' She patted her pocket, pulled out her cigarettes and set one between lips the colour of deadly nightshade. 'Have you

408

got a light, boy? Oops. What am I saying? On second thoughts, don't bother.'

'It's whatever you think it is, Elli. That's the beauty of it, and the point.'

'Right. Well, at least you still use paint, you sweet, old-fashioned, fuddy-duddy thing. I should have thought rat foetuses would be more your medium. Pigs' heads in formaldehyde. Baby sick. In fact, I didn't realise people still made pictures. Aren't "installations" more the thing? Lines of dirty washing? Fields of milk bottles?'

'You could hang it –' he gazed around him, visualising (it would look very well, he seemed to think, on this wall, or that one, or that one) – 'there, perhaps. Or there. Or over there.'

'I shall have to give the matter due consideration. Unless you would prefer, on reflection, to give it to your new employers. The . . .?'

'The Macleans.'

'To the Macleans. What with them treating you so well.'

'No. I can knock a canvas up for them another time. This one's yours. You'll see I've signed it. Some day it could be worth a fortune.'

'It could?'

'Besides, I asked him the other week if he'd commission a painting for the dining-room, and he said not just now.'

'He's an art lover, is he?'

'*She* is. Caroline Maclean. She's frightfully arty. She wears great big batik-print dresses and flat sandals for traipsing around galleries, and she ties her hair up with coloured scarves. She was in Florence the other week, mooning over the Masaccios. The money is mostly on her side, as far as I can make out. She's heir to a plastics fortune or something. She's always spending on the house, ordering redesigns of redesigns. Anyway, he wasted no time, while she was away, in moving his bit of stuff in. Brought her home under the cover of darkness. *I* know about it because I caught them at it. Walked in on them when I went up for the laundry. All over the marital bed, if you please.'

'How despicable,' said Elli feelingly, though she privately felt that a woman who went in for batik brought it on herself.

'That's what I thought. I said to them, "Don't mind me, you carry on, I'm just the skivvy." Trying to laugh it off, you see. She was quite pretty in a mimsy sort of way, the girl. Very young. Doll face. She could do much better than him. He's handsome enough for a geezer in his forties, but he's always sniffling.'

'He is?'

'He said to me the next day, "We're both men of the world, aren't we, Trevor?" I said, "Yes, Mr Maclean, we are." He said, "I'm sure I can rely on your discretion." I said, "Yes, Mr Maclean, you can." He said, "Fergus, please. We're very informal in this household." I said, "As you like, Mr Maclean. I mean, Fergus." Perhaps I should ask him again for a commission. I'm in a stronger bargaining position now.'

'Trevor,' declared Elli, getting to her feet, 'you've earned yourself a cup of tea. No, no, don't ask me why. But you are a little treasure after all. It's funny, isn't it, to

410

think how I was always going to fire you, and you ended up by firing me? Now, go put the kettle on. No, no, don't touch the cooker. Safer that we have a glass of wine. What do you reckon? A nice drop of Slovenian Sauvignon, or whatever was on special offer this week. Then you can tell me more about the nice Macleans. Fergus, you say? A sniveller? And when those idle workmen reappear, I'll get them to bang a nail in. They can hang my lovely "Anarchy" in pride of place.'

Kate wasn't very hungry, so she shared her sandwich with a quarrelsome family of ducks. She would tear off a chunk and lob it, with uncertain aim, with lamentable hand-eye co-ordination and an uncontrolled jerk of the forearm, over the hooped metal fence on to the muddy bank around the lake, which big webbed feet had slapped about and worked to slime. 'Hoy, Fatty,' she chided the biggest of them, 'this bit's not for you, it's for your little friend. Oh, blast! I missed him. I suppose they're all right with tuna. Do you think?'

'I should think they're all right with most things. I don't believe they're picky eaters.' John, with his hands in his pockets, sat back on the bench – that construction of wooden slats and rusted whorls of iron so typical of public parks – and put his chin down into his scarf. The wavelets, glugging at the bank, threw off a sort of sputtering light that lapped over his set face, lending peculiar clarity and finesse to his features. He seemed unable to look at her for holding something in his gaze (perhaps the trailing golden fronds of weeping willow). Or else he was fixing his emotions.

'I asked the sandwich man, "Is your tuna dolphin-friendly?" ' Kate related, talking for the sake of it. With John only, she was all woman. In his company she became the luscious blonde whose cigarette men rushed to light; the sultry Titian-haired beauty to whom they offered a seat on bus or train. His awareness of her bore on her awareness of herself, it made her sometimes nervous and unnatural – it was hard to take seriously this new, desirable persona – so she didn't know her own voice. 'He said, "Madam, it's not fussy, it'll be friends with anyone." '

'You surely don't expect to find a green sandwich bar?'

'No. I'm only thankful, frankly, if the sandwiches aren't green. But I do worry about dolphins being caught up in those dreadful nets.'

'I never much cared for tuna myself. I'm a salmon man. Tinned, for preference.'

'I know, it's much nicer, isn't it, from the can? Although I've never liked to admit it. What does it say about us? That we have untutored palates? Fresh salmon is supposed to be a real treat.'

'It's all farmed these days, of course. Wild salmon is quite different.'

'Ooh, here's one for you, John. Grilse.'

'Easy. It's a young salmon that's been only once to the sea.'

'I must down to the seas again.'

'The lonely sea and the sky.'

'And what are they called, up to two years of age?'

'Pass.'

'That's right.'

'What's right?'

'Parrs. Now *you* do a word.'

'Give me a minute.' He reached for her hand, took it with his own back into his coat pocket, and sat watching as the ducks drew elongated Vs upon a cold, glassed-over picture of the sky. Gaining the small, wooded island at the lake's centre, the birds broached it with a quaint, rolling gait, like fat old ladies burdened with shopping. 'Ah, yes. Here we go. Puggaree.'

'I don't like the sound of it. Can you eat it?'

'Absolutely not.'

'Would I scream if I saw one?'

'No reason why you should.'

'Is it a sort of animal?'

'Definitely not.'

'Can you live in it?'

'We-ell . . .' He wrinkled his nose, screwed up his eyes. 'You could say so, in a manner of speaking.'

'Such as what?'

'You know, you could say, I suppose, "He virtually *lived* in his puggaree." '

'But it's not a building?'

'No, it's not a building. That's five questions you've had.'

'Not five, four. And a supplementary.'

Leaning across to her, with a sudden swell of affection, he kissed the plump cushion of her cheek. 'You're freezing.'

'No I'm not.' For she almost never was. Her blood ran very warm. It was he, this thin man, who felt the cold to his marrow. 'I'm fine. So it's something you wear, this puggaree?'

'Not personally.'

'No, but you could.'

'I could. And very fetching I should look in it.'

'It's an it, then, not a they. It's not shoes. Or trousers. Is it a hat?'

'Of a kind.'

'It sounds Indian. Is it a turban?'

'You got it.'

'That's another point to me, then.'

'So it is.'

Sighing, she laid her head upon his shoulder. This version of Twenty Questions they played as a sort of surrogate, an instead-of exercise. There were twenty far more pertinent questions – such as what they must do, how be together, when and where – which they could not resolve.

In this strangely vacant park, somewhere between her home and his, at a dead time of the week, at a dead time of the year, they met in vacant mood to think on compromise. Along the tarmac path behind them, dry leaves scuttled. Across a sweep of grass a bandstand, disused, rotted imperceptibly. In the distance someone whistled and shouted for a labrador called Rusty.

'As a child,' she remembered, 'I longed for a dog. But I wouldn't swap Pushkin and Petal for the world now.'

'When I was nine I had a gerbil,' John confessed. 'His name was Gerry. I used to let him out in the front room to have a run. It was hard to see him on the carpet – it was one of those gaudy, leafy, bronze-and-gold jobs –

especially when he wasn't moving. One day I knelt down, thinking to look for him under the radiogram. And I squashed him.'

'Was he all right?'

'No, of course not. I killed him.'

'But that's terrible.' In his pocket, in sympathy, imagining a devastated little person, a highly-strung, bespectacled child, her fingers squeezed his tightly.

'I felt, then, like a murderer. No, something worse, in a way. I felt like a complete booby. I felt worthless. It all fell into place in my head. I saw the way my life would be. I was so clumsy, so inept. And I could love a thing to destruction. My mother always said "That boy will be the death of me" – then she died. For years I was convinced it was my doing. I would bring only trouble to whoever I cared for.'

'Oh, such stupid nonsense!' she protested, butting up to him, ramming her head into his chest. His scarf, of some scratchy material, nettled her cheek.

As he spoke she felt the words come boiling up inside him. 'I dread that I should do it to you. That I should squash you.'

She lifted her head once more to seek his gaze, appearing faintly flushed and tousled. 'What's my name? Squidgy? I hope I'm more resilient than that. I believe I am. And I take responsibility.' She slapped a hand over her heart. 'All this is my doing, every bit as much as yours.'

'I wish we were in bed right now,' he told her in a deep, suppressed voice that elicited in her an instant physical response (she felt as if a hand were squeezing her guts).

'Mmmm, me too.'

'But what I'm trying to say to you, Kate, darling –'

'Well, I know what you're saying, don't I? But I don't agree. Not about your being bad news.'

'I am committed now to hurting someone. If not Geraldine, then you. I've set it up so beautifully. I cannot fail. One way or another, lives will be wrecked.'

'You won't leave Geraldine,' she gently, and for the hundredth time, insisted. Her own hurt, she suggested, was inevitable and not undeserved. It would be slow and drawn out, but not insupportable. If they could not do the decent thing, they must do the halfway decent thing. They must give each other up, if not today, then some day.

'But I was meant to be with you,' he said, believing not in Fate, or in any god, but convinced of that fine thing called chance which had brought them together.

'We married the wrong people,' she mused, 'I more spectacularly than you. There's this much to be said for an outright disaster: it is by its nature just an episode, it forces on you some form of solution. David isn't a problem. Geraldine is, because she's not entirely wrong for you, and you care for her still, and your marriage hasn't been so very bad.'

'Marriage is such a weird idea, when you come to think of it,' he said, returning her hand to her, placing it neatly in her lap, patting it down, then reaching for his handkerchief. 'So unrealistic. I mean, imagine if you had to make the same commitment to your friends. Imagine you had to promise to like them and support them and hold things in common with them for ever.'

416

'I should certainly be in breach of that. With Naomi, for a start.'

'Poor Naomi.'

'Why "poor Naomi"? She's a wicked, dangerous bitch.'

'Don't be like that, Kate. It does something horrible to your face. She's selfish and confused. And very sad. She always was. She isn't coping well. You should have seen her when she came to stay. And goodness knows what's happened to her since. Geraldine's not heard a dicky-bird. Neither has Elli.'

'Yes. No one has a clue,' acknowledged Kate, with no attempt to hide her satisfaction. If Naomi Markham had left the planet, she could not have gone far enough for her.

'None.' And, for his own reasons, because there was too much else to talk over, John made no mention of a sum of money lent and – against his highest expectation – promptly repaid. The full and final settlement had come by post a month ago, drawn on a Coutts account, with no covering letter, just a scribbled note, the one word, 'Thanks'.

Nor did he disclose the secret to which he was reluctant party, and which seemed somehow, like scar tissue, to grow out of his consciousness. For, sleepless as he had been these past weeks, on a September Saturday night, slipping from his bed and making shifty progress to the stairhead, thinking to go downstairs for a scotch and water, he had heard . . . It could not have been his fancy. He had heard Naomi and David.

There had been about her, the next day, and the next, a

wildness that had troubled him. He had worried for her sanity; she had seemed to be hanging on to reason by her fingernails. 'Lend me five hundred pounds,' she had urged him, entreating with a look that he ask no questions. And he, obliging her, had reached for his chequebook. Decent of him. Gentlemanly.

Then, at last, it had seemed to him, he had the answer. There's been too much dishonesty all round, he told himself. And he was firm at last in his purpose. He would tell Geraldine he was leaving. He would play it straight. There was no other way forward. For once, when it really mattered, he would be true to himself.

She had an inoperable tumour. This diagnosis was made in an instant, with the kind of intuition that distinguishes the gifted doctor from his or her more impercipient colleagues. Geraldine's fingers, flying to the spot, seemed to have known what they would find, and where. Probing it, they were able almost mystically to divine it. To the soft pad of a fingertip it felt considerable, and yet she could see nothing. She peered into the bathroom mirror, through an anxious mist, and then, although discerning neither lump nor blemish, none the less convinced, sighing, juggled her stricken breast back into its elasticated harness.

She supposed she should go to the quack, but to what end? He would be sure to send her to the hospital, there to endure the gross indignity of tests, and more tests, and for why? Only to confirm that which she already instinctively knew, and thus to make it seem more real, somehow.

As it was, reality came and went, it zoomed up very close, dissolved before her eyes, then, receding, gathered itself up again into something tiny and intense.

This reminded her of those far-off Saturday evenings of Garvey-fest. She recalled how her father used to fiddle with the cine-projector: down the cone of light, through the blue drift of cigarette smoke, would shimmer David in cricket whites, Geraldine the plump schoolgirl, Eleanor impersonating Audrey Hepburn, a family flittering, changeful, existent and not – Uncle Sidney, hefting his great bulk out of the armchair, crossing to the sideboard for a refill, would be seen to pass right through the lot of them.

Uncle Sidney had been, until his death, a bachelor. This, the Garvey children had been asked to understand – something in the way the word was spoken gave the clue – was not a happy state. And in consideration of it, small kindnesses must be shown him, and small allowances made. Furthermore, as the only bachelor in their circle, he had come to represent for her a kind of prototype. Bachelors, she always afterwards believed – David being an honourable exception – were pitiable fat men who conjured half-crown pieces from their trouser pockets and neglected to pull the chain after they went. Married people were, by contrast, blessed, and to this day she felt sorry for her single friends, she felt herself a cut above.

Not today, however. Her illness brought her low. Overcharged with feelings, with a squeeze on her heart, she buttoned her blouse and went dazedly about her chores. She snapped some dingy late-blooming dahlias from the borders, beat out the stems with a meat mallet on the draining-board, delivering herself of the worst of her emotion, and arranged the blooms untidily in a tall yellow vase. She loaded the washing-machine with those garments that she thought of, wishfully, as her 'smalls'. She made a pie with apples from the garden, dredged it carelessly with caster sugar. She filled as best she could those womanly hours until the family should return to Copperfields, to a house redolent of baking, of cloves and cinnamon, of detergent and a good wife's honest endeavours.

Life was so unfair. She was dutiful, diligent, devoted. She had done nothing to deserve this cruel fate. And she was so young, still – or as young as she had ever been, which wasn't very.

Her relationship with God had been an on-off thing. These days it ran the course of one of those old-fashioned, over-long engagements which, having gone beyond eager expectation, beyond passion, is sustained through apathy, or propriety, or for appearances' sake, to some forgotten end. So when, raising her eyes to the ceiling, pressing her knuckles to her mouth, she dispatched a silent and reproachful prayer, when she begged Him to see reason, it was with no great hope of special dispensation.

At one o'clock, in a needy mood, she rang John at work. And was it not typical of him that he had chosen this of all days to slip out for a bite?

'The funny thing is,' she told Mrs Slack an hour later, as they sat over tea and Viennese Whirls (and she meant by this neither funny peculiar, nor, really, funny ha-ha;

she found it neither fishy nor amusing), 'that he almost never bothers. He makes do usually with a snack at his desk.'

The cleaning lady, then, in what seemed to Geraldine a quite extraordinary over-reaction, offered umpteen excuses, innocent explanations, she put up a whole barrage of reasons as to why a busy lawyer might have had to leave the office for a while.

'Well, of course,' Geraldine then huffed and puffed, feeling forced to justify her husband, to refute some nameless allegation which such strenuous efforts at legitimation subtly implied, 'he must occasionally entertain a client. No reason why he shouldn't. Only that he doesn't usually. That's all I'm saying.'

She sat back, sat tight on her fearful secret, stolidly munching, as a biscuit turned to chaff in her mouth, and she let her gaze take her out through the window on an unsteady flight up to the waving tops of distant beech trees. 'Yes, yes,' she said vaguely, and 'Goodness me', attending with not half an ear to Mrs Slack, to the singularly unapropos tale of a friend of a friend who knew a woman whose husband had an unacknowledged second family, kids and everything, a double life. Holding fast to the table edge she anchored herself; how perfectly the word 'windy' described her giddy, buffeted state!

Should she confide to John her darkest fears? He was not exactly brilliant in a crisis, being somehow too remote. He was, one must remember, a professional listener, impersonal, impassive: at times, as she shared with him her more pressing concerns, she would half expect him to reach for a pen and to make notes. But to whom else could she turn for comfort and support?

Oh, she had her friends, of course, but they would not serve. Elli would be too abrasive and determining; Kate, no help whatsoever. As for Naomi . . . Where *was* Naomi? She seemed to have skedaddled – and good riddance!

Geraldine set aside for a minute her mortal affliction; she put her mind to the rather more appalling matter of Miss Markham. All right, once, she had fancied that Naomi and David might . . . but this was decades ago. And it did not mean she could condone, today, in the very bosom of her family . . .

She had whispered to no one what she knew. To remember what had happened was to feel again a terrible affront; to describe it would be cringe-making.

She never slept through the night without once, twice, three times waking up and nipping to the lav. And on that September Saturday, when Naomi had shown up uninvited, Geraldine, passing the door of the pink room . . .

How *could* they carry on this way, her brother and that woman? Suppose the children had been woken by it? She and John had been so careful, always, so constrained. In the days when they went in for 'that sort of thing', they had done it in tooth-gritting silence, with one ear always open for a creaking floorboard, for a whimper of a wakeful infant, a footfall on the landing. Such freedom, such abandon had been, until the other week, beyond Geraldine's conception.

Thank goodness that, of all of them, she alone was a

light sleeper. It would not have done for Lucy, so much the baby, young even for her age, and still less for Dominic with his unhealthy preoccupations, to have heard what she had heard.

Discretion was not one of Geraldine's great attributes, but here was something she could never share.

It had not been half as gratifying as you might suppose. For the best part of an hour the talk had been of Naomi Markham's face. *Her* face, as it seemed, for not much longer. Once terms had been agreed, the fine print read, the contract signed, it would become the face of Jeunesse. From cinema screens, billboards, the glossy pages of smart magazines, it would stare back at her with the enigmatic half-smile of the keeper of a secret, possessor of a private joke. (What could Jeunesse do for you? That's for me to know, the smile would teasingly suggest, and for you to find out.)

This was supposed to be exciting. It *was* exciting. It was the sort of break she'd always dreamed of. So why this empty, desolated feeling?

Sitting in the light, bright restaurant – archly named The Room – at the Halcyon Hotel in Holland Park, where actors, models, socialites, drifting past the table, left faint, distracting criss-cross spoors of celebrity, she had tried to take in what they told her, to attend to Pieter Harland's 'concept', all the while, perversely, thinking, Yes, so what?

Harland, chief executive of Jeunesse Cosmetics, had had a vision. It had been, indeed, in the nature of an epiphany. He had seen Jeunesse made flesh by this ethereal creature. While rival companies might use bimbos to market their miraculous formulations, Naomi would personify the Jeunesse spirit, she would embody the Jeunesse message – that youth was not solely for the very young.

Ariadne, sitting poker straight, at a perfect right angle to her chair, cutting a crab cake into tiny pieces, had a calculating air about her, she was maybe thinking of the agency's percentage – perhaps literally working out her cut.

'Yes?' said Naomi with a faint show of interest, toying with a delicate seafood and saffron risotto, fishing the prawns out and eating them reflectively. When the waiter came to offer wine, she made a lid of her hand and, putting it down firmly on her glass, shot him a warm, complicit look, as if enlisting his support. (For ladies who didn't much lunch, the boat was being pushed out here today.)

Lowering her head she stole glances at Harland across the broad expanse of laundered napery. She saw a man in his mid-fifties, silver-haired, suntanned, aggressively well turned out, tailored and polished. She saw him shoot his starched, white cuff to flash a gold Rolex. She saw him pick in a finicky fashion at a stray thread of cotton adhering to his dark wool jacket. She saw a hand-made, self-made man (no one born to wealth was ever quite so flawless, or so beset by style).

But above all she saw, with utter clarity, the way this thing could go. Upon that arm she could very easily, acquiescently hang; around that broad shoulder drape herself.

From her photograph, only, he had chosen her as Ms Jeunesse. And, for uncounted seconds, in the lobby, as Ariadne introduced them, as he took both of her hands in his, Naomi had felt his brown eyes on her making their assessment. Then, by his tight, retentive grip, the way he put her hands apart and then together, he had told her all: he had not been disappointed. Here we go again, she had reacted dully, fatalistically.

He had a yacht in Cannes, a summer home on a green hillside of the vine-growing Napa Valley, a town house right around the corner from the Halcyon ('My local', he described the hotel joshingly). She pictured a tall, white, stuccoed building, floor on floor on floor on floor, meanly proportioned top and bottom but sumptuous in between, with iron frills about it, and an imposing portico. A uniformed Filipina would bid visitors step into the gracious, flower-scented hallway, from which the stairway would go sinuously up. For tradesmen there would be an entrance down below street level. She knew such places, after all, and from time to time had hung out in them.

She had come a long way, it seemed, since she had lived just streets from here, in a scruffy sub-let, in a botched conversion, in what she wilfully misremembered as a gloriously rumbustious, girlie ménage. (Those were the days, my friend! We thought they'd never end . . .)

If she lifted her head now, sought him out, engaged his look, bestowed upon him her full radiance, the whole game could begin again. And was that such a terrible idea? Mrs Nichols, Marjorie, Naomi Markham's alter ego, would doubtless disapprove, she would be sure to look askance. But what the hell? For two years, maybe three, they might be happy. If not love, then something aping love could grow between them. He would bring her little gifts in Tiffany boxes. He might name a racehorse after her, or – more appositely, perhaps – a greyhound. He would treat her as his pet and prize possession. It would mean, once more, she'd have no need to think. And it was thinking, frankly, that was doing her head in.

She had not planned to be, again, a rich man's plaything. But in a very real sense, in any case, as Ms Jeunesse she would be Harland's. He had picked her from that great, international catalogue of babes for sale. He had already effectively bought her, subject only to contract.

Now he was calling for champagne, imploring, no *insisting* that she take a sip, at least, in celebration of their new association. Even Ariadne, who acquired austerity at such a price, appeared to weaken (was that – oh, surely not! – a smile?).

'If you will just excuse me for a minute . . .' Naomi snatched her napkin and fluttered it ambiguously. Standing, she cast around for some sign, some direction, and 'her' waiter, enamoured, inveigled by her look, sprang forward to direct her.

In the cloakroom she stood hard against the basin, turned on the tap and held her wrists in the refreshing stream of icy water. She was filled with panic, but *why*?

Pieter Harland? Just who was he? Was the 'i' an affectation? Would he be, to his chums of old, simply Pete?

Peter, Peter, she recited to herself. Peter, Peter, pumpkin eater, had a wife but couldn't keep her.

There was no wife now, if ever there had been. He spoke in the first-person singular. Or was the 'I' an affectation? Would he be, to current acquaintants, a they?

He put her in a pumpkin shell, and there he kept her very well.

She had no idea what was meant by this childish rhyme, but she found it peculiarly disturbing. She did not fancy for herself a pumpkin shell.

I am on the very brink, she told herself. A fortune, I am being offered.

An actress, familiar from the television, bustled into the cloakroom, she watched herself in the mirror as she crossed to a cubicle. Her reflection and Naomi Markham's, seeming to know each other slightly, nodded curt hellos.

I shall be famous, Naomi further told herself. People will point me out in public places, they'll want my autograph.

She had an image, then, of a huge advertisement hoarding, her face vastly magnified, exerting itself upon a windswept urban highway, with perhaps a busy round-about. The poster might be lit, as some were, from beneath; or, by some trick of the setting sun might phosphoresce. She visualised then, riding by, in silhouette, crouched over his handlebars, the fit, strong figure of Alex Garvey. And here was the macabre part: while Ms Jeunesse watched the going of him, he would not so much as notice her. She would be a stranger to him.

Making a comb of her splayed fingers, she went right up to herself, nose to nose, to ask a question: was this truly what she wanted?

Alex, holding aloft, between two fingers, a folded banknote, muscled his way to the counter and, despite the throng around it, commanded instant service. A barmaid with a mass of amber hair and grape-green eyes came hurrying over, she summoned for him especially a merry smile (she could think of nothing jollier, the smile suggested, than to pull a pint of beer for him, or to pour a glass of wine).

It was ever thus with him; no one ignored or over-looked him. Male as well as female waiters, bar staff, shop assistants accorded him unquestioning recognition. His relaxed, unchippy manner owed much, in fact, to the favour that was shown him. He never had to try too hard with people (to try too hard being, in any case, in all human congress, fatal). He was the more person-able for being treated always as a person.

'You were first,' he said easily, to a tetchy-looking guy beside him, who had the exasperated air of one who has, as usual, waited longer than is right or just, and he held back with a good grace to await his turn. There was no rush, after all.

Having duly seen to the other customer, the green-eyed girl was back in a flash – very much a flash, of teeth, of eyes – to attend to Alex. 'You sit down,' she urged him, taking his money for a Brie and French bread lunch and house wine. 'I'll bring it over. Where will I find you?'

'We . . .' Alex, craning his neck, saw that his

companion had secured a table. A small, white hand went up and, twirling in the air, proclaimed its triumph. 'We're in the alcove. Thanks so much.'

Susie was a new recruit to the studio, a trainee, fair and pretty, with a pleasing, toothy smile. She was funny and forthright, a fantastic mimic. 'Bright as a button' would have best described her. He liked having her around but, for him, it went no deeper. 'They're bringing it,' he told her, returning to her unencumbered. 'This place is hell on earth, isn't it?'

'There's a nasty niff of damp.' She gave a twitchy sort of sniff.

'It *is* a cellar, after all.' He squinted around him at ochre walls hung with sepia-tinted photographs of a long-ago London, of tall ships in thriving docks, of horse-drawn transport, market porters, barefoot matchgirls. He despaired of such nostalgia for the days of rickets. 'It wouldn't be my choice of venue if it weren't so near the office. There's something about this Stygian gloom – don't you find? – that makes you feel drunk before you touch a drop.'

'I can't take much alcohol in any case,' she boastfully confided. 'One glass and I'm anybody's, me.' Struggling to cross her legs, to haul one across the other beneath the squat wooden table, keeling towards him, she leaned right into him – her hair brushed his face, it tickled his nose, he breathed her light, floral, feminine scent. Alex was left in no doubt as to who that 'anybody' might be, yet he felt absolutely nothing.

For how long would it be this way? Would he ever respond again to an attractive female? It seemed that

Naomi had sort of queered it for him, she had spoiled him, perhaps for ever, for her sex. Other women seemed to him to be mere holograms, with illusory substance, of neither flesh nor blood.

Susie was a case in point. He might enumerate her attributes; he quite saw, intellectually, that there was much in her to be desired. But nothing worked on him, nothing moved him. No one held for him the mystique of Naomi Markham. She alone could make his nerves quicken. Even now, when he thought of her, it was with physical anguish which caused him, at moments, in private, to double up.

'Who's the Brie?' the green-eyed barmaid queried, arriving with it at his elbow, glancing surmisingly from him to Susie.

'We both are,' said Susie smartly, reaching for the plate. 'We're sharing. Ta.'

'You're welcome.' Alex was treated to a glimpse of cleavage as a glass of wine arrived before him.

He felt so tired, suddenly, he felt he could have crashed out right there on the stone floor, in the mess of sawdust and cigarette butts. So little sleep, his fevered brain allowed him lately. But a dig of an elbow in his ribs jolted him back to consciousness. 'I think she fancies you,' whispered Susie, dimpling, nodding after the retreating barmaid.

'Yeah?' He took a swig of wine and pulled a wry face. 'Yuck.'

'Uh-huh.' She in turn sipped her drink. 'A one-glass wonder, me.'

The question remained: what, if anything, was to be

done? He could not admit defeat. He had tried upon himself the failure of his affair, but it somehow would not fit. All was not, he felt sure, as it had been presented to him.

His pride, his common sense, said to let it go, it said 'forget it'. But neither common sense nor pride would rule him. If Naomi had been cold, dismissive, he would have known himself rejected. But she had seemed, to the contrary, maddened, distraught. So what was he to make of *that*?

'. . . would enjoy it,' Susie was saying to him.

'Sorry?'

'This rave. At the Hangar. On Saturday. You should come.'

'Oh, thanks.' He took another slug of wine. Funny how its very nastiness, its growly taste, became so immediately compulsive. 'But I really can't, you know, make it this weekend.' Or the next, he might have added. Or any weekend. He simply wasn't free to date. His heart was spoken for.

London, at this grey time of year, was an unexacting city. It took almost nothing from one, and gave almost nothing back. Exhausted by the summer swell of tourists now subsided, not yet braced for Christmas madness, it sprawled listlessly about in the stale, spent air. The parks lacked a certain lustre that they took upon themselves in springtime, or by moonlight, or when frost silvered their lawns and borders. Visitors had forsaken them in droves. The deckchairs had been stacked away. Taxis queued on all the ranks, or coasted up and down with their FOR

HIRE lights showing an optimistic orange. Only the most shameless stores had begun, so previously, their annual exploitation of the festive season. It was thus possible to walk the pavements relatively unimpeded.

Naomi, stepping purposefully, put a mile behind her before slowing her pace. *Now* they would be missing her. They would be making their enquiries – of the management, the serving staff, each other. Five minutes, and they would not have raised an eyebrow (beautiful women must be granted time for titivation). Ten minutes, and Pieter Harland would have held a sneaky consultation with his flashy Rolex, Ariadne with her punctilious little Cartier. Conversation around the table would have faltered; in a strained and desultory way they would have talked, as dark suspicions crept into their minds. Drugs would have figured in their thinking, mental instability, *bulimia nervosa* (what could she be *doing* for so long in the loo, if not shooting up, or cracking up, or throwing up?).

Eventually, Ariadne, with a murmured 'Excuse me', would have gone to rout her. With that curiously smooth and silent port of hers, she would have proceeded as if on castors, looking neither to right nor left, but fiercely in front.

'That's torn it,' Naomi said happily, aloud. And, with a rush of exuberance, to an unsuspecting passer-by, 'That will be that, then.' So much for fame and fortune. She had cut loose at last; she had never been so free.

With no object in mind, no mental map, she found herself, within the hour, in Oxford Street. It had become, since she had last frequented it, a street of mixed fortunes, faintly aspirational at the Marble Arch end, more cheap and cheerful as you marched on Tottenham Court Road.

At the halfway point of Oxford Circus, where she paused to buy from a street vendor a magazine to help the homeless, she watched bleary and bad-tempered travellers coming up out of the ground, she saw them issue from the tube mouth having clattered here via tunnels from points north, south, east and west. How many years since she rode on the underground? How many years since she hopped on a bus?

She was suddenly and deeply fascinated by the way the capital functioned: public transport worked after its fashion; people got from A to B. And how shop-literate they were! They plainly knew this high street chain from that one, they made informed choices about quality and price at a level she could barely comprehend.

To idle past the open shop fronts was to walk through butted walls of loud rock music. Here and there, a rail of garments had been wheeled into the open, for passers-by to pull about. No respectful hush greeted you as you crossed the threshold. Rather, a man in uniform would eye you dubiously up and down.

With some diffidence, feeling like an alien, she allowed herself to be sucked into a bustling interior. There she made a study, for a moment, of what other, more proficient customers were doing, then, self-consciously, she copied them. That is, she riffled insouciantly through the many, crowded racks of clothing, now and then hauling out a hanger, holding garments up against her, inclining her head this way and that, chewing on the inside of her face as she appraised them. Venturing, once, too near the exit, she gazed about her in bewilderment as cunning electronic tagging set alarm bells ringing.

The fitting-rooms afforded neither space nor privacy but seemed full of flying elbows and chemical deodorant smells. No discreet, polite assistant begged her to call out if she needed help. The grey frock into which she struggled was of some man-made fabric, it was not artfully cut or thoroughly finished in the fashion of designer wear. But, what the hell? It didn't look half bad. Her pelvic bones showed through it – a reproach to her for losing too much weight – but that was not the maker's fault. The price tag, meanwhile, was a revelation.

'I'd like to wear it,' she told the girl whose job it was, apparently, to stand guard over the triers-on.

She must pay for it first, the girl told her indifferently. Security tags would have to be removed. She was extraordinarily beautiful, this young person, much of Naomi's height, and of her size, but stronger somehow, and more vital. She was black – or rather, Naomi mused, in envious contemplation of her burnished skin tones, she was golden. White skin like her own, it seemed to her, could never be so stunning.

She joined a shuffling queue and parted with a silly little sum of money, to have the dress perfunctorily folded, bagged, returned to her.

With humble apologies for her irregular behaviour, making vague explanatory noises, she slipped once more into the fitting-room and hurriedly pulled on the new frock.

Into the cheapo drawstring carrier-bag went her Ferragamo tartan skirt and body. A month's wages would not have bought the golden girl such garments. 'Here,' said Naomi, emerging flustered from behind a curtain. And she pressed the bag of clothes upon the startled shop assistant, then fled.

Ask Naomi Markham how to get from Oxford Street to Fulham, and she would tell you, 'Well, darling, you just hail a cab.' Alternatively, she might have added, you could take the Victoria line, change at Victoria Station; then District Line (Wimbledon branch) to Fulham Broadway. Easy.

In the after-darkness, Alex could not at first discern what bags or baggage had been dumped upon his doorstep. But stepping back a pace, withdrawing his own shadow, letting pass a shaft of dirty yellow tungsten street light, he saw huddled in his unaccommodating porch something of human form. And peering closer, seeing milky skin, the lucent whiteness of an eye, he knew.

He felt, then, not so much a pang as an almighty bang, a whacking great explosion of emotion in his chest, which made him catch his breath. But, steadying himself, he asked casually, in a voice that trembled only slightly, 'So, what brings you here?'

How long had she been waiting? She could not have said. Darkness had seemed to come out of the concrete several hours ago, it had crept very slowly up the walls, but the sky to the last had been light. She was frozen to the bone (the London parks might yet awake with a lustrous glaze of frost). Or was it for fear that her teeth rattled so inside her skull?

She had dreaded his arrival – dreaded more that he should not arrive. He might be out with someone – some young girl. He might not return for hours. And, when he came, he might bring his date. Then how would she appear, hunched up here? What pathetic spectacle would she present?

Naomi was very good on what was these days called the 'worst case scenario': she was past mistress at dreaming up the most dire consequences. And so vivid had been her picture of him looming over her, laughing at her, with his arm about the shoulder of an eighteen-year-old lovely, that she shrank from him into the corner and, for a moment, could not speak.

Then, finding herself, taking from him a neutral, conversational tone, although with a sort of stretching of her vocal cords, 'I was offered a job,' she ventured. 'I wanted you to know.'

'Any good?'

'Well, you know. Two hundred thousand pounds for starters.'

'Ah, I see.'

'I turned it down.'

'Well, I dare say that was wise. Er . . . what are you doing here, actually, Naomi? I do but ask.'

'I just thought . . .' She held out her hand and obligingly he yanked her to her feet. Inches apart they stood, she with her face turned up to his. His breath fanned her cheek as she scanned his features, searching for some clue to his feelings, and she could have died, just *died* for love of him. 'I felt,' she said, as tears did terrible things to her mascara. 'That is, it seemed to me to be only right. I thought I should have custody of the chicken thingie.'

CHAPTER

11

'You had better come to me for New Year,' Elli decided, swallowing the last of a doughnut and licking sugar crystals from her fingers, 'you sad, lonely, desperate thing, you. We can't have you mouldering away on your own at the stroke of midnight. We'll tak a cup o' kindness together, you and I. What d'you say? And a right guid-willie waught (though I'm not sure I like the sound of that, whatever it is). We'll dance to the chimes of Big Ben.'

'I'm not lonely,' protested Kate, mooching, crotchety about the room. She flung herself down on the sofa, grabbed for the teapot, then recoiled from the sight of her own snouty, sulky face in its bitter chocolate glaze. 'And I'm certainly not desperate, thanks anyway. This New Year business is a lot of nonsense. Just another one of life's imagined corners, if you want my honest opinion.'

'Which I don't. I have enough opinions of my own, honest and otherwise. I have too many of them, some say. No, we'll make a night of it,' Elli persisted, waving aside Kate's objections. 'In fact, I'll ask the gang along. The auld acquaintances. It will be a night of *rapprochement*, a great burying of hatchets. And a kind of house-warming, the first bash at Schloss Sharpe since the

438

rebuilding. I might even invite the wretched Trevor. Dermatologically challenged he may be, and talent-free artistically – if he would only be more avant garde, make plaster-casts of piss holes in the snow, instead of this obdurate insistence upon paint – but he can warm a house like no one else I know.'

'Poor Trevor,' murmured Kate with feeling, 'you are never going to let him live it down.'

'Nonsense. That's all forgiven and forgotten. What's a little conflagration between friends? Besides, young Pocock has done me a huge favour, if he did but know it. He has, so to speak, tipped me the wink.'

'The what? Hey, Elli, you don't mean, do you, by "the gang" . . .?'

'Absolutely. The whole bang-shoot. The Gorsts, yes. And Alex and Naomi.'

'Then count me out. I simply can't. You must see that,' Kate pleaded. Here was the problem with Elli Sharpe, she told herself, exasperated. Her sterling qualities were also her worst attributes (or should that be the other way about?). It was hard at times to tell her good intentions from her bad. 'I still can't believe they got together again. It makes no sense. I was so sure he was over her. I had such hopes.'

'And *I* can't believe you're still knocking off John.'

'If you must put it like that.' Kate winced.

'How else? Although, I have to say, it's doing you no end of good, a bit of sex, after twenty-odd years of celibacy.'

'Who said I was celibate?' She was crackling, now, with indignation.

'You did, if you remember. You shared it with me in that frank, confiding manner of yours. You said, "Elli, I have lived the life of a veritable nun." '

'I said no such thing!'

'Then words to that effect. The Poor Clares, I was given to understand, had had more fun than you in all those years. The Ursulines were living it up by comparison. But I should have known anyhow, in retrospect. One only has to see the change in you. You're so smug with it, you practically glow in the dark. It's taken ten years off you. Because you were looking, I have to say, a bit of a middle-aged frump, you were going to seed. But not now. Even your hair is in better condition. It must be all that sperm.'

'All what . . .? Oh, *really*, Elli!'

'So-o, that's settled. New Year's Eve at my place. We'll go the whole Hogmanay. You, Mrs Garvey, will be there, and no excuses. We'll have no ill feeling at the year's end. Then how – now I come to think of it – will you be spending Christmas? Ah, I see! Once again, festering on your own.'

'I shall be quite happy.'

'Sure you will. You'll have a turkey, won't you? With all the trimmings? Or a more modest bird for your solitary repast? I hear snipe is very tasty.'

'You're the expert on sniping.'

'Woo-hoo! Get you!'

'Lay off me, Elli, can't you?'

'No, I can't, you see, because it worries me.' Elli became quite exercised, all at once, on her friend's behalf – and on behalf of her sisters everywhere, who were

440

men's dupes and playthings. She was seized by a fine sense of outrage. 'It's the lot of the mistress, isn't it, to be left high and dry on these occasions? Christmas, birthdays, bank hols, you will find "the other woman" indoors washing her hair. St Valentine's Day, St Swithin's Day, Holy Innocents and Circumcision Day, she'll be there crying into her Cuppa Soup. Ascension, Assumption, Independence Day, she waits for the phone to ring. Mother's Day, Father's Day, Pentecost, Palm Sunday, National No Smoking Day, she sits like patience on a monument, smiling at grief.'

'If you say so,' Kate told her, sighing, resigned, conceding the morning along with the truth.

Elli had arrived without warning, half an hour ago, with a bag of cakes for 'elevenses', she had ambushed Kate on the doorstep, headed her off as she prepared to leave the house, proposing that the two of them pig out. This she had proceeded to do, between mouthfuls chiding Kate for being very much not a voluptuary. She seemed on top form, with a surfeit of energy and suspect good will, so Kate nerved herself to ask, 'How's work?'

'Work? What about it? It's just dandy.'

'But I thought you were having . . . that is, I understood that they were trying to . . .'

'A little local difficulty. Nothing I can't handle.' With glistening fingers Elli waved away the notion that she might not be equal to the situation, she took air up her nostrils and expelled it noisily. 'It'll all be over by Christmas, as they said of the American War of Independence.'

'Where have I heard that before? And, speaking of "the other woman", how are you doing with Martin Curran?'

'Oh, good grief, that's ancient history! *Finito*. And with, as you see, no harm done. Because we were never in love, you understand? It's through love, not sex, that we screw up. It's where you're going wrong, if you ask me.'

'Which I don't. I *don't* ask you, Elli.' Kate sort of bucketed on to the floor, upending the sofa cushion behind her, and gazed bleakly around her. Lately, intermittently, she had been seeing her home with new eyes. She had always loved this place for its adequacy, but it seemed to her suddenly that for a house, as for a person, mere adequacy was, paradoxically, not enough.

Niggardly, number 28 struck her now in its design. The architect must have foreseen – indeed, *decided* – that no one truly exceptional would ever live at this address. He had subtly reduced successive occupants. They would never aspire; they would know their place. There was about everything a meanness of scale that suggested a mean mind at work. And with the gratuitous addition of that silly front balcony, that pointless metal frippery, he must, after all, have been taking the piss.

In a similar fashion, when she reviewed her life, it seemed so small and shabby. Her two great adventures – pregnancy before marriage; an affair with her brother-in-law, her friend's husband – seemed not racy or saucy, but only banal. Banal, too, her love for John which, though she might not make Elli see it, was the point of that affair.

'Anyway,' she added, scratching with a bitten nail at a

dry curry splash on her shirtfront, 'I shall probably go away for Christmas. In fact, I may well go away for good. Move out of town. To tell the truth I'm tired of London.'

'When a man is tired of London,' pronounced Elli sagely, 'he's tired of London. And where do you plan to go from here?'

'I don't know.' Kate brought her shoulders up in a defensive shrug. 'To France, maybe. I might find work there.'

'In December? Doing what? Picking gooseberries? You're talking six kinds of shit, Kate, my darling. You don't seriously want to skip off abroad, do you? Only to run away? But it won't work, because your problems go with you, honey.'

'That isn't true. I should leave my problems. I should leave John free, at any rate, to get on with his life.'

'And does he want to be "free", as you put it? I thought what he wanted was to be with you. To leave Geraldine for you. Isn't that what he says?'

'But I don't want that. Or, at least, I do, but . . .'

'But you can't handle the guilt.'

'The price is too high. I don't care to be responsible for ruining people's lives. Not just Geraldine's, but the kids' too. Because they would be bound to be affected, especially Lucy. She's at a particularly vulnerable age.'

'They'd get over it,' said Elli, dismissing such concerns. 'You know your trouble? You're a moral coward.'

'Ah, yes, I dare say. Now, was there something, Elli? Anything in particular? Some reason why you're here? Only, I should have been at work an hour since.'

'Marriages do break up. One in three at the last count. It's an everyday occurrence.'

'I was due at Janet's at nine-thirty.'

'Whatever for? You can't do much in this stinking weather.'

'On the contrary, it's just the time, while so much is dormant, to make new beds and dig over the borders. And I have to sow some alpines. And there's pruning to be done. In any case, I need the money.'

'It's a shame you have to scrimp as you do.'

'I don't. Not scrimp. I have to earn like everybody else, that's all.'

'And there's me, paid a fortune for doing next to nothing, for putting my feet up and painting my toenails every second week. I shall be rather sorry, in that sense, to see the back of Dawn the Yawn.'

'She's going, then?' asked Kate, surprised.

'Ah, yes. Very soon,' Elli assuredly confirmed.

'Is she happy about that?'

'Oh, she doesn't know yet. It's to be a surprise. My Christmas surprise for her.'

'I don't follow.'

'No. How could you? I say, don't you want this last bun? Well, pity to waste it, though I'm sure it'll go straight to my thighs. Sugar, I read, by the by, is very good for panic attacks. You should stuff your face with cake, Kate, whenever you get panicky.'

'I'm not that keen on sweet things, actually. And I don't need to palliate myself the way you do.'

'Suit yourself.' Elli turned the bun around, inspecting it minutely, narrowly meeting its curranty eyes. 'I could

444

have gone for redundo I suppose. Held out. Boy, that would have cost 'em! I should have backed a pantechnicon up to the cashiers, loaded the loot, then driven off into the sunset. But when it comes to a choice between the purse of Fortunatus and the satisfaction of seeing our Dawn cop the black plastic bin bag, there just isn't any contest.'

'You seem very confident,' said Kate, curious.

'Yes, it's cut and dried. Or as good as. More anon. The full story when we reconvene. That may not be till New Year's Eve. It's one mad whirl of parties between now and then for me. Listen, Kate, I'd love to stay all day and have my ear bent, I'd love to hear more of your tale of woe, but I'm wanted at the office before noon.'

Kate opened her mouth to protest at such a travestying of the facts, but no words quite seemed to meet the case, so she shut it again with an audible snap.

'You should take my advice,' Elli offered, turning, resisting, as Kate shooed her through the front door. 'Keep it light. Have your fun. Don't get too emotionally involved. So long as you can handle it, there's no need to end it, is there, hm? Now, I simply must dash. Toodle-oo. Be good. And don't do anything Elli wouldn't do.'

Three minutes is nothing when you're running late and you've a train to catch. It is barely enough time to hard-boil a quail's egg. Just three minutes of sex would be a pretty poor show; it would be over, almost before it had begun. No one could run a mile in three minutes . . . could they? Yet, to wait three minutes for a chemical reaction, to spend one hundred and eighty seconds staring at a 'result window' to see if it turned purple, to know if your life was about to be blown inside-out, was an interminable, torturous process indeed.

Naomi, mouth-breathing fastidiously over the instruction leaflet, revolted by a process that required one to hold an absorbent strip for ten seconds in one's urine stream, then to lay the wet test down and watch it, drummed with her fingers on the basin edge, counting off the interim as best she could. She drove her gaze off around the tiny, boxed-in bathroom, ordered her attention elsewhere, but always it came slinking back to the test strip, the magic wand, which suddenly and, yes, magically, changed colour. The purple staining moved, as promised, through the 'result window' into the 'error control window', and Naomi felt her face suffuse with blood – she felt it, too, take on different hue, she turned a whiter shade of puerperal.

Human chorionic gonadotropin was present in her waters, in some quantity if the darkening stain spoke true. She was, in other words, up the spout. She was in the club. At this late stage in her reproductive life, she had a bun in the oven.

'Who can I call,' asked the instructions leaflet of itself, 'if I have any other questions?' And it gave itself the answer: Susan Scott, at the Feminine Care Research Laboratories in Folkstone, Kent, during office hours.

Susan Scott? Was anyone really so called? It sounded to Naomi a generic name, the sort you would make up to conjure an efficient, eminently sensible female of indeterminate age. Susan Scott was probably a whole department. Or a team. She was whoever happened to pick up the phone. Perhaps they had a rota at the Feminine Care Laboratories: today it might be Carly's turn, tomorrow, Tasmin's, the day after, Fiona's, to impersonate Ms Scott.

And if she did exist, how could she help Naomi Markham, who was expecting a baby by her young lover – or by his odious father? What comfort or counsel could this Susan offer to a bad, bad woman, who had had sex with the two Garveys, *père et fils*?

Naomi recognised the baby now. It was as if he – yes, certainly, *he* – had always been there, a notion, a baby-shaped idea in the back of her head. As a young woman, in her teens, her early twenties, she had supposed that motherhood would happen one day, much as middle age would happen, but to a very different self, a Naomi she did not yet know. She would be living in a house much like her mother's, an ancient, rambling building, with a central staircase going off in two directions to the fore, and a narrow, twisty service staircase from the kitchen aft, with a walled potager, and an orchard, and a gardener called Nelson, and with a riot of Virginia creeper up the front. She would be respectable, married – she had seen, indistinctly, a faceless couple, herself and her life partner, like the confectionery bride and groom on a wedding cake, sugar all the way through – and frightfully county, with a couple of dogs, Dalmatians for preference. She had imagined she would wear court shoes, tailored jackets, Gor-Tex, Barbour waistcoats and box-pleated skirts, she'd be adapted and grown up.

Then when, year after year, it hadn't happened, when she had neither married nor grown up, when she had

447

somehow never gone into Gor-Tex and was still so ill-adapted, the imagined baby had been put away somewhere in her subconscious and forgotten. So completely had she forgotten him, in fact, so implausible had his existence come to seem, that she had grown careless in the matter of precautions, now and then, through indolence, or in a fever of lust, omitting to insert the cap which was the only contraceptive she could tolerate. With Alex, on occasion, she had taken the most delicious risks. And then for David she had, of course, not been prepared.

'Alex will be pleased,' she said aloud, although 'pleased' was not the adjective she wanted. Overjoyed? That would not do, either. It had a tabloid ring about it: it evoked those 'miracle' babies, born against whatever odds, whose devoted parents declared themselves, invariably, 'overjoyed'. Perhaps there was not a word for what she knew he'd feel, an emotion so large and so rich that it could not be eaten all at once.

And wasn't this the worst of it? The hideous twist? Because his joy, his pleasure, call it what you will, would be premised on the understanding that this was his child, which it might or might not be. When it might in fact be . . . Slow to come to this realisation, appalled by its implications, she clutched the rim of the basin and put her face down into it. The baby might be Alex's half-brother. Or half-sister. No, not sister. And either way it could grow up to resemble him, and he might never be the wiser. Nor, for that matter, might *she*.

Even Naomi, with her somewhat tenuous grasp of ethics, could see this was a knotty one, too problematic, probably, even for the estimable Susan Scott.

The basin could be seen, up close, to be grimy; the plug-hole whispered something nasty about drains. Naomi, as the nausea passed, wondered if some gentle cleaning, a little light housework, would be therapeutic.

Then she wondered about termination. Should she stop this now? Unmake the difficulty? No, she could not bear the loss of Alex's baby. His might-be baby. *Her* baby. 'Two wrongs,' she said glibly, aloud, into the resonating porcelain, 'don't make a right.'

What was more, in her strange, intuitive frame of mind she was somehow sure that she was carrying the only child she would ever have. This unhoped-for thing seemed now to exceed all hope, to lie way beyond it, somewhere in the territory of wildest dreams.

Straightening, groaning, with a trembling hand she slipped the test stick back into its plastic wrapper, then into its box. Discover Today, it had proposed, and Naomi, for her sins, had discovered. She could dispose of the evidence, into the dustbin, but she could not dispose of reality.

Simple arithmetic might be decisive in the matter of paternity. Date of last period, that sort of thing. She had missed . . . how many? Two? Three? She was so fragile, with such low body weight; menstruation was, for her, an incalculable process, conforming to no charted cycle. And perhaps, in any case, it would be best if the truth were not established (this depended, of course – and, oh, what irony! – upon what the truth might be).

She pressed her fingertips to her forehead, closed her eyes, as if, by this charade of thinking, to promote thought. It was no good. Her brain had almost nothing useful to contribute. She was capable at this instant of only physical response; her body, with its secret charge, the life within, was already taking over.

When the telephone trilled, she went as if in a dream, out into the hall, where a bright stripe of winter cold came through the gaping letterbox, and thence to the bedroom to answer it. 'It's you,' she said faintly, in response to his greeting. 'Oh, Alex, it's *you*.'

'Yes, it's me,' he confirmed, surprised at this extreme reaction to his call. 'Is everything OK?'

'We-ell . . .' Naomi sat as heavily as it was in her to sit, down on the unmade bed, she wound the phone flex round her hand. 'Yes, everything's fine, I guess.'

The decision must be reached today. She must choose the honest course, confess to treachery, risk losing Alex, with consequent misery all round; some sense of integrity, of common decency could, at enormous cost, be served. Or he must be told only the half – that she was pregnant, that she had a Garvey baby growing inside her, and she must hope for lasting happiness for everyone, she must foster delusion, build the edifice of family upon a howling lie.

Her guilty secret would be her punishment; she would watch as her child grew, and never be sure. She must pray ever more fervently that David wouldn't tell. Not just David, for there was also Dominic, Geraldine's insufferably cocky son, who had probably seen and certainly heard David in her room on that dreadful morning when life as she knew it had seemed to end. A canny youth, he must surely have guessed that this was no mere social call.

450

Sighing, she gazed around her at the familiar, tumbled room. This flat was so small, but even with an infant would be adequate. Here was her great discovery: that adequacy was indeed, by definition, enough. And to have enough was to have it all.

'Do you love me?' she asked meekly of Alex.

'You can count on it,' he told her. And she could. He had taken her back so gladly, forgiven her so readily – had gone so far as to beg that she forgive him. Yet he had never wilfully hurt her, had tried only to urge her to find some meaning in her existence. And, if it didn't have meaning now, she told herself – if the incubation of a new life was not meaningful – then it never would have.

Glancing out at the garden, she saw two, three, four starlings rise out of the viburnum and wheel against an acid sky. One for sorrow, she thought, two for joy. Three for a girl, four for a boy. 'I mean, with all my faults . . .'

'I love you, OK? What can I say?'

'No matter what?'

'No matter what, Naomi. Warts and all. And come what may.'

'I love you too.'

Three more birds took flight.

Five for silver, she recited mentally, six for gold. Seven for a secret, never to be told.

She drew a quick, deep breath, shut her eyes and masked them with her free hand. 'Oh, Alex, I'm going to have a baby.'

*

What a sinister illness was this that gave no sign, beyond putting up one horrid little growth! It was a sly old disease that had no apparent pathology.

Geraldine Gorst felt, if anything, dangerously well. Her eyes were bright (too bright, perhaps?). Roses flowered in her plump cheeks. The tongue which she poked out at her reflection was raspberry pink with the faintest bloom upon it. The thermometer registered a deceptive normality. Her appetite, far from deserting her, seemed insatiable, as if some rude and ravening other lurked inside her, calling out all day for biscuits, cakes, hot buttered toast.

The most pronounced of her symptoms, indeed, apart from the elusive lump (now she felt it, now she didn't), was a sense of being profoundly changed. Something about her was altered. Mortality had moved in on her.

A twinge of pain would have been almost a comfort in her present state. A nagging ache, she could have coped with, she could have focused on it. What she could not stand was tricksy sickness masquerading as rude health.

So clumped was she around the private, certain knowledge that she was not long for this earth, that she could scarcely give of herself to her near and dear ones. The family's needs she met these days with duty and distraction. In the face of her children's squabbles, she could offer only silence. And, strangely, far from running riot, they were fighting rather less. Whole days went by without a hint of Dominic's teasing, or of Lucy's tantrums. A precarious peace had broken out at Copperfields. All was ominously quiet on the domestic front.

Were they at last growing up? Or had they intuited her

trouble? Were they, at a conscious or unconscious level, frantic with worry over her? She liked to think so.

Lucy had even, last night, without any bidding, cleared and washed the dishes, she had made the coffee. Now, how could one account for *that*?

John, too, had been more than usually solicitous these past few weeks. By small gestures of tenderness he had shown that he was still devoted to her. She supposed he must be very anxious. Yet she could not bring herself to speak about her private terror.

Sitting on the sofa now, mixing her fingers, mauling hand with hand, tugging as if at an invisible glove, as Mrs Slack trundled furniture above her head (she was giving the bedroom a good old going-over; floorboards thundered, castors squealed), Geraldine envisaged her own ineluctable end.

She could not for much longer put off the evil day when she must visit the doctor, after which it would be made, so to speak, official. This reluctance to seek advice was out of character, it was an index to the seriousness of her concern. She was no stranger to Dr Neville's consulting room – or he to her anatomy. Few parts of her body, over the years, had gone unprodded. Through his stethoscope he had oft attended to her breathing, the stentorious ins and outs of air, he had heard the noble beating of her heart. They had worked their way doggedly together through the pharmacopoeia; hundreds of prescriptions had been filled. 'Mrs Gorst,' he liked to joke with her, 'I can't think why you bother to discuss these things with me, when you know more of illness than I ever shall.' She could close her eyes and conjure vividly the floral pattern of his cubicle curtains, which she remembered so well and very much disliked.

She was a great believer in orthodox medicine. And no ailment was too small, in her view, to go unreported. Her GP ought, she felt, to be told how she was coming along, to take a lively interest in her general health. If hot baths made her go all woozy, if cheese last thing at night gave her the collywobbles, if strawberries brought her out in rashes, and cabbage made her flatulent, and eggs bound her up, he ought to note it. A nice, fat sheaf they had on file for her, a colourful medical history.

But this time it was different. This time it was life-threatening. She could not nerve herself to visit the surgery, to be told that there was something desperately wrong. She could not sit there while a noncommittal Dr Neville, with knitted brow, hmm-hmmming, jotted something on his pad, then, flinging down his pen, suggested she undress behind the screen.

As the most forward of the Copperfields clocks anticipated half-past twelve, she began to muse, as every day, upon her lunch. Her internal other, in need of serious comforting, signalled its desire for a substantial feed, preferably fried. She was mentally inventorying the contents of the larder when she heard the purring of a motor, the swish of tyres, the churning of the shingled drive.

Glancing towards the window, she saw just the tops of trees against a brimstone sky. The impulse to get to her feet, to go at once to see what brought the car here, was not powerful enough to activate her. Nor had she voice to summon him.

So she waited, and in a moment John came through the house, calling her name. She heard the soft thud of his footsteps, as urgently he sought her out. 'Ah, there you are,' he greeted her, on finding her at last, seeming to see her and not to see her. He looked literally washed out, faded, frayed, as though he had been too many times through the full hot cycle.

'What brings you . . .?' she wondered, for it was rare for him to nip home in the day. But, beyond the turning of her head, she did not stir.

'We need to talk.' He drew a high-backed chair away from the wall, sat on it, very tense, and rested his hands upon his knees. She saw signs of strain in his face, a little tic under one eye, the twitching of a rogue muscle.

'We do,' she wearily assented. It would be a relief, after all, to give voice to her fears, to share them with her man. She turned her own hands over, palms upwards, sort of flapped them out in a capitulating fashion. 'You're the boss,' she signalled to him.

He rocked himself back, forth, and up on to his feet again. Crossing to the sideboard, he asked over his shoulder, 'Need a drink?'

Need? She didn't think so. Want? Perhaps. It would help to steady her. 'Just a small one, maybe.' And, behind his back, she pincered thumb and forefinger to indicate the smallest nip imaginable.

He fixed a gin and tonic for her, a large scotch for himself. 'You've got wind of something, haven't you?' he quizzed her as he pressed a glass upon her.

Accepting the drink, she took a sip and choked it down. She felt her face flood with colour – although whether from the shock of alcohol or with emotion she was unsure. Tears sprang. She could have broken down. Because he had noticed. He had actually *noticed*. For years he had seemed so remote, so elsewhere, somehow. But he was very much here, now, in the room with her. She could not remember when he was last so absolutely present.

'Yes,' she confessed, dropping her head, gazing into the tumbler, inhaling fragrant gin fumes.

'Geraldine, it's time you knew the truth.'

'But I simply cannot bear . . .' she ventured faintly, touching her fingertips to her chest.

'One cannot live a lie.'

For a moment she considered this. 'I suppose one can't,' she finally allowed.

'I would not have had this happen for the world, you understand?'

When she opened her mouth there were no words within, so she simply closed it again. This lent her a fishy and an oddly vulnerable aspect which unmanned him.

'I do care for you,' he assured her. 'That hasn't changed.' But he was running out of steam, rather, and took a swig of whisky to refuel himself. He had expected weeping and recriminations, histrionics, a dramatic showdown. And he had not had the imagination to arm himself against her acquiescence, let alone her air of utter defeat.

'We both of us . . .' He tendered. But those words took him nowhere. They were sorry, he and Kate, but so what? It wouldn't make it any the more bearable for Geraldine. It might even make it worse. Better she should loathe and despise them, publicly denounce them. Two decent, abject, well-meaning, middle-aged people offered poor scope for demonisation. Geraldine could say, as she had always done, believing it to be the truth, that she'd been good to Kate. She could talk of rank ingratitude, but would that be enough?

'You must think that I've been very stupid,' she ventured with rare humility, dropping her head, staring at her knotted hands.

'No,' he protested vehemently. '*No*. I never took you for a fool. We neither of us – oh, good grief!'

For there came, from the hallway, a human cry, and a crash that seemed to rock the house. 'What the hell,' wondered John, 'was *that*?'

Elli joined the small knot of hungry workers at the trolley and, crying 'Let me through, I'm a doctor', shouldered her way to the front. 'Have you no salmonella and cucumber?' she demanded of the guy in the white overall, the catering assistant, who, accustomed to the rudeness of this abominable female, set his face against her, not deigning to reply. This was something of a shame, for she was taken with his look, which she thought of, vaguely, as Latin. She liked his sulky mouth, his dark, unfocused eyes; she related powerfully to his air of wishing to be anywhere but here.

Sorting through sandwiches in plastic packaging, finding nothing to her fancy, she settled with an ill grace for egg and cress, then stood blockishly waiting for change from a twenty-pound note, while her colleagues muttered and fidgeted behind her. She was more than usually feisty today, an effect of premenstrual syndrome, which explained, also, her sugar craving, the alacrity with which she had already this morning, at Kate's, put herself outside two doughnuts and a bun.

Many women, Elli had noticed (check Kate, who was a fine example), seemed convinced that there was something seriously amiss with them at this time of the month. Persuaded by male propaganda which put them always in the wrong, they bought the story that their rage and bitterness was irrational, they explained it away as merely hormonal, even apologising for it, seeming shamed and surprised by their propensity for outrage.

Elli, however, with a period imminent, had a different perspective. For most of the lunar month, the world was veiled in a softening and transforming haze. But for two, three days in every twenty-eight, the fog would lift, she would wake to find things as they truly were, and understandably she railed against the inequity of it all.

She had read that premenstrual depression was a disease of loss. Loss of interest, of enthusiasm, of energy, adequacy, concentration, self-control . . . but for her it meant loss of illusion, only, and loss of inhibition. Was it any wonder that half of all suicide attempts among women were made just prior to a period? Or that irritability and aggression were common in this phase? It was not, as myth had it, a response to some monstrous distortion, but a reaction against a harsh reality, briefly, acutely apperceived.

She actually celebrated menstruation, which so invigorated her; she regarded it as a big event, and was apt to boast about it. She never felt more her own woman, stronger, or more fierce, than when reaching for the Tampax. The regularity of her cycle was a source of pride to her: 'You could set your watch by me,' she liked to brag to Juin.

Herself, she set her watch by the speaking clock, and would have it not a second fast or slow. Notoriously unpunctual, she judged her lateness very, very finely. Dialling 1–2–3 now, for mischief, for the hell of wasting company money, she heard that the time, sponsored by Accurist (and wasn't this a surreal concept; what would become of time without a subsidy?), was one thirty-six and forty seconds. Pip, pip, pip.

She could cut off to the pub, or to the wine bar for a tincture. There she was sure to find, at this hour, a few old lags dispersed around the bar. But another symptom of premenstruation was a tendency to sottishness; the stuff went down, somehow, without touching the sides.

Normally, this would not bother her – the more game of her long-standing colleagues had fond memories of Ms Sharpe, teetering on a table at Fleet Street's Cock Tavern, brandishing an empty magnum, loudly proposing, 'Shall we have the other half?' – but at this moment she must keep a clear head, for she had orders to fill. And men to see. And cats to kill.

When she sat back in her revolving chair, she could take in the broad sweep of the open-plan office, the wage slaves hunched over their terminals in the unkindly fluorescent light, and, at the far end of the room, the closed doors behind which the executives were busy all day executing.

Through one of these, just under sixty minutes ago, had emerged Gus Maclean. Elli, myopic even with her contact lenses, had seen, nonetheless, a beige hand go up to a beige face, she had recognised his peculiar stoop as, ducking his head, he made for the lift.

The *Globe*'s proprietor had recently been born again. He had managed miraculously to find God, while being still in thick with Mammon. His staff, who saw almost nothing of him, knew him as a workaholic and a stickler. Whether or not Gus Maclean was by nature super-conscientious, he did well, as the proprietor's lieutenant, to be seen to be so. His lunch hour was, therefore, precisely that.

So, 'Spot on!' she crowed aloud when Maclean returned, as she'd predicted, at the stroke of one forty-five.

'Diligent to a fault, our Gus,' remarked Alan Ridgeway, following Elli's hawklike gaze. Alan was a thin, stooped man, charged with being funny for the paper, and the effort of calling continually upon his seriously depleted wit so fatigued him, that he was in person a lugubrious sort.

'Yes. I hear he's always up at the crack of Dawn,' said Elli, and laughed maniacally, incomprehensibly as, snatching her sandwich from her desk, she sprang from her chair. Then, with a more than usually sassy walk, her bright hair bobbing at her shoulders, she went right on over to Maclean's door and, rapping upon it, barged in.

'I have an idea for you,' she announced, laying a hand meaningfully upon a chair back.

'Ah, yes,' he said hastily, before she could pre-empt

him, 'please sit down. I can give you just two minutes, I'm afraid.' His tone was one of studied dislike; a ram-raider, she felt, might have hoped for a warmer welcome here.

'Two minutes will do. We need a London supplement. I hear the *Monitor* is launching one. If we move fast, get in first, we shouldn't lose too much more ground to them.'

'Indeed?' With a knuckle to his nostril, and with unconcealed dislike, Maclean considered her. It was the 'we' that got him, for it carried the suggestion that Elli Sharpe was still a vital part of the machinery, that she did not have – as must be evident to her – the skids well and truly under her. 'This possibility has, of course, been mooted at boardroom level,' he told her tersely.

'Oh, it has?'

'Most certainly.'

'Any dice? Will we push ahead with it?'

'That, I am afraid, is for the present confidential.'

'I suppose it would be.' Elli crossed her legs, she made herself comfortable, swinging her foot, flapping her shoe from her toe. She peeled the clingwrap seal off her packaged sandwich to release a noxious, eggy stench into the atmosphere. 'Eeeugh! I don't think so, do you? Suddenly I'm off my food. One has to keep body and soul together, but there are limits.' And she discarded the offending, noisome item, tossing it into the wastepaper bin, privately regretting that she hadn't gone for Brie, so redolent of unwashed socks.

'Was there something else?' queried Maclean with barely suppressed loathing.

'No, not really.' She mimed confusion. And then,

'Well, yes, as a matter of fact,' she admitted in a confidential rush. 'It's about Dawn Hancock, to be honest.'

Reading her wrong, Maclean thought, This is it! He rejoiced, She's cracking! Inclining towards her, clasping his hands in front of him, he waited with expectation – 'Resign, you cow,' he almost urged – and, magnanimous in victory, mentally resolved to slip a fiver in the envelope when they stumped up for her leaving present. (Well, maybe not a fiver, but a quid or two, at least.) 'Shoot,' he invited.

'She shows such promise, doesn't she?'

'Yes, yes. We have high hopes.'

'And so young. By the time she gets to our age, she will probably be quite as good as me. Or, if not . . . Although, of course, by the time she gets to our age, we shall be some other age. We'll be sixty. Just imagine! However, I digress.'

'Then come to the point please,' he said through clenched teeth.

'We-ell . . . It's a teeny bit embarrassing. May I speak as your friend, Gus? May I call you Gus, Gus?'

He opened his mouth to say no, indeed she might not, and open it stayed as she went blinding remorselessly on.

'This affair between the two of you. We're all so worried – we, the girls, that is – that it will end in tears for poor Dawn. Because she is emotionally such a baby. And I know she hopes you'll leave your wife. No, no, Gus, hear me out.' Elli put up her hands like buffers. 'She tells us that you have plans to leave Caroline. And we are aware how painful that would be. Then, of course, there is the proprietor, with his rather rigid views about d-i-v-o-r-c-e. Thou shalt not commit adultery, etc. You have your position at the *Globe* to consider. Now, you may tell me to mind my own business, you may say I'm a nosy old bag, and it's not my place to get involved, but –'

'Cooee.' Patti Henderson's blonde head, her silly, smiling face came flirtatiously around the door.

'Not now,' snarled Gus Maclean, waving her away. 'Push off.' Good grief, he thought, as she withdrew, affronted, this outfit is stiff with harpies. He felt himself hag-ridden. And, unbelievably, it appeared that Dawn, the gossipy little bint . . . It seemed she had been woefully indiscreet, she had blabbed to, of all people, Elli Sharpe. 'How many of you has Miss Hancock, er, confided in?' he asked, dabbing with his hankie at the drooping corners of his mouth.

'Oh, not many. Please don't concern yourself on that account. No more than a dozen of us, I should say. Make that a baker's dozen. Or fourteen, top whack. Close friends. Trusties. Which is why I'm here, sticking my neck out, to implore you not to lead her too much of a dance.'

Elli had never before used the word 'dumbfounded', it had had no place in her vocabulary, but it seemed to fit the bill. Dumbfounded was pretty much how Gus Maclean appeared to her. It would not be true to say that he turned ashen, but there was a distinct touch of green around the Maclean gills.

Folding her arms in front of her upon his polished desktop, she exuded sympathy and understanding.

These things happened, her manner conveyed. People met and fell in love. This was life. And who was she to censure?

'I think,' proceeded Gus Maclean, improvising wildly, breaking an awkward silence, 'that there has been some misunderstanding. My interest in Dawn Hancock –' He instituted a search for his handkerchief – 'My friendship, yes –' He patted his side pockets, his top pocket. 'It has been purely professional. I have sought to bring her on, to nurture her undoubted talents.'

'I see.'

'And in so doing, I may unwittingly have encouraged . . . She is, as you say, very young. Perhaps naïve. And fanciful. She may have read into my actions far more than was intended. Kindly leave it with me, er, Elli. I shall have a word with her, set matters straight. Meanwhile, I hope I can rely upon your circumspection.'

'Absolutely.' Elli, with a gleaming eye, got to her feet. 'Count on it. My lips are sealed.' She mimed the zipping of them, and in so doing erased a smirk. 'Wild horses wouldn't drag this from me. Let me know about the London section, won't you, if you decide to go ahead? I might well be able to make some modest contribution.'

Then, with a clip-clop of unsensible shoes, and an exaggerated wiggle, she took her leave of him. *Fait accompli*, she exulted.

Molly du Slack had come downstairs, as Geraldine would later lightheartedly report, 'like a ton of bricks'. She would laugh about it after, but it wasn't funny at the time to see one's cleaning lady prostrated, it was just her luck, she thought.

'Out cold,' pronounced John, feeling for a pulse. 'The poor dear must have banged her head.'

'Well, she will wear those silly shoes,' wailed Geraldine. 'They're far too tight, you see. They pinch her toes. And the straps have stretched. And she's trodden them down. You know,' she continued, parting company with truth, without a qualm embracing fiction, 'I am forever telling her about it. "You'll fall and break your neck," I've warned her a dozen times.'

'Well, I doubt that her neck is broken,' offered John, for whom the day had taken so bewildering a turn. He went down on his knees, took Molly's hand in one of his, and with the other gently pat-pat-patted her sagging cheek.

Molly, opening one eye an instant, glared at him. 'Philanderer,' she accused him darkly, and she shook him off.

'She's raving,' said Geraldine, appalled. 'There could be brain damage.'

'Nonsense. She's probably just mildly concussed.'

'Should we give her a drop of brandy? She's a bit blue around the mouth.'

'Better not. I mean, in case of any broken bones. They might have to put her under. You make her as comfortable as you can – only don't move her – and I'll call an ambulance.'

As he went to the phone he felt drained. There was nothing left in him at all. He had spent his energies on confession, but his soul felt none the better for it, if anything it had made it worse.

Geraldine, kneeling over Molly, fanned her with a copy of *The Lady*. Her quiet, unassuming man, she told herself, had all at once assumed. He had taken on a new persona, strong, supportive, *there* for her. With him at her side, she could face anything – even, if it came to it, the temporary lack of help around the house.

'You are probably right,' she said, smiling gently, girlishly up at him, when he came to tell her that the ambulance was on its way. 'I've been most dreadfully silly. Fretting over nothing, probably. I shall see the doc first thing tomorrow as you suggest. You'll come with me, will you? It would mean a lot to me.'

'Well . . .' John banged the side of his head with the heel of his hand, as people do when they have water in their ears. Or he might have been trying to dislodge a stubborn thought from his brain. He had lost the plot completely, that was obvious. He simply could not follow. 'Of course, if you want me to,' he meekly agreed. 'Anything you say, my dear.'

CHAPTER

12

Juin lifted the lid of the pan and gulped audibly as a bubble broke the surface of the brown sludge. 'What's this?' she demanded.

'What does it look like?' Elli pulled the cork of a bottle of Sancerre and sighed with joyous anticipation.

'The primordial soup?'

'Nearly right.' Sloshing wine into a glass, Elli offered it. Juin, for answer, shook her head. 'No? Really, no?' Mother, then, passed the glass back and forth before daughter's eyes, but failed to beguile her. 'Sure? OK, please yourself. Now, guess again.'

'It looks as if the monster from a million fathoms had eaten something that disagreed with him. It looks as if it went right through him.'

'In fact, it's chilli,' Elli revealed, and, lest it not be hot enough to blow her guests' heads clean off their shoulders, she heaped in another spoonful of the fiery red spice powder.

'*Con carne*?'

'Exactly.'

'And what will *I* have?'

'My dear, if you *will* be so faddy.'

'I'm not faddy. I'm a vegetarian. That's not a fad, it's a principled stand.'

'And what do you think your boots are made of, Goody Two Shoes?'

'Nnnnnyerr. I know they're leather, don't I? But I didn't just go out and buy them, I've had them for simply aeons,' protested Juin, who had a youthful tendency to hyperbolise. 'I can't throw all my old stuff out, can I, unless I can afford new? Anyway, what would be the point of that?'

'As a gesture, I suppose.'

'An empty gesture, yes.'

'Then, when you next buy shoes, you'll go for plastic? Cotton espadrilles? Or crocheted? You'll treat yourself to a nice pair of clogs?'

'Canvas,' said Juin firmly. 'Plimsolls and stuff. So what *will* I have tonight, when you flesh-eaters are all guzzling chilli?'

'You can have bread and cheese. Some salad. I can't cater especially to your whims when I have a dozen hungry mouths to feed.'

'I told you, it's not a whim. It's a commitment. Could I, at least, have a baked potato?'

'Oh, my poor, starving child, you can have anything you ask, within reason.' Elli wrapped her red silk kimono around her, she hugged herself and raised her eyes to the heavens, seeking a witness. 'When did I deny you?'

She was fresh from the bath, scented, powdered and puffy, with her wet hair wrapped up in a towel, turban-fashion, revealing her big face. Upstairs, on her bed, she had laid out her dress, a babydoll number in brown silk with a froth of creamy lace at the bodice. ('What are you coming as, a *cappuccino*?' Juin had wanted to know, but Elli had cared nothing for her disparagement. She had seen the dress on the rail and had simply had to have it.)

'I don't see why we need to go through this ridiculous performance, anyway,' Juin told her rattily. 'I never heard such a crap idea. It will be horrendous. And don't think I don't know why you're doing it.'

'Spreading sweetness and light, you mean? Pouring oil on troubled waters? Handing out the olive branches right, left and centre? It's just in my nature, honey. Like a bridge over troubled waters, tonight old Elli will lay herself down.'

'Personally, I think it's all a game to you. You're just mixing it.' Juin, with hands on enviably narrow hips (Elli, certainly, envied them), backed up against the fridge and scowled. 'You love to manipulate others, don't you?'

'Sure I do.' Elli would not deny it, for had she not manipulated the hopeless Dawn clean out of Globe Tower? If only the security men had marched her through the door, put her out like the cat, her happiness would have been complete. As it was, Dawn had quietly resigned. She had put about the rumour that the *Sunday Times* was after her (the Style section had been mentioned) and departed. Never mind, for the Sharpe End was Elli's once more. 'But tonight I have the highest motive,' she insisted. 'I'm sick and tired of all the intrigue. I'm bored witless with trying to remember which names I dare not mention in whose presence, and who's not speaking to whom. We can all start next year afresh. Won't that be a relief?'

'Not especially,' replied Juin, who felt sick, literally *sick* at the thought of seeing Alex and Naomi here together. 'It will be a horrendous ordeal for Kate.'

'It will be good for Kate. She misses Alex sorely. If she weren't so pig-headed she'd have come around to that liaison long ago. And so, I regret to say, must you. Accept it and move on.'

'What's it to me? What has it to do with *me*? Why should I be interested?' To demonstrate her complete and utter indifference, Juin lolled her tongue out of her mouth, then endeavoured to touch her nose with it, crossing her eyes.

'You're telling me you aren't? Not one teeny, weeny bit? You're cool about Alex and Naomi?'

'I think it's –' Juin began, but was spared from saying more by the appearance of Muffy in the kitchen doorway, grinning, with one of Elli's strappy sandals swinging from his mouth. With a shrill cry, Elli gave chase. With a horrible rending sound, she tore the floating sleeve of her kimono on the door handle. 'Fuck, fuck, and double fuck,' she ranted as she pounded off upstairs. 'First thing tomorrow that dog goes to the vet. He gets put to sleep.'

Juin, sighing, shrugging, reached for Elli's wine glass and took a long draught. This was going to be quite a night.

Kate had never been a frock person. The problem was not really physical – although she did have a considerable talent for choosing unsympathetic fabrics that went into chevrons around the groin when she sat down, and rode

470

up her short thighs when she stood – but was psychological: in a frock, she simply felt all at odds.

Standing in front of a square of mirror, going on tiptoe to try to see the hem, then dipping at the knees to bring the neckline into view, she could make almost no sense of what she saw. It was like doing a jigsaw of oneself, she decided in exasperation, and not even having all the pieces.

She had resolved to dress up, to make the effort, out of pride. She had to show everyone just how sorted she was. 'I don't care,' she said aloud, and then stiffened, because the house tonight was loud with creaks and bumps and spooky, swishy sounds, and all her nerve-ends bristled. As a child she had assumed she would one day grow out of her terror of the dark, her fear of upstairs and downstairs and empty, echoey rooms, but it had yet to happen. Better, she told herself sternly now, to think on real-life matters, to prepare herself mentally for the meetings in prospect.

Which troubled her more, she quizzed herself, the thought of coming face to face with John, or that of seeing Alex there with Naomi? She visualised the first encounter, then the second, and the hurt was concentrated in the first. In a strange way, without any conscious effort, she had come to terms with Naomi and Alex. Or was it that she'd used up all her rancour on the Gorsts?

'I told you, didn't I,' John had said when he rang her, 'that I should end up hurting you?'

'Well, you said you'd end up hurting one or other of us,' she had reminded him miserably. And, forgetting how she had insisted that he could not, must not leave his wife for her, she had begun to sob self-pityingly. 'I might have known, mightn't I, which one of us that would be?'

He had tried to tell Geraldine, he had said. Not just tried: he *had* told her. He had gone home to confess to her, because he'd sensed such tension in her, such trouble. He had imagined she had guessed at his affair, that she was tearing herself to shreds over it. And, one way or another, she'd got hold of the wrong end of the stick.

'So that's it?' Kate had asked him, feeling sort of broken, wondering dully how such a thing was possible. If a man went to his wife and told her unequivocally, 'I am leaving you for someone else', could she genuinely misapprehend him, come back with the answer, 'Seven pounds forty', or 'It's in the garage', or 'It's probaly an allergy to house dust'?

'I guess. Yes, that's it.' His tone had been one of infinite regret. He was aching too, she knew it. Aching and aching. But he hadn't wept until he feared his skull might split in two, you could bet your life on that. He hadn't sat all night crying, convulsing, until his eyes disappeared in his bloated face and there wasn't a shred of tissue left in what had been a nearly full box of man-sized Kleenex

In the short time she had had to reflect upon it, she had decided that, yes, it was for the best. She had accepted the inevitable. But still it hurt like very hell.

So it was important, for this little party, for her ego, that she look her best – whatever her best might be. She rootled in her bag for her car keys, then decanted the contents – money, keys, old supermarket till receipts, bound in webs of human hair – with impatience on to the bed.

Petal and Pushkin came purposefully in, nose to tail, mewing, and eddied round her legs. She picked up each in turn – they hung very long from her hands, with their shoulders bunched, their toes spread like flowers – and she kissed each of them on the top of the head. 'You're all I have now,' she told them, then was a little bit abashed at her own melodramatics.

'But you have Alex,' said a voice in her head. 'He's not lost. This has been your doing. Only through your own intransigence, you ridiculous woman, have you become estranged.'

The fact of this quite took her breath away. She snatched up her bag and scooped everything back in any old how. More tears started. So many tears. Elli was right, she realised. Elli might be a monster, but she was always right. (It was her rightness, in a way, that made her monstrous.) She would make her peace tonight with her son. She would be warm and magnanimous to Naomi, if for no other reason than that Alex loved the woman. Only, please God, let them be there.

'I might have known you'd be first,' said Elli. 'Come right on through and help me in the kitchen. Meet Darcus from next door.'

'Marcus,' amended her neighbour.

'He's a film producer, you know.'

'I have a catering business. Cook-chill dishes.'

'Yes, that's it. I knew it was something of the sort. He's

473

just popped in, Trevor, to ask to borrow an electric drill, if you can believe it. I mean, what would I be doing with . . .? And to be hanging shelves on New Year's Eve. Did you ever hear of such a thing? But, there you are. I'm sure you'll like him. You'll get on – dare I say it? – like a house on fire.'

'I'm not your slave now, lest you forget,' grumbled the erstwhile cleaner, but he caught the tea towel that she chucked at him and, nodding to Marcus, who seemed concerned to make good his escape (who looked, indeed, as if his native Jamaica would not be far enough from here), he began obediently to polish glasses. 'Do I at least get a drink?'

'Never let it be said . . . Will white do you? I can open a red if you prefer. But you needn't think you're tapping into my best bubbly until some grown-ups arrive.'

'I'd rather have a beer.'

'In the fridge. Help yourself. Now, tell me, don't you just adore my dress?'

'For God's sake tell her she looks like frothy coffee,' said Juin, coming into the room, rolling her eyes, then nodding an insouciant hi. She seemed, herself, to be dressed for a funeral, and her face was white with strain.

'I wouldn't dare,' reacted Trevor feelingly.

'Darcus,' Elli said then, conversationally, turning to Marcus, 'this is Trevor. *The* Trevor. You may remember hearing mention of him. It was he who . . . Oh, I say. Are you off? Won't you stay? Then come back at one minute past twelve,' she enjoined him. 'Promise me. Bring a lump of coal and first-foot us. It's supposed to be a dark stranger, and you can't get much darker or stranger than you. Whoops. There goes the doorbell. Who will that be?'

'Why did we have to come?' said Lucy plaintively. 'I can't endure this sort of thing.'

'It will be OK,' said Dominic, not unkindly. The impulse to tease his little sister, to wind her up, came . . . and then it went. He somehow couldn't be bothered any more.

'You are a funny child,' Geraldine told her daughter mildly. 'When I was your age, I loved to go to parties.' And she laid her hand on John's leg, rather as if they shared a secret, as if they had been all for parties in their giddy youth. She claimed him, he thought, the way one might claim a spare chair by putting a coat or hat or newspaper on it. He did not feel himself loved so much as required. Still, it was something, he supposed, to be required.

He was with Lucy in the matter of this evening: he didn't think he could endure it. To see Kate, but not to talk with her, not to hold her or touch her, would be torment. He could picture her, so bright and plucky and faintly abrasive, covertly curling her lip at him, throwing him looks of contempt (well, he deserved no better). She was more than life to him, and he had sold her out. Simply by ineptitude, he had let her down.

It was warm in the car, and fuggy, with a stifling family closeness. Out of the corner of his eye he caught, now and then, his reflection, the ghost of himself, in the side window. Glancing in the driver's mirror he saw his own narrowed eyes, his eyebrows drawn together. Behind him, his children's faces, in the street light that rinsed through the Rover's interior, were intermittently yellow.

Geraldine withdrew her hand and rustled around in her bag for Polos. 'It's just such an awkward journey,' she said. 'The wrong side of town. It's as well that we're staying the night.'

She and John had the promise of the spare room. Lucy would go in with Juin. Dominic must make do with the sofa. It was typical of Elli, Dom reckoned, to so arrange things. As a boy (she would assume), he had no want of a bed, he could crash out just anywhere, he could rough it. 'It's not fair,' he had grumbled, when given notice of the plan, '*I* want to sleep with Juin.' And, 'Go on with you!', his mother had chided, as if she found him such a wag.

'Mint?' asked Geraldine, offering the Polos. When no one responded, she took one for herself, prised it from the pack, popped it in her mouth and rattled it around her teeth. She was feeling happy, relaxed – even (she said this to herself) a little gay. What a silly billy she had been, to worry herself sick over a tiny cyst. The doctor had confirmed it. She was indeed, as she had felt, dangerously well.

'Do I look all right?' asked Naomi, fussing unnecessarily with her hair. 'Is this getting thicker, or what?'

'You'll do.' Alex hoiked her shirt out at the waist and bent to kiss the soft swell of her belly. 'You're coming along nicely.'

'Does it show?' Smiling, giving him a gentle shove, she tucked the blouse back in her waistband. 'Hey, don't mess around. The cab is here. I heard him toot.'

Then toot made her think of Tooting, and of Kate, and the faint sensations of nausea returned. 'Will anybody guess, d'you think, that I'm . . . you know?'

'Elli might. Being Elli, I mean. She doesn't miss much, does she? But it's barely noticeable.'

'How much is barely?'

For answer, he put his index fingers apart an inch, two inches.

'That much, huh? I feel so different,' she confided. '*Is* my hair thicker? It seems to take so much longer to comb.'

'It looks great, that's all I can tell you. Now, are you ready, Mrs?'

'No. I need to go.' She steered him out of the bathroom and closed the door firmly on his heels. Urination was, for her at any rate, a strictly private matter. She was not like Elli, who would plonk herself down on the loo, just sit there with her skirt bunched, with her knickers round her knees, calling out through the open door, keeping up a spirited conversation with just anybody, man or woman, with no thought of guarding her female mystery. Basic, that was Elaine Sharpe.

Nor could Naomi pee, these days, without remembering that test strip, the way it had turned so suddenly, vividly purple. Then all the same emotions would assail her. Alex was so thrilled and proud and . . . well, yes, overjoyed. She was both mortified and thankful to see him thus. And thankfulness and mortification, like oil and water, simply would not mix.

She pumped the flush handle, once, twice, as was necessary (there was a knack to it), and stood at the basin distractedly soaping her hands.

'Oy,' yelled Alex, banging on the door.

'What?' She smiled at herself, such a sad, sad smile.

'Are you going to be in there all night?'

'Just a mo.'

'Only I have to ask you something.'

'Yes?'

'Yes.'

'Well, ask me, then.'

'Very well. Naomi, will you marry me and make an honest man of me? I'm down on my knees here, begging you.'

When she flung wide the door she found him with his face pressed to thin air, and very much not on bended knee. He slid her a sly smile out of the corner of his mouth, and winked at her.

'Say that again, Alex, please.'

'I said, will you marry me? Etc., etc.'

'Is that really what you want?'

'*Assolutamente*.'

'Then I accept.'

'Excellent.'

'Will we tell them all tonight? Kate and everyone?'

'A double whammy. Why not?'

'Because Kate might . . . I mean, mightn't she?'

'She might, but I don't think she will. Elli's right. (How come Elli's always right? What a wise old owl she is.) It's time to build bridges. I wouldn't go there tonight if I didn't believe that was possible.' Tucking Naomi under his arm, he planted a loud, squelchy kiss on her cheek.

'Sometimes I think you're quite mad, Alex.'

'I'm just so excited. Here. Give me your hand. C'mon, give. We'll face this together, won't we?'

'Together,' agreed Naomi. But, deep down she knew she was on her own. There was, rather, just her and her secret.

Kate sat primly, in her stiff frock, in solitary splendor, under a painting of all hell breaking loose, turning and turning the glass of fizz in her hand, resisting the impulse to swig from it, reminding herself sternly that she had to drive. She felt like the victim of a practical joke (the party was being held elsewhere). Or like a patient in a pox clinic waiting-room ('The doctor will see you now, Mrs Garvey'). She was agitated and embarrassed, wishing that some other guest would show, yet chagrined to think who that guest might be. She should have known, when Elli said nine, to come at ten. She should have known to be late – that even late would be early.

In a moment, Elli put her head round the door and gave a ghastly, hostessy smile, showing lots of teeth. 'You all right?'

'Yes, I'm fine.'

'You haven't touched your wine.'

'I'm pacing myself.'

'There's an idea! I must try it some time. Not tonight, mind. Tonight I get ratted. Then maybe I'll give up all my vices. New's Year's resolution. What's yours? To be nicer to me? And not to go, "Oh, *really*, Elli!", as has been your wont?' Without pausing to hear the answer, she withdrew once more to the kitchen, where she could be heard to harangue poor, spotty Trevor for spraying beer from a can up the wall. (She had just had the place redecorated, was the gist of her complaint. He might remember, there had been a bit of a blaze.)

Kate heard footfalls pass below the window, voices like plumes in the chill night air, heard two, maybe more people turn in at the gate and come scuffing up the front step. And, in spite of hearing them, when the doorbell sounded she started violently and spilled her drink.

'*Entrez*,' yelled Elli in the hall. 'Step inside and give your aunt a kiss, you gorgeous hunk of manhood. Don't you just love this dress? It's like wearing coffee creams. You're not the first. Don't you hate coming first? Kate's here. Follow me. *Suivez la* pissed.'

When Alex Garvey put his head round the door, he found his mother on her knees, rubbing at the carpet with the hem of a garment made from some peculiar blue and unforgiving fabric. She got to her feet and put her hands behind her back in an endearing, childlike fashion which went straight to his heart. 'Kate,' he said, choked, and he crossed to stand by her, to give her elbow an encouraging squeeze. 'How are you?'

'I'm fine.'

'And what have you done to my nice carpet?' Elli demanded.

'I'm sorry, I'm afraid I spilled –'

'Well, not to worry, honey, it's only champagne. Hey, what a great epitaph! Write it down, somebody. Make a note of it, Alex, you young person. There is at least a chance that you'll outlive the rest of us. I want these words on my gravestone: it was only champagne. And a screamer.'

480

'Screamer?'

'An exclamation mark.'

'Oh, *really*, Elli,' protested Kate.

Glancing over at the doorway, she saw Naomi, wearing, of all things, jeans. She seemed to have gained weight, and to have done something to her hair (Kate was not sure what), and there was a sweetness, a shyness about her that was unfamiliar. This was manifestly not the spoilt, idle, feckless woman of recent memory. 'Hello, Naomi,' she greeted her in a neutral tone, suppressing her feelings until she should have a chance to analyse them.

'Hi.' Naomi gave a kind of wave, a vague circling of the fingers. Kate must be told before the rest of them, she was thinking. She should hear it before the others did. But how to break it to her? Such tact was demanded here. Such a subtle turn of phrase.

'And, now, guess what,' cried a jubilant Alex. 'Kate, you're going to be a grandmother.'

'I never met an artist before,' said Lucy, impressed. Just wait till she told her best friend Sarah about this!

Trevor, with a shrug of one shoulder, swigging lager from the can, indicated that it was, after all, no big deal. He was secretly flattered, though, by this kid's worshipful attention, her interest in his canvas, his 'Anarchy', which she pronounced 'wicked' and 'awesome'.

'Things fall apart,' he told her, 'the centre cannot hold.'

'No?'

'Mere anarchy is loosed upon the world.'

'I suppose you're right.'

'That's Yeats.'

'What is?'

'It's from "The Second Coming", by Yeats. It's poetry.'

'Oh, I *love* poetry.' She lit up at this and looked all soulful. She was really quite fetching, with her blonde hair tucked behind her ears, and her shining, schoolgirl complexion. Besides, there was no one else to talk to here, except maybe for Juin, and he didn't know where she had disappeared to.

'You do?'

'Up the airy mountain,' she recited, screwing her eyes tight shut, the better to remember, as her head filled with fairies, 'Down the rushy glen.'

Trevor swilled the dregs of the lager round in the can and said, 'That's pretty.'

'We daren't go a-hunting, for fear of little men.'

'And *you're* pretty.'

She blushed crimson. 'Dominic – he's my brother – says I look like a pig.'

'Then Dominic doesn't know diddly.'

'Do you honestly think so?'

'I honestly do.'

'He can be really gross at times. I can't endure him.'

'Take no notice of him, I should. Listen, this tinnie's dead. I'm going to get another. Shall I bring you some champagne?'

'I should love that,' she responded, imagining herself twirling the glass on its fragile stem in a frightfully sophisticated fashion. A real-life artist. Sparkling champagne. What a glamorous tale she would have to tell Sarah when the term began. How she would rub that spiteful cow Jacintha's nose in it!

'So-o,' said Elli, ambushing Naomi in the kitchen, pinning her against the stove, 'you're in what is termed an "interesting condition" – although quite what is interesting about honking your guts up every morning, I fail to understand.' She snatched the lid off the pan and gave the slurping chilli an exploratory stir. It was burnt at the bottom, but sloppy up top. Breathing a meaty waft of steam, Naomi felt her stomach turn. 'Won't you have some of this?' Elli urged her. 'No? I tend to forget your anorexia. But you ought to be eating for one, if not two. *I* would. What were we saying? Morning sickness. Then there's the chronic heartburn. The swollen ankles. The backache. The craving for dill pickles and Walnut Whips.' She counted off these trying symptoms on her fingers. 'And you do realise, I trust, that your tits will just *go*.'

'I don't care,' said Naomi bravely, caring desperately, and she glanced down at her lovely, new, full bosom.

'They'll take first-class care of you, of course, being, as you are, an elderly primigravida. Don't make that face. You're elderly at thirty-five, as far as your friendly local obstetrician is concerned. Now, do tell me, who's the father? Hey, hey, I'm only joking. Just my fun. Take no notice of me.'

'That's all right. Look, Elli, I'm going to the bathroom.'

'I imagine you're forever popping to the lav, are you? Another feature of your delicate state. How it takes me back! You wait till you start leaking from the nipples. I shall come up with you. I'm busting for a slash myself.'

'No, no,' protested Naomi, fearing that Elli would follow her in, that she would stand over her chatting as her bladder seized up. 'You go first then. I have to find Alex.'

'What a devoted couple you are! I'm serious, Naomi. I envy you, rather. I never thought I'd say that, but I do. Now I'd love to stay here chatting, I would talk you through the pains of labour, but it's going to have to wait. Of episiotomy –' Elli made scissors of her fingers, she went snip-snip – 'more anon.'

'How is Molly?' asked Kate of Geraldine, as listlessly she pushed around the plate the excoriating chilli that Elli had thrust upon her, before venturing a tiny forkful. By nibbling away at it, she hoped to make at least some inroad. She dared not leave too much. 'I say, isn't this *hot*? It's making my eyes water.' And if I should cry, she told herself, I shall use that as an excuse. Because, one way or another, she was close to tears. She stole an anguished glance at John, who hung about the fireplace giving off dejection, sort of shedding on the rug. She longed to go and tip herself into his arms. For an instant her gaze snagged on his, then fought free of it. Her heart banged about like something caged. It's over, she told herself, recalling the lines of an old Roy Orbison number. It's over, it's over, it's o-o-over.

'Too much for me, I'm afraid,' Geraldine agreed. 'I'm not a great one for hot food. Hot as in spicy, that is. Not hot as in hot. I cannot stomach a curry.' She was evidently on top form. She had had her hair done just this morning. A simply charming boy at Gay Blades had, she told Kate, proposed a fluffier, more youthful style, which had taken years off her, everyone said. The lilac dress, meanwhile, was from a shop called Toggles.

'Yes?' Kate bit down on a yawn, a great gust of despondency that billowed in her chest. If she could only curl up in a corner somewhere and sleep for about a year, through the worst of the hurt, she might be able to carry on.

'You were asking after Mrs Slack.'

'I was. How is she?'

'Ah, well, she's on the mend. Just a sprained ankle, after all.'

'A sprain can be as bad as a break, I've heard.'

'And mild concussion.'

'Who has mild concussion?' Elli enquired, bringing more plates of chilli, all up her arms like a waitress, foisting them on to John, and to Alex, looking for takers. It was like some gruesome parlour game, Kate decided. If you were holding a plate when the music stopped, you would be forced to eat from it.

'My daily help,' Geraldine told her. 'Molly Slack. No, not for me, dear. I'm not a great one for hot food. I'll have some salad in a minute, hmm?'

'The trouble with a bump on the head,' Elli told them with callous unconcern, 'is that one never quite knows. Your Mrs Dogsbody could be walking around as right as rain one week, two weeks after the event, and then pow!'

'What do you mean, "pow"?' asked Kate irritably.

'I mean, zap.'

'Zap?'

'Sudden death.'

'Oh, *charming*.' Kate put her plate down on the floor and took up her glass. Muffy, hurling over to her, sniffed the chilli, sneezed on it and turned tail.

'Bless you,' said Elli distractedly.

Now, I'm definitely not going to manage it, Kate told herself faintly.

'I'm only stating the facts. I say, Katie, this is a bombshell Naomi and Alex have dropped on you tonight. How does it feel to be expecting a grandchild? I must warn Juin, if she has any plans to make me a grandmother I shall have her sterilised. Where is the jewel of my womb, incidentally? I haven't seen her for hours.'

'I've no idea.'

But Kate had, in truth, a hunch. For she had seen, though fleetingly, in the doorway behind Naomi, as Alex made his shock announcement, a small, wan figure. As if running herself through with a dagger, Juin had brought her two clasped hands up to her breast, she had gone limp, then, birdlike, she had flown. She would be in her room now, probably, sobbing into her pillow.

In this, Kate almost envied her. For herself, no such escape was possible. She would have to sit it out to the bitter end.

'I believe congratulations are in order,' murmured John to Alex, and he wondered, as he offered a hand, why he was speaking like a silly old fart. (Perhaps because he *was* a silly old fart?) He kept trying to catch Kate's eye, to

486

signal his regret, but she just sat there, turned away from him, giving him quite literally the cold shoulder, as she toyed with this mince concoction (what was it made with, gunpowder?). If Geraldine would only push off, he would go and sit with her and somehow find the words to fix it. He would make it better. But she wouldn't. And he didn't. And he quietly despaired.

At a few minutes before midnight, Juin, having sunk a whole bottle of Bollinger in the privacy of her bedroom, in the finest Sharpe tradition, and having no head for drink, staggered out through the now-deserted kitchen into the back garden and threw the lot up in a flowerbed.

Frost silvered the grass, which splintered underfoot as, doubled at the waist, she staggered to the bottom of the small lawn, where she waited, clutching her sides, to discover if there was more to be dredged from her seething interior.

'Can I hold your coat for you?' offered a cheery voice at her elbow.

'I don't have a coat, as you see,' she said groggily.

'Your metaphorical coat.'

'Not even a metaphorical one.'

'What I am asking, in so many words, is if I can be of persistence to you?'

'Aren't you always, Dominic?'

'I do my best.'

She straightened up, groaning, and he slipped an arm about her shoulder to give her a jollying hug. They stood for a while without speaking, staring at a thin sliver of moon like a fingernail paring. Then she gave a loud belch and felt better. 'I beg your pardon,' she tendered.

'Granted,' he responded. 'Swell party, huh?'

'No more dire than I'd expected.'

'How's your old lady making out?'

'My mother?'

'No, you goof, the old lady at the home. What was her name? Mabel?'

'She's not so bad. She has a new friend. Mrs Grace. Now Miss Armitage sits alone and knits blanket squares. I took them bath foam for Christmas.'

'You're a sweetie. What are you?'

'Eeugh. I'd hate to be sweet.'

'Have it your own way. You're a sourpuss. So what about our Naomi, then? Preggers, no less.'

'I think it's ridiculous. A woman of her age.'

'Didn't I tell you, stranger things have happened?'

'Did you?'

'Yes, indeedy. I said that your mother probably wanted to have David Garvey's love child. Now Naomi's to have it, which is the same difference, agewise.'

'Except, of course, that it's not David's,' she reminded him with an impatient gesture, a flip-flap of the hand.

'Do we know that?'

'Of course we do,' she said, sounding furious. 'In this case it's Alex's.'

'Can we be sure? Can *she* be sure?'

'What are you getting at, Dom? What are you talking about? Are you drunk?'

'Sober as a newt. Now, I'll tell you something to shock

your socks off – and try saying *that* when you're pissed. But you have to promise not to tell another soul.'

'Right. I promise.'

'Cross your heart?'

'Cross my heart.'

'And hope to die?'

'Oh, do grow up. Tell me or not, but don't play games.'

'You see, she came to stay at our gaff for a weekend. It was a full house, Saturday night. People bunked in together. That is to say, David bunked in with Naomi. Then, in the morning, Alex showed up. So I, wearing my marriage guidance counsellor hat, went on up and begged her to see him, but she wouldn't. And the beastly uncle was there, going "Tell him to fuck off", or words to that effect. Then she came down and gave a fair impression of Mrs Rochester. Mad as a snake, you understand? Barking. And she screamed at him to go, so Alex went. And how they got together after that is quite beyond my ken. I did my best to broker a deal, but it seemed impossible. I'd have thought the lion would lie down with the lamb, sooner.'

Juin sucked in her lower lip and chomped on it. 'I've got the most vile taste in my mouth. And do you think she told Alex about David? Or is she having him on, or what?'

Dominic scratched his nose in a considering manner. 'I couldn't say. But I'll tell you this, I'm keeping out of the whole murky business. See no evil, hear no evil, speak no evil, me.'

'But surely Alex has a right?'

'Stay away from it, Juin. Forget I mentioned it. Let no

word of it pass your luscious lips. Hey, you're shaking like a jelly. Your tiny hand is frozen. Let me warm you.'

'I'm fine,' she protested, but her teeth were clattering like typewriter keys, and she went not unwillingly into his arms, putting her head down on his shoulder, speaking into his shirt. 'That offer you made me. Is it still open?'

'Closes December 31. This means you have . . .' He brought his wrist up to his face and squinted at the dial. 'It means you have just fifteen seconds to take me up on it.'

She raised her head once more and turned from him. 'Look,' she said, nodding towards the house. Through the lighted window they saw a great coming together, a circle was formed, hands linked with hands. The sounds of the dreary New Year dirge came to them faintly through the glass. 'Couldn't you just die of embarrassment?' she whispered.

'It's excruciating, isn't it?'

'Hear that clock striking midnight?' She lifted her finger, cocked her head, counted the chimes. 'Eight, nine, ten, eleven. All right, Dominic. You got it. I accept.'

John had made it his business, at the death of the year, to seize Kate's hand for 'Auld Lang Syne'. He squeezed it very, very tightly, numbing her fingers, and did not release his hold on her when the all singing, all dancing circle of merrymakers broke up, but dragged her to the french windows, putting up a larky pretence of flirtation, a double bluff, lest anyone be watching them.

'Here's one for you,' he told her.

'What's that?'

'Gowans.'

'Gowans.'

'As in, "We twa hae rin about the braes, and pu'd the gowans fine." '

'I don't understand anything,' she told him ambiguously. Then, 'Is it animal?'

'No.'

'Vegetable?'

'You're getting warmer.'

'You know this is killing me.'

'It's killing me too.'

She brought her knuckles up to his face and sort of tapped it. 'Will you forgive me?' he asked.

'How can I not? Now, these gowans. Are they flowers?'

'They are.'

'But I miss you. I miss seeing you. They're wild flowers?'

'They are.'

'If we hadn't gone so overboard, that would have been better. We should have kept it nice and light. A fling, sort of thing.'

'But it's not as if you can choose, can you, to fall in love – or not to fall in love?'

'I don't know. There could be some volition. Are they buttercups?'

'No.'

'Remember in the park? The ducks?'

'I remember everything. I always shall.'

'Are they daisies?'

'They are daisies. Was it worth it, you reckon? Worth all this?'

She gave the question due mind. Then, gazing right into his eyes, she gave her answer. 'Yes, John. Oh, yes, I reckon it was worth it.'

David Garvey had not had the best evening ever. It had not been exactly a riot. The Titian-haired Roxanne, whom he'd picked up at the Groucho and had since been dating in a desultory manner, had turned out to work in publishing, so naturally he'd told her of his novel. He had given her the broad outline – viz., that here would be an important work of fiction, addressing the big themes of good and evil, sex, power, war, peace, and the whole damn thing. Very interesting, she'd responded. Did he have anything on paper? Did he have, for instance, a cast of characters? The bones of a plot?

Christ, was his name not enough? Could she not see it set up in fat, black type, shouting from the bookstands? What did the woman want, blood? He had begun to wonder if she knew her job. Because he was well aware that this was not the way business was done. What usually happened was lunch at Quag's. Publisher and putative author, a media 'name', got together over a bottle of cold Chablis and threw up a couple of ideas. After which you wheeled on a shit-hot agent, and a cheque for a quarter of a million was in the first-class post before you could say 'knife'.

The suspicion that Roxanne was toying with him, that she failed to take him seriously as a property, and was after only one thing had done nothing for his humour tonight, and they had quarrelled from the word go. At half-past eleven she had hailed a taxi, crashed into it, and left him standing on the corner of Frith Street and Old Compton Street like something of a spare prick.

Soho had been sick with drunks, it had seemed an alien and terrible place. He'd seen no one he knew in the club, and was seized by the need to be among friends, to have some undemanding company at this year's end. But he could think of no one undemanding, he could only think of Elli. So he, in his turn, had flagged down a cab, and ordered it to Hackney.

'That will be our first-footer,' exulted Elli, at five minutes past twelve, when the doorbell rang. And she went tripping girlishly to beckon Darcus – or was it Marcus? – across the threshold.

Naomi was on her way down from the bathroom when Elli, with a tug at the latch, revealed to her the dark shape of a man against a rectangle of street. Her hand flew to her mouth and she reached for the banister to steady herself. It was David! David Garvey! Solipsistic, she supposed he had come here to find her. To destroy her. To wreck everything. And she went into stealthy reverse, feeling her way with one hand, flittering her fingers on the banister rail, walking backwards upstairs, step by step growing smaller.

Elli, however, had other ideas. 'Not today, thank you,' she shouted. And she closed the door smartly in David's hated face.

'Who was that?' asked Kate, drifting out, with a sort of lost air about her.

And, 'No one,' Elli assured her adamantly. 'Kate, it was no one.'

CHAPTER

13

'So here's to us,' said Elli, slopping champagne into four unmatched glasses, handing them around. 'After all these years, still the best of friends.'

'Yes,' said Kate, putting her nose into the glass, watching with mixed feelings, from under lowered lids, a dreamy and reposeful Naomi, a plushy, oddly glossy Geraldine. The best and worst of friends, she told herself.

Warm air from the garden breathed life into a curtain drawn to exclude the blistering sunshine. But it was not the early summer heat that stifled, so much as the sense of something quite momentous, invisible, female, primal in the room with them. Of course, no one had ever had a baby before.

'Did you have a truly terrible time?' asked Geraldine with a kind of smug solicitude, jabbing long-stemmed roses into a jam jar.

'It wasn't so bad.' Naomi put her feet up, winced, smiled a long-suffering smile. She was stretched out on the bed, fetchingly arranged among piles of cushions, staring at her child in a dazed and disbelieving fashion. 'It's sort of bearable,' she confided. 'The pain is unimaginable, and yet . . .'

Gravely, three experienced mothers listened to her, gravely watched as she reached out tentatively to rock the cradle.

'Did you tear?' Elli wanted to know. 'Have to be stitched? Hey, shove over.' She crashed down beside Naomi, eliminating the teddy bear that had been Kate's present, sheepishly delivered.

'Oh, *really*, Elli!' scolded Kate. Inexplicably timid, as though she hadn't the right, she peeped into the crib.

He was not, she privately acknowledged, the most beautiful of babies. He would not be winning any prizes. He was very red, and looked worried and wizened. It was a wonder that two such attractive people could spawn such peculiar offspring. All the same, she felt her hackles rise, she flushed with indignation to hear Elli say, 'He looks like a potato.'

'I think he's divine,' responded Naomi evenly. When she closed her eyes, she still saw her boy child, she held him in her memory. It was weird.

'How are you,' Geraldine wanted to know, '*in yourself*?' And she loaded the question oddly, she unbalanced it with more meaning than it could carry.

'Me?' Naomi sighed. In truth, she was not so much in as out of herself. She felt something beyond love for this scrap of new life which had displaced her in her own affections. She would have died for him without a second thought. And, in a small, obscure way, she almost loathed him.

Her emotions were more complicated, of course, by the question of paternity, by the insecurity of not knowing. She could not unpick shame from pride, or wretchedness from utter bliss. At moments this quite paralysed her. What a perfect little hell on earth she had created for herself, in which she had everything but certainty.

'The fourth day is always the worst,' pronounced Elli. 'It's your hormones, dearie. Chemically, you're a Molotov cocktail; don't worry if you go off bang.' She picked up a matinée jacket, a thing of powder-blue wool, all lace and scallops with ribbon tie, held it up consideringly. 'What's *this*?'

'Geraldine knitted it.' Naomi shot Elli a repressive glance. 'Isn't it nice?'

'He'll look like a right Nellie in it, to be frank.'

'Did you read,' put in Kate to punish Elli, 'that Dawn Hancock has been named columnist of the year for her work for the *Inquirer*?'

'Well, my dear, we *all* know about the press awards.'

'We do?'

'An annual celebration of the mediocre.'

'You've not been nominated, have you? Ever?'

'Nor should I wish to be, thank you. I should worry that I was losing my touch.'

'Don't fight,' begged Naomi weakly. 'Please don't.'

'No, girls, please don't,' Geraldine supported her. 'This is supposed to be a happy time.'

'You're right,' conceded Elli. 'Who wants a top-up? We're here to wet the baby's head.'

'Not for me, dear. I must dash.' Geraldine set the jar of roses on the chest of drawers, stood back to consider it, regretted the lack of a pretty vase. 'I have to look in at the travel agent's.'

'Will you post a letter for me on your way,' begged Naomi, extracting from under a cushion a slim white envelope.

Rudely, Elli snatched it, read the address, handed it on. 'To your *father*?'

'Yes.'

'Well! I shouldn't have thought you owed him –'

'But I do, Elli. More than even he knows. So I'm squaring it with him.' To have one thing straight, at least, she thought. To be free of my rotten past. Not to have that money which I can never account for to Alex, never enjoy. And to show that I'm not all bad. She turned to each of them in turn, sought approval, found only mild incomprehension. They didn't know the half.

'We're off to Guernsey,' Geraldine persisted, 'did I tell you? Just the two of us. Lucy is to holiday with her friend Sarah Brooke, and Dominic is old enough, heaven knows, to be left alone. So it will be something of a second honeymoon.'

Christ! Kate cringed. The pain was unimaginable. And yet sort of bearable. No worse than childbirth, probably. No worse than motherhood. Or the loss of a son to a friend.

'May I hold the little one?' she asked with diffidence. And when Naomi with an upturned hand silently consented, when she invited her please to help herself, she took up in her arms this tiny being, she held him to her breast and breathed the strange, strangely familiar, cloying, baby smell of him, she felt his waxy skin, put her cheek to his mauve-veined head, and was so overwhelmed with the purest, most profound love – more powerful than anything she'd ever felt for John, more compelling even than her love for grown-up Alex – she could have wept.

Embarrassed by her glutted feelings, by her sudden tears, she took her grandchild to the window and stood there jigging him, crooning to him. Theo, she tried upon him, as he blew a bubble through his nose. Theodore. Weren't names just too absurd on newborn infants? There was, in those unseeing blue eyes, as yet no hint of person. You should wait a year, at least, to see who someone was, not prejudge the matter in this way.

I shall have to be there for Naomi, she resolved. I shall have to help her. No matter how she works at it, she'll find it hard to cope. My precious, precious boy is going to need his gran.

'Is it a year?' she asked, gazing mistily at the tiny garden, the dusty shrubs. 'Was it a year ago you came to me, Naomi?'

'Nearly.'

'We've all passed a lot of water since then,' quoted Elli, 'as someone or other once memorably remarked. Was Alex there to hold your hand at the delivery, Naomi? To do the breathing bit, and tell you when to push? They have it so bloody easy, don't they, men?'

'I don't think he found it easy,' Naomi fondly, humorously, replied (without turning, Kate could visualise her smile). 'I was a bit afraid that he might faint and cause a scene.'

'They're such babies themselves, these chaps, when it comes to a bit of blood,' reflected Geraldine. 'They're so squeamish, physically. So intolerant of the tiniest pain. I remember when David had the snip, the fuss he made over such a minor op, the work of minutes.'

'The . . .?' asked Naomi faintly.

'You know. The vasectomy.'

'David's had a . . .'

'Oh, yes. Four, five years ago. I was very much against it, I may tell you. I said to him, "One day you'll want to settle down, you'll want to tie the knot and have a proper family of your own." But he was adamant, he wasn't getting caught like that again. He'd had one unplanned child, one "brat", he said, and that was one too many. Oh, goodness, Kate, forgive me. I forget myself.'

'What? Sorry. I was dreaming.' Kate, drifting from the window with her darling Theo, was astonished to find that Naomi was weeping.

Juin Sharpe snatched up the phone and, with a stabbing finger, dialled the number. It rang once ('You stirring shit-bag,' she heard Elli say), twice ('You blabber-mouthed toad'). But Alex ought to know the truth . . . Well, oughtn't he? It was a matter of high principle.

At the third ring he came on the line, sounding very bright, with eager expectation. 'Hello?' she heard him say. 'Hello, hello-o?'

She swallowed hard, and in so doing seemed to swallow the words. When she opened her mouth there was nothing there to say. Quickly, and with thudding heart, she slammed down the receiver. Immediately, she grabbed it up again to call Dominic.

What she knew, she would not tell. Of course not.

ROSE SHEPHERD

Too Rich, Too Thin

Caroline Charteris has so very much. She wants for nothing – except a sense of self-worth. And a trim waistline. And the attentions of eligible young men. And the approval of her mother, the bored beautiful, rapacious Laura.

Michele Fairchild has so little of anything. She has nothing – except the face of an angel. And a figure to die for. And the awesome secret which her grandmother has shared with her.

When their lives overlap, nothing, for either of them, will ever be the same again.

'A stylish and touching comedy of manners . . . I loved it'
Penny Vincenzi

'She writes assured, stylish sagas laced with wit . . . readable, witty and poignant'
Time Out

ROSE SHEPHERD

Happy Ever After

When someone with all the answers meets someone with lots of questions, you'd expect her to be happy. Wouldn't you?

Dee Rawlings is the agony aunt with the answers for everything and everybody. But nothing has prepared her for unmarried teenage mother Kayleigh Roth.

Cuckoo-in-the-nest Kayleigh starts disrupting Dee's happy family home in all sorts of unexpected ways. Husbands, brothers, sisters and lovers soon discover the full force of Kayleigh's irresistable personality . . .

Happy Ever After is a heartwarming, poignant, funny novel for the nineties.

'A funny, fast-paced fairytale with a happy ending – for those who deserve it'
Living

'Rose Shepherd is a wry commentator on the vicissitudes of life in the nineties and her shrewd, sharp, very funny book is a delight'
Midweek

SUSAN LEWIS

Summer Madness

ONE HUNDRED DEGREES OF PASSION ON THE COTE D'AZUR

After finishing work on their sensationally successful TV series, Louisa, Danny and Sarah take a much-needed holiday on the French Riviera. All they want to do is party, soak up the sun and have a good time.

Danny, the actress, with her sensual beauty and impossible temper, soon has the eligible men of the Riviera chasing her. Louisa, the scriptwriter on the rebound from a broken love affair, finds herself more and more drawn to the mysterious Jake Mallory. While Sarah, the producer, just wants to hang out and have fun.

But they quickly discover that the sparkle of Riviera life conceals a dark presence that pulls them all into a game no one can win. And when mayhem and madness begin to stalk them, to their terror they find that there is no way out.

A Selection of Fiction Available from Mandarin

While every effort is made to keep prices low, it is sometimes necessary to increase prices at short notice.
Mandarin Paperbacks reserves the right to show new retail prices on covers which may differ from those
previously advertised in the text or elsewhere.

The prices shown below were correct at the time of going to press.

☐ 7493 1447 8	**Hard News**	Tess Stimson	£4.99
☐ 7493 1470 2	**Georgia**	Lesley Pearse	£4.99
☐ 7493 1251 3	**The First Wives Club**	Olivia Goldsmith	£4.99
☐ 7493 1105 3	**A Double Life**	Vera Cowie	£4.99
☐ 7493 1098 7	**Too Rich Too Thin**	Rose Shepherd	£4.99
☐ 7493 0980 6	**Best Kept Secrets**	Sandra Brown	£4.99
☐ 7493 0919 9	**Mirror Image**	Sandra Brown	£4.99
☐ 7493 1312 9	**Breath of Scandal**	Sandra Brown	£4.99
☐ 7493 1320 X	**Obsession**	Susan Lewis	£4.99
☐ 7493 1180 0	**Darkest Longings**	Susan Lewis	£4.99
☐ 7493 0380 8	**Stolen Beginnings**	Susan Lewis	£4.99
☐ 7493 0166 X	**Dance While You Can**	Susan Lewis	£4.99
☐ 7493 0977 6	**Facets**	Barbara Delinsky	£4.99
☐ 7493 1169 X	**A Woman Betrayed**	Barbara Delinsky	£4.99
☐ 7493 1435 4	**The Passions of Chelsea Kane**	Barbara Delinsky	£4.99

All these books are available at your bookshop or newsagent, or can be ordered direct from the address
below. Just tick the titles you want and fill in the form below.

Cash Sales Department, PO Box 5, Rushden, Northants NN10 6YX.
Fax: 01933 414047 : Phone: 01933 414000.

Please send cheque, payable to 'Reed Book Services Ltd.', or postal order for purchase price quoted and
allow the following for postage and packing:

£1.00 for the first book, 50p for the second; **FREE POSTAGE AND PACKING FOR THREE BOOKS OR
MORE PER ORDER.**

NAME (Block letters) ....

ADDRESS ....

....

☐ I enclose my remittance for ....

☐ I wish to pay by Access/Visa Card Number

Expiry Date

Signature ....

Please quote our reference: MAND